THE DAY THE RAVENS DIED

BY

TIMOTHY PILGRIM

Visit us online at www.authorsonline.co.uk

An Authors OnLine Book

Text Copyright © Timothy Pilgrim 2008

Cover design by James Fitt ©

All rights reserved. No part of this publication may be reproduced, stored in a retrieval system, or transmitted in any form or by any means, electronic, mechanical, photocopy, recording or otherwise, without prior written permission of the copyright owner. Nor can it be circulated in any form of binding or cover other than that in which it is published and without similar condition including this condition being imposed on a subsequent purchaser.

ISBN 978-07552-0427-4

Authors OnLine Ltd
19 The Cinques
Gamlingay, Sandy
Bedfordshire SG19 3NU
England

This book is also available in e-book format, details of which are available at www.authorsonline.co.uk

PRELUDE

Angela Bates was having a bad morning; her husband had left much earlier than usual for his job in the city. Because of this, her normal routine had been upset and she had drifted off to sleep again, now the kids were playing up. As a result she would probably be late getting them to school; the North Circular was certain to be solid with traffic at this time of day. Her husband had taken the car so she had been left with the people carrier which she hated driving and dare not drive on the narrow back streets.

Just as she was strapping her ten year old into his seat, one of her friends from two doors along the street came hurrying past the gateway, dragging her three children in her wake, imploring them to hurry or they would miss the only bus which might get them to school on time. Spotting her friend Angela loading her two children into the huge people carrier, she decided to beg a lift off her normally helpful neighbour.

"Oh Angie, you couldn't help me out could you? My car won't start and I'm sure we'll miss the bus. You couldn't take my little monsters as well could you? Please."

"Of course I can Liz; James went early this morning and left me the 'truck', if you can help me strap them in there's plenty of room."

The two friends strapped their kiddies into the comfortable seats, for what should have been a ten-minute journey to their school. In spite of the traffic she reached the slip road for Kingsbury easily. As she turned off the chaotic North Circular, the car which had cut in front of her braked for no obvious reason; conscious of her friend's children she limited herself to, "You silly man!"

What happened next horrified her, the car which had braked suddenly lurched to the right, bouncing off the under rider rails of a petrol tanker crawling along in the traffic on the busy main road. The car swerved again, harder this time, its bonnet bending the strong rails and becoming wedged beneath the tanker. She barely had time to take the deep breath so she could scream before the big people carrier was hurled like a blazing comet across the pavement, taking the pedestrian railing with it into the small family shop.

Within a few seconds the blast wave had dissipated. All that was left for more than a hundred yards in every direction was wreckage, anything combustible in the area was burning fiercely.

Timothy Pilgrim

It was lunchtime before the fire brigade reached the main area of destruction which consisted of smouldering heaps of rubble. Of the people carrier there was no sign, it was totally covered by the collapsed remains of what had been the shop and the flat above.

It would be three days before a team working with a JCB, frantically waved at the digger driver to stop; his bucket had hit what looked like part of a vehicle of some kind.

It took most of the following morning to carefully remove the debris to reveal the burnt, partly crushed remains of Angie's hated people carrier. The first estimate of how many had been in it was based on the number of seat belt clips which were engaged, as only the metal bits where left, and the heat and the weight of the collapsed building had buckled these.

A shaken fireman reported to the senior officer co-ordinating the recovery teams. "I think you'd better come with me Sir, I think we may have found what's left of the missing mum and her load of kiddies."

"What do you mean leading fireman," the man sounded angry. "You're not paid to think, you should know!"

"It's difficult, there's hardly anything left. I can't handle that, and I'm not about to ask my men to. They are, after all, retained firemen not full timers. In my opinion it's a job for the forensic boys not my team, so if you would come and see for yourself Sir, you can make the decision on how to handle it!"

It took the forensic teams another two days to clear the vehicle of what was left of its passengers, and the go-ahead was given to lift the wreckage out of the pile of still hot rubble. As the already rusting remains were swung clear by the big digger, another gruesome find was revealed - the crushed and cooked remains of the shopkeeper's wife and teenage daughter. Saved from the worst of the fire they did at least bear some resemblance to having once been human beings.

By the end of the week the death toll was officially put at one hundred and thirty seven, with another fifteen possibly unaccounted for. The injured total was in the hundreds, hospitals for miles were still struggling to cope, and this was just the beginning!

CHAPTER ONE

"Good afternoon Sir," was the welcome General Leach received as he opened the door of his car. Paul had been sitting on the low wall beside the road facing the wild expanse of Loch Awe and smoking the inevitable cigarette, a glass with a generous helping of his favourite malt balanced on a capping stone beside him.

"Obviously you were expecting me," replied the supposedly retired General, "which is somewhat surprising as no one should know I'm here. Indeed, I didn't even suggest to anyone that I might come to see you," he reached for his bag on the back seat.

"Allow me Sir. Swap," said Paul, offering the older man the glass. "It's all right Sir, mine is on the patio table, round the back."

Taking the visitor's bag, he led the way up the path which climbed the slope around the end of the converted croft. The two men entered the sheltered haven of the carefully landscaped garden via a solid door set into the high stone wall; this offered a degree of protection from the gales which frequently howled along the loch.

"You've been busy since I was last here Paul," observed General Leach, admiring Paul's handy work in the garden.

"It was at least two years ago when you were last here Sir, and I've had the past couple of months to work on it."

The General placed his drink with the other matching glass on the table, noting the half empty bottle beside them. The thought crossed his mind briefly that Paul might have returned to his old problem which had almost destroyed his career before it had really begun.

"If you'd like to come this way Sir, no doubt you would like to freshen up first after your trip. I'll put your bag in your usual room, the wife is in the kitchen, she'll be glad to see you."

Five minutes later the General rejoined Paul on the patio, built between the two extensions to the original croft.

"Before we start, there are two things I want to clear up." The General paused to take a sample of the malt. "One, drop the Sir, and two, how the bloody hell did you know I was on my way?"

"I can hardly call you 'Boss' as I'm a civvie now. Well. I will be in a couple of weeks, and who says I knew?"

Timothy Pilgrim

"The drink already poured, room ready, and I did see what your lovely wife was preparing for tea. I don't care what you say, that's just too much to be coincidence. You knew, the question is how?"

"No mystery Sir," replied Paul, "you have to pass the post office in the village to get here; the postmaster is ex-regiment. There is a discrete camera covering the road from his garden, it's linked to the unit's computer and clocks every car that passes, identifies it, and if it's not local then it warns us. The whole thing takes less than a minute, and it's a ten minute drive, even in daylight, and then only if you know the road. As the road doesn't go anywhere else, apart from the Campbell's farm a mile further on, we don't exactly get traffic jams."

"OK, that's dealt with. The second point, now to sort out the reason for my visit. What would your reaction be if I was to tell you the Prime Minister himself asked when you were expected back from leave?"

"I'd say it was him who was pissed, and I did notice you spotting the bottle was only half full, and before you ask it's been open more than a week, even then I had some help from Gary, the manager of the trout farm!"

"Not quite the reaction I had hoped for," replied General Leach. "It was however a genuine request on the Prime Minister's part, he even suggested a promotion might sway your decision."

"That's a new way of getting a promotion," chuckled Paul. "Thump a senior civil servant and make Brigadier. What would have happened if I'd hit that idiot Yank Defence Secretary as well, I suppose the powers that be would have offered me your old job as the Chief of Staff?"

"Don't be so flippant about it, whether you like it or not Paul, you're missed."

"No doubt in the same way as one misses a toothache or piles?"

"All right, let me put it this way. You're the best there is at second guessing these bloody terrorists, even the Americans are asking when you'll be back."

"Why do I find that a little difficult to believe? I rather lost my temper at the conference, in front of the television cameras, I wouldn't apologise then and I won't now. I know I shouldn't have let fly like that, but I stand by what I said."

"To tell you the truth, it's my opinion the vast majority of Americans agree with you. The levels of co-operation have soared since the man resigned. As unlikely as it sounds, we are actually getting requests from them, for instructors to train their troops in 'low level' warfare."

"Well, all the fuss might have had some good results then, but I fail to see what difference it will make with me coming back. If I thought for one moment it could significantly improve things, then I'd think about it. I know the new engines are coming through at long last for the Canberras. I also know they're not in harmonised pairs, there is still some bloody Whitehall warrior playing silly buggers. The rig Rolls Royce use to harmonise a pair of jets is tied up for months in a pointless experimental program on Tornado engines, why? They're in the process of being phased out. So the answer is no Sir, I will not come back. If I had to deal with another episode of what can only be described as civil service sabotage, putting lives at risk, merely to serve their own agenda, then I would either develop high blood pressure or more likely simply shoot the meddling bastard."

"So you are staying in touch," replied the General, "I thought as much."

"More of a case of Taff keeping in touch with me Sir, and then it's more to make sure I'm all right rather than anything else."

"And are you, all right, that is?"

"I couldn't be more all right Sir. Just look at this place, it's bloody paradise - peaceful and a loch full of big fish twenty yards from my front door."

"The All Arms Unit needs you Paul, it was you who built it into the force it is today. Taff is brilliant at co-ordinating the various elements of the command, but he lacks your insight into the terrorist mind"

"I know what he's good at Sir, that's why he's in the position he is, he's one hell of a co-ordinator." Paul finished his drink. "We have got a choice sir. We can sit here and finish this bottle, which will mean we will not fully appreciate my wife's culinary efforts, or I can grab a couple of rods out of the shed and we can have an hour or so out in the boat until tea is ready."

"OK, I give up," sighed the General. "What are we going after?"

"Let's set our sights high and try for one of those ferox trout."

"How many of them get caught per year? I've never even seen one!"

"Granted they are somewhat elusive, but I reckon we're in with a chance, the sun will be off the water in about half an hour. The mouth of the river is solid with little roach and all the fry from this year's spawning game fish are dropping down the river into the loch. With all that food there just has to be a few ferox hanging around the drop off, opposite the river mouth, and if they're going to feed then I reckon now is the most likely time."

Paul passed a rod to the General. "A powerful looking piece of kit Paul," he remarked as he tested the bend.

"9 weight, 15 pound leader, and a couple of inches of 15 pound wire. Those things have got teeth the average pike would be proud of, talking of which we might well catch a pike or two."

"On a fly? That would be a first for me Paul, I'll bet they put a bend in the rod."

Paul took an old two-ounce tobacco tin containing a selection of large 'flies' off the shelf just inside the shed door. "Come on, standing around here nattering about it won't catch a fish. I'll just let the missus know where we're going."

The General heard her say, "All right love. Tea will be ready in two hours. Don't be late!"

After about an hour they still hadn't caught anything, although the General had lost a large rainbow trout; after several spectacular leaps, it finally threw the size two hook from its jaw.

"Oh bugger it," exclaimed the frustrated man. "That beast was well over ten pounds, easily my best ever."

"They do tend to do that if you let the line go too slack." Paul passed the still muttering General a pair of powerful binoculars. You see the little field high up on the second spur, the one still catching the sun?"

"What am I looking for?"

"Right in the very edge of the trees, see them Sir? Red deer."

The older man watched transfixed as a magnificent stag walked confidently into the last rays of the sun, followed by his harem and their youngsters.

"What magnificent creatures. It's not often you get to see them in the open like that. I take it they are never hunted?"

"If you tried, it would probably be the last thing you did. The keepers are pretty protective of that herd, you'll see why if you keep watching."

Animals were still emerging from the edge of the forest. "Good grief, a pure white hind."

"Keep looking Sir."

"Good Lord! She's got twins!"

"There's a white yearling there somewhere, though barely half the herd are out yet."

The General was so enthralled by the deer he hadn't noticed Paul was still fishing. The first he knew of it was when Paul's rod slammed down through his field of vision, followed by a loud splash.

"Don't get excited Sir, it's only a little jack pike," he used the strong tackle to bully the fish to the side of the boat. "Greedy little devil." Just as he leaned over to pick his unwanted capture from the peaty coloured water, it vanished in a huge splash as an unseen predator lunged up from the depths, engulfing the hapless jack pike.

"Bloody hell," exclaimed Paul as the wire came back minus fly and pike. "The bloody thing bit straight through the wire."

"That was some pike Paul."

"No it wasn't, it was a tiddler, not much over a pound."

"I didn't mean the one on your hook; I meant the one which ate it!"

"It wasn't a pike Sir, it was a huge ferox trout. Didn't you see the big square tail, the thing must have been pushing 20 pounds!"

"Aah, bad luck Paul," said General Leach sympathetically.

"Well, I guess that makes us even, we've both lost personal bests. Sod it let's go, tea will be ready soon. Oh, there's snowy, the yearling, see him?"

"I do indeed. What a place."

"And you seriously expect me to leave here and go back to fighting civil servants so the lads have got the gear they need to take on these nutters before they do any more damage?"

"I'm beginning to see why you are so reluctant to return Paul."

"I'm afraid you won't be able to put mission accomplished against this trip Sir. This time I am staying retired!"

In the event, the General stayed for several days, much of the time spent fishing from Paul's boat.

Predictably, the big ones eluded them. "That's why they're big Sir," was Paul's comment as his guest muttered some dark oath as yet another 'monster' made a half-hearted attempt to grab his lure and missed.

Although the General enjoyed the fishing, the highlight of the visit came in the early hours of the third day. Paul had woken him at dawn with a cup of coffee, the presumption being, an early start after the elusive ferox trout. He was a little surprised when his host handed him a pair of binoculars instead of a fishing rod. As they walked along the badly maintained road following the shoreline, curiosity finally got the better of the General. "All right, I'm intrigued. I noticed you stuffing a loaf of bread in your rucksack, any particular reason you took the whole grain rather the ordinary white loaf?"

"That 'ordinary' white loaf was one the missus baked yesterday afternoon, she would have had my guts for garters if I'd have nicked it! Anyway, I'm not too keen on wholegrain; the deer on the other hand love it!"

As they headed up the hillside towards the field where they had seen the herd of deer General Leach asked, "Exactly how close will they come?"

"On my own, some of them will actually take it from my hand, though quite how they'll react to a stranger I don't know. One thing, watch out for 'Rambo' the big stag, he can be a right evil sod and will bite you if he gets the chance. If he comes close enough, what ever you do, don't rub him behind his ears. Oh sure he likes a bit of fuss, but if he shakes his head, with the set of antlers he's got he'll take your eye out!"

"You mean they'll come that close!"

"I don't know, two or three of the hinds are nosey buggers and will probably come to give you 'the once over'. Like I said you're a stranger, most of them will probably hang about just inside the trees, we'll see."

The two men sat down on a couple of rocks protruding from the grass, about twenty yards from the trees. Paul broke some slices of bread in halves and threw them frizzbee style towards the edge of the wood. He passed the General some of the bread, with the reminder that given the chance some of the deer might well bite the hand feeding them.

In the event only about half a dozen deer came close enough to take a piece of bread at arm's length; the only one to be bold enough to accept the offering from the General was the old 'Queen' hind. To Paul's relief 'Rambo' kept a safe distance as he was clearly unhappy at the presence of the new intruder in his kingdom. The white hind, after a few moments inspecting the men from a safe distance, suddenly marched straight up to Paul, snatched the offered slice of bread and trotted back to her twins who were watching from the safety of the trees.

The yearling stag Paul had hoped would be brave enough to venture out, stayed resolutely back in the woods, he was clearly visible much of the time, his brilliant white coat making him difficult to miss.

"We'd better be off Sir, give them time to have their breakfast in peace before the sun gets properly up."

"Well, thanks for that Paul, what a treat, quite remarkable."

"The best part is yet to come, this is the dodgy bit. You'll have to keep your wits about you as more than one of this lot are likely to butt you up the backside, just to let you know this is their patch."

"Charming."

"As long as it isn't one of the stags there's nothing to worry about."

"All right for you to say!"

Only the old hind followed them more than a few yards. "Go away, you silly old sod!" Paul scolded, as she tried to grab the bread wrapper. "It's empty! You've eaten it all."

"You've got a fan there Paul."

"Tell me about it Sir. She can get a bit too friendly at times."

On their return to the croft they found Paul's wife busily cooking breakfast. "No prizes for guessing what happened to the new wholemeal loaf."

"Well the deer like it better, and I dare not take your homemade."

"I should hope not," she said giving him a sideways look. "He's a terrible man General. You see what I have to put up with."

"I do indeed my dear, and I wish you would call me Brian. Drop all this General and Sir, that goes for you too Paul."

"I know why you're here; you want him to go back. I'm right, aren't I?" The concern was obvious in her voice.

"Yes, we do want him back but so far, I must admit, I've failed to find an argument to sway him. Your husband is one of the most stubborn men I have ever had the dubious honour to command."

Paul acted as waiter. "Breakfast is served Sire," as he placed the plate before his guest, then added somewhat ungraciously, "You can help yourself to coffee."

Breakfast over, Paul was clearing up the plates. The General suggested, "You wash, I'll wipe."

"Not bloody likely," retorted Paul. Hidden behind one of the oak panel doors, under the polished granite work surface was a compact dishwasher. Having put all the crockery and cutlery he could find into the machine, he placed a tablet in its holder, flicked the door shut with his foot and pushed a button, "Job done."

"Do either of you want anything from the shop?" asked his wife. "Jean is organising a coffee morning, I did promise I'd try to get there."

"Any chance of a newspaper of some sort?" asked General Leach. "World war three could have broken out for all I know. I've only just noticed, no papers and I can only remember hearing music on the radio since I've been here."

"You might be lucky but, as far as I know, they only get papers in to order," suggested Paul.

"I'll ask anyway, see you this afternoon."

"Take care Luv."

Once the sound of the car had faded, the General turned to Paul. "You two are great hosts, but there is one thing which is really bothering me."

"And what would that be?" asked Paul with an air of innocence which suggested he had a pretty good idea what was coming.

"I know you told me about the early warning system with the shop, but you knew a long while before that, I was on my way."

"Whatever gave you that idea Sir?"

"This is me you're talking to Paul!" exclaimed the General. "How long have we known each other now? You knew! How else can you explain the sheets on the bed in my room. I've commented before on the fact I'm no lover of cotton sheets, and of course it is pure coincidence your wife happened to have all the ingredients to hand for my favourite meals. I can't imagine how, but I am certain you knew I was on my way, and a long time before I passed the shop! So come on when and how?"

"Taff told me, just after eleven o'clock."

"And how, pray, did he know? Damn it, I didn't even tell my wife, she is spending a week with her sister anyway, so I just told her I'd be away for a few days."

"I suppose I'd better tell you the whole story. Taff was getting worried. He'd had several calls from people trying to get in touch with you. No one, it seems, had any idea where you were. Not surprisingly alarm bells were ringing; all your office could tell callers was that you were away for a few days."

"I still don't know how he could have found me. My mobile was switched off so no one could get a fix on it, I am only too aware of the habits of some of our American cousins, so how?"

Paul led the General to the small room, more of a cellar really, at the rear of the house. He passed him a print-out from the communications terminal. The message shocked the older man, it read: -

'11.05 hrs G.M.T. Located target. North bound A74M, one mile north of Lockerbie. Speed 74.4 mph., playing Dolly Parton on the in car CD. Subject singing along but out of tune.'

"All right, how the bloody hell did your lot get all that information? If you have got my car bugged then I will not be very happy."

"I wouldn't dare do such a thing, although I will admit to having put trackers on in the past when there had been a need to watch your back."

"Then how? One of your newly equipped Canberras I suppose."

"That's exactly how they found you - one was up on a proving flight, headed for the ranges off Benbeccula. When Taff called them, they were some where round about Lancaster; from what I could gather, it took about ten minutes to spot you."

"However many vehicles did it check before it found me? I happen to know that system scans behind the plane first which must have included most of Greater Manchester. Then there's this business of hearing what is playing on my CD. They've made that gismo work as well?"

"That gismo, as you call it, has always worked. We've been able to 'see sound' for a couple of years. It was only the vibrations from the engines, or the air rushing past the sensor head because the plane wasn't high enough, which buggered things up. Now they've got the new engines and the latest computers are on line, the sky's the limit. It's a shattering thought, it's now possible to carry something in your inside jacket pocket with more computing power than Whitehall, Langley and the FBI combined."

"If word gets out of even a fraction of what this new technology can do, there will be hell to pay Paul."

"The question is, what do we do with it? Do we give the cops a photograph of a murderer we happened to spot? If we had a plane up within nearly a hundred miles at the time and its scanners were on, all we would have to do is run the recording backwards and we could tell them who did what to whom. The next time a kiddie vanishes, the same applies. Where do we draw the line?"

"Where indeed, it's a moral dilemma, we'll have to seek guidance from on high," replied the General. "Do you realise I had never even considered this aspect of all your new technology, it is worrying. Orwell has nothing on this Paul!"

"There's no question, if we're to defend this country against terrorist attacks, then much of the country will be under constant surveillance. It is the only way I can see of stopping them, or at least catching them. It is, as you said, a moral dilemma and needs to be kept secret, at pretty well all costs. Images taken by those planes have been used in two court cases already. In the first one nobody thought to ask where the pictures came from, it was assumed a surveillance team had taken the picture from a motorway bridge. In the other instance, the judge threw the case out as the origin of the photo was 'uncertain' and the terrorist walked free."

"What's happened to him since?"

"He flew out to Pakistan a week later to join the Taliban or Al Qaeda. He was shot as he tried to cross the border along with about a dozen others."

"How sad. But I'm still gob smacked at how easily they picked out my car."

"You know the really scary thing? Doing all that used less than one percent of the plane's on board computer power. It didn't even need the ground link."

"All this and you still won't come back! In heaven's name why not?"

"I'm pretty well burned out Sir; it happened once before. I've been there, didn't like it and I have no desire for a repeat thank you very much. So the answer is still no and it will remain no. I will however add the proviso, should a specific threat be seen to be developing, and if Taff and the others think I could help, then and only then, I will consider it."

"Well it wasn't the answer I wanted, but fair enough. I suppose you are still 'on call' so to speak, with all this gear here. I'll tell the PM you need longer to recuperate, and not mention the communication equipment. I'll also keep the location of this place to myself. As far as I know, not more than a dozen of the unit know the location. I take it you would prefer it stayed that way?"

"I'll answer that with another daft question. Do you want to go fishing again?"

CHAPTER TWO

A few weeks after the General's visit, Paul came in earlier than he planned from the garden. "This wind's getting up and it's got to my ruddy back," he moaned.

"Don't come in here with those mucky boots," scolded his wife. "Leave them in the hall, Marie has only just finished cleaning up the mess you left dinner time."

"Sorree!"

"I should think so too," she chuckled.

Having left his boots behind, he headed for his favourite chair, "Any idea where I left my painkillers Luv?"

"Where you always leave them, on your bedside table."

"I'll get them Sir," replied Marie, "and no doubt you'd like a cup of coffee?"

"That would be great, but you're not our servant you know."

"Oh I don't mind," replied Marie as she scurried off on her errand.

"What on earth are you making there?" Paul asked his long suffering other half.

"A blanket for our little granddaughter. Just because you don't feel the cold, you seem to forget, other normal human beings do! The thought of the little mite out in her pushchair with one of those lazy winds you get in Norfolk wintertime! Well I like crocheting, so I'm making her a nice warm blanket before the cold weather arrives."

"Who says I don't feel the cold? The way I'm going, you'd better make me one as well!"

Marie returned with the coffee and Paul's 'lost' pain killers.

"Thanks Marie. Didn't you make yourself a cuppa?"

"No Sir. I've got to be off to get my man's tea ready; he'll be hungry when he gets home."

"Please call me Paul, I hate being called 'Sir', everyone in the village does it as well. Any one would think I'm the local Laird!"

"They do it because they respect you Sir," replied Marie unbowed.

"Why, in heaven's name. I'm nothing special!"

"One way or another, nearly every job in the village exists thanks to you."

"How do you work that out?"

"The trout farm was on its last legs and about to close until you invested a lot of money in it. The little canning factory and smoker means it is making money and six full time and three part time jobs keep nearly half the village busy. Even the wood for the smoker comes from the trees you planted when you first bought the croft. The little workshop making jumpers from local wool, means extra income for the farms and work for more people. It was you who paid for the renovation of the building and the machines.

Widow Mac Bride's guesthouse is always fully booked. I know you bought her house when she thought she was going to have to leave because the previous landlords wanted to double her rent and she couldn't afford it. She couldn't advertise and bookings dropped off."

"Marie! Stop making me out to be some sort of saviour. It's Ma Mac Bride's cooking which keeps her fully booked, along with Ken's fishing boat trips on the Loch. As for the rest, their success is down to their own hard work. All right, granted, I invested a bit of money, which I ought to point out gives me a lot higher return than I could ever get from a bank!"

"That's the point Sir, you believed in them. You helped them when the banks didn't want to know!"

"That's the bank's tough luck!"

"One way or another everyone in the village owes their livelihood to you. Even my little job cleaning and doing little jobs for you both means I earn more, after allowing for the cost of all the travel, than I could if I travelled to Oban to work in a shop."

"And worth every penny Marie. I might be English, but I come from a small village, so I understand country life. All I've done is help the locals make a decent living from what they already had, it isn't magic or charity. I make more than enough for us to live on out of their hard work."

"Well, English or not, I'm still going to call you Sir. No one in the village is likely to lose their job, and as soon as they are old enough, there will be jobs for the kiddies, if they want them.

Most people, when they have moved into the area, have tried to change things then left when they found they couldn't. You didn't, you talked to people, found out what they wanted, then helped."

"What's the point of trying to make people do things differently, just for the sake of it? Don't fix what isn't broken! Anyway, I thought you had someone's tea to cook. There's a bag of spare vegetables on the back doorstep and grab a trout out of the freezer on your way. We'll never eat them all and while you're at it, take one for Mrs Mac Bride. I happen to know her current guests have been pike fishing, and wouldn't have caught a trout on the dead baits they've been using. Go on, away with you! See you tomorrow."

After Marie had left his wife turned to Paul. "You are awful some times. Marie is a sensitive soul; she was only saying thank you for all of the village. If it hadn't been for you, most of them would be out of work and would have been forced to move to find a job."

"OK so me chucking a bit of cash at their enterprises made things a bit easier for them, but they all work damned hard. I feel quite bad about how much we make out of them for doing bugger all, and as for Marie being sensitive! She's as tough as the local granite!"

Paul dozed off in his chair as the painkillers took effect. It was dark when he woke with a start.

"What the hell was that crash?"

"Something blew over outside. It's got really windy while you've been snoring."

"Oh damn it! I left my tools leaning up against the shed door." He returned a few minutes later. "Bloody hell, it's getting wild out there, we might as well have our tea and turn in."

"Your tea is under the grill. I got hungry and ate mine three hours ago!"

"Good heavens, is that the time? I didn't realise I'd been a kip for so long."

He had just finished clearing up his dishes and coffee cup, and was heading for the bedroom when the telephone rang. "Who the hell is that, this time of night?" he asked no one in particular as his wife was already in the bathroom.

It was a surprise to hear Taff's lilting voice on the other end of the line. "What's up?" he asked with a worried tone in his voice.

"Sorry Mate your holiday is over. There's a chopper on its way to pick you up. It will take you to Prestwick. The Lear jet will be waiting for you, you're needed Paul. Everybody, from the PM down wants you at a meeting tonight."

"It will be past midnight before I get there!" exclaimed Paul, "and I'm not sure about the chopper being able to land either, it's blowing a gale up here."

"Well get yourself sorted, it will be there in about forty minutes. See you later, gotta go."

"And good bye to you too Taff," Paul muttered as he replaced the handset.

"Who was that?" asked his wife, sounding worried,

"Taff has just informed me, a helicopter is on its way to pick me up. It seems as though my presence is required at a meeting in London."

"What, tonight in this weather? I hope you told them no."

"It appears that luxury has been denied me on this occasion."

"Oh Paul!" she sighed. "You're not going. Can't they deal with whatever it is without you just for once? It is so unfair."

"I have no idea what it's all about Luv, it must be important. You know as well as I do Taff wouldn't have called me, never mind told me to get a move on, over everyday things."

"That's what worries me, I know what you're like, and we've only got the one of you."

She watched as he filled two extra speed loaders for his revolver and slipped them into the spare holders on his web belt. "I'll be all right. If it's going to be more than a week I'll send a driver up for you. You'll enjoy seeing the other wives again."

"Stop trying to make me feel better about it. Too many of the older wives who were my friends are now widows."

"About the biggest risks I am likely to face are, high blood pressure dealing with civil servants, terminal piles or eyestrain from reading reports, so please stop fretting."

Paul saw tears in the corners of her blue eyes. "Hey, come on, this isn't like you. What's so different this time?"

She sniffed as he put a wiry arm round her shoulder and gave her a hug. "Nothing, I suppose. It's happened so many times over the years, it should be getting easier but it's not."

"In the early days I'd have said you had a point, now?" He paused, "I'm virtually chained to a desk, glued to a computer!"

"I suppose you're right."

"My main concern right now is finding a safe place for a helicopter to land. The usual place is out of the question, this gale is blowing straight into the field. The only place I can think of is on the road, just this side of the bridge. It's flat and there isn't anything for the rotors to hit; the spur should take the worst of the force out of the wind. We can park the car on the bridge facing this way with its headlights on dip beam; it should help the pilot to see what he's doing, but rather him than me."

Paul parked the car on the ramp of the little hump back bridge which carried the road over the foaming torrent, before it cascaded into the loch. With the headlights on dipped beam, the improvised landing site was illuminated in such a way the lights wouldn't dazzle the pilot, who would have to land into the wind, his nose towards the car.

Such was the strength of the following wind, the pilot overshot his planned turning point. He came in low and slowly, following the shoreline before landing, somewhat unsteadily, on the section of road illuminated by the car's lights.

"I'll ring you in the morning. I don't like leaving you on your own on a wild night like this, but sometimes..." he gave her a quick peck on the cheek and was gone, waving as he climbed into the Sea King, ducking low beneath the beating rotors.

The crewman shut the door behind him. "Welcome aboard Sir; it's a bit wild out there tonight."

"Nothing personal, but I can think of several other places I would rather be."

"It wasn't exactly what I had planned for tonight either Sir. We were the second standby crew. The duty and standby crews are both out on rescues. One is to a trawler taking water off Kintyre, and the other is picking up a medical emergency on Arran; the little air ambulance tipped over in the wind when it tried to take off. Nobody's hurt but they'll be grounded for some time 'til it's repaired."

"So it's one of 'those' nights. I was on what I thought was terminal leave but the powers that be have decided to interrupt even that. I can't imagine any reason to recall me, never mind at this time of night."

"You're the Commander of the All Arms Unit aren't you Sir?"

"I was until I quit."

"I saw you on the tele., when you put the Yank in his place. The entire mess was cheering you, even a couple of American crews who were with us for training joined in. It wasn't before time; someone should have done it long ago."

"For what it's worth I agree with you, but it should have come from our political leaders, not a serving officer of our armed forces. However you look at it, I was well out of order."

The pilot came on the intercom, "I'm sorry about the bumpy ride back there, but until I can get out of the hills it's likely to get worse. The really good news is the flight to Prestwick is going to take at least half an hour longer than it ought to on account of this head wind."

In the event, it was nearly forty minutes later than planned when the Sea King flopped onto the tarmac, as close to the Lear Jet as was safe. Paul thanked the crew of the helicopter and headed for the comfortable little twin-engined executive jet.

Instead of the crewman in flying gear and 'bone dome', a stewardess wearing an RAF uniform welcomed him aboard.

"Allow me to take your bags Sir."

"It's all right corporal, I know where they go. Both are wet and heavy, there's no point you getting yourself messed up, but if there were a chance of a cup of coffee I wouldn't say no. Strong and sweet, the opposite to me."

"As soon as we are at cruising altitude Sir. I think the pilot wants a quick word with you before we take off Sir."

The pilot was not happy. "We have a bit of a problem Colonel, you being so late means we cannot land at City Airport."

"Who says?"

"It's the rules. Only turbo props after twenty two hundred hours."

"Tough, they'll have to lump it this time. Anyway this is a military flight so they can't stop you. If they get stroppy tell them to ring Number Ten. Having been bounced around in a noisy Sea King for the last hour and a bit, I'm not exactly in the right frame of mind to deal with any bloody jobs-worth when we get to London. Given the choice I'd be tucked up with my cocoa."

"Whatever you say Colonel. If you tell me to land there then I will have to do as ordered, as you clearly outrank me."

"Fair enough, don't spare the horses."

"You'd better take a seat Colonel and buckle up. Take off could be interesting in this wind, in fact, it could be distinctly bumpy for several thousand feet, but it will be fine once we've climbed above the worst of it."

Paul sat in the seat indicated by the stewardess, his temper not improved by the increasing ache in his back. He could hear the conversation the pilot was having with those in the control tower. The controllers were telling the pilot he should not attempt take off in these conditions, in fact he should shut down his engines and wait until things improved.

After an increasingly acrimonious conversation, the senior air traffic controller finally relented, adding the somewhat worrying comment, "On your own head be it."

Paul usually enjoyed flying, especially take offs. On this occasion however, enjoyment was not a descriptive term which sprang readily to mind. He heard the pilot say, 'rotate' as the nose wheel tried to leave the ground in response to the lift generated by the increasing speed. This happened to coincide with a particularly strong, swirling gust of wind; the effect was so dramatic the 'stewardess' let out an involuntary cry of fear as one wing lifted a lot more than the other. The veteran pilot reacted instantly, applying emergency power. The equally experienced co-pilot whipped up the under carriage and the plane was flying, granted it was in a steep climbing turn rather than a smooth climb, out over the Firth of Clyde.

The controller's voice could be heard saying, 'Your turn was supposed to be to port not starboard!'

Sitting in the warmth of the control tower, he had actually reached for the emergency phone linking him to the fire and rescue services. He was sure the speedy little executive jet was going to crash. Somehow the informal, tongue in cheek rebuke for turning the wrong way seemed appropriate.

The reply broke the tension and made him laugh as the crisis was clearly over. The co-pilot's voice came clearly, 'It's his age,' referring to his long time friend sitting in the pilot's seat beside him.

Paul, his thoughts elsewhere, had noticed things had been far from smooth. The magnitude of the drama had, however, not really registered. He had been called to this meeting late at night, the only clue was it had been Taff who had summoned him, and his old friend would not have called him for anything less than a genuine crisis. Ignoring the somewhat bumpy ride he opened up his laptop, spending the next few minutes scanning the latest news stories in a fruitless search for a clue as to why his 'retirement' had been so short lived.

Attempting to call Taff or General Leach had proven equally futile, all he was able to glean from the base was that Taff had said 'Oh dear!' as he put down the 'hot line', immediately prior to calling Paul. Taff had then rushed of to collect General Leach, as both had been summoned to an urgent meeting at Number Ten.

He sat watching the lights of the towns and villages of south western Scotland slide beneath the wings, apparently slower as the altitude increased; at least it was a smoother ride now. The irony was not lost on Paul; he had at his disposal the most sophisticated and powerful communications devices there had ever been, yet he had no idea why he had been recalled, other than there was a crisis of some kind in the dark world of security.

Such was the power of what appeared to be his mobile phone, he was even able to call up the unit's spy planes, wherever they were operating. He spoke to several of the crews in his quest to find out what was going on. They seemed to be going about their normal day to day routine of watching over allied patrols in both Iraq and Afghanistan, spotting ambushes and roadside bombs for the men on the ground.

All, that is, except one. This was one of the original six rescued from the scrap heap on their retirement from active service with the R.A.F. Paul was surprised to learn this plane was about one hundred and fifty miles northwest of Cape Wrath.

"What on earth are you doing there Colin?" he asked the pilot whom he knew well.

"Keeping an eye on an unregistered freighter Boss; we thought it was smuggling something into Ireland because it was following the old gunrunner's route. Our scanners are detecting a lot of explosives in the hold. As she sailed straight past Ireland we sort of figured she is either lost or up to something else, we'll know in the morning. *Intrepid* has got ahead of the ship and is working out a plan to board her. You may be interested to know, most of the crew have been identified as either known terrorists or at least militants. We also think they may have a captive on board as there is someone who never leaves the hold where the explosives are stored."

"Thanks for the briefing Colin, sounds an odd one. It has given me something to think about, but I don't see it as anything that justifies dragging me back out of retirement."

"You love it really Boss," replied the pilot of the spy plane. "Why not just admit you can't keep away. I'll see you tomorrow Boss, and good luck hob-nobbing."

"And goodnight to you too Colin."

Paul gave up trying to work out what the crisis could be and sat chatting to the crew. It wasn't long before the glow of Greater London seemed to fill the Southern horizon.

"When you see it from up here you realise just what a vast area it covers," he remarked as the enormity of the task of protecting the capital sank in.

"My problems of getting the likes of you to wherever you need to be are more than enough for me, thank you Boss," replied the veteran pilot. "You can keep your job."

"The problem seems to be exactly that!" Paul replied. "Nobody else seems to want it!"

"You'll have to take your seat again I'm afraid Boss; because of noise regulations the descent will have to be as steep as I can safely make it. The controller is not happy about letting us land at all this time of night, but it seems as though your driver and escort convinced him it might be a good idea, no matter what the rules said."

"Quite."

As the plane was going to have to remain on the ground overnight, Paul ordered the protesting escort car driver to wait and take the crew to the 'town house', as the 'All Arms Unit's London office was commonly referred to.

The journey from Docklands to Number Ten became a frustrating stop-go affair as it seemed as though every set of traffic lights had a sensor which turned the lights to red as the car approached.

"Oh stuff this," muttered Paul, as the constant stopping began to further aggravate his already aching back. He turned to the driver, "Hasn't this thing got 'blues' fitted?"

"You know it has Boss."

"Then use the bloody things, all this stopping and starting is killing my sodding back!"

"The Met doesn't like us using them, unless we are responding to a direct terrorist incident."

"Oh Lord" muttered Paul, "Just put them on and be careful."

"Ok, you're the Boss."

"Next thing you'll be telling me they won't let us carry our guns unless they're locked in a secure compartment!"

"You got that bit right Boss, they tried to lock up a couple of our lads last week for doing exactly that!"

"You are taking the piss Ronnie?"

"Nope, it's all down to the new Assistant Deputy Commissioner."

"I can see I'll have to have a word with him and straighten a few things out."

"It's a 'her' Boss, she has overall responsibility for all armed security within the Capital. Only officers under her immediate command are allowed to carry firearms in the London area."

"Oh right!" exclaimed Paul. "Like that edict is going to survive the night. I won't do it without telling the PM first, but tomorrow's standing orders will make it clear. All, and I mean all, members of the unit will be armed at all times."

"She won't put up with that Boss; Taff tried and she sent a squad to try to arrest him."

"You are kidding!"

"Straight up Boss, there was a right row," the driver cursed under his breath. "I told you the cops don't like us using our 'blues'.

The police motor cycle pulled up beside the car and signalled the driver to pull over.

Paul decided not to put up with any negotiations, he produced his warrant and ID card, "If you want to do something useful officer, ride in front of us and get us to Number Ten as fast as is reasonably possible! You can discuss things with the PM himself when we get there."

"You can discuss things with your lawyers when they get to the station," replied the young officer. "I couldn't help noticing your gun when you reached for your ID. Carrying a concealed firearm is an offence."

"Not with the warrant I showed you it's not!"

"All those warrants were revoked last month Colonel, whatever you are. You will also be charged with unauthorised use of emergency lights and I have also been informed your aircraft broke noise regulations when it landed at City Airport."

When Paul got his voice back, he got out of the car and approached the officer. "Let me put things this way," he paused, controlling his rage. "I have just been summoned to an emergency meeting at Number Ten. I am in neither good humour or health, and as for the crap about me or my men being armed, tell the silly tart who issued the order we are talking about guns, not her bloody dildos. She might regard them as a phallic symbol but they are a vital, if unfortunate piece of kit in our less than pleasant line of work. Now you can either escort us, or get out of the bloody way! Do I make myself clear!"

Paul climbed painfully back into the front passenger seat. "Go Ronnie, drive round his bike, just get me there!"

"Welcome back Boss."

"And while I think of it, if he looks like getting in the way again, stick the sirens on as well!"

CHAPTER THREE

Paul was ushered into the 'inner sanctum' with only the minimum of checks as those doing the checking knew him only too well.

"Good evening Prime Minister. Please accept my apologies for the hour, a difficult journey."

One of the civil servants present made a comment about, 'ox carts from Norfolk,' which provoked the response, "for an intelligence officer, you are remarkably ill informed!"

Paul sat in the chair indicated by the PM. "Now, if someone would care to enlighten me as to the specific reason I was summoned here tonight, I will attempt to offer some reasonable advice on the matter."

"You mean you don't know?" exclaimed the Metropolitan Police Commissioner.

"I presume there was some pressing reason, other than to fall foul of one of your young jobs-worth's on the way here from City Airport. I believe I am currently under arrest on charges varying from carrying a concealed firearm to noise pollution."

"Good Lord!" muttered a minister.

This provoked the response Paul had been secretly hoping for. One of the first people he had noticed on entering the conference room had been the same Deputy Assistant Commissioner who had issued the 'no guns' edict. The senior members of the security and armed forces present sank deeper into their chairs, one got the feeling they had a fair idea what was coming.

Resplendent in her immaculate new uniform she rose to the bait, delivering what she thought was a speech which would result in Paul calmly handing over his revolver, and an eloquent apology. To her increasing annoyance, Paul seemed oblivious to the tirade and more interested in his laptop. Eventually, seemingly happy with what he had found, he looked up at the furious police woman. "Sorry it took so long for me to find this," he turned the screen towards her, "I'm not very good on these things."

She didn't even glance at the screen. "You didn't listen to a word I said did you Colonel?"

"No, it was a load of ill informed rubbish anyway," replied Paul evenly.

"Colonel!" she began.

Paul cut her off. "Shut up and read what it says on the computer screen."

"You do not tell me to shut up!"

"And you do not decide if I, or any of my men, carry firearms in public."

"I am in charge of ALL armed security personnel in the Metropolitan Police area, other than troops within defined garrison areas."

"Not anymore you're not. I don't care how many degrees you've got, or how good a shot you think you might be on a range. None of those quasi qualifications entitles you to command armed personnel. I know for a fact you have never fired a shot in anger, at least not one which hit its target. The only people qualified to command armed personnel be they police, military or something in between, are individuals who have had to use ultimate force themselves, and more importantly coped with it. You never know if you have coped until it happens again, so you have absolutely no qualifications or moral authority to occupy your current office."

In all her years in the police no-one had ever spoken to her like that before. For the first time anyone could remember, she was stuck for words.

"While you're trying to think of a reply, read what is on this computer. A copy of the full charter is in the PM's safe, for his eyes only; the Monarch also has a copy, as do I. They are the only two people in the country who can give the Commander of the All Arms Unit direct orders. If it comes to the crunch you, and the staff of your department, are ultimately under my command in matters relating to terrorism. Even if your targets are armed robbers or drug dealers, if the proceeds of their crimes fund terrorist activities under any guise, then you liaise with the All Arms Unit. No ifs or buts, you do it!"

"I do not believe what is on this screen. If it were true then we would be under what amounts to martial law."

"Well done, you can understand what you read. The point being, we have been for the past twenty or so years and no one has noticed. I suppose nearly fifty people actually know; now you know. The question is what are you going to do?"

"I will not accept any interference from someone like you in the way I run my department. I'll resign first!"

"In that case. Goodbye. Oh before you go, sign this pro forma, it's part of the Official Secrets Act you will never have heard of before. Refusing is not an option, neither is breaking it"

"I'll deal with you in the morning Colonel, there are more pressing matters to discuss."

"You won't be dealing with anyone in the morning. I do however agree with you about the rest, so I suggest we get on with it."

"What do you know about the current crisis Colonel?" asked the Home Secretary.

"I was unaware there was an specific crisis, which in turn means no one has been talking about it, my old unit included. I could however hazard a guess, based on traffic reports I happened to hear on the radio. Something about fuel tankers catching fire, three in a week struck me as being a bit strange."

"So you think it is the start of a campaign you predicted a couple of years ago, designed to bring the country to its knees by choking off the fuel."

"That's a bit of a leap Sir," Paul replied to the head of the Chiefs of Staff. "Of course it is a possibility I don't suppose we can ignore. Is there any evidence? As I understand it, the incident on the North Circular was caused by a car losing control on a bend and hitting the petrol tanker. A discarded cigarette is supposed to have been the cause of the explosion at a filling station in Bradford, which is about as plausible as a mobile phone sparking the Bar Hill inferno north of Cambridge."

"Your scenario as I recall, started in much the same way Paul. If you were correct in your assumption as to the methods they would employ, then all of this fits."

"Add to that a couple of recent intercepts, and a warning passed on to us via Al Jazeera, then in my opinion we have a problem," added the head of MI6.

"Have you copies of these Sir John?"

The head of MI6 handed Paul three sheets of paper. The expression on Paul's face changed to one of growing concern. "I see what you mean Sir. I take it the translations have been double-checked from the originals?"

"Absolutely Colonel, you taught me that much. Interestingly, all three were in a strange Yemeni dialect of Arabic."

"I'll bet they were not transmitted from Bora-Bora."

"Oh no, but one of our technical staff is certain the first two were sent by one of the radio operators who used to be there. Both had references to 'dealing with the guard dog' just as you predicted."

"I don't understand the point Colonel, could you explain please?" asked a minister.

"Sammy Bin Liner, Osama bin Laden to you, always describes the British as 'the great Satan's guard dog."

"The great Satan?" enquired the same minister.

"It's how Bin Laden always refers to America. You know what Sir John," Paul turned to address the head of the Secret Service again. "My first impression is, these could well be genuine."

"You don't happen to know the whereabouts of General Leach and your Welsh cohort do you Colonel?" asked the Chief of the Defence staff. "I was under the impression they were supposed to be here."

"I was expecting to see them here myself Sir, I have been trying to contact them since I left home." He turned to the PM. "With your permission Sir, I'll try again."

"By all means Colonel."

Once in the corridor, Paul tried first Taff's mobile then the General's; both times he got the same high pitched whine. He was beginning to think it was his phone which was up the creek.

More in desperation than anything he called the main switch board on the base, at least he got an answer. He quickly identified himself. The duty operator was unknown to him and was reluctant to put Paul through to the duty officer. For once he was in luck, it was an old friend who picked up the phone.

"B.J.?"

"Ah Paul, I've been trying to get hold of you, your phone has been off. I take it you've heard about Taff and General Leach?"

"I've been trying to get hold of the reprobates for the last three hours, where the hell are they? They are supposed to be at this bloody meeting with me!"

"Obviously you haven't heard. Taff is in hospital along with General Leach. They'll both be all right, but their driver and the trooper escorting them are in a bad way."

"How? I thought we trained our drivers to avoid accidents."

"I don't think any amount of training would have helped very much Paul. It seems as though a tanker exploded on the M11 just as they were about to overtake it. The car is burnt out. It seems as though they had taken their jackets off, and of course their mobiles were in their pockets. Just to compound matters, the explosion destroyed a mobile network relay mast."

"That's the fourth tanker in a week B.J. We had just been discussing the other three."

"Actually it's the fifth. There was another which went off the road and blew up this afternoon; it was full of jet fuel, which isn't exactly easy to ignite. The Yanks are dealing with that one as it was on its way to Mildenhall."

"So have the bastards started?"

"It certainly looks like it Paul, but so far there isn't a shred of evidence of deliberate sabotage at any of the sites. As unlikely as it seems, it is just possible this is simply a succession of unrelated freak accidents."

"Yeah right B.J.," retorted Paul.

"Oh, I agree with you mate. It's the proof which is missing."

"I'd better get back to this meeting. Give Taff and his Nibs my regards and tell them to find a better excuse next time. Make sure those two lads and their families have everything they need. Look after them B.J."

"I will Paul, I'll hold the fort 'til you get here. Taff and the General are being kept in over night, just to make sure they're okay."

"Thanks for the update, at least now I have some idea of what'ss going on. See you in the morning."

It was a very thoughtful Paul who returned to the meeting. "Well, where are they Colonel?" asked an obviously annoyed Prime Minister. "This really isn't good enough."

"Actually Sir, they are in hospital. Both Taff and General Leach should be all right in a few days; the same cannot, unfortunately, be said for the driver and escort."

"What on earth happened?"

"It appears a petrol tanker blew up on the M11 just as they caught it up and it wasn't the only one today, as I have just been told of another near an air base in Suffolk. As of this moment I have no idea why they exploded."

"It might be a good idea to find out Colonel."

"The police are investigating but, as far as I'm aware, no one has found any reason as to why any of those tankers should have blown up.."

"Make it your job to find out Colonel."

"Yes Minister but I am a soldier, not a scientist." Paul took a drink from his glass. "Now, before we got side tracked, we were going to take a look at this warning passed on by Al Jazeera."

"Do you think it is a serious threat Colonel? These nutters are constantly making wild statements."

"I think it would be prudent to check it out Sir"

"It seems utterly absurd to me. How on earth could a motley band such as Al Qaeda hope to destroy London? Even a sizeable nuclear bomb couldn't destroy all of it. I think we would know if they had stolen one of them, don't you Colonel? This is just another of Bin Laden's fantasies."

"Is it? How can you be so certain Minister. I'll grant you even the Russians would have noticed if they had lost one of their big nukes and as you said, it would have to be a big one. As far as I am aware, Iran does not have the ability to make one, not on a scale such as this; for that matter North Korea couldn't either. Read the letter again and you'll see, it doesn't state they will destroy London, which I agree is probably beyond them. If you read it properly you will observe it actually says 'wipe out' London, a small but subtle difference."

"So what do you think they are going to do Colonel?" asked the persistent politician.

"Frankly I haven't got the remotest idea Sir, but as soon as I get back to the unit's base I will look into it."

"More to the point Colonel, and this was the reason for your recall, what are we going to do about this threat?" asked the Prime Minister.

"The threat to 'wipe out' London, or the threat to 'destroy the guard dog' Sir?" Paul asked, "because they are vastly different things. If, as seems to be the case, they have already started, then the only way is to disguise petrol tankers as other trucks. This will upset Health and Safety, not to mention EU officials and god's dog and its puppies, as this will entail hiding the tankers in fridges, curtain-siders and the likes, and of course, removing any trace of hazchem stickers, in particular the distinctive orange markers."

"We could not possibly do it Colonel, it would be against the law!" exclaimed a civil servant.

"And blowing them up isn't?" retorted Paul.

"The obvious way is to escort the tankers Colonel."

"What good would that do, apart from killing the escorts as well as the tanker drivers, who will probably quit anyway as soon as they twig what is happening?"

"Then we'll simply have to use the army to deliver the fuel."

"How on earth do people like you get jobs such as the position you hold? I have never heard anything so stupid; what possible difference will a half baked idea like that make? The poor bloody driver will be just as dead, soldier or not. What we have to do, is find out how they are detonating these tankers; as yet, to the best of my knowledge, we have no idea. We cannot even prove these explosions are in any way linked to terrorists.

All right, the one on the North Circular was without doubt deliberate, but whether it was a suicide bomber in the terrorist sense, or some sad individual utterly determined to end it all in a spectacular way to make some point, who knows? We don't even know who he was, we may never know."

"What about the others Colonel, there must be some commonality?"

"You forget Sir. I've been away on extended, what should have been terminal, leave. As you are aware, I have been accessing the unit's computers. The latest information is, there is no known cause for any of the other explosions or the accidents leading up to them."

"Yet you think they are terrorist attacks?"

"Initially I had doubts, but five in a week?"

"What about the threat to 'wipe out' London Colonel. What should we do about it?" asked the Prime Minister.

"Before we can even begin to answer that one Sir, we need the answer to 'IF'. Once we have evaluated this first question, it then comes down to how and most importantly when? What we cannot do, is leave any warning pertaining to this lying in someone's in tray because 'it's not their department' which is exactly what the Yanks did with the information on nine-eleven."

"So you are proposing to have your armed soldiers running about all over the place again Colonel?"

"I thought we had dealt with this. Not only will the security forces go wherever the information takes them, they will be armed. Until police units have been retrained, they will not deal with any terrorist linked activities, other than in a containment role. Now this in no way denigrates the courage of the individual officers, but this is a situation they are not trained to deal with. The problem is at the top, the leadership have lost the plot. Frankly I don't think they had ever had the plot in the first place."

"My officers are trained to the highest standards Colonel."

"I don't doubt that, but to deal with highly trained and motivated nutters they require distinctly different techniques, and frankly all the degrees under the sun will never qualify you to lead them."

"Getting back to the matter in hand Colonel. What, in your opinion, should we do to counter these specific threats should they prove real?" asked the Prime Minister.

"That's a bit academic at the moment, but for what it's worth, draw up plans to disguise the tankers and protect them when they are delivering. I suppose the only thing we can do about the other threat, until it's defined, is to draw up contingency plans for the rapid evacuation of London. The only way to deal with such a threat is to identify it and stop it before it happens, and that is always a dangerous strategy without a back up plan."

"How will you investigate this latest threat Colonel?" enquired a civil servant.

"Same as usual Sir," replied Paul with a non-committal tone in his voice.

"Which is Colonel? You are not being very helpful. The committee of which I am chair will need to know, so we can evaluate your unit's performance."

If there was one thing guaranteed to upset the long time operational commander of the All Arms Unit, it was a civil servant trying to poke his nose into the affairs of his command for no other reason than to justify their own existence.

"Fair enough Sir, but first of all I will need an estimate of tea, sugar and sweeteners your committee will require. Also we will need to know whether you require fresh or long life milk, not to mention what variety of biscuits and how many packets you will require on a daily basis."

"Do not be so facetious Colonel," was the man's angry retort.

"You asked for that," chuckled one of his colleagues.

Paul simply gave him an almost pitying look and shook his head. He turned to the Prime Minister. "With your permission Sir, I think it would be a good idea if I get back to my base, if only to bring myself up to date, as clearly something is going on. The problem is going to be finding out who is behind it, and sitting around here talking about it isn't going to help very much."

"It would be advantageous if you were to stay in London Colonel."

"Advantageous to whom?" Paul asked the civil servant.

"You would do well to be more respectful Colonel as my committee was set up specifically to oversee all counter terrorist efforts in the U.K."

"Another monumental waste of public money. You lot serve no useful purpose, in fact you are an extra embuggerence to all those engaged in the fight against these idiots. Out of idle curiosity, what qualifies you to judge how well a unit is performing. Have you ever served with, never mind lead, a counter terrorist unit?"

"That is totally irrelevant Colonel. My committee are all highly qualified in assessment techniques and performance related evaluations."

"Right then, sod off and evaluate your own performance and stay out of my way, and the way of all the other units trying to keep our people safe. We do not need you interfering and generally getting in the way. The time spent giving 'evidence' or filling in questionnaires sent out by you is wasted time and could be much better spent tracking down these idiots. I'll be in touch Prime Minister, as soon as I have anything to report. I think I really ought to get moving as both Taff and the General are being kept in hospital for the moment, I wish you all goodnight."

CHAPTER FOUR

By the time Paul reached the Breckland base of the All Arms Unit it was getting light. With the dawn came the first gusts of the storm he had left behind in Scotland. It was two very tired friends who greeted each other as Paul walked into the control centre.

"Morning B.J., I hesitate to call it a good one."

"Hi Boss, you got here at last then?"

"After a fashion I suppose. I'm knackered, have little idea of what is going on, hungry and in need of a decent cup of coffee, but all that can wait. What I really need to know is the condition of Taff and General Leach."

"Taff's pretty much all right, a little scorched around the edges but nothing to worry about, last I heard he was sleeping without sedation."

"We should be so lucky, and the General?"

"According to the hospital, he's not too bad. A little smoke inhalation damage, a few minor burns to his ears and nose, nothing life threatening."

"That's something I suppose. Is my old office free?"

"Oh yes. I thought you'd want it, it's ready."

"Come on, you can brief me on what's going on."

Paul went straight to where the kettle should have been. "OK, where have you hidden it?"

"We had to take them all out Paul. Health and Safety gave this place the once over and the kettles had to go - it was deemed an unacceptable risk with all the computers around. If we want a drink then it's the canteen. The other thing was, there were no separate washing up facilities in each office."

"I have never heard such a load of old bollocks in all my bloody life! Who the hell let them in in the first place?" Paul called the stores, but, predictably at this early hour, got an answering machine. He left a message requesting a kettle.

"We didn't have a lot of choice. Some of the civvies working on base are in the union. One of the contractors was rewiring an old ammunition bunker we are refurbishing and managed to give himself a pretty severe shock. When he came out of hospital we got a solicitor's letter informing us he was suing as we had failed in our duty of care, and broken several health and safety laws."

"Like what?"

"The wiring he was replacing was in the old colours. This, it seems, is against EU law and as a result MoD legal eagles sent in the Health and Safety inspectors. The rest is history."

"I have never heard anything so bloody daft!" exclaimed Paul. "How the hell are you supposed to rewire something; are the wires supposed to change bloody colour themselves! Anyway, what the hell are civilian contractors doing working on this base?"

"A French company was awarded the contract by the MoD for all electrical wiring work on all military bases."

"Since when have we been subject to the whims of civil bloody servants in Whitehall?"

"It just seemed to happen Paul. One day we were answerable to the PM's office, next morning all logistics and building work came under the MoD," replied B.J.. "The General complained, but it did no good."

"Well the PM made it pretty clear last night we were still answerable to his office, so when those contractors turn up, they will NOT be allowed on base. No ifs or buts, their passes will be revoked; in fact, the duty officer can phone their office and save them a wasted journey. As of now this base is totally off limits to all but unit personnel. Deliveries, including the post, will be to the building next to the guardroom, the same as they used to be. That system always worked well in the past, and kettles will be available in any office where the staff ask for one. As for the 'no smoking' rules! This is my bloody office and if I want a fag, I'll bloody well have one!"

"What about the builders and associated tradesmen who work for the government agency responsible for property maintenance?"

"Do the same as we always did. Use a local firm for painting and the likes, and our engineers for anything else. Task for today. Restore the integrity of base security. I'll be damned if I'll have every Tom, Dick and Harry wandering around this place. Madness, absolute bloody madness, how on earth did this happen? I can't imagine Taff or the General putting up with it."

"In fairness Paul, they didn't have a lot of choice. The MoD were very insistent."

"I'll bet the nosey bastards were. Well this is supposed to be a secret base. A lot of our gear, even some of our planes, are not supposed to exist, so it stops right now. Shut up shop B.J., we've got some terrorists to catch and we won't do it if we're falling over, Bodge it and Leg it, Builder's Ltd."

To save a queue at the main gate Paul sent a military police unit to close the access road on the junction with the public road. The telephones nearly melted as angry contractors rang in, demanding their workers be allowed in - this in spite of the employers being informed about the base being sealed. Predictably it wasn't long before the MoD joined in the protests.

"I am the Director of Public Works," came the posh voice. "I demand to speak to whoever is responsible for this debacle."

"Then carry on talking to yourself Mate," replied Paul, "If however you want to talk to whoever is sorting it out, then you've got him."

"I beg your pardon, to whom am I speaking?"

"For what it's worth, I'm the Operational Commander of this unit, and yes, it was me who revoked all the passes."

"You cannot do that, all those staff are under contract."

"Yes I can, and I have. They might have contracts with the MoD; this unit does not come under MoD control so the contracts do not apply."

"I say they do apply. The unit was taken under MoD control to streamline administration."

"And we all know what that means don't we?" Paul responded angrily. "You lot used money from the Chancellor to redecorate your executive bogs; money which was specifically for new engines for some of our aircraft. I suggest you go and cry into your gold rimmed urinal and do not waste any more of my staff's time answering your calls. The matter is closed. Oh, one other thing, my staff are authorised to use lethal force against intruders. I suggest you pass that information on. Good day!"

Paul heard "Now just a ...", as he replaced the handset. He called the main switchboard on the internal phone and, after introducing himself to the operator, he told the harassed telephonist to put all calls from the MoD on hold and leave them there, unless it was from the Secretary of Defence in person.

Many of the contractors had equipment on the base. Paul's solution to this was simple. The unit's own transport section would deliver the equipment to the nearest site or to the Ministry of Public Works depot at a nearby army camp. If they didn't like it, hard luck!

By lunch time the number of those trying to gain access had shrunk to a trickle. Even the local police had gone, satisfied the congestion in the little market town had passed. About half past one a car pulled up at the road block, the occupants furious at being denied access."

"I don't care who you are Sir," said the patient provost sergeant. "You are not on my list of persons allowed on base, so that is the end of the discussion."

A tall, quite imposing man got out of the front passenger seat. "Now look here my good man. I insist, no, I demand you let us in. We are from the Health and Safety Executive and have a right to inspect this, or any other establishment we wish. You cannot refuse us entry, do you understand?"

"I'm not your 'good man,'" replied the military policeman. "I have my orders from a man with two pips and a crown on his epaulettes. I don't see anyone in your party out ranking him, so I'm sorry gentlemen you have had a wasted journey."

"Get your commander here at once sergeant, and stop messing us about!"

"If you insist, but it won't do you any good. In fact I don't think it's a good idea at all, as he is not in the best of moods at the moment."

"Get him!"

"On your head be it." The sergeant used his radio and informed Paul of the problem.

"Put your phone on speaker Alan so the dipstick can hear what I say, as I am not in the mood to repeat myself."

"OK Boss, and welcome back."

Paul grunted what sounded like 'thanks'. "Right, I presume you can hear me, I am only going to say this once. Get back in your car and go back from whence you came. This base is sealed to all those not authorised to be on site, we are under operational security. Put in simple terms, the guards are authorised to use lethal force against any intruders or anyone attempting to enter the base illegally. In other words they can shoot if they wish!" The click as the line went dead was audible.

Paul's attention was drawn to a VDU on his desk as a message flashed up on the screen. Another tanker had blown up. In the next five minutes three more such incidents were reported.

"How the hell are they doing it B.J.?"

"Pass, but at least two of them will be on video. Possibly all four could have been in the area covered by 'eagle eye four'."

"I presume the data is being processed as we speak."

"Should be, I'll go and check. I'll also make sure we have the video all the way back to the depots."

"I don't suppose we had coverage overnight did we? There is always the chance someone snuck in and planted bombs with timers when the trucks were parked up."

"I'll check that too Paul."

The intercom buzzed again, it was the main gate. "Yes Alan?"

"It's this Health and Safety lot Boss. They refuse to leave until they have spoken to you."

"All right, I'm on my way."

"Thanks Boss."

Just for a moment the military police thought the land rover Paul was driving was going to crash into the gates. He jumped out, clearly not in a good mood. "Right! What part of go away didn't you pillocks understand?"

The reply was lost in the thunderous roar of a heavy jet beginning its take off run. He watched as the old Victor tanker roared into the sky trailing black smoke behind it. The brilliant blue flames of its after burners, which apart from its speed, were the only visible signs this was a different beast to the old RAF machines retired after the first Gulf War.

"Now," said Paul, as the noise abated. "You were about to tell me which part of go away you didn't understand."

"You do not have the right to refuse us entry Colonel," replied the big man.

"Yes I do. Your car is obstructing access to an operational security forces base. Shift it, otherwise I'll get a forklift out here and shift it for you, into that ditch!"

"Do not threaten me Colonel."

"I'm not threatening you mate, I'm telling you the way things are. If you want to do something useful, why don't you go and tell the terrorists to stop blowing things up!"

"Don't be ridiculous Colonel."

"I'll tell you what is ridiculous, me standing here arguing with you. In the last half an hour four petrol tankers have blown up on major roads. I have the task of stopping it happening again.

"Alan!"

"Yes Boss."

"If this lot does not leave within the next five minutes, throw them in the cells in the guardroom, if they resist shoot them!"

"You can't do that!" the big man complained. "Surely those guns are not loaded!"

"They had bloody well better be," retorted Paul. "Mine is!" as he produced his faithful old .357 revolver. "Last chance. Bugger off while you still can!"

"You cannot carry loaded weapons Colonel."

"Of course we can, stupid sod. The bloody terrorists do, go and harass them." Paul turned to go. "Sort them out Alan, do what you have to do, but get rid of them. Keep this access clear."

"Will do Boss," he turned to the man from the car. "You heard the CO, I do not recommend upsetting him further. You will not be allowed onto this base without his specific permission, and I wouldn't think that is very likely to be forthcoming."

"I'm going back to London sergeant. I'll be back in the morning with written authorisation to make sure our previous directives have been complied with. Woe betide your Boss if they haven't."

"You can bring as many pieces of paper as you like Sir, the answer will be the same, and I cannot guarantee whoever is in charge of this detail tomorrow will be blessed with my patience. Goodbye!"

On the return to his office Paul was given the phone by an agitated B.J. "The PM for you Boss."

Paul groaned, "Yes Sir," as he took the handset.

"What's going on Colonel?"

"At the moment all I know is four more tankers have blown up and there has been heavy loss of life in at least two of the incidents."

"I meant what is going on with the MoD Colonel? I've had many angry officials phoning me up; even stopping me in the House to complain about you. It seems as though you have been denying their contractors and inspectors access to your base."

"That is correct Sir. None of them have security clearance to have access to the base. We are under operational conditions until the current threat is dealt with, and will remain so until further notice. In the meantime we will revert to our previous practice of using our own local contractors if needs be. Apart from anything else, this is also a much cheaper option. Most of these

Timothy Pilgrim

so-called contractors were not engaged in any projects which mattered. They were merely a confounded nuisance, not to mention a security risk. I will concede, tact is not my strong point, but none of those refused entry added in any way to the efficient running of the base. The same applies to a party from the Health and Safety Directorate who also attempted to enter the base. I have no doubt you will be hearing from their boss shortly. Please inform them this base is a highly restricted area for the foreseeable future and very definitely off limits."

"I do see your point Colonel, and as you say, tact is not your strongest point. I will however inform the Secretary for Defence that your unit has returned to its former status. I must confess, I had no idea the MoD had moved in to such an extent. It seems as though certain officials omitted to tell me about certain changes they had implemented. I trust you will have some results shortly regarding these exploding tankers."

"As soon as I have anything I will let you know Sir." Paul heaved an audible sigh of relief as he replaced the handset.

He turned to B.J. "Any news on Taff and the others?"

Taff is on his way here. The General is due out in a couple of days, but will need to rest for a bit. The driver and escort are both in a bad way but they are hanging in there."

"Having Taff back will help. Have we got any indications on the cause of the tankers exploding yet? Are there any common factors?"

"I'll get someone in Intel to send us all there is on these incidents Paul, but we have got a good team of analysts, they don't often miss anything."

"I know, but there must be some sort of pattern emerging. Last I heard the only one with a known cause was the suicide car bomber on the North Circular. There is no sign of a missile or a bomb at any of the other incidents. Don't forget, one was full of central heating oil and another full of jet fuel, neither of which burn easily as liquid. What could be a cause, other than an explosive charge of some kind?"

"Damned if I know Paul. Add to that the fact that, they are not only from different depots but for the most part they belonged to different companies."

"There just has to be a link. If it's not explosives, could it be the fuel itself?" Paul answered his own question. "But then two weren't petrol, and they are all over the place."

"A team is checking security tapes from all the depots, they might come up with something," B.J. said optimistically.

"I had hoped we might see something on the Canberra's films, but I'm damned if I could see anything. We zoomed in to maximum resolution, went over every inch of the tank immediately prior to the blast, not a damned thing. The tank was as clean as a new pin."

Paul brought up the recording of one of the explosions on the plasma screen. He stopped it on the actual frame showing the exact mille second the tank ruptured. He rewound the recording and played it over and over, nothing!

"Beats the hell out of me B.J., there has to be something. These things don't detonate for no reason!"

"The team have had all sorts of theories Paul - micro-waves, ultra sound, nothing. The only anomaly was a couple of the tanks had hot spots prior to blowing up. Nothing which could have set them off though."

Paul brought up pictures of four of the tankers prior to their dramatic demise. One of them was the tanker hit by the suicide bomber.

"All of them clean as a whistle Paul, what have you noticed?"

"They are all very clean. Well, one of them is clean because it's been through a washer, that one," he pointed to the one with the known cause. "The others are clean because they're new. See the difference?"

"I think so, it's the wheels which give them away. You could have something there Paul."

"Like what? Could a chemical reaction with the paint make them blow up? But then they are all different colours. The military one was matt paint, so that one doesn't add up either. It could be worth checking who made them. A new lining possibly, but then something like that must have already been checked on, surely?"

Two minutes later B.J. had the answer. A Dutch company had made all of the trailers. Further checking revealed the tanks had actually been made in a brand new factory in Croatia, part of an EU initiative to help re-generate the area. Only the final paint job had been carried out in Holland; this had been the application of the company's liveries.

"I suppose they did inspect the things before they were shipped over here? Get onto the company and get them to e-mail copies of the inspection reports to us. Also check if trailers destined for the UK have a different spec to continental tankers. If they have, then we could have our first lead."

"Bloody brilliant Paul. There is a significant Muslim population in Croatia. All right I know, the vast majority are perfectly honest, decent folk but it would only take one or two."

"Get on with it B.J.," scolded Paul. "While you're out, see if you can find a fuel tech., we must have some around here; no doubt there's a lab rat amongst them, I'd like a word."

"I'll see to it Boss."

As soon as B.J. left on his errand, Paul used the internal phone to call the stores in search of his elusive kettle. He got the duty store man. "Corporal Lines stores clerk. How can I help?"

"Is the QM handy? I'd like a word please."

"He's a bit busy just now, sorting out the new rosters. It seems as though all our civvies have been banned from the camp."

"I know! It was me who banned them. Now give Brian my compliments and tell him to get the kettle I asked for earlier, with a lead into my office, like yesterday!"

"Health and Safety banned them Sir," replied the young storeman.

"And I banned Health and Safety. I've got coffee, coffee mate, lots of sugar, I've even got mugs and water in the tap but no bloody kettle! Unless you fancy Deepcut or Catterick, I suggest you get your arse into gear and supply the missing item, and make sure the bloody thing works! You've got five minutes!" He sat back in his chair and lit a cigarette. He was about to take his second drag when a high pitched peep-peep went off. In his absence smoke alarms had been fitted pretty well everywhere. For a moment he considered shooting the offending sensor but settled for switching it off. While he was on his feet he used his combat knife to prize both 'No Smoking' signs off the wall, and consigned them to the rubbish bin.

There was a furtive knock on the office door. It crossed Paul's mind that the new storeman had been unusually swift in delivering the desired kettle so he was surprised to see a very young looking Major enter in response to his "Come".

"Oh," uttered Paul. "And you are?"

"Major Andrew Courtney Sir." The young man seemed as confused by Paul's presence as Paul was by the Major's.

"What can I do for you Major?"

"It would seem your smoke alarm went off Sir and is now malfunctioning." The young man was suddenly unsure of himself as he belatedly noticed the cigarette in the senior man's hand. "I've got some fresh batteries in my pocket if you would like me to reset it Sir?"

"What I would like you to do Major, is send a sparkie over and remove it! That, or fix an on/off switch beside the door to enable me to switch it off when I'm in my office, and reset it when I leave."

"You are not allowed to smoke in here Sir."

"Stop right there son. This is my office, and if I want to smoke then I will bloody well smoke, and I don't give a flying f.. you know what, what Health and Safety, much less some interfering bloody do-good busybody says. Now what is your position here, and who posted you here, and when?"

"I am the camp Health and Safety Officer. I was posted here by the MoD safety directorate last week."

"Right. If you want to stay around here, you will report to the training cadre at 0700hrs tomorrow. They will evaluate you to see if you have got what it takes to be a soldier, rather than yet another candidate for an attack of terminal piles. If you don't like the sound of that, then you can return to your quarters and start packing. I'll have your orders and travel warrant ready for you first thing in the morning. The choice is yours."

"What sort of evaluation would that be Sir? I am, after all, a major."

"Everything from computer skills to free fall parachuting, weapon skills, general fitness and the likes, a general evaluation, to establish if you are of any use to us."

"My chosen field of expertise is in safety in the work place Sir. I and my team are badly overstretched here to the extent I have requested some additional personnel who will arrive tomorrow morning."

"I am absolutely gob-smacked Major. If we need anything in the way of equipment from an outside source, it can literally take a year to supply, no matter how vital, yet you request some additional deadwood and it arrives straight away!"

"It has been determined this establishment is an extremely dangerous work environment, there are many safety procedures which need implementing."

In the most patronising tone he could manage Paul said, "Son, it may have escaped your notice that being a member of Her Majesties Armed Forces carries with it certain dangers. If training was made risk free, then it would be pointless as no one would know how an individual would react to danger, or even if they would recognise a situation as being potentially dangerous until it was too late. It is no good finding out you can't cope when the shit hits the fan, is it?"

"I suppose not Sir."

"By the way, how many are there in your team?"

"Twenty in all Sir, with another ten due tomorrow."

"Right, now you run along and gather up your flock and tell them the options. It is of no consequence what you do if you are not the best in your chosen field. Equally you must also be capable of defending yourself and your colleagues against any threat. If you fancy having a go then you are welcome, otherwise you can go and make a pest of yourself elsewhere. Good day Major."

The young man didn't move. "The smoke detector Sir?" He held out his hand with two new batteries. "Or maybe an electrician to fit an on/off switch beside the door?"

"Now that is a workable solution Major, I'll see you in the morning."

Timothy Pilgrim

CHAPTER FIVE

The next furtive knock on the office door turned out to be the fuel technician Paul had wanted a chat with.

"Come in son. Contrary to rumours I do not bite!"

"How can I help Sir?"

"I'm told you know about fuels and how they burn, more to the point what makes them burn."

"That is my trade Sir."

"Right. I have a tanker full of fuel - petrol, diesel or aviation kerosene, and I want it to blow up. There are no explosives, bullets or other projectiles involved. As far as we can tell there is no faulty wiring either, how can I make it go bang?"

"What you need is heat Sir," replied the young soldier nervously.

"What sort of heat? Could a binding brake generate enough?"

"It would have to be well alight Sir. Even if the tyre was on fire, it would have to burn very fiercely to set off the petrol. The other fuels would need much more than one tyre to set them off."

"OK you have now ruled out my ideas."

"Sorry Sir."

"Don't be sorry son. At worst you've narrowed the cause down to something we haven't thought of yet."

"It could be caused by a chemical reaction Sir. It is possible to generate very high temperatures with the right mix of chemicals."

"Brilliant, did I sense a 'but' in there?"

"Well, yes Sir. I can't see how anyone could get the chemicals into the tanker. Obviously we are aware of the exploding tankers at the PO.L section. Our CO has had us checking all incoming fuel, just in case it is contaminated."

"Well done him. What if the contaminate was in the tanker before it was loaded?"

"Can't happen Sir, they are always checked. They must be clean and dry before they can be loaded. Health and Safety are very strict on that point Sir - a single violation could cost an operator his licence to run tankers. If it had been just a single incident then it could possibly have been a case of inadequate inspection, or even an opportunist terrorist, but not all these incidents. The latest one at Fawley was still in the truck park when it went up, and there is no way their procedures are slack."

"Could these chemicals be applied as a coating on the inside of a tanker? Would it escape notice?"

"I really don't know Sir. It is possible I suppose, depending on which combination of chemicals you used, but you would have to be inside the tank to do it, and it needs at least two different agents to react with each other. If they mixed while they were being applied it could be fatal to those doing it."

"OK," Paul paused as he thought it through. "You spray one section with chemical 'A' then the next with chemical 'B'. You would have to allow the first to dry so there was no danger of mixing. The tanker is then filled up and sets off on its delivery run. Could the fuel act as a catalyst and dissolve the chemicals, thus mixing them?"

"Yes, but you would have to do the spraying in the factory Sir, during the building or a major refurbishment. Those tanks are full of baffles to stop the fuel sloshing around; there are so many of them in the new tanks, checking them is a right pain in the arse. Sorry Sir," The young soldier blushed at his perceived gaff.

"That's all right son, tell it how it is. I started off as a very ordinary squaddie. It might have been a lot of years ago, but my memory isn't failing yet. Anyway, thanks a lot, you figured out how, I had already worked out where. I take it you were unaware all the exploding trailers were new ones?"

"I didn't know that Sir. For me, it confirms your theory of a dry coating applied during manufacture. I don't see how it could happen, but if that is how it was done then everything else adds up."

"Thank you son, now if you will give your section commander my regards, I would like you to go to your lab and work out what the likely chemicals involved could be. Once you have a list of possible combinations of chemicals, if you could let the forensic teams, on a list I will get printed out for you, know what they are looking for, I would be very grateful. The list should be at the front desk by the time you get there. Thank you again, you have been most helpful."

In his haste the young soldier almost collided with the returning B.J. "Steady on soldier, the Boss isn't that scary is he?"

"Sorry Sir, but he did say as soon as possible."

"On you go son, and take it easy."

B.J. wandered into Paul's office. "You really must stop scaring the youngsters Paul.

"What?" replied Paul, his thoughts elsewhere.

"The fuel tech., he was bricking it, panicking in case he displeased the legendary leader."

"Oh, belt up you idiot. He was the one who came up with a likely answer, he's simply keen to prove his theory. Anyway, what did the Dutch have to say?"

"British tankers are indeed built to a different spec. than Continental ones. The metal is thicker, and they have extra baffles."

"I don't suppose you got a list of customers for this particular batch did you?"

"I might not be Taff, but I do know how you think most of the time Boss. Not only did I get the list, but every trailer is being located as we speak. Eight are still in Holland. Two on the ferry and four on the docks at Harwich, awaiting clearance for delivery. At least eleven have exploded, so there are twenty-five to account for."

"Half of them are still out there, get a team on it B.J.."

"Already done Paul."

"Well done Mate."

"So how are the explosions being set off? I suspect you have a pretty good idea."

"The likely explanation is, at least two chemicals have been sprayed on internally during assembly, as the British ones have a different spec. they are easy to identify during construction. Once dry they would not be detected during normal examination, and when mixed there would be a violent chemical reaction, producing a lot of heat, result, BOOM. Until the tanker was filled, the chemicals would remain inert, add a hydrocarbon, petrol, whatever, which would then dissolve and therefore mix the chemicals," Paul gestured, indicating and so on. "Too bloody easy Mate."

"So it seems. I take it this explains the haste of young Sherlock, scuttling back to his lab to see if you're right?"

"It was more his idea than mine, but you've got the general idea. Better let the manufacturers know. They can check the trailers still in their yard and then get onto the docks, those trailers do not move!"

"I hate to be boring Paul, but..."

"Already done?" Paul finished the sentence. "Tell me something else, oh great mind reader. How come with all of this technology around here, information at our finger tips, it still takes over an hour for a store man to deliver a bloody kettle?"

"You've got me on that one Paul. Maybe he is still following the directive from Health and Safety?"

This time Paul stabbed the internal intercom button. "Brian, good to hear your voice again my friend," he replied to the QM's acknowledgement to the call.

"I heard you were back Boss, welcome home."

"Do me a favour."

"Of course, what's up?"

"My boot, right up a certain young corporal's arse if I haven't got a working kettle in my office within the next ten minutes."

"Consider it done Paul. He did come to me about it nearly an hour ago, I told him to get a move on and get it over to you, ASAP. He muttered something about Health and Safety, but I assumed he'd do as he was told."

"Thanks Brian." He turned back to his old friend. "I cannot do with all this crap at my age mate. If there is one thing I cannot put up with, it's a bloody job's-worth!"

"They do tend to cause a rise in blood pressure. I must admit I hadn't noticed quite how bad things had got. It sort of crept up on us."

"Talking of creeping up, open the door B.J., I have the distinct feeling there is someone on the other side."

B.J. walked quietly to the door, then quickly snatched it open. There stood a smartly dressed bespectacled corporal, clutching not the desired kettle, but a copy of the directive issued by the Health and Safety officers regarding the use of kettles in office areas.

"Where the bloody hell is my kettle corporal?" Paul almost choked trying to control his temper.

"I would draw your attention to the directive..."

"Stuff your bloody directive!" snapped Paul. "And if you don't know where, I am more than willing to show you!"

"You cannot expect me to carry out an unlawful order Sir as defined in the army act of..."

Again Paul cut him off. "This is the All Arms Unit, you bloody muppet. We are not part of the army, not under the control of the Mo.bloody D. We are answerable to the PM and the Monarch"

"It is still an unlawful command Sir, as it infringes the Health and Safety at Work Act."

Paul stabbed a button on the console on his desk, "Security, my office, now please."

"Where did you come from son?"

"Why Sir?"

"When I ask you a question, you give me the answer. You do NOT ask me one in return. At the moment your next destination is in the balance between your previous abode and Colly nick, your choice."

"I came straight from Deepcut training establishment."

"Thank you, then that is where you will be returning to. You are no use to me on this base Private, so I will send you back for retraining. They should at least teach you not to piss off Colonels; it is not a good career move. Senior officers, especially ones with grey hair, tend to get upset when jumped up little jobs-worths start quoting rules and regulations."

There was a firm knock on the door. In response to Paul's call of "Enter", it swung open to reveal two military police. One a 'red cap', the other a 'snow drop'.

"Ah gentlemen, please come in. I would like you to escort Private Lines to his quarters and supervise him packing his kit. Ensure he takes only what is his. Get him a travel warrant for Deepcut. Take him to Thetford railway station and ensure he catches the next London bound train. On your return if you would then be so kind as to inform Deepcut of his likely e.t.a I would appreciate it. Carry on."

"Yes Sir."

"You cannot do this Colonel," the young man was still unbowed, "and I'm a Corporal, not a Private. These are trade stripes so you cannot demote me without an article..."

Yet again Paul interrupted him, "If you tell me what I can and can't do once more!"

The 'red cap' had been with the unit for some time and knew Paul well. He grabbed the corporal in an arm lock and hustled him out of the door. "Leave him to me Boss," he called back over his shoulder, "I'll take care of it."

B.J. had been on a computer terminal whilst all this was going on, staying in touch with the search for the remaining trailers. "You do know who his father is, I presume?"

"Can't say that I do, not as it would make a difference."

"Brigadier, soon to be Major General, Sir Philip Lines."

"That pompous little shit is Phil's son? I thought his nipper was down for Sandhurst?"

"By all accounts he failed the entrance exam. All he could get was store man or infantry. I think his dad had a hand in posting him here. The idea was maybe we could do something with him."

"Phil is a good friend B.J.. I'll get the MPs to keep him in the guard room over night and I'll see if I can straighten the little shit out in the morning."

"Phil must be a friend if you are prepared to go that far Paul."

"He is a good man and deserves better. We'll see if a night in the cooler brings a dose of reality with the dawn."

"More than he deserves. Oh by the way, Taff should be back within the hour, thought you might like to know."

"Thank heavens for small mercies. Anything on those trailers yet?"

"We've traced all except one, which was delivered to Milldenhall three days ago. They are tracing it as we speak. There is a potential problem with two of them as they are on the road and loaded. The instructions to the cops are to get them off the road in as isolated a spot as possible. One of them only left the depot ten minutes ago soon after loading. We are going to try to get it onto an old airfield, park it as far away from anything as possible, get the driver out and allow it to burn out. If the tank isn't getting too hot, the driver will drop the trailer and save the tractor unit. We have stressed no heroics."

"What about the other one on the road?"

"There is hope for that as well. It is loaded with central heating oil, so it will have to get hotter than it would if it were full of petrol, this should buy us a little more time."

The phone on Paul's desk rang making him jump. On answering it he was surprised to hear an American voice on the other end. "The trailer you are looking for is on your base Colonel."

"What?"

"It is one of three we sent over to collect fuel for a Presidential flight due

The Day The Ravens Died

in this afternoon. All the aircraft in the President's flight use the same fuel as your big jets. They have special, more powerful engines and need the better quality fuel; we always get it from your base as it's the nearest depot where stocks are held."

Paul conveyed the message to B.J. adding, "Find it and park it out of the way, then load one of our tankers to replace it."

"I'm on it."

Paul spoke again to the American. "Any chance of speaking to your head of security?"

"That's me Colonel."

"Good, here's something for you to think about. I presume the tanker which blew up a few days ago was on the same task as the ones here now?"

"What's your point Colonel?"

"I'm not quite sure myself, but if the only use you have for externally sourced fuel is for VIP flights, it seems to me you would use a new tanker, if you had one, to refuel such a flight, if only because it looks good. Now I happen to know the tanker which blew up last week, broke down on this base. I am reading this as I speak, this information is all news to me. It seems as though we sent one of ours as a replacement. According to this report it took our mechanics nearly four hours to repair the braking system on your truck."

"It was one of the lines of investigation Colonel. The thinking was, the faulty brakes could have caused the problem which resulted in the incident. However, checks on what was left suggest the brakes where working perfectly at the time."

"I'm pleased to hear it, but would I be right in thinking the VIP flight was back in the air before the tanker exploded."

"Hell yes, they normally turn round in a lot less than an hour. You're saying this was a deliberate attempt to bring down one of our aircraft?"

"I'll send a helicopter over for you and I'll share what we have with you. See if you reach the same conclusion."

"I take it you do not want our Feds involved just yet?"

"I'd prefer they were not involved period, as you would say, but if it looks like there is something in this theory, then I suppose they will have to be involved. I'll get the Lynx moving to pick you up."

"See you soon Colonel."

The young fuel tech. was rushed out to the suspect tanker. He quickly confirmed the fuel was beginning to heat, but was far from critical. As soon as the tanker was moved to a remote part of the airfield, he not only took some samples of the contaminated fuel but also placed a remote sensor to monitor the temperature of the load and transmit the data to his lab. Within ten minutes of his return he had isolated the chemicals causing the reaction and e-mailed Paul the results.

"That boy is a bloody genius." Paul called the officer in charge of all fuel-related matters on the base. "I know you're a bit on the busy side just now, but make sure the young lab tech. gets two stripes; he's earned them. If a dozy bloody storeman gets two on completion of his course how come someone like that young tech. is rated as a craftsman?"

"I have no idea Boss. I've been saying as much for years, it's just the way things are. I'll get the paper work done, want me to tell him?"

"Nah, not yet. Wait until it's sorted, then give him a tongue in cheek bollicking for not wearing his rank."

"Evil sod Boss. Ok I'll sort it."

"Cheers Frank."

Paul called the communication centre. His instructions were to get the young tech. in the fuel lab to speak to the manufacturers of the tankers in Holland and advise them of the chemicals sprayed onto the insides of the as yet un-dispatched tankers.

"Have we got a team in Croatia or anywhere near?" he asked.

"Yes Boss. They are part of the UN team looking for Serb. War Criminals."

"Tell them to get their arses to the tanker plant and find out who sprayed that shit on the inside of those tanks. Yesterday will be soon enough!"

His next meeting was with the American Security Chief; between them they went over every detail of the tankers.

"I suppose it's just about possible it was a deliberate attempt to bring down one of your planes. The only difference between yours and the rest of the batch was the tanks destined for you had an undercoat of paint of a much heavier type, to take the final coat of military spec. paint. But then why risk getting caught by doing the entire production run. I suppose they could have designed the entire thing around the fact it would take a lot longer to detonate aviation fuel than petrol, the idea being to bring down the plane.

I know this lot are devious, but this would have been smart, too bloody smart, I think it was simply a plot to cause mayhem before they start for real attacking tankers. The suicide attack at the beginning was designed to throw us off the scent, it worked too. Sneaky bastards."

"So I can tell my superiors what?" asked the American.

"We have identified the cause and this particular problem is over. We know how, when and where the problem occurred and a team has been dispatched to pick up those responsible. All the other suspect trailers have been located and are being dealt with. As to whether it was a deliberate attack aimed at your VIP flights, in my opinion it is unlikely. I think it was purely down to chance that two of the trailers were destined for this purpose. However I cannot totally rule out the possibility, although I stress it is highly unlikely. I will of course keep you up to date with any developments."

"I think I agree with you Colonel. It could be interesting to know what the suspects have to say when your lads pick them up. You know the State Department will want them transported to 'Gitmo'."

"And you know that won't happen."

"I know, but every agency will be wanting a piece of these guys. They will all be wanting to score a few, what do you call it, brownie points?"

"They will have to catch their own. Doing things our way might upset some of your hawks, but even they have to admit we have had some good results 'turning' some terrorists."

Taff arrived having been released from hospital and the conversation revolved around his lucky escape and the condition of the others, General Leach in particular, as even the American Major knew him.

The call they had been waiting for came in. It was as disappointing as it was unsurprising. The two men tasked with spraying the protective coating on the insides of the tankers had both called in sick the week before and had subsequently vanished, along with their supervisor.

"Oh bollocks," cursed Paul. "Let me guess, all had given false names and had equally false IDs?"

"We were never going to be that lucky Boss," came the reply on the radio.

"Get anything you can on them, send it here, then I suppose you had better get on with whatever it was you had been doing."

"Sorry we missed them Boss. By the way, how are Taff and his Nibs?"

"The bush telegraph at work again I suppose?" replied Paul. It was virtually impossible to keep anything regarding the welfare of any member of the unit a secret from the others.

"You know how it is Boss, a small unit, at least in terms of bodies on the ground, we're bound to be worried about each other. Are Davey and Sam going to make it?"

"As long as they don't pick up any infections they have a chance of making a reasonable recovery. 'His Nibs', by which I presume you mean General Leach, should be discharged in a day or so and 'Taff' is sitting opposite to me."

"Glad you're all right Sir."

"So am I corporal," replied Taff with a grin.

"It's Sergeant Ingram Sir."

"I know who it is, twit! Get on with it, out."

"Rotten bugger Taff."

"Yeah, and who taught me?"

"I suppose I had better let Downing Street know what's happening before they have another panic attack," Paul turned to the American military police major. "You had better give your lot the all clear before they start panicking as well."

"Can I use your telephone Colonel?" asked the American.

"Better than that. Taff will show you how to work the terminal on the other desk. On our system you can talk direct to your base commander, and to the Pentagon, one at a time or together, it's up to you."

"I'd sell my Grandmother's false teeth to have just some of the kit you guys have got about here."

"I'm not sure if you would get the court order to dig her up Major, based on those grounds."

The reaction to the various phone calls was varied to say the least. The American base commander was very relieved; the Pentagon official was at first confused as he had known nothing of the exploding tankers. The confusion was replaced by blatant disbelief of the fact all the suspect trailers had been located and dealt with one way or another. This was accompanied by a demand for all the relevant documents and full co-operation with a team of military investigators who would leave the USA to arrive on the All Arms Unit's base in the morning.

Paul had been telling the Prime Minister what had gone on and how the threat had been removed. He could of course hear what the American Major was saying to the Pentagon. "I have to go Prime Minister. I'll get you a full report, it will be on your desk in the morning."

"Thank you Colonel, and very well done to everyone involved."

"Thanks, bye Sir." He walked over to the console and asked Taff what the problem was.

"What do you think?" replied the stocky little soldier.

"Having trouble Major?" enquired Paul, sensing the growing frustration in the American Major's voice.

"The guy on the other end of this is a permanent secretary to the joint chiefs intelligence committee, he is unhappy because he doesn't know what's been going on."

"Ah bless 'im," said Paul sarcastically. "Want me to have a word?"

"If you would Sir."

Paul took the hand set. "To whom am I speaking?" he asked in a patently false accent.

"I am the senior..."

Paul cut him off. "I asked WHO, I already know what!" he snapped. "What's all this crap about sending a team over here to investigate events surrounding these exploding tankers. We know exactly what happened. We know how many tanks were treated and we know what with, and the effects it had on the different fuels. We know where and when the chemicals were applied, we even know who by. The only thing we do not know at the moment is exactly where the culprits are and we are working on that!. A full report will be on the desk of the most senior military officer who deals with fuel in the morning. It will detail the chemicals and how to check for them and neutralise them should they try the same trick again."

"That will not be satisfactory Colonel."

"It will bloody well have to be old son, because it's all you are going to get."

"I've just realised who you are. You are the Colonel who launched the outrageous attack on our former secretary for defence. Our information indicated you had been removed from command."

Paul laughed, "Just goes to prove how bloody useless your particular section is. Funny how shit always rises to the top. Just so it is on the record, none of your investigators will be allowed on this base, I've had dealings with them in the past after nine-eleven. We sent your section the names of six of the hi-jackers, pictures, addresses, flight numbers, even the numbers of their boarding passes, and this was three days before the attack! If you think I'm going to let the same lot of investigators who cocked it up then, come on to this base again, then you really are nuts! Good day."

"Another shining example of Anglo-American co-operation!" commented Taff.

"Some of our lot are just as bad, I take it you knew I had all the civilian contractors sent by the MoD prohibited from entering the base."

"I had heard, how'd you manage it? I couldn't stop them, believe me I tried."

"Easy, revoked all of their passes. This business with the tankers gave me the excuse to put the camp on lock down, on the grounds of security of course."

"You can be a devious bugger Paul. I'm just glad you are my friend, well most of the time."

The knock on the door turned out to be Brian, the QM delivering Paul's kettle and an apology, in person.

"You see Taff, there is a god, even if he does masquerade as our QM."

CHAPTER SIX

The next problem to surface came in the form of the all too numerous inquests, the question everyone was asking was, 'Why did the tankers explode?'. With the help of the young lab tech. an information sheet was prepared and forwarded to all the relevant courts. For the most part the explanation was accepted, the usual verdict was unlawful killing by persons unknown. As is often the case, there is always some lawyer who spots a chance to make either a name for themselves or a lot of money, ideally both, and so it was with a case which was heard in Uxbridge. The case had dragged on for over a week by the time Paul heard about it. The means by which he discovered his presence was required did not amuse him.

He was sitting in his office, talking to the Skipper of *Intrepid*, trying to decide whether or not it was worth the risk boarding the old freighter which they had been patiently shadowing for a week, or simply sink it and say nothing.

"We have positive IDs on everyone on board Paul."

"Even the one who never leaves the hold?"

"You are right of course, whoever it is, could well be a prisoner. Our team of Marines seem certain they can board her tonight as long as the sea state doesn't get any worse, The swells are at least ten feet at the moment. The 'crazy gang' say this will actually help them, personally I think they are all certifiable."

"I agree with you, they are nuts, but then they are the experts in this sort of thing. Me, I'm feeling sea sick just thinking about it."

"It's your call Boss," replied the Skipper.

"I'll tell you straight, it's a bloody sight harder sitting here and ordering young men into harm's way than it ever was doing it myself. Damn it Skipper, if they say they can do it, go for it, with the proviso they all carry individual emergency beacons. Getting shot is one thing, goes with the job - drowning or dying of exposure because a rigid raider tipped over is not in the job description. Do whatever it needs to ensure there are no accidents."

"Fair enough Boss. I'll make certain both choppers are in the air as long as the Marines are in their small boats, and far enough away from the freighter so they won't be heard."

"Okay, I'll leave it up to your lads, good luck. I'm curious to know who is being kept in the dark, never mind why Al Qaeda have taken to the sea in an old rust bucket like this one. What the hell are they planning to do with about three hundred tons of what appears to be high grade explosives? I take it you've seen the scans? I can't work them out. The explosives are on top of a lot of scrap metal. There is a container of some sort holding explosives and metal together in one great lump. The hull shows signs of having been modified in such a way so as the cargo can be dumped out through the bottom of the hull. What possible target can they be after, a pipe line may be, but surely so much explosive is over kill in the extreme for such a target?"

"I'd have thought so Boss. One thing is for certain, they are up to no good."

"I've got to go Skipper, seems as though I've got a visitor, I'll catch up with you later."

Claire, the lady who acted as secretary for both Paul and Taff, was hovering in the door way to Paul's office. The piece of paper in her hand looked horribly official even from across the room.

"What the hell is this?" Paul asked no-one in particular. "Where did this come from Claire?"

"A court bailiff Paul, he is in the outer office with a guard who escorted him here from the main gate."

"Show him in."

"The man strode confidently in. "I am here to escort you to Uxbridge court Colonel. If you will come with me, we should get there before the court closes for the day. Arrangements will be made for you to stay in a hotel over night."

"Why?"

"Why what Colonel?"

"Why have I got to attend a coroner's court on a victim of terrorism? We have sent all the information we have on the exploding tankers, I can add nothing. And as for being away from here tonight, it is totally out of the question; before you ask I will not give a reason as to why. You can go back to the court and give the Coroner my regards and inform him, depending on what the outcome of certain operations are, I may be able to attend later in the week. I will let him know."

"That is a high court order Colonel, you must comply with it and come with me."

"Go back into the outer office and wait until I sort this out." The man showed no signs of moving. "I said get out of my office and wait. Now bloody well move."

"No Colonel, you must come with me NOW."

"Raise your voice to me again and you will regret it. Out!"

Once the bailiff had rejoined his escort Paul rang the court. The clerk confirmed the warrant was genuine and Paul must attend. The clerk was informed it was impossible as there was no way Paul could be back on base in time.

"While you're on the 'phone explain to me exactly why I need to attend and whose idea it was please."

"The barrister representing the family of the deceased is suggesting your unit was negligent in protecting the public, and is likely to put in a substantial claim for damages. I think it was the barrister who applied for the warrant."

"I've never heard anything so bloody daft in all my life. I was on what was supposed to have been terminal leave prior to retiring when the nutter committed suicide. We have no idea who he was, if indeed it was a he. As far as I am aware, forensics couldn't find anything which might even have been any remains of the bomber. It took nearly a week to identify the car as one which had been stolen several days before. I am at a total loss to see how I can help."

"Be that as it may. You still must attend court today Colonel."

"As I already told you it is not going to happen, it is utterly impossible for reasons I cannot divulge. If there is somewhere within a reasonable distance of the court where we can land a helicopter, and where it can wait for me, then hopefully I can be there about lunch time tomorrow. That is the best I can offer."

"I'm not sure it will do Colonel," replied the clerk of the court.

"I'll see you lunch time, I hope. My regards to the Coroner, and good day."

The head of the base security detail stuck his head round the door. "'Scuse me Boss, what is happening to this court bailiff? He is beginning to make a pest of himself."

"I'll come and sort him out, I'll need a couple of your boys to escort him off base." Paul led the way to the outer reception area. "Right Mr. Bailiff, I've been in touch with the court and explained I will not be attending today. I will however, if circumstances permit, be there by lunch time tomorrow. Enjoy your drive home."

"That is not an option Colonel, as I explained to you, you must return with me today, to Uxbridge."

"Had you have arrived at a reasonable hour, it might have been possible. I am trained in pursuit driving and well used to powerful cars, I am telling you there is no way on this earth we can get to Uxbridge before every one from the court goes home. I very much doubt whether we could get there using a chopper, so save every one a lot of grief and go home. I will be there, terrorists permitting, around lunch time."

"It is your fault I was late arriving. Your base should be clearly sign posted, there do not appear to be any signs whatsoever relating to this establishment. You are in breach of numerous regulations relating to places potentially dangerous to anyone inadvertently straying into a danger area. Now you will come with me Colonel, I always produce the required individual on the required date. I have never failed yet, and will not fail on this occasion."

The Day The Ravens Died

"Hells teeth," muttered Paul as he turned to the security men. "One of you drive his car off base, escort him out of the gate, and stick him in his car before I stick my boot up you know where."

"Will do Boss. Come on Sir, this way."

"If he uses his car to obstruct the road shove it into the ditch and him with it. If he attempts to re-enter the base, refuse him entry. If he tries to sneak in through the wire you may shoot him or throw him in the cells until someone comes for him."

"Get your hands off me soldier, that is assault!"

"Actually I'm Air Force not Army, and I will only use such force as I deem necessary to ensure you comply with my instructions. Now come along Sir."

Hardly had Paul returned to his office, when the door again swung open. He turned from making himself a cup of coffee to see Taff and a battered looking General Leach. "You two must have smelled this or heard the kettle. Good to see you Sir."

"One day he will shock me Taff, by getting his priorities right!"

"I was going to suggest you took your good lady up to the croft for as long as you liked, but if that's how you feel about me Sir."

"Good to see you haven't changed Paul. I understand you've sorted out the mystery of the exploding tankers, well done m'boy."

"As usual it was a team effort Sir. What do you know about the unregistered rust bucket *Intrepid* is shadowing?"

"Other than the fact it has a lot of explosives on board and goes to great lengths to stay out of regular shipping lanes, not a lot."

"Where is it now Paul?" asked Taff.

"Just to the north of the Faeroe Islands and has resumed its original course."

"They are definitely terrorists?"

"Without a doubt. The only person on board we haven't identified is the one who stays in the hold. My opinion, for what it's worth, is he is a prisoner."

"Could they be planning to attack an oil or gas platform, maybe a distribution platform?"

"Damned if I know Sir, I have no intention of waiting to find out. The Marines on *Intrepid* are confident they can successfully board the ship, so I gave the go ahead for them to go tonight."

"Is it worth the risk Paul, what if it blows up?"

"I have already had this discussion with the Skipper Sir, and we agreed it is a lot easier to do the job yourself than it is to order brave young men to take the risks. It's even tougher in a unit such as this as we tend to know most of them."

"You're right as usual, but what can we gain from a successful operation?"

"For a start we should be able to trace the explosives. Hopefully we will find out where the ship was modified. Scans suggest the explosives can be dropped through the bottom of the ship, the whole stack is attached to several hundred tons of scrap iron as far as we can tell. The only reason I can think of for that is so the stuff will sink quickly into deep water, which again begs the question, what is the target? More to the point, we should find out who the mystery guest is."

"What on earth can they be after so far north and in such deep water Paul? There isn't anything up there is there?"

"Nothing I know of Sir, unless they're looking at cracking open some of the old Russian nuclear subs which have been dumped, in the hope of releasing significant radiation."

"Surely those things are too widely spread for a single charge to crack open more than one, even if they could find one."

"I think it was Ballard's team tasked to locate them and check the condition of the wrecks. As I recall he had a hell of a job finding any of them in water so deep and rough. There is usually a Russian deep sea research ship monitoring the wrecks, and they can't find them every time, even with all the gear they've got now and GPS. No, this lot know what they're after and it's nothing we've thought of yet."

"Who was that we saw being escorted out of the building Paul, just as we drew up?"

Paul showed the General and Taff the paperwork and informed them of the conversation.

"You'll go of course?"

"It depends a little bit on how things go tonight. I'll stay on until we know how it went, then if all is well I'll hand over to B.J.. If you could organise a landing site as close as possible to the court, and a car from the Town House for me, I would appreciate it Taff. I've got a few things I need to get together for my day in court. Basically I want to load the CCTV. of the car ramming the tanker. It's about all we've got, apart from the strong suspicion it must have been waiting in the car park in front of the shops, a couple of hundred yards before the blast site."

"Waiting for its target?"

"It seems so Sir. There are marks on the curb suggesting a car similar to the bomber's crossed the curb onto the main carriageway shortly before the blast. As there is no sign of the car having passed the previous camera it seems the most likely explanation."

"So why has it got to be you going to court Paul?" asked the General. "Surely any officer could do it."

"I would have thought so Boss, but a barrister seems to think it has to be me, and got a high court warrant to that effect. According to this anonymous legal eagle, it's our fault their client lost his wife and kiddies in the explosion. Exactly how it's our fault is something of a mystery to me, but I believe a figure of several million pounds has been mentioned as compensation for allowing this terrorist attack to take place."

"So you are going? Tomorrow I presume."

"I might as well Taff, drop in on Downing street on the way home. I can personally deliver the report on the tankers to the PM. This other matter will have been resolved by then, so I can at least brief him before the news gets out and we're branded as pirates."

"So what's to do now Paul?"

"I'll get the stuff I want to take to court tomorrow ready. If you don't mind taking over for a few hours Taff, I can catch up on a bit of kip, then I'll come back for when the Marines do their thing with the floating bomb."

"Rather them than me mate," observed Taff.

"I thought you would have been right at home with them, seeing as how you were navy, on the *Endurance* weren't you?"

"Just because you get sea sick in a boat on your local pond!"

"All right you two," chided the General. "I think we can safely assume normal service has been resumed."

"I take it you will be accepting the offer of the croft Boss?"

"Better see what my Boss has to say about it first Paul. Maybe the end of the week would be better, it will give me a day or two to get a bit stronger, it is quite a trip up there."

"Fair enough Sir, you get off home to your wife, we'll be all right here. I'll get a car round for you."

"Thanks Paul, that would be appreciated. I'll let you know when, or I suppose that should be if, I'm ready to take you up on your offer."

"Okay Sir, you know you can fly up if you don't fancy the trip in a car."

"Can you see her ladyship in a Lynx for three hours?"

"Well, maybe not. You get home Sir and take it easy, I promise I will let you know if anything serious happens. I won't call you if all goes well tonight, so as long as you don't get a call you can assume all is well. The doctors said you need rest more than anything else so, starting tomorrow, I'll give you a briefing every evening at twenty hundred hours."

"That sounds like a good idea Paul. I'll be off and leave you to get on, and good luck, give my regards to the Marines."

"Will do Sir, bye for now."

After the General's car had left Paul commented, "He's a tough old bird, I know a lot of men half his age who would have been laid up for months with burns like those."

"None of us are getting any younger Paul. I wish you would accept promotion, you are the General's natural successor."

"Don't talk rot Taff. For a start you out rank me, but you know as well as I do, if the General does finally retire then it should be who ever is OC. Special Forces who should take over. My temper would make life impossible around here, you know I get a lot of peoples' hackles up, you have to be a diplomat for that particular job, and diplomacy is not one of my strengths. My patience has decreased in direct proportion to my age."

"You could have a point," replied Taff. "Go on, sod off and get your head down until the fun starts. Don't worry, I'll call you the moment things start."

"Fair enough, Oh and while I remember, ask B.J. to come in an hour early in the morning please, to give me a bit more time to sort myself out for the court."

"Will do, now get some kip while you can."

Within minutes Paul was asleep on the bunk bed in the back office.

CHAPTER SEVEN

Far to the north the weather had taken a turn for the worse; the Skipper of the *Intrepid* was all for calling the attack off, the senior marine asked to see him.

"Your men are crazy Captain, those seas will tip a rigid raider over before they clear the well deck."

The commander of the Marine detachment seemed unmoved. The Skipper decided on one final attempt at reason.

"I'm not even sure we can open the stern doors in this sea state, not without risking damage to the hover craft. Even if we could get the rigid raiders away safely, and by some miracle you are able to them get along side the target ship, they will be smashed to pieces against her hull."

"That is why I came to see you sir," replied the Marine Captain. "We reached the same conclusions, which is why we were planning on using the Geminis."

"You are bloody mad!"

"Not really Sir. Being flexible they will cope better with the swells, also hitting the sides of the ship should not present an immediate threat to the integrity of the craft. Our plan has been modified, it will now consist of a four man team, plus a coxswain in each inflatable. If we use the storm covers then the assault teams can stay reasonably warm and dry."

"Exactly how do you propose crossing the greater part of forty miles of less than calm North Atlantic Ocean?"

"Would it be possible to calculate the point to drop us off? The idea being, we allow the wind to blow us into position. The recon. plane can track us and relay instructions to keep us on course. The outboards on the Geminis are quite powerful Skipper, we've talked it over and are sure this is our best option, if we all carry beacons and wear safety lines we'll be all right. The other plus is we'll be harder to see, not that they'll be looking in this weather, a rigid raider might show up on their radar, a Gemini won't, not in these seas."

"The Boss will have my guts if I give the go ahead and you lose a man to the weather."

"Relax Skipper, it will be fine."

"All right, have a talk to the crew of the recon. plane first, if they say they can track you and maintain contact, fair enough."

Timothy Pilgrim

The crew of the old Canberra miles above the storm tossed ocean pointed out their equipment could track a storm petrel, even in these seas. In fact they were getting fed up with tracking the tiny sea birds to relieve the boredom. It would mean breaking off now to refuel, if only to ensure they had enough fuel to allow for any problems, they would be back an hour before dark.

Typically, the Marines used the time the Canberra was away refuelling going over their plan, better to discover any flaws now than later. The navigation team on *Intrepid* double checked their calculations on the exact point to release the Gemini craft so they would drift into the path of the target vessel. The more accurate their calculations, the greater the safety margin on fuel for the Marines in their flimsy craft, should things go wrong.

About an hour before sunset the Canberra floated unseen above the southern horizon and reported she had contact with both *Intrepid* and the target vessel. The old plane was already far higher than any U2 had ever been but was still climbing effortlessly in spite her full load of fuel.

Such was the power of the optical devices fitted to the old plane, the crew were able to inform the Skipper of *Intrepid* at least two of the crew on the target vessel were being violently sea sick as a result of the rising seas.

One of the bridge watch crew on *Intrepid* heard the message from the airman. "Wait until they get on this old bath tub and have to eat the stuff they serve up in the brig, they'll beg to go onto bread and water."

"Some people are never happy. All right the old girl rolls a bit, but have you ever been on her when she's really opened up?" replied one of the old hands.

"Can't say as I would want to Chiefie. I've heard tales of stupid speeds, but I don't want to believe them, not in this weather," was the less then enthusiastic reply.

To the surprise of most of the crew, the order came to 'heave to'. The twin divots on the lee side of the ship swung out the Gemini inflatables complete with the assault teams, and dropped them remarkably gently into the stormy seas.

The Chief turned to the sailor who had been moaning. "Wouldn't you like to be coxswain in one of them lad? The wind in your hair, which could do with a cut, and the spray in your face?"

"Yeah-right Chiefie, you forgot the icicle for your nose and the odd finger snapping off with frostbite! No thanks."

"I don't know what the younger generation are coming to, no sense of adventure. Maybe you'd be happier on the QE2 cruising around the Bahamas?"

"On an evening like this, even you will have to admit it would have its attractions Chiefie."

"Oh I don't know. If things go horribly wrong for those boot necks with more balls than brains, then life could get exciting. Have you been on board when she has properly let fly with her main battery. Two 4.5s each chucking out ten rounds a minute, and you really will be surprised just how fast this old 'bath tub', as you call her, can go. The Royal Navy haven't got anything which can get near her."

"Come on Chiefie, she's as old as Noah's Ark, she's an assault ship, not a destroyer!"

"You'll see. Just ask yourself why is the engine room out of bounds to anyone who doesn't work there?"

If the 'chief' had been hoping for a spectacular naval gunnery exhibition he was in for a disappointment. Guided by the 'eyes in the sky' the Marines drifted directly towards their approaching objective. Certainly it was not a pleasant experience, being bounced around in their little boats, but these were the very best of the Royal Marines. The assault groups were managing to stay tolerably warm and dry. The same could not be said for the Coxswains, in spite of the thermal diving suits and numerous other insulating layers, they were beginning to feel the numbing cold. Somehow they managed to keep in close touch with each other as well as on course. The fact it was now pitch dark was no problem to the watching Canberra, guiding them unerringly towards the old coaster.

On *Intrepid* the duty crewmen watched on the display screen the images relayed from the aircraft. It was the Skipper who noticed their speed had dropped, allowing the gap to close. He immediately ordered an increase in speed, and called the Officer of the Watch to the control centre.

"I understand your concern, and the desire to be available as quickly as possible should disaster befall our Marines, however, we know the radar set they have on that old rust bucket is capable of picking us up at forty nautical miles. With this in mind you will maintain a minimum gap of at least forty five, not a yard less, do you understand?"

"Yes Sir, sorry Sir."

"Don't be sorry Number One, do it right. Carry on."

"Sir," the young officer acknowledged the Skipper and returned to the bridge.

"Do you think they spotted us Sir?" asked the Marine Captain.

"We have sensors which should have alerted us if a radar sweep went over us, but I can't rule it out. We were very close to the limits of their radar; if nothing else, it proved the need to watch every detail. If they had got a solid 'hit' on us and turned away, your men would have suffered for nothing. Let's face it, the size of the return the old girl would make on a radar screen could hardly be mistaken for a trawler."

They need not have worried. The success signal came through so quickly after the 'contact' signal no-one had a chance to get any more nervous than they had been already.

"Repeat please," said the radio operator, not daring to tell anyone without confirmation.

"I said 'target secure', cloth ears."

"Your status?"

"Seven fine, one cold and wet, but otherwise fine, and two very cold and wet, but will be fine as soon as we get a brew inside them."

"What about the crew, the terrorists?" asked the Skipper.

"Four dead, eight captured and secured, two of the lads have gone down into the hold to check out the mystery contact."

"What about the explosives?"

"They are checking that out as well Skipper. I'll let you know as soon as I hear from them."

"Well done. I'll get a couple of Ordinance Artificers over to you as soon as possible."

"You'd better send a medic as well Skipper. The lads are back from the hold with the captive. He's an American agent of some kind, he's one hell of a mess, but get this. He twigged straight away what unit we were; says he knows 'the Boss', and could we send the Colonel and Taff his regards."

"Well I'll be buggered," muttered the Skipper. "I wonder if the Boss knew all along?"

Paul didn't know, he was still sleeping on the bunk. Somehow Taff had missed the fact things had been brought forward several hours and was still blissfully unaware the operation had even been launched, much less it was completed.

Thinking he still had an hour or so before he was due to wake Paul, Taff had decided to take the opportunity to catch up on some of the paper work which had accumulated during his brief absence. He was rather surprised to get a call from the Skipper of the *Intrepid* informing him of the successful seizure of the ship and the release of the prisoner.

"Do we know who the prisoner is Skipper?" asked Taff.

"I don't, but it seems as though he knows you and the Boss. His message was 'Arnie sends his regards', if that means anything to you Taff."

"It certainly does Skipper. Last I heard he was a Captain in the Yanks Navy Seals. I haven't heard anything from him for years. He rejoices in the name of James T Alexander the third. He's a good guy, one of the rare breed of Yanks in his line of work, take good care of him Skipper, I'll tell Paul."

"I'll be in touch Taff as soon as we rendezvous with the ship."

"Well done to all of your crew Skipper, take care."

Back on *Intrepid* the 'new boys' on their first detachment with the All Arms Unit were about to get an education. The Skipper called the bridge, "Batten down the hatches Number One, then bring her about. Take up station a hundred yards off the coaster's starboard side. As soon as you are ready, take her up to half speed, no point bending her in this sea."

"Aye-Aye Sir."

Two minutes later the familiar throb of the four propellers which normally drove her along at an economic maximum of eighteen knots faded. For a moment an eerie silence descended, quickly replaced by an increasing hum.

The Day The Ravens Died

The stern of the ship seemed to dig into the sea as eighteen thousand tons of steel healed over in a turn. The stern seemed to skid sideways, then the great ship straightened up and seemed to bound forward. For the first minute or so it was quite alarming for those who had never experienced it before. Huge sheets of spray where hurled into the night sky, higher even than the bridge, then she settled, bow riding high, shrugging aside the twenty foot plus swells as though they were ripples on a village pond.

The forty miles between the ships seemed to just vanish and again the stern skidded round. With a shudder the bow dropped back and the familiar throb of the propellers returned. There, barely one hundred yards away, was the ship they had shadowed for nearly a week.

"She doesn't look dangerous," commented a young sailor. "Any idea what they were planning to attack Sir?" he asked an officer standing beside him.

"It's our job to find out. She's got three or four hundred tons of high explosives in her hold, complete with detonators. The only thing I can think of is an oil rig, but it seems a bit extreme for such a target."

"Could it be a bridge Sir? Maybe the Forth Bridge, detonate it just as she's passing under it, an explosion like that might bring it down."

"As far as I know, no one had come up with that idea before, but why come so far north and, apart from the day or so she spent circling, she's been steady on the same course for days"

"It was just a thought Sir."

A couple of hours later Paul and Taff sat staring at the main display screen in the operations centre. "I can't figure it out Taff. The point on the map marked as the detonation point is in the middle of nowhere, there is nothing there except several thousand feet of water. It is smack over the deepest bit of the Norwegian trench, according to the charts. Beats the hell out of me, any ideas?"

"The Americans haven't got an exercise in the area have they?"

"Not as far as I know Taff. You're thinking they were planning on ramming an aircraft carrier?"

"That or a sub, but then if they got too close to a carrier, they would get blown out of the water, and how could they find a sub?"

"It doesn't make any sense does it?"

"Not a lot Paul, but you're the one who normally figures these things out."

"Not this time Mate. I'm as scuppered as everyone else."

The two old friends sat reading the reports from the Marines involved in taking the ship, "These guys are bloody nuts Taff, two and a half hours, virtually drifting around in an Arctic gale in those flimsy things. Mad, totally bloody mad!"

"You're telling me you wouldn't have done the same at their age? I can remember an incident years ago. A small matter of parachuting into the Atlantic, miles off the Irish coast, no matter you can barely keep afloat in your skivvies, never mind swim!"

"Yeah, well, it had to be done."

"And so did this, and before you say it, I agree with you. It's harder in a lot of ways, sitting here with a cup of coffee, knowing the risks brave young men are taking to obey our orders. In a way I'm glad I didn't know about the change of plan until it was done and dusted. It stopped me worrying and you calling it off."

"I suppose you're right Taff, I would have taken a bit of convincing. But as it turns out, leaving it to the men on the spot was, as usual, the best way. At least they used safety lines until they were aboard. The thought of falling into the sea is enough to make me reach for the bottle again."

"You never were much of a sailor were you?"

"A fishing boat, in fairly calm water, fine. Something like that, I feel queezy thinking about it."

The printer purred again, it was the initial report on the explosives, a mixture of semtex and C4, all with batch numbers and manufacturer's marks still on the wrappings. It was the means of detonation which spread confusion.

"Here Taff, what do you make of this? According to the explosives boys the charge was set to detonate on or very near the bottom. Why for heaven's sake? What on earth could be the point?"

"Clearly there must be something down there."

Paul turned away from all the high tech. gear on his desk, to a 'normal' computer hooked up to the internet.

"What are you looking for Paul?" asked Taff as he filed the reports from the Marines.

"Found it already, on Google. Geological surveys… the lot, now I know what the clever bastards were up to. Set off their explosion which in turn could well have detonated several tons of methane hydrate. Either way the aim was to trigger an underwater landslide, bigger the better. Look here, there are even the survey results showing the exact spots these slides have occurred before. According to this report, the last big slide was half a million years ago and sent a tsunami over three hundred feet high down the North Sea. Of course there was still a land bridge to Europe then, so it stopped round about where north Norfolk is today."

"Would it have worked? Seems a bit far fetched to me Paul."

"I don't know, do I? They had picked the deepest spot, with the biggest deposits of that methane stuff, add to that the highest under sea cliffs and the thickest sediments on the cliff top, it could have worked I suppose. Even a fifty foot wave would have caused chaos. The North Sea gets narrower and shallower as you come south. Looks like we got a right result, admitted there was an element of luck in it."

"Don't knock it."

"All down to one hawk eyed coast guard in Gibraltar, spotting it was the same unregistered ship the Yanks stopped years ago off the Yemen, with those missiles hidden under cement from North Korea."

"Why did he report it?" asked Taff.

The Day The Ravens Died

"I don't know, boredom?"

"What did happen to those missiles Paul?"

"The Yanks had to let the ship go. From what I can remember some supposed Yemeni official produced papers proving it was a legitimate deal. I presume the Yemeni forces were equipped with the Scuds and Silkworms. No doubt the CIA kept tabs on them."

"Why don't you grab a bit of kip for another hour or so, I'll hold the fort until B.J. comes in?"

CHAPTER EIGHT

The helicopter landed at Northolt near enough on time. The car scheduled to collect Paul and take him to Uxbridge courthouse was irretrievably stuck in a huge traffic jam, caused by a spectacular accident on the notorious gyratory system where the North Circular crossed the A40. Finding a replacement car was easy, getting from the airfield to Uxbridge across grid locked roads full of frustrated motorists was a different matter. As a result it was past eleven o'clock when he finally arrived.

He apologised to the Coroner, briefly explaining the problem, and his apology was accepted as being perfectly reasonable. No mention as yet of his refusal to come with the bailiff the previous day. The thought crossed Paul's mind it had indeed been the barrister for some of the victims, as the Clerk of the Court suspected, rather than the Coroner, who had obtained the court order to compel Paul to attend. So it proved to be the case, as soon as the Coroner had finished asking his questions to establish Paul was who he claimed to be. The young, not unattractive, barrister representing the families killed by the suicide bomber, began her attack on the Security Services and Paul in particular.

Completing her opening tirade with, "What have you to say Colonel?"

Predictably much of what she had said had annoyed Paul, no doubt deliberately. "Have you finished, or just paused for breath?" was his immediate response. "I have here a video of the incident which resulted in the tragic deaths of so many innocent people." He turned to the Coroner, "with your permission Sir, it will clarify matters a great deal and save us all a lot of time."

"We do not have the facilities immediately to hand Colonel."

"The wall on the side of the courtroom is more than adequate Sir, and my computer has a built in projector. It is battery powered, so there is no need for a power point Sir."

"Very well Colonel, I will allow it."

"What is the source of this film Colonel?" asked the lawyer.

"It is from the CCTV camera monitoring the traffic on the section of the A406 where the incident occurred."

"I have seen the video Colonel and it shows nothing to help understand what happened, the quality is extremely poor." Confident she had scored an important point over Paul, she continued, "I see no reason why my clients should be subject to further distress by having to view it again."

"That's the point Sir," Paul addressed the Coroner. "She had the video, this is a digital recording, vastly better quality, and I agree with her. There is no need for the families of the victims to suffer the pain of seeing this material. However I feel it is vital for the court to see it, to understand exactly what happened."

"You are suggesting my clients leave the court Colonel? Is it so they do not see just how incompetent the security forces, of which you are a senior commander, were in this case?"

Paul ignored her and spoke to the presiding judge. "This is distressing footage Sir."

"My clients will stay."

Paul turned to the families, "I had to ask. If you are sure, then I will start the recording. It begins shortly before the tanker comes into shot. Several people gasped as they saw the cars stuck in the right hand lane, recognising them as their family cars. The big tanker crawled into the shot as the left hand lane edged forward a few cars' length. As it moved again the people carrier full of kiddies came into the edge of the coverage. Just as Angie, the driver, began to accelerate up the slip road, a car under took her and swerved across in front of her, hitting the tanker.

Paul stopped the recording. "I would like to draw your attention to the exhaust pipe, note the angle, it is clearly broken, note also it is a new car. The general condition is such the exhaust must have struck something to have broken. Now it gets distressing, I will wait in case any of the families chose to leave. Very well"

He tapped the 'go' button and the recording continued. The car backed up in front of the now stationary people carrier, Angie could be seen clearly gesticulating at the man in the car. What happened next shocked everyone who saw the recording. The big Mercedes shot forwards, its wheels spinning. The tough steel under-rider on the tanker was never designed to cope with this and finally bent inwards. The badly damaged car was now firmly wedged under the chassis of the tanker, just in front of the trailer wheels.

A small but deceptively powerful explosion went off under the bonnet of the car, the force directed upwards. This split open the compartment directly above the car, releasing a torrent of petrol through the gaping hole. For what seemed like an age, in reality no more than a couple of seconds, nothing happened, then everything vanished in a blinding fireball.

The previously undamaged compartments began to explode in rapid succession. As the one over the trailer wheels detonated, the people carrier was hurled, like a leaf in the breeze, into the shops. Of the occupants there was no real sign, it was difficult to see anything inside in the mass of flames. There was the suggestion of a black manikin in the driver's seat, the flames obscuring the real horror within the big vehicle.

The camera continued to record for another minute or so until it too melted!

Paul turned to the Coroner. "There are a couple of other points I would like to draw the court's attention to. Firstly this picture of a gouge in the kerbing outside the shops. The kerb is there to prevent cars leaving the car park and exiting directly onto the A406. This gouge matches what one would expect, if a car of the model which instigated the incident had driven over the kerb. As you can clearly see the gouge is fresh. Tests on residue recovered from the gouge indicate it was hit first by a catalytic converter of the type fitted to the car in question. It also indicates the vehicle to which it was fitted had been driven for less than one hour, in other words it was new. The court will recall I pointed out the damaged exhaust on the new car which instigated the explosion."

It was the Coroner who replied. "Thank you Colonel, most helpful." The man paused to regain his composure. "What do we know about the car and the bomber?"

"The car was stolen from a dealership less than two miles away. It appears it had been valeted prior to being collected by its new owner. The keys had been left in it for the salesman to take it back to the showroom at the other side of the building. It seems as though this was normal practice, so the salesman didn't have to go into the valeting area and get his shoes wet, which would have soiled the interior of the car. It was not regarded as a risk as the front main entrance has a security guard on the barrier, and the rear goods entrance is kept shut. A storeman opens it for deliveries, and the gates open automatically for their own parts vans. What appears to have happened is, one van went out followed by the Merc., the barrier had stayed up as another van was waiting to enter. The assumption being, it was a salesman driving the car, taking it 'round the block' to the salesroom, rather than through the busy yard, again not an unusual occurrence..

As to the driver, we know almost nothing. All we could learn from such images we have is it was almost certainly a man, he wore a gold ring on his ring finger on his right hand and had brown skin. Estimates suggest he was about five foot ten inches tall and of slight to medium build. Nothing identifiable has been found of him, indeed very little has been found of the car."

"Thank you for attending court Colonel, your evidence has been very helpful."

The barrister rose to her feet. "I have some questions for the Colonel, with the court's permission."

The Coroner gestured his consent. 'Here we go,' thought Paul.

"Your long experience in dealing with such atrocities seems to have rendered you emotionless in dealing with such scenes of horror."

"I wouldn't say that," replied Paul.

"Then how do you account for your total lack of any visible emotion to the video you showed the court?"

"I didn't watch it."

"Your unit has the reputation of always being one step ahead of the terrorists, so how was it, in this case, you seem to have been powerless to prevent the carnage. Indeed, why was this terrorist not identified and arrested before his cowardly attack?"

"For a start we don't know it was a terrorist, I'll grant you it is the most likely explanation, but it could also be some sad individual who decided to end it all in spectacular fashion. Do not make the mistake of linking this incident with the other tankers which exploded. As far as we can tell, this had nothing at all to do with the others, unless it was intended as a diversion."

"Surely, there must have been some indications from your much vaunted 'sources' which, had they been acted upon, could have prevented this outrage."

"Like what?"

"Don't Al Qaeda members release videos or send messages to their loved ones saying they will meet again in Paradise?"

"Where on earth did you get the idea this was Al Qaeda? If you've got Osama bin Laden's phone number can I have it? As to the rest of your statement, you have been reading too many tabloid newspapers. Next you'll be telling me the sun is shining because the forecast says it should be, when in fact it is raining!"

"It is my clients contention, the security forces and your unit in particular, were criminally negligent in failing to prevent this outrage, and this being the case are liable to punitive damages."

"I don't know how many university degrees you have got but clearly one is in clairvoyance, and another in optimism. If you could tell me exactly how I could have known this was going to happen and, more to the point, who was going to carry it out, I would be very interested to have the benefit of your doubtless superior intellect."

"The fact remains, you failed to stop this and the other attacks."

"You are quite wrong. As I said, there is absolutely nothing to link this with the other tankers. We got twelve of the other tankers before they could be activated, three more were moved to a place of safety before they could detonate. Granted, nine others exploded before we identified the cause. We know the names of the individuals responsible and what they look like. As yet we have not found them, the world is a big place to hide. You have also to answer my question as to how we or any other security force could have known about, never mind prevented, this horrific incident. We still have no idea who the driver of the car may have been. So exactly how I or my unit can be held in anyway responsible defeats me."

"You were away from your unit at the time I believe?"

"I take it you never go on holiday, being the dedicated ambulance chaser you are. For your information, I hadn't had anything in the way of proper leave for five, maybe six years. An occasional long weekend but that is all. I was, it is true, away on what was supposed to have been my severance leave when this started, and was recalled to take command of the operation."

"So your successors are incompetent Colonel? Your re-call suggests they do not command the confidence of the authorities as you obviously do."

"As usual you could not be more wrong. You clearly, for all your degrees, have not the remotest idea of what is involved in an operation such as this. There is a limit to what any one individual can do. It is a question of capacity not competence."

"So you are saying there is nothing your unit could have done to prevent this?"

"Well, at least we can agree on something."

"There is another matter Colonel," she continued "Your failure to attend this court yesterday as ordered. The subpoena stated quite clearly, you were to accompany the high court bailiff and present yourself here yesterday. Incidentally, where is the bailiff who served the writ ordering you to appear?"

"I have no idea where the idiot is, probably lost again! How could I possibly get here before the court rose, when he didn't turn up at our main gate until fourteen thirty hours? That's half past two to you. You saw how long it took to get here from Northolt today. What was I supposed to do, parachute into the court car park? Use a bit of common sense!"

"Had you complied, you would have been here this morning when the court opened, instead of holding proceedings up still further."

"My presence was required last night on other matters."

"What were these other matters Colonel?"

"Frankly, none of your damned business. Now if the Coroner has any more questions for me I will do my best to answer them. I have an appointment in Whitehall I am expected to attend."

She marched confidently towards Paul with a folded piece of paper in her hand. Paul guessed what it was. He held out his hand as though to take it, as she released it he withdrew his hand allowing the paper to drop to the floor.

"Nice try. If you want to claim damages so you can inflate your bank balance, I suggest you find out who was driving the car and give that writ to his 'group'. Seeing as you're so obsessed with Al Qaeda, find old Sammy bin Liner and give it to him, he's got plenty of money. Good day."

"Actually Colonel I do have one more question for you."

"What is that Sir?"

"The recording of the horrific incident. Can you explain how you were able to provide such a horribly clear picture of the events, yet Counsel was only able to provide a poor, often indistinct video of the incident?"

"Yes Sir, the answer is perfectly simple. She asked for, and received, a video tape. We obtained the digital recording of the incident. I trust it answers your question Sir."

"It is remarkable, the difference."

"There is a degree of enhancement Sir, though nothing of significance."

"I would like a copy of your recording Colonel so independent experts can determine precisely the changes you made."

"We didn't 'change' anything, merely enhanced some aspects of the recording, so it was easier to see exactly what was going on."

"Is it really necessary Ms Smith-Parkin?" asked the Coroner.

"It's no problem Sir," replied Paul; "it will be worth it, if it shuts her up."

"Quite."

Paul took a spare disk out of the lid of his laptop, and inserted it in a slot on the side, tapped a few keys, "Your copy."

"I wanted the entire video Colonel, not a couple of still photographs."

"There is no pleasing some people," muttered Paul. "You have the entire coverage on that disc, not just the bit I showed the court. It will take half an hour to watch it all. There is also a selection of still photographs taken later, such as the scrape on the curb as well as copies of reports on various tests carried out by the forensic boys. Basically all I know about the incident is on that disk."

"Then what did you remove from it before you gave it to me?"

"I didn't remove anything, Ms Smith-Parkin. The machine made you a copy of what was stored on the memory, of all the information relating to this case. You really should try to keep up with technology."

"My name is Smythe-Parkin!"

"Must have been a typing error. I'm sure it was Smith on the paper work."

"It is pronounced Smythe!"

Paul chuckled as he gathered up his papers.

"What is so funny Colonel?" asked the angry woman.

"I just couldn't help but make the connection with Mrs. Bucket, pronounced Bouquet." He turned to the Coroner. "My apologies Sir, I really must be going. It would not do to keep the Prime Minister waiting,"

"Thank you for attending Colonel, your evidence has clarified matters somewhat."

"I still have some questions for the Colonel Sir."

"Are they relevant to establishing the cause of death of the family of your client?"

"I believe they are very relevant Sir"

"Make sure they are."

"What steps are you taking to identify the driver of the car Colonel?"

"Other than liasing with the police, not a lot. There is very little we, or anyone else, can do. If you have any useful ideas on how to identify the driver, I am listening."

"You are not making any efforts to identify him then?"

"I'm not sure what we can do. All CCTV cameras in the area have been checked since the theft of the car, an eye is being kept on missing persons, what else can be done?"

"What about satellite surveillance Colonel. I'm sure the Americans will have pictures."

"Then ask them. I have the CIA's phone number if you would like it."

"So you are doing nothing to protect us from any more attacks from Muslim extremists?"

"Who said anything about this being an attack by an extremist, never mind a Muslim? It is just as likely it was a local who had blown the family fortune in Las Vegas. All we know is, the skin on his right hand was brown, and it could just as easily have been suntan as natural pigmentation."

"I ask again. What are you doing to prevent further attacks?"

"At the moment nothing as I am wasting my time repeating myself. Also there is no way I will discuss the way my unit, or any of the security forces, operate with the likes of you. If you have no further questions Sir, I'm afraid I must get to my next appointment ."

"Thank you again Colonel."

As Paul left the court house, he was aware of someone behind him. He was not surprised to find the young lawyer following him. "Colonel! Wait!"

"The only thing I am waiting for is my car," he replied.

"The Coroner may have accepted your explanations for your incompetence, I do not!"

"And?"

"And I will see you in a court of law, I will get justice for my clients and the compensation they deserve. You may think you can hide behind a cloak of secrecy to cover your ineffective methods, I will see to it you do not!"

"Seeing as you are such a bloody expert on these things, would you mind telling me exactly what we should be doing to catch these murderous bastards?"

"If you increased your surveillance of terrorists to the proper levels, then attacks such as the one which wiped out my clients families would be prevented."

"Fine, you point the terrorists out to us and we will watch them like hawks."

"Don't be ridiculous Colonel. I don't know who these terrorists are."

"It may surprise you to know that, apart from a handful, we don't know either. When was the last time you saw a terrorist?"

"I haven't ever seen one."

"Are you sure? How do you know? Living within the M25 I would say it is virtually certain you have passed one in the street. Of course you didn't spot him or her, that is the point, they look just like anyone else. With a few exceptions they keep a very low profile, often their own families are unaware of their activities. They are extremely cautious contacting each other, very few know more than one or two others in their 'group', which makes it almost impossible to monitor any network, much less penetrate any specific gang."

"Make all the excuses you like Colonel. It is my opinion your total incompetence is the reason my client's family were murdered."

"Right, I've had enough of this," snapped Paul. "I refuse to be lectured by some silly money grabbing little tart like you. You, in common with most of, your profession, have never done a day's real work in your lives. Yet your salaries are many times greater than those of the brave young men and women who risk their lives on a regular basis, attempting to remove these murderers from our streets. Then having caught one and brought them to court, they see over paid smart arses like you con judges into letting them go, because we infringed their human rights. What about the rights of your client and his wife and kiddies? One thing your experts may detect as a change on the recording I gave you, was the blackened face of the wife, clearly screaming - the remnants of her hair still burning and the skin falling off her face, some of it stuck to the glass which was already beginning to melt. Now, if you want the unedited version I can supply it, here and now. I resent you implying I do not care, I care a very great deal! I very much doubt whether you have the strength of character to deal with such horrors on a day to day basis. Now bugger off, and allow me to get on with the task of trying to identify the next batch of idiots before they cause yet more mayhem and suffering!" He turned to go in search of his car, then as an after thought turned back on the shocked young woman, "And just for the record, events such as this do get to me. Even I need a break, it is difficult to stay objective when constantly bombarded with such sights, and then having to deal with holier than thou, pompous, self righteous idiots like you all the time does not make the job any easier."

"If you were more successful it might make it easier."

"That's another thing which makes this job more difficult. Much of our success goes unnoticed, it has to stay secret to protect our sources. Not like the Yanks blurting it out all over the media, 'We have found Osama bin Laden's hide away by monitoring his radio phone and matching the geology of the rocks behind him to a particular spot.' Every time some one gets clever and tries to get credit for some success against this lot, another door closes and it gets harder still. Think about it before you go off on your next crusade."

He was very relieved to see his car approaching, even more so as he settled into the comfortable passenger seat; his back was beginning to 'play up' again.

The traffic, for once, wasn't too bad, the accident having been cleared and he arrived at the Cabinet Office in good time for his meeting to brief ministers on the exploding tankers. He had three folders in his briefcase, all for the Prime Minister. The first was the thickest; this was the completed report on the tankers. The second was what he called, 'the preferred draft', for a speech the Prime Minister was due to make in 'the House' that evening regarding the tankers.

The third was the one which intrigued the Prime Minister, he had noticed the rarely seen 'eyes only' stamp on the cover and there were only four names on the 'viewing' list. He could see the names, Paul and Taff he knew, the third name he didn't recognise then there was his own. When Paul motioned him to follow to a quiet corner, the politician gladly followed.

"Before you show me whatever it is you are guarding so closely, allow me to go first."

"By all means Sir."

"I received a call an hour or so ago from the American Secretary of State. I had no idea what she was talking about, so I couldn't give her an answer, other than I would establish the facts and report back as soon as I could. It would appear elements of the unit you command rescued an American undercover agent last night from the Al Qaeda cell who were holding him captive at an undisclosed location. Is this true?"

"Off the record, and for your ears only Sir," he paused for effect, "Yes."

"Then why all the mystery? I would have thought this was something to cheer about. Think of the effect on Anglo-American relations."

"In the wake of my very public spat with their former Secretary of Defence, I would say this would probably tip us over the edge of the abyss."

"What on earth are you talking about Colonel?" asked a confused Prime Minister.

"It's all in here Sir, and it is not pretty." Paul stopped as an aide approached, both he and the PM waived the man away. The civil servant ignored the gestures and continued towards the two men. "Go away, right away! Now," growled the Prime Minister, "I don't care what it is, GO!"

"We are due to convene the meeting in five minutes Sir, I must insist you take your place."

The PM was about to explode. Paul held out a restraining hand, "Allow me Sir." He covered the couple of paces to the man before the PM had a chance to respond. "Obviously you do not understand the Queen's English so let me put it this way, fuck off! Go while you can still walk, move it. Now!"

"Well really, how uncouth of you Colonel."

"Your reluctance to leave leads me to one conclusion, you wish to know the substance of the conversation between the Prime Minister and myself. In spite of both of us making it abundantly clear the subject was no concern of yours. There can be but one conclusion; you are the most inept spy I have ever encountered." Paul pushed a button on what appeared to be his mobile phone, two security men were there in seconds. "Well done lads, very prompt. Escort this pest out into the lobby and hold him there until I come out please."

The protesting civil servant was unceremoniously frog marched out. Most of those present in the room had heard both Paul and the PM tell the man to keep his distance. The collective decision to allow the two men to complete their conversation in peace was unanimous.

"Sorry about that Sir, now where were we? Ah yes, our American friend. A detachment of our Marines did indeed rescue an American agent, a man known to us. The down side is the circumstances of his rescue; he had uncovered a most unlikely plot to cause massive damage to all the countries bordering the North Sea, the plan was to trigger a massive tsunami."

"That is ridiculous Colonel."

"I thought so too Sir; however it is not as impossible as it sounds. Detonate a large enough explosion in the right place and this would trigger an underwater landslide which, if you got it right, would send a wall of water down the North Sea anything up to a hundred, or more, feet high."

"Is this possible?"

"Oh yes. Now here is the interesting bit. It seems as though the agent sent a message to his masters with all the details of the plan, and included in the message a request that the 'All Arms Unit' be informed immediately. This message was never sent to us."

"How can you be so sure, could it have been missed?"

"I shouldn't tell you this really Sir but with our technology it was easy to check the Americans' signal logs. They received his message when he said, to the minute, however, they positively did not relay it to anyone else. In other words they had the information which, if they had passed it on, would have enabled us to have prevented something much worse than 9/11."

"How did you find out about it Colonel?"

"Pure chance Sir, it is all in the folder, there is however worse to come. As you said, we rescued the agent last night. He was being held captive on the ship carrying the massive charge which was to have triggered the landslide. The question is, how did the Yanks know we'd got him?"

"Aah, I see your point. Did he ring home to let his family know he was all right?"

"No, he was in no condition to and he has been kept under sedation on *Intrepid* until he can be transferred to our medical facility. The other way was if the crew of the ship had got off a signal, I can confirm they did not."

"Then how on earth did the Secretary of State know?"

"I think I might know the answer to that one Sir. As you know we have a detachment in the states, a liaison group, it's mostly one way traffic from us to them, at least anything useful. One of the team out there is a friend of the agent in question, in fact he is godfather to the couple's little girl, the officer in question often pops in to see his god daughter."

"That could look bad Colonel with the father away."

"Worse than you imagine Sir, the little one's mum is our Officer's sister!"

"Then she must have said something."

"Nope. Carl has stayed with her, she has told no one, and no one has called her."

"Then how? You indicated you knew."

"Carl called in; he found a bug right next to the telephone. We monitored it and guess who is listening?"

"CIA. The FBI?"

"I must admit they would be top of my list. Would you believe the

Department of Homeland Security on the orders of the Department of State. The grounds being that Ellen, that's the wife, is British by birth and is therefore an alien in a position in which she might become aware of sensitive material. Incidentally she used to work for us on the most sensitive stuff until an 'Arnie' look alike, swept her off her feet and married the girl."

"Are they safe? I take it she is still a British citizen."

"The answer to both questions is yes. Their plane left Goose Bay in Labrador over an hour ago. Our detachment is on board with her and the baby."

"Do the Americans know? Won't they try to intercept the plane if they find out?"

"If I tell you they will be landing at our base in a little over an hour from now," Paul paused with a little gesture inviting the Prime Minister to work out the rest.

"So it is true, there is still a Concord flying."

"Not exactly Sir. Not one, we've sort of nicked three, by various means."

"Ha splendid, absolutely splendid." There was no pretence of secrecy in his reaction, although he did promise not to tell anyone what had evoked such an ebullient response.

"I'd better let you get your meeting underway Sir. If you could keep that file and its contents to yourself, it could come in very handy in the future. Clearly not all is as it should be at or near the top of the American intelligence community. It might be expedient to find the rotten apple before we let them know that we know, if you see what I mean Sir.

"I do indeed Colonel, but it is galling not to be able to shout our success against the terrorists from the roof tops, however I concur with you. Low key on the tankers and no mention of the ship. One thing before you go Colonel, was the ship the source of the threat to wipe out London?"

"Not in my opinion Sir. I think there is much worse to come before that attack, whatever form it takes, is launched."

"Keep me informed Colonel and well done to all of your men."

Paul passed the furious civil servant in the lobby. "Let him go lads, and next time you are told to mind your own bees wax, take the bloody hint. Nosey old sod!"

"Well really!"

"You certainly know how to make friends Boss."

"Well it's been a long day"

CHAPTER NINE

By the time Paul reached his Breckland base it was dark and raining, his back hurt and he was thoroughly fed up. Settling back in his comfortable chair he lit the inevitable cigarette. Spotting the stack of documents on his desk he muttered a quiet, 'oh shit', as he reached for the top folder. Just as he picked it up, there was a loud, insistent repetitive peep-peep-peep, 'blast the smoke alarm!' In his absence the electrician had been in and fitted the requested on/off switch by the door leaving the alarm, quite correctly, switched on.

The duty officer in 'the watch room', noticed the indicator light for the smoke alarm flashing. "I see the Boss is back," he commented casually and dispatched the sergeant to check all was well.

Paul was half way across the office to switch the offending alarm off when the sergeant knocked on the door.

"Come in," called Paul. "Ah, sorry about that sergeant, my fault, I didn't realize the on/off switch had been fitted while I was out today. Please convey my apologies to the duty officer. Oh and while you're at it, see if Taff is still around, I'd like a quick word if he's still available, tell him I've just put the kettle on, that should hurry him up!"

"Will do Boss, good evening."

Taff arrived about ten minutes later, looking a bit concerned. "What's up? I thought you would have been here like a shot with a brew on the go," Paul chided his friend.

"Normally you would have been right. I was down in 'ops'. You remember the UN asking for a scan of Somalia the other day, so we could give them a more accurate estimate of the number of refugees?"

"Yes, there wasn't a problem was there? Other than the number being rather larger than anticipated."

"It wasn't so much a problem as some bloody odd readings. We used the flight to test some of the new scanners, chemical detectors and the likes."

"I take it all of this is in the report on the top of the pile marked for my attention?"

"From that, I assume you have yet to look at it."

"I've only been back long enough to go to the bog and make a cuppa."

"And set the smoke alarm off. Half the camp turned round and said, 'the Boss is back', in perfect unison."

"Yeah well, you know what I'm like. So what's odd about these readings?"

"The readings for some rather nasty things went right off the scale on the initial flight. Our first reaction was an electronic malfunction or something had interfered with the transmission. When the plane got back we checked the on board logs and the computer hard drives, all said exactly the same thing. So we checked the images for the location where we had got the readings. The only thing visible in the area was a derelict factory. The long and the short of it is, I sent another plane over there this evening to do the most detailed sweep possible, and guess what?"

"The same readings?"

"Pretty much, but more so, if you know what I mean?" Taff replied

"Frankly NO. But no doubt the folder you are clutching in your sweaty mitt will throw some light on the subject."

"I doubt it, this only confuses the matter further. There are so many different chemicals present it rules out any legitimate use, or anyone with the remotest idea of what they were dealing with. To say some of the compounds present are incompatible is something of an understatement. As well as the confusing cocktail, there also seems to be a liquid fuel used in unsophisticated rockets and considerable quantities of thin broken glass. Best guess is Hammas are producing chemical weapons to attack Israel, we know they train in the area, as it's well away from Israeli eyes."

"You're thinking we will have to put in a team on the ground to find out what's been going on?"

"There's a problem with that idea Paul; the area is crawling with militia. Neither UN nor African Union peace keepers go anywhere near the area, it's reckoned to be far too dangerous."

"Oh bloody great, so we can't put a team in to have a look because the UN forces aren't strong enough to protect themselves against a militia. Even if we can work out a way of getting our lads in and out intact, we still can't do it in case there's a brush with the Ganjerweed, or whatever they are called."

"That pretty well sums it up Paul. About all we can do for now is to keep monitoring the place. At least we'll be able to work out the rate the various compounds are degrading, which in turn should enable us to work out when the stuff was there and precisely what was there."

"It goes against the grain but I suppose it will have to do for now. Get one of the analytical teams to give all the data a really thorough going over. I hate anything to do with Bio or Chemical weapons, give me a good old fashioned nutter with an AK47 any day."

"I must admit they give me the creeps as well, I might feel easier myself if we had more information."

"Well Taff someone somewhere knows what was going on there. Our dear friends at Langley should have some high resolution pictures of the place;

once your boffins have narrowed it down a bit on the time scale, we'll ask the CIA if they've got anything which might help us."

"You're hoping Paul. All that will do is make them look for themselves."

"What will they see?"

"Not a lot. Before I forget, what the hell is going on over the American rescued off the floating bomb? I was informed just as I left Ops., a 'speed bird' was requesting permission to land, seems as though it has a load of fugitives escaping surveillance by the FBI on board. Now I don't know how I got the idea, but something tells me their visas haven't got exit stamps on them."

"I'll bet the Canadians stamped them, in and out."

"All right what's going on?"

"The P M knew we had got 'Arnie' off the ship, well 'rescued him from an undisclosed location' was the term he used. The Yanks had asked him, more accurately their Secretary of State asked him, when he would be returned."

"How the hell did they know we'd even found him, never mind got him out?"

"I've had all this already Mate. The long and the short of it is, they were watching our lads and had bugged 'Arnie's house, on the pretext his wife is an alien."

"You mean to tell me they have bugged the house of one of their best operatives, because he's married to an English girl! I've never heard anything so bloody daft in all my life!"

"That is more or less what I said so I pulled the team, and brought his missus and sproggy as well." Paul lit up yet another cigarette. "You knew 'Arnie' told his lords and masters about the ship before he was caught, asking them to pass it on to us?"

"I didn't know about that bit, I must have missed it. Sometimes it's hard to tell just whose side they're on."

"Tell me about it," replied Paul. "If you're going to hang around for a bit, why don't you and I have a quick look through the stack of files which magically appeared on my desk while I was out today. See if there's anything which matters, then we can have a clean start tomorrow and see if we can come up with anything on the missing container we thought was full of RPGs."

"Sounds like a plan Paul."

In the event it took nearly three hours for the two old friends to work through the files.

"Was that a waste of time, or what?" commented Paul as he initialled the last of them. "I found two which mattered. Both were quotes from local builders for doing some, somewhat overdue, repairs to some of the quarters. All of it, allegedly, already done by 'bodge it and legit', contracted by the MOD. The best bit is, these guys are known to us and charge less than a quarter of the price and do a bloody good job."

"I take it you OK'd them?"

"Any reason why I shouldn't?" asked Paul.

"I hope not, because I OK'd three."

"Right I'm off. We'll drop these files off in admin on the way out, mark them up for immediate action."

"Sounds good to me, see you in the morning Paul. I'm in at nine."

It was about six thirty the following morning when the first indications were picked up in the control room that all was not well. For a few moments no one seemed to know where the voice on a radio link had originated from, everybody in the room heard, 'oh shit,' a bang then an ominous silence.

B.J. was the duty officer. Looking forward to a couple of days off after this watch was over, he stood up and in his quiet but authoritative voice said, "Would one of you gentlemen care to find the source of that signal?"

"I know who, B.J." replied one of the team, "It's just I don't know where it came from."

"Elucidate," suggested B.J.

"It came from one of the long range Sea Kings. The pilot's name is Adam, a big ginger haired Jock from the Western Isles, that's all I can tell you B.J."

Another radio cracked, "*Fearless* calling you B.J. line three."

The call answered the question of the first fragmented call. One of her helicopters had reported being shot at! *Fearless* and the Units' other ship, an old destroyer rebuilt to the units requirement and renamed '*Kelly*' in honour of Louis Mountbatten the original champion of combined operations, had been on station for weeks in the Indian Ocean.

Both were on duty with the UN off the 'Horn of Africa'. Their brief was to protect the ships ferrying in the aid to the ports from the growing number of pirates operating in the area. There had already been one violent confrontation when *Fearless* had pushed herself in- between one of the pirate vessels, and a freighter, painted white, with the large black letters on her hull UNHCR.

The pirates were furious at being pushed aside from their prize. Their ship may have been only a couple of thousand tons against the eighteen thousand of *Fearless* but they were confident they could out manoeuvre the larger ship and board the freighter. The anger of the pirates grew as they realised they had no chance with 'plan B' either. Previous encounters had proved they could do more or less what they liked without fear of retaliation, even American warships had only fired small calibre warning shots.

Whoever the crew were on this strange ship with lopsided funnels, and a large flat deck for helicopters on the stern, it did not seem as though they were in the least intimidated by a burst of heavy machine gunfire from the pirate. To the consternation of the thwarted thieves, the twin four point five inch guns, mounted near the bow of the big ship, swung round and pointed at the bridge of the pirate. The captain of the pirate spoke good English, he used a loudhailer and ordered the *Fearless* to get out of his way so he could examine the cargo ship for contraband; he claimed this was on behalf of the Somali government.

The Day The Ravens Died

The Skipper of the *Fearless* was not impressed, as the ship was flying a flag none on board *Fearless* recognised. His reply was a burst of twenty-millimetre cannon fire across the pirates bows.

Whether the pirate captain ordered one of his crew to fire the RPG at *Fearless* or not was a point of some contention among the critics. The Skipper of *Fearless* was in no doubt; he ordered, "Return fire! Three rounds HE per gun, FIRE!"

The modern four point fives mounted on his ship were devastating weapons, firing at the same rate as the famous Bofors gun. In less than half a minute the pirate ship was blown clean in half and was already sinking rapidly. Critics could say he over reacted. What they could not argue about was the five-foot hole ripped into the side of his ship and eight injured crew. He also had seven survivors of the pirate crew under lock and key.

Now it seemed as though he had another problem to deal with. The Sea King which was under attack was nearly two hundred miles away to the south, he had another helicopter away to the north, watching another suspect ship. *Fearless* herself was with two UN ships loaded with food and medical aid from Australia. He couldn't leave these two ships as it was known at least three probable pirates were heading his way, and none of his helicopters, still on board, had the range to assist their friends.

B.J. was straight on the radio to the Canberra doing yet another sweep of the suspect site at Taff's request. Although many miles away, it was capable of mach. point nine as long as it stayed at its extreme altitude. The old plane wheeled onto its new course and sped to find out what was happening. An hour later the scene was in range of its scanners. Paul was by now in the control centre, alerted by his radio phone to the problem, he had rushed in from his old home.

Taff appeared shortly after, both of them requesting coffee which was promptly produced, in defiance of the no food or drink signs erected by the Health and Safety purge.

"Before you light a fag Boss," began B.J, "there are two things. One, we haven't got any ashtrays in here and two, our smoke alarms can't be switched off If you want a fag, it will be your own office or outside."

B.J. braced himself for the expected outburst. He was caught totally off balance by the reply, "Fair enough mate," even after all these years together Paul could still surprise him.

Initially the pirate ship seemed to crawl over the horizon. The radar had been able to detect it some time before it had become visible. First a mast then the upper works, now the entire ship was visible.

Then they spotted the Sea King, its floatation devices had at least prevented it sinking, the crew could be seen in their dingy, trying to keep the bulk of the Sea King between themselves and the Coaster. As the range rapidly closed, it was obvious why the helicopter was bobbing on the sea. The rear rotor was missing and judging from the clearly visible damage, a missile must have exploded nearby.

The crew of the recon. plane were now able to speak to the four men in the inflatable yellow dingy. Everyone was horrified to learn the crew of the Coaster were still taking pot shots at them with rifles, as well as trying to get the helicopter to sink by shooting at the buoyancy tanks. Alarm grew as they learned two of the helicopter crew were wounded.

"I don't suppose by some miracle there are any weapons on the Canberra?" Paul asked.

"No such luck Boss."

Taff had been on a terminal away from most of the others. "You might want to look at this."

Another video screen lit up displaying another image from the Canberra's multi lens optics.

"This will still be well below the horizon to those at sea level. That gentlemen, is *Kelly* at absolute maximum speed," Taff announced proudly. In truth there wasn't much of the ship to be seen.

Somewhere, in between two towering sheets of spray, was some eight thousand tons of ship and it was travelling at the sort of speed an offshore power boat would be delighted to match.

"Her guns will be in range in about two minutes, we are aiming them using the data from the Canberra. I have given permission to open fire as soon as they are in range and have a solution."

Time seemed to stand still to those watching, helpless to assist their friends and colleagues in desperate trouble. Two more rifle bullets found their mark injuring the radio operator for a second time and adding the co-pilot to the injured list.

Brief flashes of light twinkled between the towering clouds of spray flung up as the sharp bows hurled the water aside.

"She's opened fire at last," someone said with relief.

"Why has she stopped firing?" Paul asked.

"Those shells have got to travel over twenty miles Paul. Don't worry they'll be on target," Taff sounded confident.

His confidence was well placed as a chain of explosions detonated all along the centre line of the pirate. The old Coaster simply disintegrated and, apart from a scattering of wreckage and a lot of foam, there was little evidence to say it had ever existed.

Still the *Kelly* came on at full speed, only slowing when about two miles from the damaged helicopter. Twenty minutes after their assailant vanished beneath the waves, both the crew and the damaged Sea King were on board *Kelly*. The men had been rushed to sick bay.

The Skipper of the *Kelly* had acted quickly as the Sea King was obviously beginning to sink. The starboard crane was swung out with a diver clinging to the shackle above the hook. As much by luck as judgement he landed right beside the emergency lifting point, the link snapped shut and the crane took the strain. The lift was a slow job initially, as time had to be allowed for the water to drain out, but it was soon secured to the helipad at the stern of the ship.

It was Paul who called the Skipper. "Well done, I don't suppose there are any survivors from the pirate ship but you had better check, and keep an eye open for anything which might help to identify them. It seems as though the Sea King was brought down by Stinger missiles. We thought our countermeasures could protect us from them, but it seems not to be the case, which is a bit worrying."

The *Kelly* launched her two motor boats, which spent a little while chugging about amongst the spreading patch of oily wreckage. Various bits were fished out as they looked interesting, enthusiasm for the task waned with the appearance of several large sharks which set about clearing up the scattered bits of what had been the crew, with a little bit too much relish for the comfort of the sailors in the small boats.

To the great surprise of everyone, one of the ammunition tubes recovered contained the latest mark of the deadly Stinger missile, the tube had retained just enough air to remain afloat.

When Paul heard about the discovery of the latest American hi-tech. hand held missile he went, as Taff described it to the young Major Courtney, 'gently ballistic'.

"Why do you want to see the Boss, knowing your role here and his mood, the smart thing to do would be to keep out of his way for a bit."

"I'm sure you're right Sir," replied the young officer, "but I was told to come to see the Colonel about the future of my unit's detachment. All except two would like at least the opportunity to attempt qualification to become part of your command Sir."

"I'm delighted to hear it Major, I presume those folders are your assessments from the training cadre?"

"Yes Sir. I am proud to say all of us who wanted to, were accepted for training."

"Not bad for a bunch of pen pushers. You know you are bound to get some extra stick from the instructors because of the way you arrived here in the first place?"

"We have sort of figured that much out ourselves Sir, we have already had a taste of what's to come. I suppose the biggest shock is the discovery one's rank doesn't count for much around here, as I have found out personally. I mean things like, you being a Brigadier and yet everyone calls the Colonel, 'the Boss'. It's all a bit confusing, it seems to be mostly first names, irrespective of rank."

"The only things which matter around here are how good you are at what you do, and your face fits. We are such a small force spread so thinly, it is absolutely vital we all get on and we trust each other, totally. If not, then the system doesn't work."

"Do you think the Boss will be long Sir?"

"Drop the 'Sir' and I'd wait until he has made his call to the Pentagon. An hour or so ago, we had a helicopter shot down by an American missile so you can imagine, he's not very happy at the moment."

"Blue on blues are always bad, but if proper safety protocols are observed most such incidents are avoidable."

"I wouldn't say that to Paul if I were you, this wasn't a blue on blue. This was one of the very latest, still secret, versions of the 'Stinger', so new it hasn't even undergone acceptance trials with the Yanks military yet."

"So how come one was used to shoot down a helicopter?"

"The very question the Boss asked. You are, I take it, beginning to see what we are up against?"

"Not really Sir," replied the young man, "but I can see why you said I would be better waiting for a bit."

Paul's call to the Pentagon followed a fairly predictable pattern. The initial reluctance to put him through to the duty commander was eventually overcome. The one star Marine General in charge was at first confused as to how he could help, then after Paul explained he became obstructive. Not in the mood for being messed around Paul got straight to the point. "There is a humming thing on the desk in front of you called a computer, log in with your password. I am going to transmit a very long serial number to you, which will come up on your screen as soon as you have logged in. All I need is the information on who is supposed to have that particular missile and the rest of the batch please. Clearly something has gone badly wrong as some of the others were used to shoot down one of my bloody helicopters."

"Just a moment Colonel, I have a top priority flash coming through on the Satellite link." The American was still holding the telephone. The first comment Paul heard was, 'What the Sam Hill is that?' then as the *Kelly* opened fire and the resulting explosions filled his screen, 'my god'.

"I'll have to call you back Colonel, there's been an incident in the Indian Ocean. A cargo ship has just been blown to pieces by an unidentified warship. I've never seen such speed," the man paused; "it was so fast, incredible."

"What do you think I've been trying to tell you? The warship was the *Kelly*. The rust bucket she blew out of the water was the ship the Stingers were launched from which shot down our Sea King. The crew of the cargo ship were shooting at the helicopter and the crew in the water. *Kelly* had no choice but open fire to save the lives of our men. What I need to know is, how the bloody hell several of your latest missiles came to be in the hands of bloody pirates?"

The number Paul sent flashed up on the Marine officer's screen. "How did you do that Colonel?" asked the confused American.

"I haven't got the remotest idea how it works. I just think of it as an advanced e-mail, what does your humming machine say about the number?"

"Oh , that's not good."

"What's that Sir?"

The Day The Ravens Died

"What have you done Colonel? The computer is telling me access denied, and highly classified. Hell, the who is top secret! Just trying to trace it has set off security alarms on the system."

"I guess that answers one question Sir. Only the CIA are that paranoid. If they run true to form, they'll be there to arrest you in about five minutes. Don't worry, I'll have a word with the duty Deputy Director in Langley's ops room and straighten things out. I suppose I should have guessed it was them behind it. Thank you for your help Sir."

Unfortunately the Duty Officer at Langley was not one Paul got on with too well. The American began to lecture Paul on how he shouldn't meddle in such affairs and warned him to drop any further enquiries, he didn't actually say 'or else', but the implication was there.

"O.K.," replied Paul. "I'll tell you exactly what I am going to do. As from now, my men will check every UN marked container landed anywhere near Somalia. Any and all weapons found in them will be confiscated and destroyed, unless they are clearly marked for, and collected by the official UN peace keeping forces. Preventing illegal arms entering the area is within the remit of my orders from the UN, as is preventing piracy in the area. Now either you tell me how your missiles came to be in the hands of someone trying to shoot down one of my bloody helicopters, or the shit will very publicly hit the fan."

"It must have been a case of mistaken identity Colonel, easily done. Clearly the crew of the ship you sank made a mistake and over reacted."

"You epitomise all which is wrong with your agency. How the bloody hell can you mistake a Sea King, painted white with UN in ruddy great black letters on its side, for anything other than what it is?"

"It must have opened fire on the Coaster Colonel."

"What with, missile decoy flares? It was unarmed you idiot! Where did those bloody pirates get those missiles from? And don't give me a load of bullshit about classified or need to know. Your kit was used to try to kill some of my men and I will find out how the pirates got them. Now are you going to tell me or do I start dumping your illegal arms shipments in front of the world's media?"

"You won't do that Colonel, you won't be allowed to."

"Who is going to stop me? Not you. Inform the Director I will be calling him when he gets in to work later today."

By lunch time Paul had his answers. It transpired CIA teams were at work in the west and south of the country. Fed up with seeing helpless civilians being bombed out of their villages by a handful of old migs of the government air force, they had decided, not unreasonably, to do something about it. Typically, rather than equip the UN teams with a means of defending themselves openly, someone in the corridors of Langley took it upon themselves to use the UN food shipments to supply the missiles covertly instead.

"Don't you think the UN have a hard enough job as it is Director, without having to explain illegal weapons hidden in food shipments for the starving people in the area. Damn it , it calls into question the credibility of the UN aid programs world wide. Now some of my lads came close to paying the ultimate price, rest assured I will not let it happen again."

"I'll check and see if there are any more consignments en-route Colonel. If there are, can you find a way of discretely removing them, as I share your concerns as to the credibility of the UN. You have my word those responsible will be dealt with."

Paul thought 'yeah right' but contented himself with, "Thank you Sir."

He called Taff in, intending to discuss the affair with him, but Taff brought the young major in with him, still clutching the bundle of assessments on his unit's members from the training cadre.

CHAPTER TEN

"Declared a cease fire with the CIA Paul?" asked Taff innocently. "Major Andrew Courtney has some good news for you, it seems as though all except two of his detachment would like to join us. Their evaluations are pretty good, I've been browsing through them while you have been cooking the airwaves between here and Langley."

"Fine, I'll leave it to you Taff. Anything interesting?"

"Oh yes," replied Taff, sounding quite pleased about something. "It seems from these, at least two of the Major's gang are accomplished chemists, both specialists in chemical weapons, and the Major himself has a degree in the subject of toxicology. I can see you are thinking the same as I am, as things stand we have to beg information from various government labs, and they can take forever to get back to us, no matter how we pester them."

"Taff you are a genius. There is a spare office a couple of doors down, Andy, scoot and get your chemists, I want them in here in ten, GO."

"I'll get tech. services to start installing the computer terminals, I take it you'll be assigning a photo analyst?" Taff suggested.

"I think it would be a good idea, don't you? What about the big blonde sergeant who transferred in from the RAF, by all accounts she has an eye for detail."

"I wonder what attracted her to your attention?"

"I'm a happily married man, dirty minded sod. But seeing as how you asked," Paul picked up a folder from the pile beside him marked 'read'. "This is a recommendation for a commission for the lady in question, from her section commander. Mind you, I'll concede you have a point, she is quite difficult to miss. Tell you what, why don't we put her in charge of the task group to try to work out what was going on in those scans?"

"Why not, we'll be able to evaluate her command skills and gauge the reaction of the Major to working with our way of doing things."

"Get her in here Taff, let's see if we can have this team up and running before tea time."

"Okay Paul. You're worried about this, other than the obvious, any particular reason?"

"Sounds daft in these days of hi-tech. gismos, but my gut is telling me this is bad, seriously bad. We've missed something which would help us unravel it, but I'm damned if I can think of anything which even begins to make sense."

"There was the suggestion it could have been Hezbullah or Hammas trying to up the anti against Isreal."

"I know, but it just doesn't sit right. Let's see what our lot come up with, there ought to be something in all those scans recon. have been doing. Have you any idea what all this stuff is about? What for instance is multi facet laser spectographic scanning, or remote spectral analysis. There's one here I can't even pronounce, much less tell anyone what it does. Here look, what the hell is multi frequency remote scanning graphic cromotography when it's at home?"

"Don't look at me Paul, I haven't got any more idea than you have."

A knock on the door signalled the arrival of the sergeant from the analysis team, Paul noticed her name tag, in truth it was difficult to miss. "Tell me this is a wind up."

"No Sir" she replied, worried by the reaction of a senior officer she knew only by reputation. "My name is Helga, my mother was German, my father a British soldier. I am sure you have not called me here because of the way I look, I try to dress down for work but some would say nature has been kind to me."

"No, no, of course not sergeant. I have a job for you, an extremely important job. We are setting up a new section to deal with a specific task, it seems from your file you will be ideally suited to lead this team."

"Sir?"

"You are up to speed with all these new fangled scanners on the recon. planes?"

"As much as anyone Sir, I find them fascinating."

"I'm glad we have got some one in the building who knows what they are looking at because most of it's Greek to me. Here's the task, you are no doubt aware we have taken an interest in a partially destroyed warehouse in a remote area of Somalia. I am told by people who claim to know about such things there are high concentrations of some rather nasty chemical agents present. I need to know everything there is to know about that site. What is there, what it does, how it degrades, where it came from and more to the point it's uses and where it went.

We will give you everything we have on the place. If you know of any scan which can be carried out, but has not been done and it even might help you answer any of my questions, you may request them without further reference to us. You will be in sole charge of this project, you will have a team of three chemists to tell us what was there and what to do about it. One of them is a major, so I suggest asking him to do things rather than telling him. Think you're up to it Sergeant?"

"I don't know what to say Sir. Of course I will do my best, thank you Sir, the only thing which bothers me is I have my flight sergeant's exams coming up next week Sir."

"Two things, stop calling me Sir!, I bloody hate it. My name is Paul, all right call me Boss in front of lower ranks but in here or in meetings it's Paul or Boss, and don't worry about the crown to go with your stripes, we'll take care of it. Ah, your team have arrived, we'll show you to your new office. It's a bit bereft of equipment, sort out what you want and I'll send the QM over to sort out furnishings etc.. Tech. services will have your terminals up and running by morning along with a double plasma screen and a communications terminal."

Paul led the way and ushered them into their new home. "If you three can get your minds back, I was going to say to the job in hand, but maybe not! As you know we don't take much notice of rank around here. I can fully appreciate you will find it difficult to adjust to this but make no mistake, Helga is in charge of this team for very good reasons. Granted, I will expect her to ask Andrew to do things rather than tell him, but if it comes to the crunch and the situation warrants it, she is the Boss. As soon as tech. services have you kitted out, no-one, and I mean no-one other than Taff, myself or the duty officer, are allowed in here, and you will discuss your work only with each other. If you need outside help then clear it with Taff or myself, other than any additional scans which Helga has already been given permission to authorise. All that remains to be said is 'carry on'. You all know where to find me, good luck."

"One thing Boss," asked Helga, "Are we allowed a kettle?"

"The thing on the wall over the draining board looks awfully like a socket to me. You'd better get one and a spare mug, I like my coffee strong and sweet, the opposite to me. Good luck all of you. Back to my office Taff, there are a few things I need to catch up on."

Once settled down in his comfortable chair with a fresh cup of coffee and a cigarette Paul started on his list. "Right, the two lads who got hurt with you and his Nibs, how are they? Is there anything we can do to help?"

"They are both still poorly, but holding their own. Transport for their wives is available on request. Hopefully we will be able to move them to our own medical centre in about a week, if all goes well."

"The General, how is he? I heard a nasty little rumour he had pneumonia."

"He had a bit of a scare but it seems he's fine. The medics are keeping an eye on him. They have been told not to take any chances with him and he has been told to do as the medics tell him, for what good that will do."

"How is our illustrious American friend getting on? I take it his wife and kiddie have been allocated a quarter out at 'the farm'," he asked, referring to the unit's original base, a few miles away.

"We gave them your old quarter, and James T Alexander the third should be arriving in one of *Intrepid's* choppers round about now. The medics are ready for him. We've also arranged for the cargo ship to dock in Kings Lynn where we will remove the explosives and store them in our bunkers here. A survey reports it's all in excellent condition and should satisfy the needs of our armed forces for some time. The scrap iron used to weight it down will be sold at market price to a dealer based on the docks. We will then see if we can find a use for the ship. The Yanks want the prisoners, it seems as thought they can make a kidnapping charge stick. I'm inclined to let them have them, after we've had a chat of course."

"Any more news from *Kelly* or *Fearless* on the condition of the crew of the Sea King?"

"One is perfectly all right, two who got shot are sitting up and complaining about the coffee, so they sound in pretty good shape. The radio operator is out of surgery but under sedation. He is expected to make a full recovery, but it may take a bit of time. Initial assessment of the Sea King is it is beyond repair, but most of the equipment is salvageable."

"Anything else I should know about?"

"Like what?"

"I don't know, that's why I asked?"

"Well there are no more writs outstanding as far as I know. The bailiff was found hiding in the bushes beside the approach road and has been convinced his hundred per cent record is in tatters and he should go home. The last bits of contractor's equipment have been removed from the camp and returned to it's rightful owners. The MoD are still bleating about all manner of things, and the Health and Safety Executive are crying outrage at being refused permission to come snooping around. Oh yes, and the MoD want to know when they can have their safety inspectors back. They have only got two, and would like the rest!"

"Tell them tough, the team are on detached service. Some may be returned, depending on how they do on their course."

"That's exactly what I told them," chuckled Taff.

"You are getting nearly as bad as I am Mate."

Taff just laughed. "I suppose we'd better try to find out what happened to the missing container of RPGs we thought snuck in through Felixstowe a couple of months ago."

"Have we got anything at all which might help find it?"

"Nothing you don't already know about Paul. The last thing was the burnt out tractor unit on an old industrial estate in West Bromwich. The CCTV footage showed it shortly before it entered the estate, already minus its trailer and with the same man driving it as it was who drove it out of the port. Of course, we now know he wasn't who he claimed to be and the truck might have matched the description of the truck the registration belonged to, but that was a con as well."

"Whoever was behind it had done their bloody homework. They knew the real truck with that registration was off the road for a couple of days. Anything on where they might have switched the trailer to another tractor unit?"

"Every possible sighting has been ruled out after it left the port."

The Day The Ravens Died

"Too neat. Get a team to check them all again Taff, I'm sorry I just don't believe it. Someone, somewhere must have seen it; a bloody great thing like that cannot travel half way across the country and no-one sees it!"

"They'll love you Paul but you're right, as usual, we must have missed something. I'll get them to start at the port gates and check everything along all possible routes, there are so many cameras these days, it just has to be on one of them. The thought of what chaos could be caused with a hundred or so RPGs doesn't bear thinking about."

"Correct me if I'm wrong, but haven't we got half a dozen Canberras fully fitted out with the new 'sniffer' gear but still waiting for the new engines?"

"Yes. You are wondering if it will work at more normal altitudes?"

"Why not? As I understand it, these sensors are not as sensitive to vibration as most of the other gismos. Why not stick one up and do a couple of orbits of the base, it will be interesting to see if it will detect traces of explosives, say inside a container? I'm sure we have one or two on base. If it does work then we have another way of possibly finding the bloody things; if it doesn't, then we've used a ton or so of fuel finding out. It's got to be worth trying, if only to help calibrate the equipment and train the rest of the crews."

"Fair enough, I'll get things started, you never know what might turn up."

Taff left Paul alone with the inevitable stack of files and reports to read, how he hated this part of the job.

It was amazing how varied the subjects were. Could the unit provide pictures and maps detailing the precise location of new poppy fields in Helmand province? Could a plane be provided to help the detachment of Marines operating in the Shat-al-Arab Waterways, to enable them to be more effective against the gun runners smuggling arms in from Iran? This one he attached a quickly scribbled note to. 'No further action required, aircraft already on station.' Weapons are entering in the north of the country over land and by-passing American check points, using the simple expedient of travelling across country."

Another which caught his eye was a request from the Metropolitan Police for replacement instructors involved in retraining the firearms teams in the techniques for dealing with terrorists. The current team were deemed to be 'too abrasive' in their approach. As he had to be in London that evening for yet another meeting, he decided to go now and check it out himself. There was no mistaking the signature of the Deputy Assistant Commissioner with whom he had argued previously.

He told Taff what he was doing. The response from his long time friend wasn't quite what he expected. "Not on your own you're not, you take a driver and no arguments."

"Yes Sir, certainly Sir!" he replied, somewhat taken aback by the forceful tone in Taff's voice.

"Cut it out Paul, the days of us swanning around on our own are long gone. I'm not doubting your driving but we're not getting any younger, and you are short of rest since you've been back. Anyway, this is precisely the reason we have staff cars and drivers."

"Oh all right mother, I won't argue, I might even grab a bit of kip on the way down."

"Good, and try not to get too wound up with 'Madam', she's becoming a royal pain in the arse, firing off more memos than the cops are using bullets in training."

The roar of a jet taking off reached them even in the double glazed office away from the runway. It sounded a bit different to the familiar sound of the Rolls-Royce Avon jets.

Taff noticed Paul's enquiring look. "That one is still a B59 Paul, with its American J47 engines, they sound different. Supposedly they produce more power, they certainly make more noise and they smoke worse than you do, but they are reliable. We'll soon see if they can do the job of 'sniffing' out explosives. By the way, what time do you think you'll be back?"

"No idea Mate, you know what these meetings are like, most of those attending haven't got anything better to do with their time."

The journey was remarkably free of significant hold ups for once. Having parked in the designated spot, Paul sent his driver to get himself a cup of tea, whilst he went in search of his training team. One was giving an introductory lecture to a newly arrived fire arms team, the remainder were on the range trying to change the way the police teams operated, all under the watchful, disapproving eye of the officer in overall command of the Mets.' armed units.

Spotting their Boss, activities were halted briefly. "Come to sharpen up a bit Boss?" asked the soldier in charge.

"Not really Rick. I've had a complaint from on high," he said motioning more with his eyes than anything, to the senior police officer. "It would seem as though you are being too hard on her 'boys', have you lot got any complaints?" Paul asked the officers. "Now would be a good time to let me know if you are not happy with the training my lot are giving you."

"It is certainly different Sir," replied a sergeant. "If nothing else, it has made us realise this is potentially much more dangerous than the usual armed robbers, or even the less committed terrorists we have faced so far."

"That will do sergeant." The stony faced woman approached Paul. "Why are you here Colonel?" she asked.

"Oh, just came to see if there was any truth in this," he waved the folder. "My first impression is, it's a load of ill informed bollocks so you can have it back to recycle with your own rubbish." He tossed the thin folder gently to her.

"How dare you talk to me in such a manner?"

Paul ignored her reply. "Out of idle curiosity how well did you score in your evaluation shoot?"

"There is no need for me to re-qualify Colonel."

"I disagree. You either re-qualify or I pull your permit to carry a firearm.

You have no authority to command people if you cannot do the job yourself, especially when the job involves the use of weapons, the sole purpose of which is to kill people. Now let's see if you're as good a shot as you claim to be. Ten rounds against the clock, five targets, two into each target."

"I haven't got my personal weapon here Colonel."

"I'm sure the range officer can provide an identical weapon. I thought you all still used the standard Berretta 9mm."

"We do."

"Very well, here's the challenge, I'll shoot with my Smith and Weston three fifty seven magnum, I haven't fired since before I tried to retire. You use your automatic with a ten round clip. Let's see who gets the highest score in the shortest time, five points off for each second after the first one is finished."

"You cannot possibly win Colonel, you will have to reload."

The instructors had seen Paul do his 'party piece' before. They moved the men they were training well back from the firing point. The range officer passed Paul a set of ear defenders and goggles, he accepted the ear muffs but declined the goggles.

"I must insist Sir."

"If, heaven forbid, we ever have to do this for real, the odds are there will not be time to follow all the regulations. Fair enough for when you are learning the basics, but those things do alter your vision. We are talking advanced rapid reaction shooting here which is a different task all together."

"Very well Sir but I am not happy about it. As long as you accept, it is at your own risk."

"Duly noted."

"Very well, five targets, two rounds per target, ready, shoot!"

Paul had removed two rounds from his revolver, the speed loader in the palm of his hand held six. With a fluency from years of practice, he ejected the four spent cases and in one smooth motion pushed the six rounds into the chambers, allowing the loading cage to drop as he snapped the now full chambers back into position. The last two 'bangs' were from the nine millimetre.

Those who had not seen it before were amazed, even more so when the targets came whizzing back along the twenty meters of wire on the winders. The DAC was dumbfounded, she had shot as well as she ever had. In truth she had done well, an average of less than two inches between shots. True one shot had gone a bit high, only just on target. It would probably have stopped the target had it been for real. She gaped in amazement at the Colonel's targets, each had a neat figure of eight shaped hole, vertically between the eyes of the target silhouettes.

"I didn't do that to make you look bad but to prove my point. It is your attitude which needs adjusting; your shooting is nearly good enough. You hurried one shot when you realised it was a lot closer contest than you expected.

It is possible something like that could cost you your life or the life of one of your officers. Had the target been a suicide bomber, the high shot might not have prevented him detonating his bomb, the margin can be that small."

"I still do not approve of your methods Colonel."

"I can't ever recall saying I liked them. The point is, on some occasions, there is no choice and even less room for mistakes. Carrying one of these things around brings with it one horrendous burden, you literally have the power of life or death, and the worst part of it is having to live with it afterwards. You absolutely have to get it one hundred per cent right, nearly, is never good enough, so stop bleating if these guys training your lads seem to be hard task masters, they have to be.

They know first hand what it's like, but I'm sure none of them will thank me for mentioning it, I'll let them get on with their job. If you want to keep yours, I suggest you train with them, you will then have a better chance of coping when the day comes, as it surely must with the way things are going. You have to lead your people in these situations, you cannot do it from an office. We will talk at length later as the training progresses. Good luck to all of you. Carry on."

Paul, unusually, was first to arrive for the meeting at the Cabinet Office. The PM welcomed him into the conference room. "I'm glad you are early Colonel, I understand from our American friends you have had a helicopter shot down, are the crew safe?"

"The answer to both questions is yes Sir. Three of the crew were injured, one quiet seriously but the last I heard he should be all right."

"That, at least, is good news. Do we know how it was brought down and by whom?"

"Yes Sir. It was brought down by a Stinger fired by pirates. More worryingly, it was of a new type not yet issued to American forces in general. It would seem as though a consignment was destined for a group of CIA operatives in Somalia, the idea being to use the missiles to protect civilians from air attacks."

"Forgive me Colonel. I cannot understand how the missiles came to be in the hands of the pirates. Do we know?"

"Oh yes. Last month a ship load of American aid was hi-jacked by pirates. They ran it aground, removed all the aid then sold most of it on the black market. In the process of unloading it they discovered the crates of weapons, including the Stingers bound for the CIA."

"The CIA had secreted weapons onto a UN aid ship?"

"Seems that way Sir."

"How sure are you Colonel? This, if true, is very serious."

"There is no doubt at all Sir."

"How can you be so certain?"

"The crew of the *Kelly* fished one of the missiles, still in its tube, out of the floating wreckage of the pirate ship. With the help of the Director of the CIA we were able to unravel the entire sorry tale."

"I take it from what you said, your forces sunk the pirate? It was hoped you could take prisoners Colonel."

"We didn't have much choice Sir as they were firing on the helicopter crew. *Kelly* sank her from maximum range with her four point fives. I have it on video if you want to see it?"

"That implies you had a plane on station. I was unaware of the deployment."

"We turned up an anomaly doing the refugee count for the UN. We were doing another set of scans, hopefully to resolve the problem when the helicopter reported being under attack. We simply told the pilot of the Canberra to go have a look."

"Well I hope it was worth it Colonel, because the entire operation took place directly beneath an American 'Big Bird' Satellite. They want to know how our plane could have been at such incredible altitude, yet still manoeuvre so freely. More to the point, how it is possible for an eight thousand ton warship to travel as fast as an offshore power boat and even more remarkably, shoot so accurately at such a range? We have a treaty with the Americans Colonel whereby we exchange technology."

"We supply their armed forces with all manner of bits and pieces ourselves Sir, but we would no more give them our latest gear, than they would give us the secrets of 'Aurora'."

"Surely Aurora is just a myth?"

"They would like it to stay that way, and why not?"

The meeting which followed was, by normal standards, relatively peaceful and free from argument for once. The only topic which stirred a degree of curiosity was the nature of the 'anomaly'.

Paul explained, "The new sensors on the Canberra had picked up strong readings which indicated substances which should not have been there."

"What substances Colonel?"

"It seems as though someone has been messing around with what appear to have been chemicals, the type used in chemical weapons. The results are being analysed and as soon as we have them I will let the Prime Minister know. It may be necessary to insert a team to obtain actual samples. This will be decided when we have the results."

"Is this a threat Colonel?"

"I have no idea Sir, it certainly is not good news, so yes it is a threat. Exactly who is likely to be threatened, I have no idea. At this stage I will not speculate as I have insufficient information."

"Keep us informed Colonel," said the Home Secretary.

"Of course Sir. If there are no more questions I will bid you all good evening."

"One more point, if I may Colonel?" asked the deputy Prime Minister. "Are you certain there will be no more exploding petrol tankers? I went to the scene of one explosion, it was the most terrible thing I have ever seen. I would like your assurance there will be no more."

"There will be no more Sir, at least from the same source. However I can give no such undertaking from attacks by suicide bombers or rocket attacks."

"You mean there is still a risk of more such outrages?"

"Personally I think these were little more than minor diversionary attacks. We are as sure as we can be of an entire container load of weapons, mainly RPGs that came in through Felixstowe a couple of months ago. We cannot prove it and, as yet, we cannot find it. We are however looking very hard. I believe the weapons in the container which 'went missing' will, if not found, be used to carry out a sustained and damaging attack on the infrastructure of the country."

"You have been predicting a major attack for some time Colonel. Do you believe it is now imminent?"

"As I said Sir. I believe the tankers were merely a preliminary. The question is, what did we miss when we were all preoccupied solving the problem with the tankers?"

"Stop them Colonel."

"Certainly Sir, if you can guarantee no more hold ups in supplies of equipment. Then we will do everything within our power to stop them."

"Anything specific you need Colonel?"

"New batteries for my crystal ball Sir. I must be going Sir. There are matters requiring my attention."

CHAPTER ELEVEN

The next few days were hectic to say the least. With a few minor adjustments to the sensors, the old American built Martin B59s could indeed detect explosives concealed around the base. Within a week all were operating in the search for hidden caches of explosives. It was amazing how many contacts the initial sweeps produced. The back-log became so great the crews were given three days off to allow the search teams to investigate most of the suspect contacts.

"This is crazy Taff. We have brought half the country to a halt waiting for bomb disposal squads to deal with unexploded bombs which have been laying around for over sixty years. The media are getting more than a little curious as to why so many are suddenly being found. Some are being explained away easily enough. We have got to think up a plausible explanation which won't give the game away. Any ideas?"

"The truth?"

"Why not, or at least a bit of it? Say we have been testing some new equipment designed to detect road side bombs in Iraq and Afghanistan, and it is working better than expected as far as detecting unexploded Second World War bombs are concerned."

"I suppose that is about as good as we'll get, it should at least shut up a lot of the speculation in the media," replied Taff.

"Get a press release ready to that effect and get the Minister for Defence to release it. Make certain there is nothing to connect us to it, or any mention it is an airborne system. If the hounds of the press want to think it is mounted on a land rover then it's fine with me."

"Works for me, I'll get on with it. I should be able to beat their deadline for tomorrow's papers; if I time it right there won't be time for a lot of awkward questions."

There was a startled, 'Oh!' as Taff opened the door to head off on his errand. Helga had been about to knock as the door opened before her.

"Come in Helga," Paul called as he headed to the kettle to refill his coffee cup. "Want one?" he enquired.

"Sorry Sir, do I want what?"

"A coffee. I presume the folder you are clutching so tightly contains at least some of the results of your team's analysis. As I am no scientist I will

Timothy Pilgrim

certainly need to ask questions which I will expect you, as head of the section which produced the report, to answer, hence the offer of a cup of coffee, and drop the Sir!"

"Yes Sir, sorry," she hesitated then sheepishly added "Boss".

"Milk, sugar?"

"Black, just a half a teaspoon of sugar please S...Boss."

"Take a seat." Paul waved his hand in a gesture to take her pick of three chairs. "Any one you like, except mine."

Paul brought the coffees over, placing them on the appropriate beer mats, then to the obvious disapproval of the big blonde sergeant he lit a cigarette. As he sat down he prodded the button marked 'E' and an extractor fan started up, dragging the offending smoke out.

"This is my office and if I want a fag I'll have one. I'll happily put the fans on, as you clearly do not like it, it's called compromise. Equally I would not smoke in another office if it was a smoke free one, I trust this is satisfactory?"

"I think it's called common sense Sir, I mean Boss. It's a much more practical solution than a blanket ban, which costs hours of lost time with smokers nipping out for a quick puff, or bad feeling if they're not allowed out."

"My feelings in a nut shell. Now your report please"

She handed over the folder, obviously nervous as this was the first one which she had written which hadn't been checked by an officer before being passed on.

"I hope you will find it satisfactory Boss."

Paul scanned the neatly laid out pages. "How certain are you about these results?"

"If the readings were accurate, then there is no doubt about any of them on the first three pages. The next two pages are less definitive but reasonably sure, over ninety per cent probability."

"I think we have a problem looking at this. You name it and it's been there." He looked at some hi - definition enlargements taken from the photographs. "What exactly am I looking at here?"

"A piece of packing case not totally destroyed in the fire when the warehouse burnt down. The markings are North Korean. We are fairly certain the box contained gyro stabilising units for scud missiles. The traces of hydro carbons detected were the residue of the major fuel component for the old mark one scud."

"What is this?" Paul asked, examining another picture.

"The remains of a container which held a catalyst to activate a foam packing agent. It was manufactured in Switzerland. It is harmless and virtually inert on its own but mix it with liquid foam base and the mixture froths up to ten times its volume or more, then sets protecting anything embedded in it."

"I take it this is glass, like glass ping-pong balls?"

"Yes Boss."

"Oh bloody hell. This place was used to fit or rather fill chemical warheads, probably to scuds."

"That was our conclusion too Boss, it's on the last page. There is a bit more Boss, we think the warheads are refrigerated as there are traces of powerful CFCs, of a type long since banned in the west. Its main use was in small mobile fridge units."

"I don't know, but I would say we are in deep, deep shit. Any idea how long ago all this happened?"

"It is difficult to be precise, but we have been monitoring the readings and calculating the rate of degradation. The fire was at least twenty eight days ago but no more than thirty five. Then there is this Boss," she passed Paul another photograph.

"Dead locusts, hardly surprising considering the chemicals present."

"True, but that was taken an hour ago. The site is still highly toxic and they were not there yesterday, which suggests toxins must still be escaping from something on site, those chemicals degrade quite quickly once exposed to the air. Also, the particular species of locust in the picture is very resistant to chemicals."

"Have you any idea of the quantities involved?"

"Not really Boss, there really isn't any way to tell. We are, however, fairly confident there must have been in excess of one hundred truck movements in and out of that place, judging from the wheel tracks."

"Have you got anything to cheer me up?" Paul asked.

"You make a good cup of coffee Boss."

"Good to know I can still do something right. Tell me, is it possible to get clear enough readings on any of the chemicals present to identify a source?"

"I don't think so Boss, but I will ask my team. They are the experts on things like that."

"How near are you to producing your final report?"

"Two, maybe three days. We are going to check everything again to make certain we haven't missed anything because we are still finding small anomalies. I think we have found out as much as we can without having actual samples."

"Ask your team what more useful information samples could provide. Also ask them, what they would want in the way of samples should it become possible to obtain them. Let me know before we knock off work for today."

"Will do Boss. If we have finished, I would like to get back to my team."

"Carry on."

She was halfway to the door when Paul called her back. "Working on this report meant you missed your flight sergeant's exam didn't it?"

"Yes Boss, I'll get it next year. I'll still be young enough to try again."

"Not if you do time in the glass house for being incorrectly dressed on duty!"

"Sir?" she sounded puzzled.

Paul frowned at her.

"Sorry, Boss," she quickly checked herself over, fearing a button had given up on her tight blouse. "My uniform seems to be in order for an RAF sergeant Boss."

Paul chuckled. "Here catch," he tossed an envelope to her with a gentle lob. "Congratulations, you are no longer in the RAF. You are now a lieutenant in the All Arms Unit. All the papers are in there, along with your badges of rank and mess cards. I thought you had a report to finish!"

"I don't know what to say Sir, sorry Boss, thank you." As she reached the door she turned, "Thank you again Boss."

Paul sat going over the report again, no matter how he tried to find a different explanation for the results from the scans of the burned out warehouse, he always came up with the same answer.

Taff reappeared. "Helga looks happy, I presume you told her?"

"I did." Paul slid the report across the desk to his friend, "See what you make of it?"

"How certain are they about VX and all this other crap?" Taff was visibly shaken by what he had read. "If they are right, then we have one hell of a problem."

"I asked the same thing Mate and they are positive. As to the purpose of all those bits and pieces there is only one conclusion, obviously you arrived at the same one I did."

"It says here, the fire was four or five weeks ago, those chemicals could be just about anywhere by now, how the bloody hell can we find it?"

"The CIA have a 'Big Bird' over there several times a day, the easy bit is getting them to send us the pictures of the site for the past six months. The hard part is going to be explaining how we know what was there. The place used to be a UN food depot. It was the hub of a network in the area, and the main depot for cooking oil for the entire northern region. It used to be brought in by tanker and bottled for distribution. Militia moved into the area six or eight months ago and drove the people out, killing those who didn't go quickly enough. UN forces were too weak to stop them so they pulled out with the refugees. I think we're going to have to put a team in to physically bring back samples before we ask the CIA for the pictures, if only to avoid a lot of bloody awkward questions."

"Getting them in is the easy bit, a night time halo. How the hell do we get them out? It is far too far for helicopters and the terrain too rough, even for a Herc.. The entire area is teeming with militia spoiling for a fight, and don't forget they probably have Stingers."

"I'd already worked out choppers were not an option as far as getting them out was concerned, there isn't anywhere we could refuel them. The Yanks have some Jolly Green Giants, which can be refuelled in the air, they have the range but they are sitting ducks for missiles or even heavy machine guns."

"Can we come in from Ethiopia?"

"Then it gets political. I think I might have an idea. *Fearless* is in the area, I don't know if she has her three Harriers on board or not. If she hasn't then get them out there, plus any RAF Harriers which are available. Hang on a tick. I seem to remember seeing something about the Yanks having one of their massive Marine assault ships out there, what's it called? Ah! yes, the *Kearsarge* is pootling about somewhere in the area."

"You have thought of something I missed?"

"I believe she has at least one of those weird Osprey things on board, as well as half a dozen Harriers. Drop the team in at night, get the American Marines to go get them with an Osprey. If we put a Canberra up and an AWAC, between them, they will be able to spot any threat to the extraction team. We can protect the Osprey with the Harriers, the Canberra can target mark any threat and the Harriers can take it out. The Yanks have six, we'll have three. We can easily sustain the Harriers and the Osprey with tankers based on Sahlala. The refuelling systems are compatible, and *Fearless* can go quite close inshore. The Harriers, ours and the Americans, can land on her to re arm if needs be and refuel while they are down. Those new rockets will fit the Americans racks as well as they do ours. I know the Yanks Marine corps have been testing them for just such an operation. Get things moving Taff."

"One thing Paul, who is going to be running this operation? With the Yanks involved there won't be any room for cock ups."

"Why don't I get my arse out there? If I go and see the Skipper of the *Kearsarge*, sort out the Osprey and the Harriers, then he comes with me to *Fearless*. Her ops. room is more than good enough to be forward tactical command. If the American Skipper is with us, then he will be able to see and hear everything which is going on and talk to anyone he wants to. Doing it this way he won't feel left out. He can even speak to the Pentagon if he needs too, and I can show him what we've got, even if I don't tell him how we got the data."

"And you'll want me here making sure everything is where we need it, when we want it."

"You are the best there is at getting things in the right place at the right time."

"Fair enough. You're not planning to do anything stupid like going in with the Osprey are you?"

"The thought had crossed my mind but, before you get all excited, there wouldn't be the room if there were any casualties to bring out. We'll put a team of three medics on the Osprey, one trauma specialist, one chemical expert and a male sick berth attendant. There's no way I'm risking a QA nurse on this one, they can scream sex discrimination all they like!"

"Sounds fair enough. I'll leave you to pick the ground team Paul, four or eight?"

"Four to collect the samples with full NBC gear, air tight containers for the

Timothy Pilgrim

samples and their gear, which they will have to take off before they board the Osprey. The other four will be to cover them and to mark the landing site, we can use the 'black' lights. I'll make sure the Osprey pilots have the correct goggles so they can see the markers."

"How will we divide up the Harriers? In pairs but keeping four with the Osprey?" asked Taff.

"It would mean putting a Victor over Somalia."

"This operation is going to need three tankers Paul. A high altitude version for the recon., a Herc. to cope with the Osprey. A Victor cannot fly slowly enough to do it safely at night, but a Herc. can also refuel the Harriers. It will have to be a Victor which goes inland with the package, a Herc. would be too vulnerable. We can use our single 'spare' Harrier as missile 'cap'. We are as sure as we can be, the new anti missile system will be totally effective, even against the latest Stinger. He can always give the launch site a burst from his cannon to avoid repeats."

"Right, let's get moving."

"Out of idle curiosity, how were you planning on getting out there? There is no way the authorities will allow military planes into Mogadishu."

"Well I guess that has stuffed plan 'A'. I'll get going, in the mean time, you find the nearest place where a Herc. can land and get a chopper from *Fearless* to pick me up."

"Just hold on a tick Paul. I know time matters, I know you and the way you like to do things, you are planning to go on the Herc. with the team, well, I'm saying no way. It's no use arguing, your place is indeed on *Fearless*, but you need to be there before the team drop in. The timing of the pick up is critical, and you won't get it right if you're on the Herc. Also there is the possibility the Yanks won't play ball; you are planning to get the Skipper of the *Kearsarge* to do what needs doing and then ask for permission?"

"That was the general idea."

"If you're there face to face it might work, but if you're swanning around in a Herc. landing miles away, then I'd say he will ask first. Even if the answer is yes it could take several days while their top brass figure out a way to cover their arses if the operation goes belly up. They are worse than ours when it comes to dodging blame."

"All right I'll behave, promise, I'll take the jet stream. If we refuel in Cyprus it will give us extra time; if there is a problem landing in the area, I'll leave you to organise it"

"Have you picked your team yet?"

"Picks itself really doesn't it? The stand by squad and our NBC team, one of whom is off sick at the moment, so we'll send the Warrant Officer from Helga's team. He's one of the top chemical agent experts in the army, he says he wants to join the unit, one more drop and he will have qualified. He'll be all right, and his presence and knowledge of safety in dealing with such 'orrible things just might make the difference."

"All right get going, and be bloody careful."

As Paul approached the door there was an urgent knock. It was Helga and she looked very worried.

"What's wrong?" asked Paul, having stopped in his tracks.

"We've identified something else at the site Boss, we didn't notice it before because we weren't looking for it. Do you know what Di-oxin is?"

"Surprising as it may sound I do. It's the stuff which escaped from the factory in India and killed thousands, and is still killing as far as I know. It is just about the deadliest crap around."

"That's the stuff. The thing is, the entire site is contaminated with deadly concentrations of it."

"Thanks for the timely warning but it begs the question. What the hell is a by-product of the manufacture of weed killer doing on this site? I also have to ask could your readings for nerve agents, in fact, be accounted for by spillages of concentrated insecticides?"

"There was the suggestion it had been used as a UN distribution depot for more than just food aid."

"Not even they could be daft enough to mix food aid with lethal chemicals Taff."

"No one is suggesting they did Paul. One story is, it was originally food. As the situation eased, it was used as a depot for agricultural supplies, seeds, chemicals and the likes to help rebuild the local economy."

"Sounds and looks perfectly plausible, apart from the glass ping-pong balls and the other bits and pieces. I think it was used exactly how we originally thought. It would be typical Al Qaeda to take advantage of such a heaven sent opportunity"

"Thanks Helga, keep at it. Oh, we'll be nicking your Sergeant Major for a few days, he'll be going on a field trip. Tell him to get down to the stores and pick up the kit the QM will have ready for him."

It was remarkable how smoothly everything went. Contrary to Taff's assertions, the Jet Stream was allowed to land at Mogadishu, and the authorities simply turned a blind eye to the Sea King which picked Paul up. As Taff pointed out later, this co-operation could have had something to do with the fact Paul personally handed over the landing fees in dollars.

The Skipper of the *Kearsarge* was intrigued at Paul's request. He knew something of the unit and decided he would be justified in claiming he was helping the UN efforts to stabilize the war torn region, if his bosses in Washington didn't like it and made a fuss.

So the mission was launched. The ever watchful Canberra co-ordinated its scanners with the old nimrod AWAC so successfully, diverting the Osprey and its escorts around possible threats, not a shot was fired on the way in. The Harrier pilots sounded almost disappointed over their radios.

"Don't knock it," Paul told the American flight leader. "You're not back yet, we are adjusting your refuelling schedules, so there will be six of you for the last leg to the coast. We are picking up indications of Militia activity. To fly round it would take you too close to centres of population, so you could well get to try out your 'Slim Jims', just don't get too excited. Wait and let our recons mark the targets."

"Fair enough Colonel, they have done one hell of a job so far. The Osprey has just taken off, we are on our way home Sir."

Apart from a couple of small detours, the flight out was as quiet as the flight in, until the last ten miles to the coast. In the event all eight of the Harriers, equipped with the 'Slim Jim' missiles, were with the Osprey for this last and most dangerous part of the journey. The Canberra detected the anti aircraft missiles as they sought to 'lock on' to their intended targets. The information was relayed via the AWAC and technology did the rest. Having all eight of the deadly little attack planes together meant they could operate in pairs. When the element leader made a firing pass at a missile launcher he had a wing man protecting him from small arms fire. Three of the Harriers were shot at. A quick, well aimed burst of cannon fire convinced the militia it wasn't such a good idea after all, and after the brief skirmish peace returned to the little group of aircraft.

One of the American Marine corps Harriers had taken a couple of hits in the tail fin. As he and his wingman were the lowest on fuel, they were told to return to the *Kearsarge*, a job well done.

The weary air crews began to relax as they headed towards their ships. This nearly ended in disaster. What everyone had supposed to be a perfectly ordinary coaster, suddenly launched two anti aircraft missiles at the flight of aircraft.

The two leading Harriers easily avoided the 'sams' and both missiles now homed in on the Osprey which seemed doomed. High above, the little Harrier from *Fearless* had been maintaining its lonely vigil, it now dropped like a stone. The crew of the Osprey were out of options as to how to avoid the missiles. Suddenly they spotted two brilliant blue streaks coming down from on high at incredible speed. They really were doomed it seemed. The glow from the new missiles was so brilliant it left the crew of the transport nearly blind as they watched them flash past, both hit their targets causing smaller than expected explosions. Through the spots in front of their eyes they saw a diminutive version of a Harrier climbing up in front of them, headed back to his lonely watch far above. From its small size they knew it was from the British ship. The other two from *Fearless* could be clearly seen against the sky as the first signs of dawn showed.

"I don't know if you can hear us little buddy, but we owe you one."

"Only one?" came the quick reply.

Two of the bigger, McDonald Douglas built versions had turned to attack the ship, which had launched the missiles, and were asking permission to fire.

Another voice came on the radios ordering all of the American planes to keep clear of the coaster.

The Day The Ravens Died

Warned of the activity in the air by her own Mini AWAC, Hawkeye air craft, one of the American battle carriers had decided to help out. They had sent a pair of F18 Super Hornets to investigate and had told them to sink the ship.

Most of the aircrews in the Ospreys' group had seen the flashes away on the south eastern horizon, it looked a bit like lightening. All of them heard Paul order the two F18s to break off their bomb run.

"Negative, we have a clear run, target lock in twenty seconds."

"Abort you bloody fool. Emergency power, climb like hell. It will blow up in less than ten seconds.

"BREAK!" Both Paul and the Skipper of the *Kearsarge* shouted in unison.

The wing man did as he was told, the element leader came back on the air. "Why? Scared we'll show you Brits and leathernecks what a real war bird can.... shit!"

All eight of the four point five inch shells, fired by the twin guns on the fore deck of *Fearless,* hit more or less together, ripping yet another of the pirate ships to pieces. The explosions also ripped a wing off the Hornet.

The *Kearsarge* already had one of her rescue helicopters in the air in readiness for the returning Harriers. This was speedily despatched to hopefully rescue the downed Naval pilot.

Paul looked at the American Skipper. "What a total pillock!" he exclaimed.

"I have no idea what a pillock is Colonel, but I guess it sort of covers it."

Paul turned to his radio operator. "Get me the Skipper of the carrier which sent those planes Mickey"

He didn't need to, an extremely angry senior officer called *Fearless* first. It was, it seemed, all Paul's fault.

"How the fuck do you work that out, you didn't call us to ask or offer assistance, not that we needed it. Your bloody cowboy ignored our instructions to abort, yet you say it is my fault! We know he ejected, there is a black knight on its way to pick him up. If it was up to me I'd leave him until he went all wrinkly, but I suppose the sharks would have found him before then. What on earth possessed you to interfere in the first place?"

"Firstly Colonel you do not swear at me and you address me as Sir. I am the Senior Allied Officer in theatre, and you should have cleared any operations through me. As you have the Captain of the *Kearsarge* on board I am going to order him to place you under arrest until transport can be arranged for you. You will be charged with the wilful destruction of a United States aircraft."

"This operation had nothing whatsoever to do with you or your battle group. The *Kearsarge* is out here to support the UN force in Somalia. Your remit is in the Gulf, not out here in the Indian Ocean. Sir is a term of respect, and has to be earned and as for swearing at you. All I can say is, an idiot is an idiot, no matter where he comes from or what fancy title he may have acquired."

"One of your missiles shot down one of my planes. I'll see to it you pay Colonel"

"I see. It's all right when one of your cowboys shoots up and kills British or other allied troops, but when one of your lot gets knocked out of the sky because he can't obey a clear and direct order, it's my fault. And it wasn't a missile as such, it was a salvo from the main guns on this ship. They had already fired when your man came on the radio. As far as I know, it is bloody impossible to stop artillery shells once they have been fired!"

"Lying won't help you Colonel. Your vessel is twenty miles from the ship which was sunk."

"Twenty two actually, eight shots, eight hits. Now piss off and do something useful, we are a bit busy just now. Oh bye the way. Your pilot has just been picked up, he is rather damp and I understand he has shit himself. Apart from that he is, by all accounts, in unreasonably good health. As soon as we have finished getting everything and everybody back where they belong we will be heading for the Oman, so we can return your fly boy on the way."

"I demand you return him immediately, and supply a full and complete report on the entire operation which resulted in the loss of an extremely expensive aircraft."

"You'll have your man back in a few hours. As for what we were doing, it wasn't and still isn't, any of your bloody business, nosey bugger, what is it with some of you lot? Contrary to the popular belief, you do not own the world, goodbye"

Paul went up on deck with the Skipper of the *Kearsarge;* he expected to see helicopters collecting his men and their hard won samples from the American ship. Instead he was amazed to see the Osprey, literally reversing onto the flight deck, it was a very tight fit!

In a matter of moments his men were off, bringing the containers holding the toxic samples with them. The medical team unloaded their kit with the help of the Marine gunners and medics, muttering about a wasted trip and a lost night's sleep.

"Some people are never happy," commented Paul. "I'll tell you what, we've got an American pilot due on board soon. He had to eject in a hurry, so you can check him over Doc then you won't have lost a night's sleep for nothing."

"Ah, thanks Boss!"

"Any time. Skipper, while I think of it, as the Osprey is on board, how would you like a couple of crates of those 'Slim Jims'? They fit in standard rocket pods and can be targeted with a bog standard laser designator. If you do have to go in to rescue UN workers they could come in handy."

"Thanks a lot Paul, should help a lot. Any chance of one of your recons overhead if we do have to go in?"

The Day The Ravens Died

"Sure, if there's time. We could have one on station in a couple of hours."

They said their farewells and the Osprey left to be replaced by the Black Knight rescue helicopter. Paul passed a DVD in a case to one of the crew, "Give this to your Skipper with my compliments, please. It is a recording of this idiot flying into our salvo, complete with radio messages, frequencies and times."

"Thanks a lot Colonel. I know our Skipper is a bit worried about the Admiral; he's one of these guys who just has to be in charge of everything, nothing can be done without his approval. Then I guess that's why he is an Admiral, if he does make a fuss, then at least our Skipper can defend himself with this."

"He can also call me, make certain he understands all he has to do is make the call. Okay, you take care, we'll look after cloth ears and return him to his Carrier; we'll let them know we're on our way, I can do without another run in with the great 'I am'."

"See you around Colonel. Oh, is it true your guys rescued a seal AL Qaeda had captured?"

"Might I know the reason for you asking Commander?"

"I know it is just scuttlebutt, but my brother is, or was married to an English girl. He went missing nearly a year ago, now she's vanished along with the kiddie. The rumour is, it was some of your guys who spirited her away, right under the noses of the Feds and CIA guys who were watching her. Her old man, my brother, is called James T Alexander."

"You missed out 'the third'," replied Paul. "Of course I can neither confirm or deny such rumours. But for the benefit of your family, let's just say they are safely and happily reunited; of course I will deny we ever had this conversation. He was in pretty bad shape but is on the mend, slowly. His 'action man' days are gone, as are mine, but he is or will be, a valuable member of our team once he has recovered."

"You have my word Colonel. The only people I will tell are those dear to Jamie, and no one will know who told me, I'll just say I overheard it in a bar."

"Right, you had better get going, we will be going up to full speed shortly. If you haven't gone by then you might find taking off a little difficult, happy landings Commander."

"Bye Colonel, and stay safe. I hope you found what your guys were looking for."

"Personally, I don't!"

The Black Knight helicopter lifted away into the clear blue early morning sky. The aircraft hung around as arranged, while the three miniature Harriers landed on the small flight deck and vanished into the hangar, having crossed from the very much larger *Kearsarge*. *Fearless* wasn't exactly small, and at eighteen thousand tons fully loaded was no light weight herself, but was dwarfed by her powerful American counterpart. The big assault ship began to pull away from her smaller companion, as she recovered the search and rescue helicopter. Her big ensign fluttering from her mast head - she certainly was an impressive sight as she headed back to her normal patrol line some one hundred miles north.

Some of her officers were watching the *Fearless*, discussing how her twin guns could have delivered such devastation at such a great range. "I'm certain every shell hit," commented one, "I didn't see any shell splashes," added his friend.

"They certainly have some advanced weaponry for an old ship, she's supposed to have been scrapped after the Falklands war. That odd ball unit have her sister ship, the *Intrepid*, as well."

"I heard they've got a destroyer out here as well. She's called the *Kelly* and is supposed to be the fastest warship afloat."

One of the American officers was still watching the old *Fearless*, now far astern. "Oh my god" he muttered, "What the hell has happened to *Fearless*. Look!"

All they could see were the highest parts of the ship, the rest was obscured by huge sheets of spray, illuminated by the early morning sun. The ship seemed borne on huge brilliant white wings as her great broad bow hurled the water effortlessly aside. Within minutes most of the crew and nearly all the Marines were on deck watching the spectacle.

"Holy shit!" exclaimed someone, "Look at that thing go! That just isn't possible!" It wasn't long before *Fearless* was hidden by spray, nearing the horizon, soon she had gone.

"Kinda makes you wonder just who is the best," observed the American Skipper. "Their Harriers are half the size of ours but pack the same punch, and I'm certain the one flying high cover was way over design speed when it shot down those two 'SAMS', just like swatting flies. They gave us a couple of crates of those ground attack missiles. I wonder what they took out the 'SAMS' with? I've never seen anything like it, and as for the gunnery. Make a note not to upset those guys 'exo'."

"We'll have to write a report Skipper."

"I know, but what do we say? If we tell it like it happened we'll get drummed out of the service for taking drugs!"

"We've got the missiles they gave us. Nearly everyone on board saw the eighteen thousand ton speed boat. I'll bet there are a lot of pictures, if not videos of it, among the crew and there is the video disc of the destruction of the pirate, right from when it fired the missiles, up until the Black Knight picked up the F18 pilot. It's even got all the signals on it with times, everything."

"What took the film?"

"Aah, I hadn't thought of that Skipper. I assume it must have been the recon. which was guiding every move of the operation."

"You are probably correct, but did you see it, even on radar?"

"The Pentagon will go spare, Congress will have enquiries. I hate to say this Skipper but it looks very much as though the Brits are way ahead of us when it comes to technology, and they are making sure we know."

Not long after this conversation had taken place, a puzzled radar operator on the huge Carrier reported a large contact approaching rapidly from astern.

"What sort of contact?" demanded the Admiral who was, as usual, getting in the way on the main bridge. "Be specific man!"

"A large ship Sir. At least fifteen thousand tons from the contact Sir, and she is catching us fast."

"Check your set man! We are at flank speed preparing to launch aircraft, even our own cruisers and destroyers are struggling to keep up."

"Contact closing fast Sir. You must be able to see it from the bridge, it's coming straight up our wake!"

The scenes of disbelief from the crew of the *Kearsarge* were now repeated on the *Reagan*. The old *Fearless* swung off to one side, taking station about a mile away from the giant Carrier.

The radio on the bridge of the Carrier crackled briefly, then a voice asked permission for a helicopter to land to return the downed pilot.

Initially the Captain of the Carrier gave permission, but was overruled by the Admiral in command of the battle group.

Paul had been half expecting this. He called the American back, "Please yourself. Either we bring him over now in our Lynx, or he comes home with us and we leave him at Mildenhall to catch the next flight State Side. I have better things to do with my time than argue with a self important old fool like you. Now do we bring him over or not?"

"Bring him over Colonel," replied the Skipper, "and thanks for fishing him out of the drink."

"Thank the crew of the *Kearsarge* Skipper. If it had been up to me I'd have left him a bit longer, it might have taught him a lesson."

"Bring him over Colonel."

"On their way Skipper. He has a package for you personally, a recording of what happened, it will play on any DVD or computer. Sorry about your plane but the shells were already in the air. There really wasn't anything we could do, other than to get them to break away under full power. It's all on the recording. For what it is worth, our medics have given your man a thorough check up, he's pretty well intact. Our medics reckon a week on traction, to allow a compressed lumbar disc to get back into shape, and he will be fine. It's all in the folder we have sent over, scans, x-rays and the likes."

The speedy little Lynx had the unfortunate airman back on board in no time. It never really landed, its wheels kissing the deck of the giant Carrier as the man climbed out, ducking low under the rotors as the helicopter lifted off and returned to the *Fearless*. As soon as the Lynx was secured, the British ship repeated her high speed vanishing act in the general direction of the Oman, to the utter disbelief of those watching from the American ships.

At the insistence of the Warrant Officer who was the chemical expert, all those who had been on the ground had undergone an extremely thorough decontamination procedure on their return, as had their kit. He had left nothing to chance, which both pleased and worried Paul. Pleased that such a 'new boy' to the unit should be so thorough, and worried as to what they had found to have brought about such a level of caution. Now freshly scrubbed, he was ready to give Paul his preliminary report, it did not make pretty reading. There wasn't a living thing within an area roughly fifty yards wide, and nearly one hundred yards down wind.

"We found four bodies Boss, far too toxic to recover. They were badly decomposed but there were no maggots. We have samples of dead insects, birds, even rats, never mind all the different nerve agents and VX traces. The worst thing is, the entire site is heavily contaminated with at least two forms of Di-oxin, it will be lethal for years."

"So we are talking chemical weapons rather than agricultural chemicals."

"No doubt at all Boss. I can't read Korean, or Chinese, whatever it is, on a couple of bits of crate we recovered, but I could understand the pictorial instructions for priming the spreader units and compressors. We have brought one of each back. The stuff in our containers will have to be handled carefully as a lot of the contaminants have no known safe exposure levels."

"As bad as that? Ugh!" he shuddered. "I hate chemical weapons, frankly they scare me shitless. Before I let you go, you are saying that site is a serious hazard?"

"No Boss. I'm saying it is lethal for the foreseeable future," replied the Warrant Officer.

"Bloody well done to all of your team. Go get a bit of rest. Even at this speed we've got a few hours until the Chinook picks us and your samples up to take us to our plane home.

As soon as the chemical expert closed the door, Paul called Taff.

"Hi, how did it go?"

"I thought you were watching?"

"I was, but I meant what did they find? Was it as bad as the scanners suggested?"

"As far as I can tell, it is a good deal worse."

"Bloody hell!" exclaimed Taff. "How much worse can it get?"

"Apparently quite a lot. How soon can you get a Vulcan up? I take it those special bombs designed to destroy chemicals are ready?"

"You mean the plasma weapons? Yes, they are ready, but we haven't got very many of them."

"I'll probably regret this but, have we got eight, two thousand pounders?"

"Probably, I'll check. By the sounds of things the site needs totally sterilizing, and is a lot bigger than we thought."

"Stick eight in a Vulcan with J-dam units; mark it, using a recon. to make certain. Drop four to explode together then turn him round. Get the Canberra to scan for any residual contamination. If you think there even might be anything nasty left, stick the other four onto it just to make certain. Don't forget to check for Di-oxin."

"All that will be left after that lot will be a sterile, glass lined pit! All of those bombs in one spot; it will be hotter than the sun!"

"Good, do it."

"Now?"

"A month ago would have been better."

CHAPTER TWELVE

The crew of the RAF VC10 made one of their softest landings ever, very conscious of the unpleasant nature of the contents of the cargo bay. The pilot had known Paul for several years and couldn't remember him ever being even slightly worried about anything before. Whatever was in those containers strapped tightly to the pallets in the cargo hold, had done more than worry the ageing Colonel. If the man said, "For heavens sake be careful, no bumps," then he was going to be very careful indeed. At the same time, he knew better than to ask what these men had been up to.

Usually a plane returning men from a mission would have parked near the headquarters building. This time the VC 10 taxied to the far end of the airfield, its cargo quickly unloaded and transferred to the deepest, most secure bunker on the base, cleared specifically to receive the deadly samples.

Paul got out of the car sent to fetch him. He was met at the door by the duty officer. "Welcome home Boss, you've got visitors."

"Like who?" then he noticed several 'official' cars in the park. "Oh lord, not bloody Whitehall. I don't need this."

"What have you been doing, Colonel?" demanded one civil servant.

"Yes, we had a good trip, and I am delighted we are all home safe and sound," replied Paul.

"What sort of answer was that?" demanded the man in a light weight suit.

"It was the answer to the question I could have reasonably expected you to ask. As to what we have been doing, the answer is simple, our job. Now, why don't you all piss off back to London and do yours, for once!"

"The Americans are furious with you Colonel."

"That's a bit strange. We parted company on the best of terms with the senior officer of the East African task force. He should be pleased as we gave him fifty of our new ground attack missiles for helping us out. I believe his parting comment was 'anytime, or look forward to the next time', something along those lines. So what's the problem?"

"We've had complaints from the Secretary of State, the Pentagon, Middle East command, to name but a few. It seems as though you shot down one of their multi million dollar F18s."

"No we didn't. We told him to get out of the way, but he kept on, tough luck. He's all right, we returned him to his carrier."

The Day The Ravens Died

"The American Admiral in command of the task force wants you arrested, and I have to say, I think he has a point Colonel."

"I think he needs a brain scan, but it would be a total waste of time, there is nothing between the senile old fools ears to scan, and you can tell the Secretary of the Navy that from me!"

"Colonel!"

"NO! Shut up and listen. Some forces from the *Kearsarge* helped us extract one of our teams who had been on a vital fact finding mission. The *Kearsarge* is the Command ship of a small task group, on a mission to take out these bloody pirates who keep hi-jacking UN aid ships, running into the ports around the Horn of Africa. Ships engaged in this task, are nothing what so ever to do with the idiot in command of the *'Reagan'* battle group. He had no authority from anyone to come poking his nose into what we were doing, he's a bloody glory hunter. 'I am, so you will do as I say'. Well I have some bad news for him. No I bloody well won't!"

"There is also the matter of secret technologies being revealed to a foreign power. That is treason Colonel!"

"Like what? The fact our ships can travel at stupid speeds in the open sea? Do you really think the Americans didn't know that already? If you fart out there, one of their satellites photographs the gas cloud. They know about our Canberras, damn it they gave us most of them, and work with them all the time in Iraq and Afghanistan."

"What about the two anti-aircraft missiles destroyed by one of your Harriers?"

"What about them? It was an American aircraft they would have hit, with a dozen of my men on board, I don't see the problem."

"The problem is, you have made their administration look stupid by blatantly displaying the huge gulf between their technologies and ours."

"They don't need me to make them look daft, they are almost as good as you are at making fools of themselves. Most of their hi-tech. targeting gear is of British origin as it is, the fact we don't sell them our latest stuff can hardly be a crime, now can it?"

"You sell equipment to the Americans! How come my department is unaware of this trade in secret equipment Colonel?"

"Probably because it is bugger all to do with you, or your department. Now you will have to excuse me, I have a rather important call to make."

Paul pushed past the civil servants and went into his office. He actually remembered to switch off the smoke alarm. Lighting the inevitable cigarette, he settled back in his chair and opened up his laptop. He had just begun to compose the message to the friendly head of the CIA photographic section when the door opened to reveal the posse of civil servants.

"Colonel!" exclaimed the leader of the pack. "You are not allowed to smoke in here."

"It is my office," growled Paul menacingly, "and if I want to smoke, then I will bloody well smoke. Now get out before I have you thrown out, smoke is allowed in here, you are most definitely not, out! And close the door behind you."

He completed his e-mail then turned to the stubborn civil servants. "What is it with you people? You have to stick your bloody noses into things you know do not concern you. There is nothing here which has anything remotely to do with any of you, so go back to your offices and try to find something useful to do."

Taff came in. "I've got the pictures of the bomb run Paul, absolutely spot on, the site is now safe, a bit on the hot side but sterile." Then the little Welshman turned to the civil servants. "I distinctly remember ordering you lot to get off this base."

Taff called security, who arrived with commendable promptness. "Find a secure room for this lot and remove any mobile phones and the like. Hold them until we get round to sorting them out."

"Be a pleasure Boss, any idea how long they will be staying?"

"The rest of the week at least, Bin Liner permitting."

Paul chuckled. "I'm proud of you Taff."

"Yeah, well I can get pissed off by the nosey bastards as well."

One of the civil servants who had been quiet up until now stepped forward. "Colonel, I am..."

Paul cut him off. "I know who you are, what's your point?"

"Colonel, you are in direct and deliberate breach of the law. You are not allowed to smoke in any building on a Military base, you are also in breach of several Health and Safety regulations, this office is not correctly fitted to allow you to make drinks. Even if it had the correct fittings, it would still not be allowed because of all the electronic equipment in here. I will personally see to it you are prosecuted for all of these violations. There is also the matter of the military team posted here to monitor your compliance with the directives issued by my department. I insist you release them immediately, I presume you have incarcerated them as only two returned."

Paul pushed a button on his com link panel. "Helga, get your team in my office, like yesterday!"

"On our way Boss. I'll be right behind the rest, the pictures you requested from Langley are coming through, I'll bring them with me."

"Thank you Helga, don't bother to knock, come straight in."

First in was the Sergeant Major who had parachuted into the suspect site the previous night, Paul had to admit the man looked the part as he lead the others in, all dressed in plain green fatigues, none of them displaying any rank.

The civil servant's eyes locked onto the Major who had been in charge of the detachment. "What happened Major? Your uniform, and you are not wearing your rank; have you been on a working party?"

"In a manner of speaking, I suppose I have, we all have. The Sergeant Major here is just back from a mission, which I believe was a success."

The Day The Ravens Died

"What is going on? I demand an explanation!"

"The Colonel here very generously offered us the opportunity to go through the selection course, almost all of us accepted the challenge. Some of us did better than others, but he found jobs which suited all of us who tried, I have to say it is a good deal more rewarding than our previous tasks. We are learning so much about real security work and I believe the unit as a whole is also benefiting from our knowledge of safety in the work place. The point is, we are able to identify potential hazards, and by talking to those potentially at risk, find common sense solutions to lessen the hazard."

"I trust that answers your questions. Now you can either bugger off back from whence you came, or spend the night in the slammer as I am far too busy to deal with you tonight. Ah Helga, the pics from our friends at Langley?"

"Sorry it took so long Boss, there were rather more than we expected. The director sent six months worth, rather than the six weeks you requested. He said he thought you would find them interesting, and if you could figure out the meaning he would like to know."

"Aah, that was my fault Helga, I did ask for six months worth, not the six weeks I mentioned to you, sorry about that, even I have 'senior moments' from time to time."

The Major approached. "May I Boss?" addressing Helga, rather than Paul.

"Sure Andy," and she passed over the bulky folder. What really caused confusion was the fact Helga was now wearing her new rank of Lieutenant. Spotting the confused look on the face of her teams previous Boss she couldn't resist the chance, "We don't take too much notice of rank around here."

"You're right there Boss," added the Sergeant Major. "It was a trooper who booted me out of the plane last night, several miles up over the desert, most impatient on his part. He was right though, the extra couple of seconds would have scattered us."

"All right you lot, I want my office back. Out! And I do not want you lot here again, clogging up the works. What happens here is nothing to do with any of you, or your nosy, meddling departments. Next time, if you are daft enough for there to be a next time, you will be slung into the slammer, no ifs or buts. If you want something useful to do, go and find some terrorists and advise them it is dangerous messing about with explosives in flats or garages. Do what you like but stay out of my bloody way!"

The disgruntled civil servants were herded back to their cars and shepherded off the base, Paul had asked Helga and Andy to stay behind to assist him and Taff in looking at the CIA satellite images of the site destroyed by the Vulcan.

As they were pouring over the images the telephone on Paul's desk rang making them all jump, it turned out to be the director of American Home Land Security.

"Hello Sir, what can we do for you?"

"Cut the crap Colonel," the man began, sounding quite hostile. "What exactly did you do in Somalia yesterday. Judging from reports, you mounted an operation against something or someone. The Admiral in charge of the battle group has put in a formal complaint about you, but knowing you, you will say he was sticking his nose into something which had nothing to do with him."

"You are exactly right Sir. So what's up?"

"Would I be correct in thinking you launched an air strike at whatever installation you were checking out, and the strike involved a tactical nuke, maybe two?"

"You are right about the air strike Sir, but we are not a nuclear armed force. Although I suppose if the need arose we could be."

"Then what the Sam Hill did you hit the place with? And why?"

"We detected traces of what appeared to be, chemical weapons Sir. We put in a team to check, just to be certain, elements of your armed forces assisted us in extracting the team."

"From the *Kearsarge*?"

"That is correct Sir, and their help was invaluable, the results confirmed our initial scans, the place was saturated with several lethal chemicals and would have remained deadly, maybe for years."

"So you nuked it?"

"No Sir, the bombs we used generate just as much heat as a nuke, but no radio active materials were used."

"So what did you find, and should we worry?"

"VX, Di-oxines, various nerve agents, blister agents, all manner of nasty things of which I know little and want to know less. As to if you should worry? Until we find the bloody stuff, I would say something a good deal stronger than worrying was called for, even panicking seems somewhat inadequate."

"You think we are the target?"

"That's the problem, I have no idea. All we have is the threat from Al Qaeda to wipe out London, note the wipe out, as opposed to destroy. If you believe the threat, then this seems to fit, until we find the stuff then no one is safe."

"How much was there?"

"No idea Sir," replied Paul, "and before you ask, it seems as though the place was abandoned and torched at least six weeks ago."

"Any chance of a report Colonel?"

"I don't see why not Sir. It will be a few days before we have analysed the samples accurately, even then my guess is, we will have more questions than answers."

"Thank you Colonel. Might I ask why you asked the CIA for all those wide-angle photographs?"

"The idea is to check for any suspicious goings on in the area. Tight shots wouldn't show anything, as the terrorists know better than I do when a 'Big

Bird' comes over the horizon, and would have dived into their bolt holes like the rats they are."

"Good point, stay in touch Colonel and good luck."

"You too Sir. Bye."

"He was pretty quick off the mark for a Yank," observed Taff.

"They are not all total idiots."

"What, total or just plain idiots?"

"I know you don't like them Taff, but some of them are all right. Let's face it some of our lot are as bad."

"True."

Several cups of coffee and half a packet of fags later, the quiet concentration was shattered. Most of the telephones on Paul's desk began ringing more or less simultaneously, both Taff's and Paul's mobiles joined in along with their pagers.

"What the bloody hell has happened now?" He grabbed a phone, signalling the others to do likewise. As soon as the mayhem subsided and they had chance to catch their breath Paul looked at his friend, "The bastards have started Taff."

CHAPTER THIRTEEN

"I'll get down to ops Paul, if I get some more recons up tracking them will be easier. I take it you'll be sorting out the teams to take them out?"

"Go, I'll be all right here. I'll send B.J. down to Colchester to brief the Paras. Two Para are at home. They're just back off leave after a tour out east. Brummie is around somewhere, he can find out which Commando is at home right now, I think it's forty. I know forty-five are in Helmand at the moment, and I'll phone Hereford, see what they have available."

The attacks were much more diverse than had been feared, and had targeted the evening rush hour, rather than the expected morning peak. At least eight suicide bombers hit the underground and no less than twenty buses were ripped apart across the Capital. Some were parcel bombs, others by remotely detonated car bombs. Three gasholders were set ablaze, one of them exploding in a fearful fireball. The national grid came under attack, transformers became a favourite target for rockets as they burned well, being full of hot oil. Pylons in awkward spots came crashing down, usually with three of their four legs blown out.

The chaos spread as three trains were derailed, one a high-speed passenger Intercity bound for Kings Cross. Another was a packed commuter train blown up by several big explosions right on Clapham Junction. The third, and worst, was a train loaded with fuel from the massive refinery at Fawley. It detonated like a nuclear bomb as it passed under the motorway bridge carrying the M 27. Traffic was almost stationary in both directions. At least five packed buses were engulfed in the fireball. The bridge had collapsed or, in the case of two massive concrete beams, blown into the air, landing on the motorway jammed with the evening rush hour traffic.

Throughout the length and breath of the country there were, what appeared to be random attacks. Inevitably petrol tankers and filling stations, especially urban ones, were favourite targets.

In this first wave of carnage two attacks failed. One was an attempt to shoot down a Jumbo Jet which had just taken off from Heathrow. Since a previous threat, it had been standard practice for at least one team from the Household Division to patrol the area under the flight path. Today, in the light of the increased threat, there were two teams. By pure chance both were close by when the recon. Canberra, circling over the west of the city, spotted the

The Day The Ravens Died

launcher being set up and guided both teams of soldiers onto the terrorists. The soldiers may have outnumbered the terror squad two to one, but they were badly outgunned against the AK47s of the terrorists. One soldier lay dead and three others injured, two very badly, but they stopped the attack and killed three of the four terrorists. The other escaped, although the soldiers thought he was wounded, there would be no hiding place for this one however. The unblinking eye of the Canberra followed him with ease, at the same time guiding in a team of armed police.

Paul watched as the net closed, "Now we should see if the retraining has worked."

It did. The second they saw the gun in the man's hands, one of the police fired two shots. The first hit squarely between the eyes, the second an inch above the first.

The attempt to bring down a plane at Stanstead was comprehensively stopped by a sharp eyed trucker. The lorry driver was ex-parachute regiment, he knew what a Stinger looked like, he had been in a helicopter hit by one in Afghanistan and had been lucky enough to survive.

For a moment he knew why tank crews felt so safe, a forty ton truck against a 'Chelsea Tractor' was a 'no contest'. Being high up in his cab he could see what car drivers couldn't, the man kneeling beside the four by four was about to stand up to launch the missile when there was an enormous crash and his vehicle was thrown over on top of him. The big truck skidded to a halt, the driver leapt out and ran back towards the tangled wreck. One terrorist lay under the mangled remains, still holding his broken missile, the driver of the four by four was also clearly dead, his head flopped at an impossible angle, his neck broken by the huge impact. The third terrorist was badly dazed but seemingly unhurt, as he crawled from the wreckage, AK47 in his hands.

He never had chance to use it. The tough ex-para knew just what to do, and he didn't hold back. A single well aimed kick, the heel of his boot connecting with the man's jaw, resulted not only in a broken jaw but a snapped neck as well.

"Bastard," muttered the old soldier as he moved the gun out of reach of the dying terrorist, just in case.

"Get a recording of that for the cops, just in case some smart arse tries to arrest that driver."

"Will do Boss."

Retribution for many of the terrorists who had launched attacks that evening was swift, and in many cases fatal. Teams of soldiers, guided by the recons, went unerringly to the killers' hideaways. All night the raids went on, by dawn many of the army teams had carried out at least three raids, and were rapidly becoming exhausted.

By brilliant management of his limited resources, Taff had managed to keep continuous surveillance over most of the country. True there were some gaps, there had to be, as the aircraft at their immediate disposal were the ones still waiting for the new engines, blocked for nearly a year by civil servants.

The police were simply overwhelmed, there were so many incidents. Then the army started turning up with suspects, each with a reference number and instructions to contact the All Arms Unit for details. In addition there was the need to secure every property raided and deal with weapons and also several large caches of explosives.

Often innocent women, the wives of the terrorists, and their children had to be cared for. By dawn the manpower situation was getting critical. For all their raids and capture of arms and the men who had used them, the attacks continued. By diverting teams from raids or guarding installations, several attacks were thwarted.

One hawkeyed operator spotted a response on her monitor coming from a car heading into central London. She double checked, there was no doubt it was carrying a large bomb. The car behind it also showed small responses on the scanner. Zooming in to maximum resolution, it was clear there were four heavily armed men in the second car. By using everyone available in striking distance, the cars were forced to stop as they came off Westminster Bridge, approaching Parliament Square. The driver of the car carrying the bomb surrendered instantly, not so those in the car behind. It was unclear whether they failed to realise the strength of the forces ranged against them, and decided they could fight their way out of the trap they had driven into, or to go down fighting, killing as many police as possible.

The Volvo carrying the gunmen reversed rapidly back onto the bridge, the driver executing a hand brake turn, side swiping a police car on the way and running over one officer who was in the road.

The gunmen were hanging out of the windows, firing at anything which moved. Paul was watching the unfolding disaster in total disbelief. Not a shot was returned because the police following the cars had not stopped as ordered, at the southern end of the bridge, but had closed up behind their targets. None of the police blocking the exit from the bridge could open fire as their colleagues were within their field of fire.

The result was three dead police, five more with injuries serious enough to keep them off work for weeks, and worst of all the driver of the car bomb was dead as well, shot in the back with three bullets from an AK47.

One of the operators, acting on Paul's orders, diverted a team preparing to raid a lock up garage, to intercept the fleeing Volvo. The terrorists, jubilant at their narrow escape, were also concerned as to how the police could have been waiting for them.

"I've just had a thought. I don't suppose it's possible they're heading for the lock up the Paras were about to raid?"

"I was beginning to think the same thing myself Paul," replied Taff. "What do you think, let them open it up for us, in case it's booby trapped?"

"Get me the commander of that squad, quickly please," the signaller handed Paul what was little more than a hi-tech mobile phone, and the trap was laid.

"Dead or alive sir?" asked the young sergeant in charge of the two land rovers.

"You and yours alive above all else. Those men are killers; they have killed already tonight and will certainly be prepared to kill again. It could be useful talking to them as they are doubtless hard core, but they are not worth any of your guys sustaining anything other than split knuckles. It's your call sergeant. No risks to your guys, all right?"

The trap laid by the Paras worked perfectly. They stayed hidden and allowed one of the gunmen to open the lockup and deactivate the booby trap. As soon as the terrorist waved his friends in, the Paras struck. Only the driver survived and he was wounded - the lock up contained the biggest cache of weapons and explosives seized during that chaotic night.

Paul's first conversation with the Prime Minister had been earlier, in fact shortly after the first attacks. "Can you stop them Colonel?" he asked.

"Not with what I've got Sir; sure, given a day or so, we will get most of them. We have, as you well know, the technology. What we lack is the manpower."

"You have access to army assets Colonel, use them."

"All Special Forces are being deployed as we speak, to the extent they are using recruits nearing the end of their training. I have a call into OCUK land forces, and the head of the RAF so we can use RAF regiment personnel. The police are also over stretched to a very serious degree."

"What do you suggest Colonel?"

"Call up all TA and reservist units. There is a massive amount of clearing up to do, and over a hundred sites to guard for one reason or another. The other thing is to issue a total curfew, nation wide for at least tomorrow. Allow trucks to travel to their next stop, then stay there. Everyone at home should stay indoors, of course there will have to be exceptions, but make it as total as common sense allows."

"We can't possibly do that Colonel, it would cause chaos."

"The terrorists have caused that already Sir," Paul spotted Taff waving frantically at him. "I have to go Sir, I will call you back."

It took most of the night before the 'Cobra' committee even got round to considering the 'stay at home' order. In truth, there was little option as most major routes were blocked at some point and many rail links were cut. Airports were closed to all traffic, all ports were closed and ferries suspended.

As dramatic as the shutting down of the country may have seemed, it did virtually stop the attacks, as more and more were intercepted before they could strike - mostly due to the all-seeing eyes circling out of sight far above the carnage, one or two were down to luck.

The team sent to poison the huge Queen Mary reservoir west of Heathrow literally ran into the leading land rover of the team sent to pick them up. The same gang had earlier planted a bomb on a nearby railway line but as they hadn't used guns or rockets, the address they were using had been given a lower priority. Their old Fiat car came off second best in the collision; the team of Marines had been up all night and were tired. The leader of the section had a few choice words for the equally tired operator, as he received the warning about thirty seconds after the collision.

The attempt to introduce some very nasty poisons into the Lea Valley lakes was also prevented by the simple expedient of adding sniper rifles to the vast array of tackle carried by some 'carp fishermen'. All four of the 'would be' mass murderers died from single gun shots. The same Canberra, back in the air after a major service, which had identified the chemicals at the site in Somalia, had spotted them; its sensors had easily picked up the poisons carried in plastic containers by the terrorists.

Far away the leaders of the terrorist groups - you couldn't really describe it as an organisation - were initially delighted as the reports of the devastation began to appear on the news programs. This would bring Britain to its knees; the destruction was not as great as they had hoped for. The casualties, civilian and police, already heavy, were still growing quickly. News of the trains reached them and was greeted with a cheer. It was however becoming clear some attacks had failed, more than could be put down to chance or good luck on the part of the security forces.

Increasingly, cell members could not be contacted to launch their follow up attacks. News was filtering out of raids by the security forces which were only to be expected. Clearly some of the 'safe houses' were not as safe as the terrorists had supposed. As one might have expected, much of the work of the security forces that night went unreported. The other nasty surprise the leaders of the terrorist groups had coming was headed their way, as they celebrated the 'success', at about sixty thousand feet at roughly mach point nine, in the shape of a modified Vulcan bomber.

Even higher was an ancient aircraft with huge broad wings. The plane was of a type a good deal older than its crew, both of whom had retired from the RAF after twenty two years. This Canberra was equipped with its proper Rolls Royce Avon engines, cruising effortlessly on the very edge of space. Its sensors transmitted every word the men in the luxurious hunting lodge of the former Shah uttered. As well as the conversations between those present, every call on their hi-tech scrambled satellite phones and every e-mail was being monitored - in spite of the elaborate precautions they had taken by routing all their communications through remote servers. The CIA had failed to intercept any more than a tiny fraction of their calls; even these had proven to be untraceable.

Paul called the pilot of the Vulcan as he approached Iranian airspace. "You have the green light. Your target will be marked by 'eagle eye one'. It might be a good idea to get as high as you can, we are not sure exactly how high their radars can see."

"Thanks for the good news Boss."

"Good luck, out."

"You did clear the air raid with the Prime Minister?" asked Taff sounding worried.

"Damn, it must have slipped my mind with all that has been going on."

"Oh you idiot. Have you any idea of the consequences if it goes wrong? Come to that, if it goes right?"

"Taff, the Shah's old hunting palace is inhabited by the most wanted terrorist leaders on earth. The only one missing is Sammy Bin Liner. There are the leaders of the Taliban, Hezbullah, most of Al Qaeda's top thugs, not to mention Al Sadder and his henchmen. We have been after most of the nutters holed up there for years."

"I know all of that Paul but who will get the blame?"

"The Yanks most likely. The world and his wife will say it was one of their B2 stealth bombers, because as far as the Iranians know, it's the only heavy bomber which can over fly them without being seen by their radar."

"What have you done? I know you, let me guess, all the B2s are sitting on their home base in full view."

"Yeah, right first time but you missed the best bit. The Russians will be able to verify the fact, all those nasty stealth bombers are definitely at home and the Iranians are big mates with Ivan."

"You evil sod."

"Oh yes. I can be just as evil as they can. You know as well as I do that we are unlikely to ever get a better chance. If the shit does hit the fan over this, then we can prove the signals launching the attacks came from that precise location. We can also prove much of it was done with the knowledge, if not co-operation, of some Iranian authorities. The world will be a better place without those twisted old bastards calling the shots, we will be better off as it will destroy the cohesion of the attacks."

"You still should have cleared it first Paul."

"You have seen the intercepts. By the time any decision would have been made they would have all split up again."

"I still say you are wrong, but what the hell. The PM will be calling in half an hour for an update; he gave me a long list of figures and statistics he needs for a press briefing this evening."

"Oh cheers," replied Paul. "Where is this list?"

"On your desk."

"Where else? Look Taff stand down half of our lot, those who have been on duty the longest absolutely must have a proper rest, the same goes for all the other forces. If we keep this up every one will be out on their feet. We have got to get a shift system working again; this in turn will require a team to prioritise our response. I know it isn't ideal but we have pretty well exhausted all sources of manpower available to us, and this isn't over yet. I've been doing some sums and I don't think the terrorists have used even ten percent of their explosives or RPGs as yet."

"What was the calculation based on Paul?"

"Simple really. I added up all the stuff on the manifest discovered at Felixstowe in the container we did intercept and deducted the weapons we seized at the time. I also added up what we have discovered since and what we think they have used so far. The result is frightening; they have tons of stuff left."

"Won't all the terrorists we have taken out make a difference? It's well over a hundred, in fact it must be approaching two hundred by now."

"Sounds as though we are doing all right, until you take into account the fact that less than twenty of them have been identified and were known to the security forces. There is no way of knowing how many of the bastards are out there."

"There must be a way of coming up with a reasonable estimate Paul."

"Sure. The way the statistics boys work it out would be to compare the percentages. Ten percent of those killed or captured were known, the total on the security services list is in the region of two thousand, less the twenty we've got. At the ten percent rate, it means there are roughly twenty thousand out there."

"That's crazy!"

"Quite," replied Paul. "Now do you want to hear something scary? Apply the same mathematics to the intercepts and guess what? You come up with the same answer."

"Oh shit!"

"If the theory is correct then we are up to our necks in it," replied Paul. "I have used every set of figures we have, knowns against previously unknowns. They all come out with similar results, which means the theory is flawed, or we are stuffed."

"What about casualties? The figures I have are around two thousand two hundred dead and rising, and eleven members of the security forces, mainly police are dead. . I haven't got any definitive figures on those injured yet, but it is in excess of three thousand."

"That ties up with what I've got."

The two friends reached Paul's office. To his annoyance the printer was going flat out and was in danger of running out of paper.

"Oh for crying out loud!" he exclaimed, "this is getting bloody daft. Most of this is from civil servants. Look at it. How long before normality returns? When will the trains be running again? Can we reopen Heathrow? How the hell should I know?"

"Calm down. I'll make the drinks."

"I've got a better idea. You empty the 'in tray' into two piles, one for you and one for me. Put another wad of paper in the printer and I'll make the drinks as you have never made a drinkable cup of coffee in all the years I've known you!"

"Bloody ingrate," muttered Taff, sounding hurt.

The Day The Ravens Died

Their chores completed, Paul slumped into his comfortable chair. Just as he fished his packet of cigarettes out of his pocket the door opened quietly and a slender, obviously female, arm reached in and flicked the switch for the smoke alarm to 'off'.

"Thank you," he called as the door began to close. "How did you know?"

The head which belonged to the arm appeared. "You forget so often, I got Al to rig up a light on my desk which shows me if the smoke alarm in your office is on or off. This means we are not being constantly disturbed by the alarm going off every time you light up."

Taff chuckled as the door closed behind Paul's loyal secretary. "I guess that's told you!"

Paul began scanning quickly through the mass of messages Taff had dumped on his side of the desk. Most were simply re-stacked but one stopped him dead in his tracks. He read it twice to make certain he had read it correctly the first time. It was from the Deputy Commissioner of the Met.

It read. 'Sorry to have to inform you the following terrorist suspects have been released on the orders of a Law Lord, on the grounds of illegal methods were used either in their detection or arrest, thereby infringing their Civil Liberties and Human Rights.'

Paul went 'ballistic' as Taff put it. Within a minute he was ringing the Law Lord's private ex-directory number. Taking a deep breath Paul introduced himself and promptly received an ear bashing for operating illegally, and the likely consequences if he continued. Before Paul could reply the man hung up! When Paul redialled, the receiver the other end was simply lifted and replaced, this happened four times.

"If you want to play silly bastards, so can I" cursed Paul.

"What are you doing Paul?" asked Taff as he watched Paul typing something into his computer.

"A little press release, informing the media of what has happened and why. I have also mentioned we cannot disclose exactly how we find the terrorists, because if we did they would become even harder to detect. I have also mentioned the fact that eight of those he released have deportation orders against them, upheld by the courts. He has lifted them and refused the Government leave to appeal. I have of course included his name and address as well as all the telephone numbers, including mobiles, which he uses, and just to add a bit of interest, his salary, expenses and projected pension - all paid by the tax payers he is supposed to protect - the release includes a picture of him in normal clothes, and the same information on the barrister who brought the actions on behalf of some Civil Liberties group I have never heard of. If I can figure out how to, I will also send them a copy of our attempt to talk to him about the problem."

"You are mad! Have you any idea of the power of these people!"

"Taff, there are at least two and a half thousand bodies in morgues throughout the country who should be still going about their daily business, and this senile old bastard releases some of those responsible on a whim; I don't think so. I'm ordering them to be picked up again and those with deportation orders against them, with appeals turned down, will be flown back to their country of origin. The only relevant country we cannot land in is Iran. The two Iranian nationals will be handed over at one of the crossing points from Iraq. We will not even inform the Courts until the job is done."

"You are not really going to send the press release are you?" asked Taff.

"Not going to? I already have. I might hate computers, e-mails and the like, but contrary to popular belief I do know how to use them."

CHAPTER FOURTEEN

The relieved politicians praised the security forces, assuring the public 'things should be back to near normal in a few days'. This statement was issued the morning following the Vulcan strike in Iran. By the time the press received it, most of the cabinet were once more at the base of the All Arms Unit for yet another meeting.

"I think you are being a wee bit optimistic if you don't mind me saying so Prime Minister. This lot are nowhere near finished yet, they are simply taking a bit of a break to figure out their next move; one way or another we have managed to seriously disrupt their plans. Many of their leaders have been removed and we have succeeded in breaking up such structure as existed. Those left, and I believe there are many more left than we originally thought, do not know what the overall plan was. I think most of them might well lie low again - the hot heads among them are, however, likely to follow their own agendas. Therefore we must redouble our efforts to detect and intercept as many of their attacks as we can. As to the nature of these attacks we can only guess, I am certain some will be high profile; the one thing the terrorists need is a propaganda victory to boost their credibility. We must take steps to prevent any such occurrence."

"Your unit has done a superb job co-ordinating operations Colonel, however, there are a few issues which must be addressed," began the newly appointed Home Secretary. "I take it you do not deny you were in some way responsible for the hysteria still sweeping the media. You are aware the judge has not only issued a warrant for your arrest but has also lodged a writ against you for everything from libel to infringing his human rights?"

"There is a perfectly simple solution - fire the senile old bastard. I'll be damned if I will be dictated to by an idiot like him. I have never heard such garbage from someone in a position of power in all my life, and I've heard some rubbish."

"So you intend to fight these charges Colonel?"

"No ma'am. I intend to ignore them!"

"You are aware, he is demanding you release the prisoners you re-arrested."

"I haven't got them so I can't release them. If he wants to get them I can tell him which countries they are in."

"What have you done with them Colonel?" asked the Prime Minister. "You've repatriated them haven't you?"

"Which is, I believe, exactly what the Courts ordered? Indeed, the Home Secretary herself signed the papers within hours of taking office. I can also tell you that all foreign nationals we currently hold, and who are wanted in their home countries, will also be repatriated without recourse to the Courts."

"What happens when the Americans ask for some of theirs? I suppose you will hand them over."

"No way!" replied Paul, to the surprise of many of those present.

"Might I ask why? I was under the impression you got on well with our trans-Atlantic cousins."

"Generally that's true Sir. However, their legal system is more screwed up than ours. They resolutely refused to extradite at least seven mass murderers of Irish origin. Four of them are escaped prisoners, tried and convicted by the Courts. According to them the crimes were political, so they walk around as free men. Until common sense takes over, they can go and whistle - what is good one way must operate the other way round as well. There is nothing political in blowing up women and kids. I am certain, if it had been you who had to pick up the head of a six year old girl from the middle of a rubble strewn road so her injured mother didn't see it, you would feel the same way. The man who planted and then detonated the bomb is one of those the Yanks won't hand over. Until they do then, as a general rule, we won't be sending any of our captives to them."

Paul's pager went off. He grabbed the telephone from his desk, "Yes?"

"Sorry to disturb you Paul. I know you are in a meeting, but the civil rights lawyer who got those prisoners released is here and demanding to be let in."

Paul cut off the guard commander. "Nick her for aiding and abetting terrorists. She can be on tonight's flight to Islamabad with the others; she is a Pakistani national, let them have her back. There is an old deportation order against her which has never been revoked, the woman is a total pain in the arse and has no legitimate right to be here."

"What about the police she has with her, to arrest you?"

"Give them a cup of tea, let them use the toilet, then send them home. They have better things to do with their time."

"I love this job," replied the guard commander.

"You really are extraordinary Colonel," said the Prime Minister.

"You gave me a job to do Sir, to rid this country of terrorists - to have any chance of achieving this I don't need such distractions. While we have been sitting here discussing niceties, a total of fifteen attacks have been launched. From what is on my screen, six were intercepted before they could strike and two more teams have been caught.... well, shot in the aftermath of their attacks. The remainder are being pursued and will be caught. The worrying thing is, in eight of these attacks, the targets were police in rural areas. Four of these attacks targeted PCSOs on foot patrols in little market towns. One was a rocket attack on a small police station not very far from here, the rest targeted police patrol cars. This is a new departure, not unexpected but difficult to counter."

"Use more soldiers Colonel," retorted the Home Secretary.

"Which regiment would that be?"

"I don't know, do I? You're the soldier!"

"Every fit and trained soldier in the UK is deployed, even they have to sleep and eat. Every unit is split into three shifts - one active, one on stand by and the other resting. An Infantry battalion is on its way from BAOR, they should be retraining for rotation to Iraq, and the last battalion stationed in Northern Ireland is landing as we speak. They are not too happy as they have only been back from Iraq for three weeks."

"Are you saying the British army do not have the resources to combat a hand full of terrorists? That is utterly outrageous Colonel!"

"I couldn't agree more Sir. It's not just the army, we are using every trained RAF regiment man left in the UK. Defence of the air bases is in the care of a handful of RAF police, supported by local auxiliary units. Virtually every fit Marine on British soil, supported by trainees who have nearly finished their training, have been deployed. The same is true of the airborne forces; there are no more deployable reserves. Like I said, we might appear to be doing well. Frankly it will be a bloody miracle if we don't get our arses well and truly kicked."

"I was under the impression your magical 'eyes in the sky' were following every terrorist who had been involved in these attacks Colonel, and troops were supporting the police in raids to arrest the bombers, then we hear soldiers are shooting the suspects on sight. I believe men from this unit were involved in one such incident early this morning. One of my constituents contacted me to say two soldiers shot four men dead without warning in the street outside his house. These men wore plain green fatigues, were bare headed and used armalite rifles. He went on to say no warning was given; there was an explosion and gunfire from just around the corner from his house. He went on to claim two other soldiers, dressed and equipped the same as the ones who opened fire in front of his house, destroyed the van which had just dropped off his near neighbours returning from work."

"I am aware of the incident. Did your man also tell you the four who died in the street fired first, well one of them did. They were all armed with modern, folding stock, AK47s. Their 'work' had been an attack on a police car carrying four officers who assisted in securing the site of an attack on a petrol tanker earlier this morning. We have the entire thing on video, I will arrange for you to see a copy before you leave."

"That is very kind of you Colonel. I still don't understand why there is this supposed manpower crisis. It frankly beggars belief, we are unable to protect our infrastructure assets from attacks such as these. Surely all your technology acts as… what do they call it: a force multiplier?"

"It does just that Sir. When you consider the minimum number in a team is four, and you need a minimum of three teams to protect any installation, the numbers required spiral rapidly.

Remember these are troops simply protecting potential targets. Add to these numbers those required for the rapid response teams, those securing sites for the police and helping the clear up operations. Then you very quickly start losing the numbers game."

"You didn't include all those sitting watching the screens in your control room Colonel; surely some of them could be spared - there must have been fifty in there, at least." The Minister for Defence suggested, "If you were to deploy half of them, you would have six more teams. Surely it would help?"

Paul looked at the Prime Minister, shaking his head in despair. "I presume our esteemed minister sat on, and broke his glasses on the way up here. There are roughly one hundred terminals in the control room you were shown. It is one of three such rooms, one for Afghanistan, one for Iraq and the one you saw for the UK. The operators are mainly local civilians and military personnel who are not fit for active duty. That is why most of the military age men in there are in wheelchairs, which the minister failed to notice. Quite how someone like him ends up doing the job he is supposed to do totally baffles me!"

Paul had walked over to the windows and flung them wide open. It was a beautiful day, and apart from the occasional Canberra coming in to land, or one taking off, the airfield was generally quiet.

"So what am I to tell Parliament and the media this afternoon Colonel?" asked the worried Prime Minister. "I can hardly say we will all be living in an Islamic Republic by the end of the week, run by gun carrying militants can I? To hear you talking, it would be an easy conclusion to draw."

"Am I to presume from that, you want me to lie to you regarding the current crisis Sir? As far as living in an Islamic state run by militants, I'll remind you, there are an awful lot of people who will not live until the week end. All we can do is keep taking them out as fast as we can. Now I don't care greatly if the terrorists survive or not, I do care if our troops and the people we are trying to protect survive. It is getting to the stage where I am seriously considering using tactical air strikes to prevent some attacks if the opportunity arises, if only to relieve the pressure on some of the troops. However, I consider it to be counter productive no matter how precise these strikes might be. For a start it would send the signal saying we are getting desperate, which we are, but if the terrorists discover that, then they will redouble their efforts, and blowing yet more holes in the motorways isn't exactly going to help."

"So, what should we say in our communiqué Colonel?"

"We are eliminating the terrorists as fast as we can. People should stay in their homes as far as is possible and remain patient and vigilant. Report anything suspicious to a national help line we can set up. Power will be restored as soon as possible, repairs are in progress."

He turned to the minister who had queried the manpower situation. "The repair teams demand armed guards, as do many fire crews, not unreasonable given the situation, but this puts yet more demands on limited resources. I don't suppose we will ever know for sure, but I'll bet who ever planned all this, had worked out we would have insufficient men to cope. Draw in everything we have available, change tactics to stretch us to our limits then escalate the attacks, I'm sure that is the basis of their plans."

"Maybe this isn't the time to bring this up Colonel. Could you and I have a word in private?"

"Certainly Prime Minister. Taff can take your party to the canteen or better still, you and I can go for a walk while your party collect all the figures they obviously crave for."

As the two men wandered out onto the grass at the edge of the airstrip, the Prime Minister began. "I know you don't particularly like me or my government, and I don't really know exactly how you got on with my predecessor but I must insist you are always straight with me. I am not implying you have lied to me, but you have failed to tell me everything your unit does. I do not understand what has been going on in Somalia; some segments of the American administration are still after your blood over the destruction of their F18."

"We've been over this Sir. Point out to them, one of their part time cowboys destroyed two of our armoured carriers in the first Iraq war, killing several of our soldiers. What did they do? They promoted the gung ho fool. This, in spite of an enquiry which proved his wing man called on him to abort his first run and physically tried to block the second run, all the time telling him they were British troops he was attacking.

The idiot in the F18 was warned by me personally, and the Skipper of the *Kearsarge*, to pull out as there was incoming ordnance. Tapes and video have been sent to the Pentagon and State Department, if they don't like it, then they can take a hike."

"I still don't really understand the need to have sent in a team in the first place. You should have cleared it with my office. Can you justify the risk you took?"

"I believe so Sir. There are still tests on going on the samples the team recovered. Early indications seem to prove we have found where Saddam's missing WMDs disappeared to. Some partly destroyed containers have Iraqi markings, and forensic tests have proven the presence of sand from Iraq's Western Desert."

"Oh dear, this is bad."

"And it gets worse. Some of the equipment definitely came from North Korea; we have bits of manifests and packing cases. My worry is, this has something to do with the threat to 'wipe out' London, as opposed to destroying it. If I am right, then all this crap going on at the moment is designed to make us take our eyes off the ball, and to an extent it is doing exactly that!"

"Have you anything to support such a theory Colonel?"

"The debriefing of the American Special Forces officer is only just beginning. He is in the medical facility at our old base. He is out of danger, but in a bad way; he has warned us of a massive attack on the UK, aimed at 'wiping out' London.

It has been suggested to him, this was the purpose of the ship he was being held on which was, incidentally, the same vessel the Americans stopped off the Yemen during the invasion of Iraq. It had a load of scuds and silk worm missiles concealed under bags of cement, again from North Korea. However, James insists this attack was supposed to have triggered an underwater landslide sending a massive tsunami down the North Sea."

"It still sounds far fetched to me Colonel," replied the Prime Minister.

"I thought so too, except it seems it is a real possibility. Funnily enough we had come up with the same theory before we were able to talk to James."

"You talk as though you know the man."

"I do indeed. I've known him years; he is very good at his job. I trust him, and if he has said something else is on its way, then count on it."

"Why then, if you got your samples and these confirm your suspicions, with further confirmation from your released captive, did you bomb the place? The Americans seem to think you used a tactical nuclear weapon."

"In fact we used a new bomb we have developed, designed to totally destroy any known chemical agents which could be used as a weapon."

"So why use it on the site in Somalia? Were chemical agents still stored there?"

"The site was heavily contaminated and would have been lethal for years. There were four bodies around the site if I remember correctly. They were so contaminated, flies trying to lay eggs on them had died in swarms. There were dead birds and animals all over the place, not a maggot in sight. The site is now 'clean' according to our scans, regard it as a successful field test Sir."

"Very well, Colonel. I have to concede, you and your men seem to have done an outstanding job, however, I must insist you consult with me and the Cabinet before you launch any future expeditions. I take it you are aware of the current diplomatic furore regarding an alleged bombing attack on a residence in eastern Iran?"

"Off course Sir"

"At first the Iranians accused the Americans of using a B2 stealth bomber for the attack. The Russians promptly confirmed the American's statement, all of the B2 fleet was on the ground at the time, on their home base. The Iranian rulers are now accusing the Russians of lying and have ordered their diplomats to leave, along with all their engineers. What is confusing everyone, the Iranian air defence radars didn't detect an aircraft or a missile, and they have some pretty sophisticated equipment. It has crossed my mind you might know what really happened?"

"If you look up Sir, you will notice an aircraft on its final approach. It could answer your question, but I will, of course, deny it."

The Prime minister watched in awe as a huge black bat floated gently down onto the runway. Only when the pilot reversed thrust was there any real noise. "What on earth is it?" asked the man, "I thought it was a Vulcan when I first saw it."

"It was a Vulcan, we simply modified it a bit, to suit our needs."

"Am I to believe, the plane which has just landed was responsible for the raid into Iran?" Paul guessed he was about to get a major rocket himself, judging by the Prime Minister's expression - he was not wrong!

"Colonel. We had just been discussing the need to get Cabinet permission for such acts of war! If this had gone wrong there could have been catastrophic consequences. Who was in the building you destroyed in such a cavalier fashion? What possible justification could there be for such a wanton act of aggression? I am seriously considering relieving you of command, the trouble you have caused since your return defies belief."

"Fair enough. You and you alone have that power, but before you start throwing temper tantrums aimed at me or this Unit, just stop and think for a moment. Do you honestly think I am stupid enough to risk a war with Iran, merely to prove we can destroy any target we chose? Who do you think is orchestrating all these attacks at the moment?"

"I don't like your tone Colonel, this could have serious consequences for you."

Paul snapped back, much to the man's surprise as he was unused to direct dissent. "For once in your life answer the bloody question! Why would we attack somewhere like that, particularly at this moment?"

"Are you saying the terrorists were being sent instructions from that building?"

"Well done. You have figured it out, and it was all with the connivance of the Iranian secret service, and yes I can prove it. I would rather not have to, as it will give away yet more of our technology secrets. The only significant terrorist leader not there was Sammy bin Liner. The leaders of every crackpot terrorist group who hide behind the good name of Islam were there. We took them out in one quick clinical strike - no one except us knows who did it, keep it that way! Give it a couple of days and these attacks will peter out, by then we will have got most, if not all, of those involved so far. Thanks to the intercepts from what is now a hole in the Iranian desert, we have the names and addresses of a lot more potential terrorists. Those we have traced so far are, for the most part, here illegally and we can simply send them home. To hell with their alleged human rights, the right of our people to go about their daily lives without fear greatly outweighs the rights of these lunatics to be free to blow us up as and when the mood takes them."

"I really don't know what to say Colonel," replied the shocked Prime Minister.

Their stroll in the bright East Anglian sunshine had brought them close to the huge hanger doors. Paul led the way to a pedestrian door. "You say I have got to trust you Sir. I am going to show you some things which, as far as the rest of the world is concerned, do not exist. You already know we saved some of the Concords from the knacker's yard, you have just seen one of our converted Vulcans land; you also know we use old Victors as our principle tanker, nothing else can get so high or fly as fast." Paul opened the door with a swipe card, only to be met by two armed soldiers.

"Hello Boss. We don't see you in here very often," then he recognised the man with Paul and came smartly to attention.

"At ease. We'll be half an hour or so; sign us in please. I can do without one of Andrews' crew giving me earache about fire regs."

"Will do Boss. I'd better take your cigarettes and lighter as well please, just to be sure."

"Fair enough Billy," he laughed, well aware it was the young trooper protecting his own backside. They both knew, when the safety officer checked the 'visitors book' he would spot Paul's name, then check to make sure he had left at least his lighter with the guards.

"This way Sir." Paul led the PM to the back of the hanger. A crew were swarming all over a Canberra which was the only aircraft in the building. "There is what makes the cameras so special; we call this lens a 'flies eye'. It is in fact many small lenses and, thanks to our computers, we can use any of the lenses individually. As long as each lens used to obtain a close up, is surrounded by lenses left on general scan then the big picture is unaffected. This is how any one plane can follow up to fifty individual targets miles apart at any one time."

"What happens at night, or if it is cloudy?"

"Night time is no problem. There is nearly always enough light. Cloud however means all our images are in black and white, and various shades of grey." Paul indicated another box of electronics on the bench. "The targeting system - It can mark up to....." he paused, "To tell you the truth, I have no idea how many it can mark now. It used to be about thirty at a time, I know it has increased but by how much is anyone's guess. There are also various sensors in another package which fits in the nose - ground penetrating radar, a specific infra red package. I'm told it can detect me smoking in my office when the plane is over London, though quite how baffles me."

"Quite remarkable Colonel, no wonder you went for the civil servant who delayed the deployment by cancelling the new engines."

"Everything you have seen so far works perfectly well with the old engines Sir. Even this sensor, which is the one we use to detect mines and explosives as well as the chemicals, works all right. It's this little gismo which wouldn't work. Don't ask me how it works, the only way I can describe it is, it 'sees' sound, which means we can listen to conversations as clearly as if we were sitting next to whoever is talking. Then there are all the usual bits and pieces to listen to… radios and telephone conversations, even if the cable is buried a few feet beneath a busy road. This is the device which generates the data stream. We sort of borrow any handy satellite to bounce the signal off back to here."

"Surely there is the danger of detection?"

"No one has noticed yet. The on board computer filters the data so only the bits we want are streamed home, otherwise we would never cope."

"I presume the computer is housed in what used to be the bomb bay?"

"No, it's in the panel beside the systems operator. It is smaller than your lap-top. Come on, there's a lot more to see yet Sir and if we are not back at the security check point roughly when I said we would be, they will send out the search parties."

They headed once more towards the back of the hanger, passing through another small door into a much larger building, in fact it was vast.

"This is under the low hill behind the outer building, you would never know it was here."

He gazed at the aircraft neatly parked along each side, noting the gap which he presumed was normally occupied by the Vulcan he had seen land. His eyes seemed locked onto two strange aircraft, long and slim with high mounted wings, canards and a flattened 'V' shaped tail. The tips of the thin delta wings were turned down. All these features, along with the strange shaped air inlets to the twin jets, gave the planes an air of menace, almost evil.

"What on earth are they Colonel, they look like they belong on the set of star wars?"

"I would have thought you might have recognised the basic design Sir, after all it was your lot which scrapped them the last time you got in. I'll give you a clue, they can, 'hedge hop', at mach2 plus a bit, all the way to Moscow and back. The original was called the TSR2, we call them TSR3. Just like the original concept they can take pictures from a low angle, which is potentially dangerous in a Canberra, or, if need be, carry a good bomb load internally. These can be a few big ones in a conventional rack, or specials in a pre-loaded revolving rack. Useful bits of kit. You have seen every other type which lives in here. Below us are the munitions bunkers, and deeper still, the ready to use fuel stores. I'm not at all sure what you will make of what is next door. There is another hanger identical to this. I might as well warn you it's largely staffed by our American friends."

He stood transfixed by what he saw. Along one side stood a line of the ten remaining operational Blackbirds, facing them were four giant Tankers, specially adapted to carry the unique fuel required by these extraordinary old planes.

"Who is in command of these things?" asked the awe struck man.

"I am I suppose. We operate them on behalf of the UN as a rule. They can carry a couple of bombs if need be, or our new anti-missile system, but it is usually used for taking pictures of conflicts or disasters for the UN. They can get to wherever a hell of a lot quicker than a Canberra, but they can't loiter over an area for hours, like the old Blue Birds. The TSR3s are strictly low level, but these are our tools for getting a quick 'snap shot' of what is going on at any given location."

"Amazing, utterly amazing. One thing Colonel, how do you get all your electronic equipment? The devices you were showing me are far in advance of anything else I have heard of. Do the Americans supply you?"

"No Sir, we supply them. The RAF have our previous generation equipment, and we flog the Yanks the stuff from the one before that, it pays for most of the running costs of this place."

"You mean you make it here? Good heavens, how? Come to that, who thinks up all the incredible sensors?"

"Several storeys below the HQ block is a room, well an entire floor they call the 'clean room'. It is inhabited by strange ephemeral creatures who spend their working days clad in white overalls and wearing masks, they look as though they are from another planet. They can talk to me for hours and I don't understand a bloody word they say; as far as I know, they could well be from another planet. If I need to be able to look at something, take 'Big Ears', the system which sees sound for example, I mentioned the idea and within a week, one of them turns up in my office with a foot long, well sort of a cube with a pipe sticking out, and announces, 'Here you are Boss, you can listen to anyone now. All you need to do is to tell the pilot to fly above 100,000 feet to reduce air noise, and to link it to this new computer.' He gave me a thing like a four pint thermos flask with a plug dangling from a piece of multi-cored cable, and that was it. Job done, and you know the saga of the engines we needed to get the planes up there. They are a weird bunch, we hardly know them, they keep to themselves. Their idea of a good night is to sit in front of a blackboard writing huge equations, to prove most quantum physics theories are a load of 'fanciful nonsense,' I think was the expression they used. They are happiest yakking on about 'quarks' and 'nuetrinos'. Don't even ask; all I know is they are something to do with sub atomic particles, whatever they are. All this seems to have something to do with making our equipment do what we want it to do."

"How did they end up working for you?"

"Do you know I really haven't got the remotest idea. They sort of appeared; a couple of them have parents who have worked with the Unit for years and I think the others were their friends. They seem happy enough doing whatever they do. It helps us so I leave well alone!"

"Remarkable."

"And then some. Come on we'd better be getting back, the search parties will be out soon."

Having retrieved his cigarettes and lighter, the first thing Paul did on reaching the fresh air was to light up!

"I take it I have your word you will not mention anything you have seen on your little tour Sir."

The Day The Ravens Died

"My predecessor was aware of all this?"

"Oh yes. I was curious as to how much you knew Sir. You had after all, attended at least three meetings here and one at 'the farm'."

"I might remind you. The previous meetings I attended here were all at night. I was aware you had a powerful, if rather limited, force under your command. If you take your registered strength as your actual strength, then you gain no meaningful insight into the size of your unit. As soon as you get the chance, it would be helpful if you could supply an accurate list of your personnel Colonel."

"Is this list to consist of permanent military staff, or do we include those on short term detachments. Others are here on indefinite detachment, and we must not forget those posted to us by their units for training. What about the civilians? Some of them are regular full time, others are on fixed period contracts. A lot of them are part time, some are instructors, lecturers and the likes, as well as advisors."

"You are not going to do it are you Colonel?" asked the annoyed Prime Minister.

"Probably not, but you did add the rider, 'as soon as you have the time'. As things stand, I think we are going to be rather busy for the foreseeable future."

"Very well, just for my own information. How many combat troops could you put into the field, as a unit?"

"We have between a hundred and a hundred and twenty, depending on fitness at any one time. At the moment virtually all of those fit enough are deployed, mostly in pairs or teams of four. These teams are spread all over the place, acting as liaison between our aircraft and ground units. Some are, of course, operating in the UK against the terrorist cells. Personally I cannot remember the last time more than a dozen of our combat team members were under the same roof together. It just doesn't happen with the way we operate."

"There are those in the government Colonel who are of the opinion your unit is an expensive luxury we can ill afford. The general consensus being, any useful equipment you may have should be handed over to the relevant units of the conventional forces. All of your obsolete aircraft scrapped. The same with the assault ships which are, by any definition, a long way past their sell by date. Personnel of military age should be redeployed, to address the current manpower shortages, into the ranks of the regular forces."

"And your opinion? Now you have a better idea of the Unit's true potential."

"I can see the points a lot of your critics make do have an element of truth in them, some of your equipment is very old."

"So are some of the staff, me for a start. Just remember one thing Sir. There is no point replacing a piece of equipment with something else just for the sake of it. Newer is not always better."

The two men were by now almost back to the headquarters building. The

PM turned to look at the Vulcan bomber he had watched landing, taxi to the hanger doors and cut its engines. He looked at his watch. "If that really is the aircraft which bombed the target in Iran, he has been travelling very fast all the way home. You have certainly given me food for thought Colonel."

The crackle of small arms fire carried to them on the breeze, followed by a sharp explosion. "What the hell?" exclaimed Paul. "Quick, inside Sir, come on, quickly!"

A couple of seconds later they heard alarm bells ringing somewhere. A radio message came clearly in his ear piece, 'Urgent assistance required, main gate, under attack.'

A Landrover came tearing towards them from the direction of the hangers with two men in it. The driver and a sergeant from the RAF police, hanging on grimly to the point five BAR mounted on the vehicle. Paul ran towards it and flagged it down shouting at the Prime Minister to get a move on and get inside. With surprising agility for a man of his age, he jumped into the back of the open topped Landrover, "Okay I'm in, get going," he shouted to the driver.

They were soon at the main gate. Paul was horrified to see the state of the police car; it had been riddled with bullets, presumably from AK47s. An RPG detonated on the framework of the camp gates as they approached and the guard room showed signs of having been hit by another rocket. The over confident culprits seemed unaware of the threat the approaching Landrover posed to their survival, and apart from an un-aimed burst of automatic fire in the general direction they did little to counter this new threat.

"Take them out sergeant," ordered Paul as he took careful aim with his borrowed M16, which was the driver's personal weapon - it was all over in less than ten seconds. The sergeant with the BAR fired two short bursts and the terrorists where hurled around like rag dolls as the heavy bullets struck home. Most of the terrorists had stayed in or near their cars feeling a false sense of security from the presumed protection offered by the vehicles. Bullets from a point five BAR can penetrate armour plate at half a mile. The bodywork of a modern car was about as effective as a sheet of newspaper against this devastating weapon barely fifty yards away.

Two of the gang had moved about ten yards away from the cars to get a better angle on one of the guards who was still firing an occasional shot from his 9mm hand gun, hoping to keep the gang at bay until help arrived. Paul saw one of these two raise his rocket launcher to take another shot at the guard room. The old armalite cracked twice. The terrorist's partner, ten feet away, winced as something hit the side of his face as he was re-loading his AK47. Just as he realised it was a chunk of his friends skull, everything went dark. He too was dead before the second round blew the back off his skull.

Paul handed the rifle back to the driver with a casual, "Thanks Eddie." He jumped out of the Landrover. "Come on, let's check those two wrecks to make sure there is no threat. Keep us covered sergeant."

The Day The Ravens Died

The checks were, as Paul suspected, a formality. The risk of a terrorist having survived the onslaught was minimal, but assumption was the mother of most cock-ups, as Paul was always saying. So he had to practice what he preached. In this case however, these terrorists would never threaten again. Such was the power of the old machine gun, most of them were a terrible mess, a bullet hitting the shoulder joint would, quite literally, blow the arm clean off.

"I'm glad I haven't got to clear that mess up," Paul said to the ashen faced driver. "Come on Eddie, you've seen worse than that in your time. Let's check on the lads in the guardroom."

They were passing the shot up police car. Paul had noticed the driver's shattered door hanging open and assumed, quite rightly, the driver had made it to the guardroom. He had noticed the blood indicating, not surprisingly, the driver had been injured. In such rural areas Panda cars usually had only one officer in, unless it was a Saturday night then often they were twin crewed.

Eddie motioned towards the passenger side of the car, then turned away to be sick. Crumpled in the foot well was, what was left of the young female PCSO - it was more a collection of pieces than a body. An RPG had come in through the thin door panel and literally exploded in her seat.

"Augh man!" muttered Paul, as he turned away and headed again towards the guardroom door. He was nearly there when the door burst open and a distraught young constable rushed towards his car shouting for 'Sandra?'

Paul intercepted him and led him back into the guardroom. It turned out, the dead PCSO was the officer's girl friend, and he had known she was dead before he took cover in the guardroom himself. The first burst of fire from two AK47s had come straight into the passenger side of the Panda car. At least ten bullets had hit the girl, mainly in the head and neck, blowing most of her head into the foot well.

"You can't help her now Mate," said Paul. "There's nothing I can say or do to make things better, at least she won't have felt anything. You stay here, the medics will be here any moment. Are you two all right?" he asked the two who had been on duty.

"Mine are just a couple of nicks Boss, they smart a bit but nothing serious. Phil stopped one, and has some other injuries from flying bits when the grenade hit. The young copper is in shock and has two or three wounds. How badly are you hit Boss?"

That was when Paul noticed blood running down his wiry forearm. "Fuck me, I didn't realise I'd been hit!" It turned out to have been a ricochet. The razor sharp edge on a flattened bullet had sliced across his upper arm after bouncing of the steel of the guardroom door. Until now he hadn't felt a thing!"

Substantial help was now arriving including a helicopter, should a caz-e-vac to the farm be necessary. The medic assigned to Paul insisted he get it seen to properly. "It needs a few stitches Sir, as well as a proper clean-up."

Timothy Pilgrim

"Look. Clean it up, tape it together, and slap a bandage round it. I've got half the bloody Government in the HQ block."

Ten minutes later Paul was back in his office, inevitably smoking. Taff was first in. "Are you bloody mad!?" he asked. "What were you thinking of, running off and leaving the PM of all people?" Then he noticed the rip in the arm of Paul's shirt and the bandage showing through. Are you hit?"

"Nothing serious, I'll live."

"You bloody old fool. Why do you think we have troopers?"

"Oh shut up bloody whingeing Taff and get the bottle out. As you no doubt already know, all three of us in the first 'rover to get there have grey hair, something tells me we are a bit more stretched than we ought to be around here."

"That's as may be, and yes I do know you got two of them. If you hadn't then the guardroom could well have taken another RPG, so I suppose I should say well done. You may also be interested to know, General Leach will be here in about half an hour."

"Is he up to it yet?"

"He is just as stubborn as you," retorted Taff.

"And you're not I suppose?"

The disturbance outside the door proved to be the party of ministers and their aides, demanding to be allowed in to complete their fact finding mission. Paul stabbed a button on the console on his desk. "Let them in."

A very senior civil servant was first in. "Put that cigarette out at once Colonel," he demanded.

"No," was the monosyllabic reply.

"I demand to know what happened Colonel."

"You'll be told in due course," replied Paul.

The Prime Minister approached. "Tell me Colonel," he began, "just how could such an attack happen? Here of all places. I am surprised you didn't pick up the attackers before they struck. Also, I have been given to understand, there were only two of your men on duty in the gatehouse at the time. Surely with us on a visit, there ought to have been more."

"We didn't know about your visit prior to your arrival, so I think you will agree, it is unlikely the terrorists would have known. All of our aircraft are already deployed. Those on the ground are all undergoing maintenance. You can't pull into a lay-bye, several miles up, if you break down.

The reason the plane which would have been covering us wasn't, is the pilot is at the other end of his patrol line. This plane still has its old engines and therefore cannot achieve the required altitude to cover us properly."

Three flat bed trucks passed the window, followed by a skip truck and a covered seven and a half toner.

"You haven't cleared the scene already have you Colonel?" asked a shocked Home Office Minister. "You couldn't possibly have collected the evidence yet. It will be needed for the trial!"

"What trial would that be Sir?" Paul asked innocently.

"The terrorists of course. I heard someone say you 'got them all'. You will need to prove which one fired the shot which killed the young policewoman. I am correct in saying a policewoman was killed?"

"She was a PCSO, only been on duty a week! There will be no need for a trial, all the terrorists are dead. They tend to ignore you if you say, 'Oh do be good boys and put those nasty guns down'. Do that and you end up dead, very quickly, so we don't need to know which one shot her or anyone else, do we?"

"But you shouldn't have touched anything until the police completed their investigations, think of the information which could have been gained."

"What information could possibly have been gained which would have been of any practical use? We will soon know who they were and where they came from. We already know the rocket launcher was from the consignment which slipped in through Felixstowe, from its serial number. To put things in perspective a bit, that makes a total of twenty one recovered out of a consignment of hundreds. The sooner dozy old buggers like you wake up to the fact we are, in effect, at war the better. To all intents and purposes we have already been invaded! The vast majority of those we have captured or killed have been here totally illegally. Don't ask me how they all got in unnoticed, because I have no idea."

"It is my belief, you are over dramatising the problem Colonel," said the senior civil servant in a superior tone of voice. "I simply do not believe many of your claims as to the numbers of attacks, actual or supposedly intercepted. In fact, I do not understand why the police cannot deal with this problem. It is, after all, a civilian matter."

"There is nothing civilian about it, other than most of the victims being civilian, assault rifles and rocket propelled grenades are, by any definition, military." Paul called B.J. into the office. His long time friend appeared with commendable promptness. "Do me a favour, take this numpty down to the MT section, and make sure he has a good look in the passenger side foot well of the police Panda car, and I mean a good look not a quick glance from a distance. Go on, go with the Major and get a quick reality check."

The man went, somewhat reluctantly, it has to be said.

The Prime Minister turned to Paul as the top aide left with B.J. "What do you hope to gain by letting Sir Jonathon see a dead policewoman; what is the point?"

"The point Sir is every day for the past couple of weeks some poor sod under my command has had to sort out something similar. I don't care how tough you are, or how well trained, things like the mess he is going to see for himself leaves an indelible impression and will, in the end, take a severe toll on those who have to sort it out. It is not like the movies - only rarely do people hit with high velocity rounds, lie down and die quietly, with a little patch of blood around a nice neat bullet hole. There might well be a small entry wound but there is, more often than not, a hole you could put your fist in where the thing came out, probably taking a lump of bone with it!"

"I take it from what you have just said, the poor girl has a particularly horrible exit wound."

"It is hard to tell Sir. One of those rocket grenades exploded in the back of her seat. Most of what is left of her is in a random pile of body parts, blown into the foot well, like I said, reality check time. We cannot fight these bastards with one hand tied behind our backs, never mind both! We may have a chance if, and only if, we can keep up the pressure. Most of those involved in attacks are being dealt with quickly, either intercepted or a raid soon after they go to ground. They are beginning to realise they are being watched and tracked. The point is, they have no idea how we are doing it, I believe this is the reason for the change in their targets over the last few days. Traffic and CCTV cameras are favourites; police are also being attacked as we know only too well. One incident involved a TV detector van looking for licence dodgers, pretty well anything with an aerial is a target, they are getting paranoid about their security. This combined with the drying up of orders from their leaders will greatly reduce the number of attacks which in turn will allow the police to raid the list of addresses we have from the intercepts.

What this unit must do is concentrate on the threat to wipe out London, a threat I happen to believe is very real. We must also speed up the camouflaging of petrol tankers, as these will continue to be the primary targets for the hundreds of RPGs still in their possession; we are a long way from winning."

"So, in your opinion Colonel, these are little more than diversionary attacks, designed to make us take our eye off the ball, so as to speak?"

Paul turned to the speaker, the Minister of Defence. "I'd say you are fairly accurate in your assessment Sir. I believe these were the attacks supposed to bring the country to its knees. I know there has been, and still is, massive disruption. I am also convinced the levels of destruction are far below what the terrorists hoped, indeed planned for.

The reasons for this are as varied as the attacks; some credit must go to the clear up and repair gangs, many of them have worked long hours. Of course the policy of simply clearing a site, for example as on a motorway, without the usual extensive forensics has helped enormously. It enables repairs to start, more or less, straight away. This is only possible when the culprits have been identified and are being followed, or have already been dealt with.

Our ability to respond rapidly to an incident and, increasingly, to intercept their teams has thrown them, as has the loss of their leaders. It is also possible we have managed to hit something or someone vital to their campaign. I have no idea who or what it might have been, but something is slowing them down."

"I know you will never admit to it Colonel, but could it be down to the timely demise of so many leaders in a single stroke?"

"Personally, I think it is far too soon after the event for it to have made any significant difference as yet. If attacks peter out in a few days, then, yes some of it will be down to the loss of direction. I think the most likely scenario is we have unwittingly taken out either one of the principle quartermasters, or the distribution system they used for shifting weapons around."

The meeting continued in a similar vein for what seemed like hours. Mostly the same old questions, repeated over and over. Paul took advantage of the brief lull, created by a jet landing, to refill his coffee mug. "If any of you gentlemen want a cuppa, feel free to help yourselves, I'm afraid I don't do waiter service."

The varied reactions were quite interesting; it was the civil servants who didn't like it. Paul was surprised when most of the senior politicians simply laughed and did indeed help themselves.

The jet had stopped quite close to the building, its engines running down to idling speed, just long enough for a passenger to disembark. A few moments later, the jet had powered up its engines to taxiing power and headed off towards the hangars.

The office door opened as a battered looking General Leach entered.

Paul immediately offered him his comfortable chair and made him a coffee. Everyone was happy to see the greatly respected Senior Officer back.

"There you are Boss," said Paul, placing the cup near the General.

"I can think of two explanations for this sort of treatment. The first is I must look worse than I feel, and the second more likely option is, this reprobate," indicating Paul, "is in serious trouble and is hoping I can extricate him," then after a pause, the General added, "Again!"

"Why did you come back so soon Sir? It's not that we aren't glad to see you, but if anyone deserved a break you do. I can only assume the fish were not in the mood."

"The fishing, as I am sure you were well aware, was fine, as was the accommodation. I'm afraid my early return is largely down to her ladyship."

"I'm sorry to hear that Sir. I'd have thought she would have enjoyed the peace and quiet with all that's going on."

"Well, I suppose it was my fault really. You know she's not much of an outdoor sort, except for her garden, and she's not exactly an animal lover. I had this silly idea an encounter with the deer might change things. It was very much like the time you took me to meet your four footed friends. I forgot what you had said about watching your back as we were leaving; mercifully it was the old hind, not the stag which butted her ladyship. The rest you can probably imagine, so here we are."

Before Paul could regain his full composure the door opened again. This time it was B.J. returning with the civil servant. The General spotted the ashen grey face immediately. "What..?" was as far as he got before Paul held up his hand.

"Well?" enquired Paul, "Are we a little bit wiser now?"

"That was totally disgusting Colonel, and totally uncalled for!"

"It was also totally your fault!" Paul snapped back. "Had the aircraft nearest to us been equipped with the proper engines, it would have spotted the bastards who did it before they attacked. Now you have seen first hand, the direct cost of your refurbishment of your executive bogs, I hope you think they are worth it. I have a bloody good mind to take you to her parents' house and let you explain to them, how it was you who spent the money earmarked for equipment which would have saved their daughter's life on your own toilets!"

"You wouldn't!"

"Watch me! Well Prime Minister, are you still prepared to defend this worthless, self opinionated piece of shite?"

"Why did you have one of the aircraft with the old engines nearest to your base? You must have known it couldn't cover you for most of its patrol?"

"Oh I knew alright, but I had to ensure the overlap with the adjoining patrol. We hadn't had any attacks around here until today; it was a risk I had to take. By the same token, I had to strip the base of almost all of its combat strength to nail as many of them as quickly as possible. It's a fine balancing act. The trick is to make us appear very much stronger than we actually are; if they knew our actual strength we would be overwhelmed, of that I am certain. Now I hope you all understand the true state of affairs. We are, it seems, gaining the upper hand, but this is largely down to a bluff. All depends on the skill and courage of the handful of combat troops deployed, and their ability to maintain the currently unacceptably high level of operations.

The reduction in our surveillance capabilities, due entirely to this idiot, could yet prove to be the margin between ultimate success and abject failure, resulting in total carnage. It really is that close!"

The badly shaken civil servant wasn't ready to go without a fight it seemed. "How was I to know what a difference such things could make? In these days of hi-tech remotely controlled aircraft and satellites, who would suspect an aircraft designed over fifty years ago could make such a difference."

"You didn't have to know. The whole point is no-one, other than those who needed to know, would even be aware of the project. Your crass stupidity and disregard of instructions from your political masters is now costing lives. Believe me, the policewoman killed here is not the only one dead because of you!"

The man turned to the Prime Minister expecting, at least, a degree of support. He was to be bitterly disappointed.

"I'm sorry Jonathon, I am going to have to accept your resignation. It grieves me to say this, but the Colonel was right all along."

"You can't just sack me Prime Minister. I only have two years left before I retire on full pension."

"A compensation package will be worked out. I'm sure there will be generous severance terms."

"I'd like to sever something," muttered Paul, under his breath; only the General heard the comment and raised an eyebrow in gentle rebuke.

The PM turned to the military leaders. "Is it possible to give us an idea when we might be able to resume, something approaching normality?"

"Ask me in a couple of days Sir," replied Paul. "We should have a better idea by then. In the meantime, I suggest you draw up contingency plans to evacuate London in the shortest time possible. I would suggest a two phase plan. Everything inside the North and South Circular roads, then extend out to the M25."

"I would say it is probably impossible, although I suppose it depends on how much of a warning we get," replied the Prime Minister.

"Exactly Sir. If we get a reasonable warning, evacuate from the centre outwards. If we don't get an adequate warning, then work from the outside inwards, until the affected area is reached. Like I said, it is just a contingency plan."

"With the current level of disruption not many people would get out Colonel. Most of the motorways are closed, as is Heathrow and three of the main lines. Our options are somewhat limited."

"Exactly Sir. If I have read the situation correctly, the current spate of attacks is little more than a trial run. As I have already said, I believe these attacks will almost cease by the end of the week. I think it is inevitable there will still be a few, to keep us occupied as much as anything. They will be analysing our response; the loss of a lot of their leaders will, I hope, have bought us a little time. Let's use that time wisely and prepare for whatever is coming our way."

CHAPTER FIFTEEN

Sure enough, by the end of the week the attacks had all but ceased. Maybe it should have been... the attempted attacks had almost ceased. Four were intercepted before they reached their targets. One of the other two targets was a large electricity sub station. Sensors on an orbiting Canberra picked up the tell tale signs of explosives in the two cars approaching the remote sub station. A sharp eyed operator monitoring the aircraft's sensors spotted the signal in time to flash a warning to the four tired Marines nearing the end of their stint on guard. The drivers turned their stolen cars around, ready for a quick getaway. The remainder of the gang approached and prepared to fire their rockets at the vulnerable transformers. The moment they raised their launchers their fate was sealed. Forewarned of the impending attack, the Marines were in perfect positions, the terrorists never had a chance. Paul, watching on a monitor in the control room, grunted with satisfaction at the result.

The two drivers, after a moment's hesitation, tore off along the access road as though they were on a rally. Rounding a bend, made blind by some large bushes, the leading driver suddenly jammed on his brakes. His escape was barred by a land rover parked across the road, flanked on either side by a pair of determined looking Marines, rifles at the ready. So suddenly had the first car braked, his friend following had no chance of avoiding a crash. Swerving hard under braking, he slammed into the leading car and rolled into the ditch on the left, the angle he hit the leading car at launched it into the ditch on the right.

"Bloody Sunday drivers!" commented the Marine sergeant. Then he instructed his team to grab the would-be terrorists, before they drowned!

The other attack was, in a way, symptomatic of what Paul had been saying about 'over stretch' of the forces available to counter this threat. Although it has to be said, it was more a failure of equipment than the men. A team of four young soldiers had been dispatched to intercept two terrorists who had attempted to bring down a pylon across a busy road. For whatever reason only one of the charges had gone off. The pylon survived on the remaining three legs. Rushing to intercept the inept pair, the army driver of the big four by four didn't notice the wheel wobble until it became quite severe. He tried to slow down and pull over, but this only increased the strain on the already damaged wheel hub. Seconds later his vehicle was, like the pylon, propped up

The Day The Ravens Died

on three corners instead of four because the front driver's side wheel had come adrift. Later examination of the service records showed the problem had been spotted at the last service, but because of a back log coupled with the need to have every usable vehicle available, the decision was taken to let it go for now. As long as it was driven gently it should, with any luck, last until the mechanics had more time.

The crew of the Canberra covering the sector were looking forward to going home. It had been a long day. They had agreed to do the extra sortie, their third of the day. This was to allow the hard working ground crews to complete the upgrading of the plane which should have been carried out before this particular flight.

It was a strange quirk among the men who flew these old aircraft - all of them would do an extra flight rather than let another crew fly 'their' plane. Paul did nothing to discourage this as it showed a pride in their particular aircraft. It also helped, as each of these old planes seemed to have their own little peculiarities, which of course the regular crews were used to.

The systems operator on this plane kept his all seeing 'eye' firmly locked on to the fleeing terrorists as they headed home with a misplaced confidence that they had got away with their attempted sabotage.

Aware of mishap to the interception team, Paul re-directed two other squads to the general area in rural Suffolk. Hopefully they could intercept the fugitives before they went to ground, and thus avoid the potentially hazardous job of raiding houses.

The teams were rapidly closing in when, to everyone's surprise, the car turned into a country estate. For a moment there was some concern they might be headed to the stately home, however they pulled up outside a range of farm buildings, converted into small industrial units.

Paul called the crew of the Canberra, "Run a scan over that place."

"Already doing it Paul" came back the voice of a veteran pilot. After a brief pause the same voice from the ether announced, "There are three people in the unit, two of them from the car. It would seem to be a fertilizer store judging from our readings. You'll have them any second Paul."

"Are you thinking the same as me Boyo?" asked Taff who had walked in, just in time to hear what had been said.

The raid was swift and devastating. One of the diverted teams was from the SAS, backed up by four Paratroopers - it was one of the greatest miss-matches of all time. There wasn't even a flicker of resistance as all three meekly surrendered.

The radio link from the soldiers crackled, confirming the suspicions of Paul and Taff.

"You won't believe this place Boss. I guess we've just found the missing contents of that container. Some fertilizer store!"

"Taff, how the bloody hell did we miss it? I must be going daft in my old age."

"You've been that for years Mate, but it proves the point. Even you see what you expect to see most of the time. Farm buildings, strong nitrate readings, a perfectly reasonable assumption. It's full of fertilizer."

"And we all know whose mother assumption is?"

"I'll send a squad with trucks to bring everything back here, and a chopper to pick up our guests, before someone else claims them."

"Good idea Taff. I'll tell his Nibs and let the General pass on the glad tidings to the PM, as soon as those trucks are back on base. This is just the lucky break we needed to ease the pressure. I for one will sleep a little easier tonight, another couple of days then we should be able to concentrate on the other problem. I just hope we have the time."

"Me too," replied Taff.

Predictably, following the seizure of the large arms cache, a meeting of all the Security Chiefs was called for the following day. Paul's reaction was equally predictable. "I can hear it now Taff," he began. "I am pleased to announce, the end of the period of emergency measures, implemented by this government, to enable our security forces to deal with the crisis."

"You are getting cynical in your old age Paul."

The even older General Leach added, "He's been like it for years Taff. Mind you, I'm not saying he's wrong. I agree with him. I'll take any bet you like, our dear PM will take the credit for dealing with the attacks. Success will be, as Paul said, down to special measures and announcements, made by him and his Ministers."

"Frankly, I can't see much point in going Sir. At best, it is going to be a nauseating back slapping session, followed up by a kicking aimed, mainly, at us for going in too hard. Oh, and I nearly forgot, yet another ear bashing for infringing the human rights of the terrorists, probably from some senile old fool who was found sleeping in his 'chambers'."

"Try to stay calm m'boy, you'll be fine. I presume you have all your facts and figures on your laptop."

"Of course Sir, and pretty grim reading they make. I will however, make my peace with the woman in command of most armed cops. She did well in one of the early incidents. We have got it on video. She nailed one herself, a quick, double tap to the head saved several of her squad, now she is better qualified to lead, she knows how it feels. It will be interesting to see how she copes. There are likely to be a lot more bust ups yet, as the police haven't had a chance to mount raids on all the addresses we gave them, mostly the ones from the intercepts from Iran."

"How do you plan to deal with these raids Paul?" asked Taff. "Don't forget you asked for a total scan of the British Isles to see if we can find any more arms caches or chemical weapons. It is going to be one hell of a task and will take a couple of weeks at least."

"I know. My other idea is to assign one of the older Canberras to the task of doing an intensive scan of each house due to be raided. We have a mobile control unit in a small truck with the police task force assigned to the operation. In addition, we will have an assault team with the truck, to take the lead if the scans show up anything out of the ordinary."

"Do you think the offer will be accepted by the Met?"

"After the last few days, I should think so; would you revert to being all parochial again?"

In the event the meeting went much as expected. Most of the effort seemed to be directed at playing down the casualties, damage and disruption caused by the multiple attacks.

"What is your opinion on our draft communiqué Colonel?" asked a young Minister, sounding very pleased with the document he had just presented.

"I suppose the general content is more or less accurate, but try to tone it down a bit. Apart from over glamorising the carnage of the past week, you make it sound as though you, and your mates, bored them into submission with your daily, 'announcing new measures'."

"What do you suggest we do? Attribute our victory over these terrorists solely to you? My predecessor warned me you were a glory hunter."

"Just for the record," replied Paul, "If no one, other than those present, were even aware of the existence of my unit, I and all those under my command would be delighted. I will leave you to work out the implications of this, in regard to the load of rubbish you just came out with."

"Why don't we leave the Minister to redraft the communiqué, more along the lines the Colonel suggested. I believe refreshments are ready." The Prime Minister was directing his guests to the buffet.

Having grabbed a cup of coffee, Paul, predictably, headed for the garden and lit up. He found a quiet corner and tried to make some sense of the bits of a signal he had been handed just before he left the base.

"Mind if I join you Colonel?" asked a soft female voice. He looked up to see the Deputy Assistant Commissioner with whom he had rowed violently in the past.

Paul shuffled along the bench a little. "Feel free M'aam."

"That's a bit of a change in tone Colonel, might I ask why?"

"Okay, the strident shriek trying to exert authority has gone, and now you know what it feels like to take a life, however justified."

"I suppose you were bound to find out sooner or later. Now I understand you, at least more than I did before. Theory counts for nothing in the real world does it?"

"Not a lot, but for what it's worth, you did damned well. You saved the lives of most of your team, maybe your own as well. To take down a hardened killer like him, you're good."

"And he is dead."

"You and your team went home to your families. That's the job; put bluntly, sometimes it sucks! He chose to dedicate himself to running around killing innocent women and kids. You chose to dedicate yourself to stopping him and others like him. Answer me this, who is right?"

"When you put it like that it doesn't sound so bad, but it still has to be lived with, just like you said. It's not easy is it? I'll tell you now, as you will find out soon enough. I'm resigning from my current post. I remember the other part of what you said about leading armed units, and I am not sure I could do it again."

"I never said it was easy. If it hadn't bothered you at all then, never mind quitting, you shouldn't have been carrying a gun in the first place. Equally if you had turned into a gibbering wreck at the time, or latter, then again I would say quit, but you didn't. You did everything right and the job was done. The doubts are good, don't dwell on them, but don't forget them… you'll do!"

The Prime Minister approached, glass of mineral water in hand. "There you are Colonel, I've been looking for you. I must admit I am surprised to see you two cosying up."

"Do me a favour Sir," said Paul, "Have a word with her boss, and warn him she is about to do something stupid; she is intending to quit because she shot a mad man with an AK47. She did everything absolutely right."

"How do you know Colonel, you sound so certain."

"I am certain, I was watching. One day you might become privy to some more of our secrets. For now, just accept things as they are. You will do me this little favour Sir?"

"I take it you are now of the opinion the ADC can do her job?"

"Just about Sir. She's forgotten one little point, you might like to mention this to the Commissioner as well Sir. She ensured all her teams received counselling after involvement in fatal incidents, but omitted to go herself!"

"Colonel!"

"Leave it with me Colonel. You have my word, I will speak to the Commissioner. We need people who lead from the front," replied the PM.

"If you are not at the head of your team, the only thing you can lead is a retreat Sir."

After a moments thought the PM laughed. "Oh yes Colonel, very good, very good indeed." The man paused as though trying to remember why he had been looking for Paul in the first place. "Were you aware, Sir Jonathon committed suicide this afternoon?"

"No Sir, I was not."

"This in itself has created a new problem; his family are demanding a full judicial review and have engaged two top barristers to represent them. The claim is he was unfairly dismissed and I acted unlawfully in sacking him."

"The only complaint anyone could justify is, you should have done it at least a year ago. Tell you what Sir. When I get home I'll draft a statement outlining how he misappropriated funds, how many soldiers have died as a result, and a copy of the tape of his, now infamous, comment, 'Well they are only soldiers'. If that won't shut them up, I'll send the same stuff to every media outlet I can think of, and no judge's order will stop it."

"I would be grateful if you could send me such a document Colonel, it could be very useful."

"Well it will cover your arse Sir, just as the media will cover mine. Of course it will be put down to yet another, 'Whitehall leak'."

"You are an extremely devious man."

"Thanks for the heads up on that Sir, and don't forget having a word with 'frilly britches' boss."

"What did you just call me!? How dare you? There are serious consequences for making such blatantly sexist remarks!"

Paul burst out laughing, "That's more like it, still going to quit?"

"You did that on purpose, the PM was right you are devious. Worse....positively under hand!"

"Absolutely, you have proved you can do the job, and no matter what they say in there tonight, this is not over by a very long chalk. I fear a great deal worse is to come. The worst thing right now would be to have someone in your job who might, or might not, be up to the task - you see my point?"

"I do indeed. What comes next, another wave of attacks?"

"Oh there will be more of the same, no doubt. I think they are planning something so huge we haven't cottoned on to it yet. I have an idea what, but can't figure out how and I have no idea when."

"What do you think this big attack will be, crashing hi-jacked planes?"

"Don't you breath a word of this to anyone, and I mean anyone, alright?"

"I promise."

"If it was me attacking, I would go for the water supply and I have to admit, what little we have, suggests this is a likely scenario, however, they tried in this last wave of attacks and failed. This, of course, does not mean they won't try again, which ties up resources to ensure we stop them next time. The bottom line is, I believe this is exactly their tactic, tie up most, or as many of our limited assets as is possible. The idea being we won't see the 'big one' coming, as to what it could be? I have a few flimsy pointers which make me think it could have something to do with chemical weapons. Forget suicide bombers, car bombs and the likes. This is much bigger… the aim is to knock Britain out of the fight against these nutters. They are after the Yanks, but they fear us much more. Bin Liner, that's Osama bin Laden to you, has ordered his militant crackpots to 'rip the heart out of the Great Satan's guard dog', that's us. To do it, his forces have been told to 'wipe out London'. Note 'wipe out', not destroy … the problem is how?"

"I find the entire hypothesis terrifying. How sure are you?"

"I'm certain the old bastard is up to something. I am however, having a little difficulty in discovering exactly what."

Paul lit another cigarette. "The point is, we must keep up the raids, and this means your teams. I will provide an assault squad and a liaison team, so they can tell your lads exactly what they will encounter. I can't tell you how we get the information, all I'm asking is that you trust it. If it is going to be a hard target, that is where the suspects are armed for certain or alerted, then my team leads."

"I can live with that Colonel. I can foresee problems with the legal system, but I suppose it will send a strong message to the terrorists. I presume any illegals we sweep up in these raids will simply find themselves on the next flight home?"

"Unless there is a good reason to keep them, I can't see the problem. At the end of the day, a lot of so called human rights cases are nothing more than money grabbing exercises on the part of greedy lawyers."

"My my, we are getting cynical in our old age Colonel," replied the senior police woman. "Mind you, I'm not saying you are wrong," she added, almost as an afterthought.

"Come on, we'd better be getting back inside, or tongues will start wagging... you know what this lot are like."

"Really Colonel, I think my husband might have something to say about it!"

"You haven't met my missus. I KNOW she would have something to say."

As they approached the 'back door' of number ten, an aide came rushing out. "Ah Colonel, Ma'am, I have just been sent by the Prime Minister to find you. The meeting is about to reconvene."

"What did I tell you Ma'am?"

Once back in the meeting, Paul was called to give what the Minister called, 'an overview'.

He began with the casualty lists. "These figures refer to all terrorist activities starting with the suicide bomber blowing up the petrol tanker on the North Circular, prior to my recall, and are, as far as I know, currently accurate. The total civilian death toll is two thousand and ninety one. This is likely to rise as bodies are still being discovered in the wreckage of the train crash north of Watford. There are also about twenty of the injured whose survival chances are not good.

The total of civilians whose injuries required hospital treatment is in excess of two thousand.

The police have lost twenty four dead, and a further thirty five are currently off duty and receiving treatment. Military casualties are five dead and a further twenty or so injured, to the extent they are currently unavailable for duty."

"Have you the figures for the terrorists Colonel?" asked a junior Home Office Minister.

"I have. Two hundred and four known dead, this includes suicide bombers. Four hundred and two captured, of these fifty one are injured, and a further sixty two have been deported to countries with outstanding warrants or, in some cases repatriated, if they were here illegally and we caught them before they actually injured anyone."

"I understand you took it upon yourself to deport one well known human rights lawyer Colonel, would you care to explain?" asked the same minister.

"Certainly Sir. She was here illegally. There was an existing deportation order against her; we had a plane leaving for her homeland with four others on board. Exit one royal pain in the backside."

"You cannot act in such a manner Colonel."

"Even the Court of Appeal turned her down. Where is the problem!?" It was this sort of thing which really annoyed Paul. "It may have escaped your notice there is, by any definition, a war going on out there. The lawyer you are referring to was totally dedicated to helping the terrorists, end of story."

"I must admit, your unit have got a grip of these terrorists very quickly Colonel, but I think you need to exercise a degree of caution from now on," observed another junior minister.

"For a start. My unit has done little more than co-ordinate the efforts of others, and if you think the current lull in attacks signifies any sort of victory, then I am afraid you are in for a very rude awakening Sir."

"So you believe we will suffer more attacks?"

"Without a doubt. We will attempt to contain or pre-empt as many as possible, to this end the police will continue to raid suspect addresses, supported by elements of the 'All Arms Unit'. At the very least, this will keep them off balance and looking over their shoulder all the time. This will enable my lot to devote the bulk of our efforts into working out the meaning of Bin Liners' edict, to 'wipe out' London and hopefully prevent the attack."

"You don't take this threat seriously, do you Colonel? Surely, as bad as the recent spate of attacks have been, they have exposed the limitations of the terrorists."

"It was more a case of defining our limitations. We calculate they used barely fifteen per cent of their people, it was us running out of suitable man power. Now I'll grant you, our bit of luck yesterday finding what is, undoubtedly, a major arms dump, maybe their principle cache, will have hurt them but it will not stop them. Their leadership may be in disarray, some of them dead but they will regroup, and quickly. We must take full advantage of the pause forced on them by keeping up the pressure. Your focus should be to get everything back to normal as quickly as is humanly possible."

"You know as well as anyone Colonel, many of the sites will take months of detailed forensic work before reconstruction can begin."

"My point exactly Sir. As most of those responsible have been captured or are already dead, most of the effort will be a waste of time. We can liaise with the police and CPS, it will soon become clear which sites, if any, need work. If the gang responsible for say, blowing up a train, are all dead then why bother? Get the line reopened without delay; the more disruption caused, the greater the victory we hand to the bastards. Put maximum effort into reducing the disruption to an absolute minimum."

"Quite extraordinary Colonel. I'm not sure the law will allow us to do as you suggest."

"Then change it! I thought this was what you lot get paid for! Anyway, I've said all I have to say, with your permission Prime Minister I had better be getting home, there is much left to do, and sitting around here repeating myself is not getting the job done."

"Very well Colonel, if you feel you must go, I will not detain you any longer and thank you for attending."

"One thing before I go Sir. Have you got contingency plans for the evacuation of London? Obviously I know about getting the VIPs out in a hurry, but what about a mass evacuation?" asked Paul.

"To be honest, I have no idea Colonel," replied a puzzled Prime Minister. "Do you think it could become necessary, and if so how much warning would we have?"

"In answer to your first question, possibly and the second one, I don't know, but not much seems a reasonable guess."

"I presume from your tone you are taking the threat from Osama Bin Laden seriously Colonel," said the Minister of Defence.

"I think it would be folly to do otherwise."

"The general feeling around Whitehall is it is an empty threat. How could he possibly destroy London? It is utterly impossible, don't waste your time on it Colonel."

"You see the problem? I agree with you, it is impossible for him or anyone else, to destroy London. That was not the threat… the threat was to wipe it out. Now this is far from impossible. We know someone was messing about with large quantities of deadly chemicals in Somalia quite recently. We do not know who or where those chemicals are now and this worries me, a lot! Like I said, we do not know who it was but, what if it was Sammy Bin Liner's lot? Our calculations suggest there were more than enough chemical agents present to wipe out London several times over. If it is Al Qaeda, then how are they planning to carry out the attack?

The truth is we have no idea, and it may not be Al Qaeda who have the chemicals. I believe we should take the threat seriously until we at least discover what has happened to those chemicals."

"It is such talk which sparks panic Colonel, the country would be ungovernable. We would have to put the army on the streets to keep order."

"Just where would you find the troops Sir? I'll remind you, it is taking every fit man available to track down and contain the terrorists responsible for the current attacks. Don't forget many are guarding vital installations. Where will you get the troops to handle your 'panic'?"

"So it is possible Colonel, but is it likely?" asked the Prime Minister.

"All I am saying is, plan for the possibility."

"Have you any idea of the population of Greater London Colonel? What on earth do you do with so many people?"

"Get them out of the danger area, and provide them with the basics to stay alive until it is sorted."

CHAPTER SEVENTEEN

The following morning Paul called a meeting of all the old hands, plus one or two of the new experts, such as the Major who had arrived as a Health and Safety Officer and turned out to be a chemical expert.

"Alright, settle down," he said calling the meeting to such order as was possible. "As many of you will already know, a threat was received a few weeks ago, to, and I quote, 'wipe out London'. This was sent via Al Jeerzera, and allegedly originated from Sammy Bin Liner. It is our task to evaluate this threat. Is it genuine, can it be done and if so how? More to the point, can we stop it?"

"I suppose you want the answers by dinner time Paul?" asked General Leach.

"If possible Boss," replied Paul.

"Assuming the message was sent by old Sammy, then how did he do it? We know everything he says. I'm certain every means of communication he has is monitored, and we know everything one of his minions types into his computer. Radio, telephones, even texts and e-mails are intercepted. If he had used a dictaphone or taped it, we would have heard."

"One of you, get onto our contact at Al Jeerzera and find out what format the message was received in. Kenny...." Paul spoke to a wiry, tough looking man in a wheelchair... "Get the best team you can put together, and look back over all the stuff we have on intercepts from Sammy. Maybe around the time we think the place in Somalia was being used. Helga's team can help you with that."

"Should keep us out of trouble for a bit. How many bodies can I have?"

"As long as you leave enough to cope with the 'on goings', as many as you think you need."

"Buck passer."

"Al, you get your electronics gang to check everything you can think of, relating to this warning. Is there any way we could have missed a signal or been blocked. Again we are interested in serviceability records from about six months ago."

"I get all the fun jobs!"

"Sorry mate, but it has to be done, we must have missed something. We knew about the ship full of explosives and didn't believe it. We even had

The Day The Ravens Died

some warnings of the current bout of carnage. Somewhere in all the intercepts there has to be something about this. I don't care how clever he thinks he is, you cannot deal with something as complex as this without communicating in some way!"

"I'll go and have another word with our American guest. The medics say he's well on the mend. He might have overheard something."

"Good idea Taff, give him my regards."

"All this is based on the supposition, the site in Somalia has something to do with Bin Laden; have you anything to support this theory Paul?" General Leach asked.

"Only some doubtful intel., which suggests some of those guarding the place were from Al Qaeda. I know it's thin Boss, but it's all we have right now.

I was going to ask Keith if we could sustain a Canberra to over fly the area long enough to do a survey of the wheel tracks in the area, maybe the new ground radar gismo could pick up the tracks of the trucks. I suppose there is a faint chance if several went off in the same direction we might be able to follow them and at least get an idea where they headed off to, but I suppose I had better let Seb handle it."

"You are hoping."

"I'd call it clutching at straws myself Boss," replied Paul. "I suppose another way we could tackle this problem, is to put ourselves in Sammy's place and ask the question as to how to get several tons of chemicals from the Sahara desert and spread them over as much of London as possible."

"Correct me if I'm wrong, but didn't our team recover equipment which suggested chemical weapons were being fitted on missiles?" asked a voice from the back of the room.

"Yes but where is he, or anyone else, going to get an ICBM to hit London with it?" asked General Leach.

"I was thinking more of a scud Boss."

"Which would have a range of not much over a hundred miles Paul. It takes a bit of time to set one up and launch it; there is too much risk of being discovered. He must have figured out we are using our reconnaissance aircraft to spot his teams operating in the UK. It therefore follows we'll spot a scud if they try to launch one over here."

"Damned if I know. They can't use light aircraft or they'll be picked up by radar. Car bombs and the like would cause panic but the area would be limited. Such bits and pieces we did find suggested arming scuds with chemical war heads. He's thought of a way of getting them in range, I'm sure of it, but how?"

"Alright Paul, but where would Bin Laden get scuds from?" asked General Leach.

"What about the ones on the ship the Yanks intercepted. For all I know he might even own the ship."

"Where is the ship now, do we know?"

"I thought you knew Sir. We're still unloading the explosives from it in King's Lynn docks. It is the same ship we rescued Major Alexander from."

"How did I miss that?" replied the General. "It does put a different light on things. Do we know if it actually unloaded in the Yemen? I believe it was its official destination."

"The C.I.A. will know. There is another link to Sammy... his family are Yemeni, I think they moved to Saudi around the time he was born."

"So if you are right about all of this, then he could have all of the missiles which were on the ship?"

"Now I am worried. From memory, there were forty eight short scuds and sixty silk worms; this is not good Boss, not good at all. Both of those missile types can carry a warhead of nearly a ton for the best part of a hundred miles. As an alternative, you can fit a chemical warhead of half a ton, as well as a spreader unit."

"As I recall...the scuds on the ship were made in China and shipped from North Korea. I remember seeing the report on them. It said they had no warheads and were old models, almost certainly decommissioned from the Chinese Military. They were Mark Ones, with many similarities to the V2.... in as much as it takes a little while to prepare the launch site to get any degree of accuracy, and you cannot fuel them until they are mounted vertically on the launcher. Now how on earth can he get them within a hundred miles of London and go through all the rigmarole of launching them, without being noticed?"

"I suppose the same thing applies to the silk worms. You need a ramp of some sort to launch them; they are lumbering great things like an over weight Cruise Missile. The damnedest thing is, with all these circumstantial bits and pieces, the only thing we can prove is someone was messing about with a lot of nasty stuff in an old UN depot in Somalia.

We have a load of photos courtesy of the CIA, we'll give them a closer look. The only traffic on the pictures was some UN tankers used for bulk cooking oil, and some containers with UN markings. I'll get our analysts to take a closer look. We've missed something, I'm certain of it, and on past performances it is staring us in the face."

"Of course, your original guess of it being Hezbullah targeting Israel could still be right Paul."

"I bloody well hope not Boss. I've got a lot of admiration for the Israeli armed forces, but a lot of their leaders tend to go totally O.T.T. when it comes to retaliation."

"Alright, let's lay it out. What exactly have we got? Bin Laden has threatened to 'wipe out' London, as opposed to destroying it. From this, you concluded it would have to be a chemical attack. You have found a site in Somalia which had definitely been used to process chemical weapons. The people using the site are unknown. Also found at the site were materials, suggesting the weapons being fitted with the chemicals were missiles. The glass spheres and a broken spreader unit, made in North Korea, support this theory. You think, although there is no proof, these missiles may have been from the same shipment intercepted, and subsequently released by the Americans during the invasion of Iraq several years ago, because they seemed to belong to the Yemen, and we know Bin Laden has strong links with the Yemen. The same grubby little unregistered Coaster then turns up crewed by Bin Laden's pirates and carrying several hundred tons of explosives, on the most improbable attack I can recall. One which experts say would, in all probability, have worked had they sunk their charge in just the right spot. We had intelligence on this attack, just as we had some on the current spate of attacks aimed, if Bin Laden is to be believed, at bringing us to our knees.

Yet there is nothing in the intercepts about this, other than his broadcast warning that he would wipe out London. If I understand you correctly Paul, in your opinion, the current attacks were little more than diversions, launched to gauge our responses. Maybe even an attempt by Bin Laden to learn more about us, to enable his attacks to be more effective in the future."

"That about sums it up Boss," replied Paul.

"You are of course totally mad!" observed General Leach, "But then I must be just as mad, because I think you could at least be on the right track. As you rightly pointed out, there are only two ways capable of getting the coverage to do what he is threatening. Aircraft, which would in all probability be shot down, and missiles. The only trouble is, we haven't worked out how he could get them in range!"

"Yet!"

"As you say, yet," added the General. "So what now? Bring home some of the recons from the Middle East?"

"I don't see how it would help much Boss. We have more than enough to give us detailed coverage of the entire area they could launch from, plus another fifty miles in all directions. Four flights of four, they can stay on station for six hours without refuelling, it works nicely. We still have our flight of old RAF models for back up and odd jobs. If we stick any more up there, all we are doing is duplicating most of the data."

"So what will you do?"

"Bring the TSRs to readiness loaded with those new bombs, and the Tornados. Probably fit three with bombs, and three with as many missiles as we can hang on them, in case the attack is with Silkworms. Pair them up, one of each, they all have cannons and should catch a silkworm, even with a full bomb load. All three of our ships have been ordered to take up positions in the channel to form a missile screen. It will be nearly a week before *Kelly* and *Fearless* get home even at their speed, but it will have to do for now."

"Have they the ability to shoot down a scud?" asked General Leach.

"A new system they have fitted could, under certain conditions, take one out but it's at best a fifty-fifty chance. The best chance is with the Harriers off

Fearless and *Intrepid*. As things stand, they are the only things which can carry the new anti-missile system; we know it works on anti-aircraft missiles, whether or not it can deal with a Scud remains to be seen."

"So what you are saying is, the only sure way is to find them before they are launched. What would happen if the Americans could deploy Patriot batteries around London?"

"They might well hit some of them as they come in. All that will achieve is to spread the chemicals over a different area, and probably in a wider pattern than the spreaders. Our only real option is to find the damned things before they are launched. We are in desperate need of some solid intelligence Boss, it's all guess work at the moment."

"Well, you've been saying for years now, someone nicked Saddam's stockpile. According to a report I read yesterday, at least some of the stuff which had been at the site in Somalia came from the same source as samples analysed by the UN in Iraq."

"I know but we don't know who had it. We think we might know, which isn't the same thing. As to where the evil shit is at this moment, we have no idea, we have been trying to follow the tracks the trucks left, but this is proving almost impossible. We have got a couple of possibles, and the pictures the CIA sent us are helping; we are looking for tankers. I think it was Helga who noticed some of the more recent photographs showed a different sort of tank. She, or one of her team, picked up on the fact they were looking at de-mountable slurry tanks, rather than the thinner skinned, larger bulk liquid tanks used by the UN to transport cooking oil. I don't know why, but I think this is significant. For what it is worth, the only ones of this type seem to have headed off north west, the others generally headed off south west. I have no idea if this is significant, but there are no UN relief operations to the north west."

"Well good luck sorting all that out Paul."

CHAPTER EIGHTEEN

The next few days were tedious in the extreme. Every picture sent by the CIA was examined in minute detail, trying to match any of the trucks in the pictures with tracks spotted on the films from the Canberras. Eventually a pattern began to emerge. Five trucks matched tracks which seemed to be heading off into the heart of the Sahara; all five were of the 'slurry tank' type and all had, what appeared to be, a small refrigeration unit attached.

"Could someone work out an average bearing, and project it. We might be able to work out where they were going?"

Ten minutes later B.J. returned, "You are going to love this Boss," he chuckled.

"Don't choke on it, spit it out!" Paul was well used to being made to wait for interesting tip bits by the original members of the unit. "Let me guess, Libya?"

"Better than that Boss, it's headed straight for Wavell el Kabir."

"Bloody hell!" exclaimed Paul, "That name brings back some nasty memories."

"I thought you might remember it, right in the heart of the desert camps where all sorts of nasties used to train. If the operation there had played out any differently, it would have been the end of this unit before it had really started."

"Wouldn't it just?"

"What now?"

"Get the C.O. of the recon. unit in here. We'll have to send a plane along the route, see if we can learn anything useful. There must be a chance of finding a truck or two. Those things are not going to travel at any real speed in those conditions, and they are going to have to be some sort of drivers to even make the crossing at all."

The relatively young Group Captain who was in command of all the old Canberras arrived in the outer office, unsure of what was coming. For one reason or another he had never met Paul. He had taken some time to settle and adapt to this strange hybrid unit. When he had discovered he was to be in command of a group of aircraft of a type his father had flown, he had been quite upset and requested a transfer, twice. The absence of any reply suggested his plea had been ignored. It had taken him some time to realise

Timothy Pilgrim

that these old airframes carried within them what was certainly the most hi-tech package of sensors of any aircraft. He had been fascinated by technology all his life, and once the realisation of the capabilities of his new command had sunk in, the last thing he wanted was a move. Now 'the Boss' wanted to see him.

Paul's secretary merely commented... "The Colonel is expecting you." That was another thing he found difficult. There were, to his certain knowledge, at least one Brigadier, Taff, and the Senior Airman who out ranked Paul, yet they all did this man's bidding. He took a deep breath and knocked on the door.

"Come!" came the voice from within. Somehow the man behind the desk did not match the mental image he had fostered over the past few weeks. He had heard a lot about Paul, not least, tales of his ferocious temper. In his imagination he had pictured someone a bit larger than average size and probably very smart in appearance, as he was always meeting VIPs. It caught him a little off guard to see someone a little below average size, wiry and definitely needing a hair cut, if one went by Queen's regs. He wore no rank on his shirt and was actually smoking!

"I'll be with you in a minute. Get yourself a cuppa, the kettle is hot."

"Would you like one Sir?"

"I'm fine thanks, still got most of my last one left. Drop the Sir, my name is Paul and, if I've worked things out correctly, we must be pretty well equal as to rank... mind you. RAF ranks have always been a mystery to me."

A couple of minutes later Paul levered himself out of his chair and went to the spare table near the window. "I'd like you to have a look at this Sebastian." He rolled out a large map, using an ashtray at either end to prevent it rolling up again.

"What are we looking at Sir, I mean Paul?" he asked as he placed his coffee cup on a slightly curled corner of the map. "I can see it's North Africa, what can my planes do for you?"

"Starting here, the site we removed in Somalia. We have, by various means, plotted the supposed route of some of the trucks which left the site. Ground radar has, as you must be aware, picked up some traces of their passing. This solid line shows the route we think they took... the dotted line is the projected route. What I would like is the most complete coverage you can give us of this projected route."

"Surely it ends up in Libya. That could be a bit tricky. They have equipment which could detect us at anything less than maximum cruising altitude."

"I know, which is why I asked you in for a chat, apart from the fact we kept missing each other. What I need to know is... does this fancy gismo work at such a height? I know the cameras work fine, it's the scanners following the buried tyre tracks I don't know about."

"I think we can follow them Paul. If I use two planes flying parallel

The Day The Ravens Died

courses, about ten miles apart, and use a new computer program to combine the two images. We should be able to follow the tyre tracks much better. This will give us a stereo image and we will be able to see them much clearer than a single image from directly overhead."

"Do it," was Paul's simple reply.

"Just like that Paul, you're not going to ask permission?" asked the astonished airman.

"I wasn't planning to. You said it could be done; I took you at your word. If we find nothing then no-one else will ever know, no fuss. It is the very reason we use those planes, we can be nosey wherever we like and no-one, not even our friends across the pond, know what we are doing, unless we want them to…. which suits me fine and allows us to get our, often less than pleasant, job done."

"Now I know why things happen around here. A clear objective, you ask the relevant department head can it be done, depending on the answer you get. A clear order."

"If there is another way of getting things done I'd be interested to see it. Prattle around in endless committees, discussing every detail, and endless 'what ifs' gets people killed in this line of work. Our somewhat unorthodox methods apart, how are you settling in? I gather you were less than happy with your secondment when you first arrived."

"It was a bit of a shock at first, I'd worked so hard for this promotion. The first thing I see of my new command is an ancient aeroplane my father flew when he was a pilot officer in the RAF, before I was born. It is the same airframe according to its number. There is a photograph on my parents' wall of my father and his co-pilot standing beside the aircraft on their return from a flight over Russia, during which they set a new altitude record. It was all very secret of course, as is much of your work here. With your permission, may I take a photograph of the aircraft with the call sign 'eagle eye one', and send it to my father?"

"Depends on where he lives I suppose, but first of all I must correct you on one little point you got wrong. I presume you wish to remain here now you've a better idea how things work?"

"Of course I do Colonel, sorry Paul. I can't imagine anything more challenging or rewarding. I would even go as far to say, I would drop a rank to stay here doing this job, and I would certainly turn down a promotion to stay," replied the young airman. "Oh my Dad lives in Lincoln, he is a volunteer with the Battle of Britain memorial flight, I am puzzled as to what I got wrong?"

"You said, 'your work here', implying my work was secret, I think you meant 'our work'. One other thing…. you were not posted here because you had upset someone in high places, the unit asked for you."

"Why?"

"Because you are the best there is, and 'No' you may not send your father a photograph. As soon as those recons return from Libya, you can take it yourself. You haven't had a day off since you got here. Get your picture and get the current crew to sign it, the photo lab can find a frame for it."

"Thanks Paul, he'll love it. I'm glad we have met at last. I'll get those planes sorted out to get you your pictures."

"My door is always open Seb, no appointment required."

Late that afternoon most of the surviving old hands had gathered in Paul's office. It seemed as though the terrorists had finally got the message, they had attempted three attacks earlier in the day, all had failed.

The 'would be' suicide bomber had travelled into London from Slough and was shot dead as he got out of his friends' car. The man attempting to deliver a car bomb didn't even get out of his drive, as it was a residential area, a different solution was devised. The team dispatched to stop him were tipped off he was about to leave by the old plane orbiting far above. Thinking quickly and for ever the opportunists, they 'borrowed' a furniture van parked a few yards away and blocked the drive. The terrorist gave the driver some bull s..t story about having to get to hospital, "so would he move?" Two more of the team walked round the truck and arrested the shocked man, less than gently it has to be said. To compound the discomfort of the hapless individual, they made him watch as they disarmed the device, having cleared and sealed the street before removing the detonators.

The third team were intent on destroying a tanker on the M25 near the Heathrow flight path, just as the morning rush hour got going. They too were spotted by the 'eyes in the sky' and two teams were dispatched to stop them. Seeing the approaching cars they guessed they had been spotted and chose to fight. It turned out to be their last mistake. As the man raised the RPG to fire at the leading car, he was cut down by a brief burst from a Heckler and Koch MP5. His friends managed a few shots before they too were shot. The security forces did not escape totally unscathed as the leading car took several hits which wrecked the engine and wounded one soldier. Those in the police car following the soldiers were all fine, and their car only needed a new wind screen. Two of the police had fired more or less simultaneously, killing the last of the gang.

"How's the lad who got hit?" asked General Leach.

"From the reports, not too bad. He might recover well enough to rejoin his unit, if not we'll find him a job, assuming he wants one of course."

"So, have we got the measure of this lot Paul?"

"I doubt it Boss. We know so many of them from the intercepts, it will take weeks to round them all up. We are then saddled with the problem of what to do with them all. It's easy with the illegals, simply ship them home. Granted doing this upsets the 'human rights' groups, and it upsets the legal eagles even more, as they seem to think the entire thing is for their benefit, to enable them to further inflate their already bursting bank accounts."

"When did you become so cynical Paul?"

"When I started working for you Boss."

"Oh thank you very much," replied General Leach, "but I suppose I set myself up for such a reply."

"You did Boss," chuckled Paul. "Right you lot, I want some ideas. I stress, at the moment this is largely guess work but for the purposes of this meeting, we think London is about to come under attack from scuds, armed with chemical warheads. What are our options?"

"There is only one viable option Paul. Destroy the things before they are launched. We might be able to get some of them in the air, but that's as bad as them hitting, worse if an evacuation is attempted."

"So you are saying evacuate London?"

"Is there a choice Paul?"

"Assuming it proves feasible to do it. When do you do it, and where do you put all the people? There is also another problem. If we evacuate and the terrorists are, for whatever reason, not ready to launch, then why bother? They will know we know, if you see what I mean, and retarget the missiles and kill just as many, if not more."

"So, if we can't find them before they are launched, we're stuffed."

"Not quite the correct military terminology Brummie, but it just about sums it up," observed the elderly General.

"We have to rely on the recons Paul, I can't see any other way. Can we keep enough up to cover the area from which a scud could be launched? Come to that, have we enough operators to man the screens?"

"The answer to both questions is maybe."

"Is there any way we can narrow down the 'when' part of the equation? If we can, then we could save a lot of our resources until it mattered."

"A pair of Canberras are being dispatched to try to follow the wheel tracks. The hope is, they will lead us to the damned things, but personally I wouldn't hold my breath. Having said that, I suppose there is a good chance they will find something."

"Do you think old Daffie is behind this Paul?"

"I doubt it, in fact I'd just about take a bet he knows even less than we do."

"That would mean he knows nothing at all," replied Taff. "What happens if those planes turn up something, like a couple of scud transporters?"

"I can always rely on you to ask an awkward question Taff"

"Well, what would you do?"

"Right. We're not doing any good sitting around here chewing the fat. Just hang on for a tick while I call Seb to find out when those planes begin their run." After speaking to the officer in command of the recons, Paul replaced the phone. "You will be delighted to know, we meet in here at 0600hrs tomorrow." Having waited for the groans to subside he added, "I thought you would be pleased."

Although Taff had moaned the most about the early start, he was the first

… of the others to wander into Paul's office next morning. Noticing the extra large plasma screen installed over night, he couldn't resist making a comment. "Oh goodie, are we going to the pictures?"

"Pillock," retorted Paul. "The kettle's hot, help yourself."

"What have you got there, anything interesting?"

"I've been taking another look at the stuff the Yanks sent us. We couldn't see a pattern before, but I think there is something in them, get your cuppa and I'll try to explain."

Taff settled into the chair beside his long time friend. "What have you noticed, everyone else missed?"

"I'm not quite sure; there are a couple of oddities. Now, the 'big bird' which took these pictures comes round roughly every four hours. It is reasonable to assume the 'bad guys' know this. In most shots there is a trailer with a standard forty foot container, backed into the door way of the warehouse." Paul slid a picture in front of his friend, "and four hours later," sliding the next picture across the desk…. "The same container, you can read the number."

"We checked all of those numbers Paul. We know they are faked as we matched every one of them to genuine UN aid shipments."

"I know, spot the difference."

"There isn't one, it's the same trailer!"

"Yeah I know, look closer."

Taff stared at the two pictures for several minutes. "I'll be damned if I can see what you're on about…. hang on!" There was an air of triumph in his voice. "Got it, it's the same trailer alright, but it's been moved. Why?"

"Check the tyre marks on the two pictures."

"How did we miss that?"

"I don't know, but we did. Granted it's not exactly obvious, but every time I've managed to identify when a trailer has been moved there has been a fresh set of tracks heading off to the north west. The other thing is, if you look where the trucks leaving the site turn, you can see they are different to the ones with the containers. This is the clearest one I've found," he slid another picture to Taff.

"Even I can see it now. Wider tyres, and I'd say more of them. They are shifting them across the Sahara. They have plenty of guts, I'll give them their due. The timing must have been spot on as well, because we didn't see one on the pictures. This lot are bloody good Paul. I wish people would stop writing them off as a load of suicidal rag heads. The planning they must have put into this."

"Quite!" remarked Paul. "I do however have one more little titbit. Check this picture out, see anything out of place?"

"Not really, what am I looking for?"

"Try the extreme top left corner, right on the very edge."

"Is that a dust cloud?" asked Taff. "No doubt you've enlarged it and found a truck?"

"The back half of a trailer. White slurry tank, UN markings on a tri axel trailer, with twin wheels on each hub."

"He almost made it. A couple of seconds and he would have been out of the shot. So we know what we are looking for, it's a start."

"Check the date Taff."

"Oh bloody hell, this is nearly six weeks old."

"I've given the co-ordinates to the recons, to use it as a starting point."

"What are we hoping for Paul? Following the wheel marks in most, if not all of the area is going to be next to impossible, isn't it?"

"Maybe, but if we can spot just enough to get a general direction. There has to be a chance at least one of them has broken down. No doubt they allowed for this as well, but we might get lucky."

By nine o'clock everyone's eyes were beginning to ache, however, there were still four distinct sets of tracks visible on the screen. As it was a warm morning the windows were wide open. A flight of four Canberras had taken off over an hour ago and the four they had replaced 'on watch' over England had returned, all was now quiet, only the sound of the ever present sky larks drifted in through the windows. Then came the distinctive noise of an approaching helicopter.

"Who the hell is that?" asked Paul fearing a visit by self appointed VIPs. In the event it proved to be the Prime Minister and the Defence Secretary on their way to a meeting on a nearby RAF base. As they were early with nearly an hour to spare, they decided to 'drop in' for a chat.

"Oh no, not now!" muttered Paul. "He certainly knows how to pick his moments."

General Leach bravely volunteered to escort the visitors to the officers' mess, but the PM was having none of it. Eager as ever for an up to the minute report, he headed for Paul's office.

"Anyone would think you were trying to keep me away General," he said as he declined the General's offer to show the PM the refurbished canteen.

"There is a meeting going on in Paul's office at the moment Sir."

"Oh good, it will be interesting to sit in, to gain an insight as to how this unit functions."

The old soldier's heart sank. What would the PM say when he realised what they were doing; come to that, what would the Defence Secretary say, as he was unaware of a lot of the technology being used?

The new Defence Secretary had, up to now, never dealt with Paul except by way of several acrimonious phone calls, mostly over the removal of the civilian contractors and more recently, over the deployment of regular troops in the most recent wave of attacks. He had several points he wanted to raise with Paul. He was also a stickler for following the rules.... to say he was horrified to find at least four of those present smoking would be to understate matters. The fact that almost all of those present virtually ignored the new arrivals failed to impress the man, before the PM could stop him he went for Paul.

"Put that damned cigarette out at once! It is against the law to smoke in such an office, especially an MOD building."

"Will you shut up so my staff can concentrate on what they are doing!" was Paul's response. "This is my office, and if I want to smoke then I will bloody well smoke. As I am smoking, I can hardly refuse the others permission to smoke can I? And before I forget, this is not MOD property!"

"Let it go Geoff," the Prime Minister intervened. "What are we looking at here Colonel, as most of your senior staff are here, clearly this is of considerable importance?"

"It is all a bit vague at the moment Sir. You are of course aware of the site we destroyed in Somalia, and why we obliterated it. The theory is, the facility was being used to fit chemical warheads to scud missiles; we think we may have worked out how they are moving them. This is an attempt to follow the route they took. As you can see, the tracks they left behind are visible, at least intermittently, hopefully we should be able to find at least some of them."

"Where is that Colonel?" asked the Defence Secretary, "and who are 'they'?"

"That is the central Sahara Sir and we believe Al Qaeda is the 'they'. If we are right then the target is London."

"This all sounds extremely problematic Colonel. I presume it is Libya we are looking at. You cannot infringe on another state's air space as and when you please, on a whim such as this!"

"They won't know, and I for one won't tell them, will you?"

Before the shocked politician could reply, Helga suddenly jumped to her feet. "There Paul, see it, almost buried in the sand. It just has to be a truck."

"You've got bloody sharp eyes girl. I'm damned if I can see it." Paul turned to his computer terminal and locked onto the spot Helga indicated. After a couple of enhancements, watched by their visitors, he sat back.

"How the bloody hell did you spot it? On full enhancement there is only a tiny bit of, what might be, a. piece of a tanker showing. Alright I've got it, four sets of tracks leading up to the sand dune and only three come out the other side. Well done Helga!"

A phone on his desk buzzed urgently. It was the control room which was also monitoring the many sensors on the aircraft.

"We have detected a strong anomaly Boss. We are certain it is one of your tankers. It is the right size and, hang on a tick… Oh bloody hell, according to the 'sniffer' it's leaking VX."

"Thanks Sammy, keep me posted," he replaced the receiver. "Now this is what I call a problem. The truck is over a hundred miles into Libya, leaking a lethal chemical agent, and we really do need a look at it."

"I don't think it would be very wise trying the same thing you did in Somalia Colonel," said the Secretary for Defence.

"For once I actually agree with you."

"What will you do Colonel?" asked the Prime Minister.

The Day The Ravens Died

"Dear old Daffie is always trying to cosy up to the UN these days. He even claims to be a friend of the Yanks on a good day, all of which has given me an idea. Why don't I go to see him personally, with just an interpreter, and tell him what we've found in his patch of desert? I can explain the aircraft which found it was following the tracks left by the truck. With his permission I would like to fly in a team of UN weapons inspectors, assisted by a small team of my own specialists, to make it safe. These could land nearby in a Hercules transport, we could bring protective gear for some of his own troops, to assist in the recovery of the truck and its deadly cargo. If he is prepared to assist, we could then fly in our C17 and remove the entire problem. This would all be done under the auspices of the UN weapons control committee. Doing this would not only prove it was nothing to do with Libya, but would go a long way in establishing his new credibility in the eyes of the UN."

"What happens if he says no and decides to do it himself?"

"He'll have a hard job Sir. I didn't say I would tell him where it was and I doubt they will be able to find it. If they do, by chance, happen on to it or the sand blows away to uncover it, then anyone going near it will die, as their gear certainly won't keep that stuff out. The other point is, doing it without us and the UN will make it look as though he has something to hide. If he won't let us and the UN in, then we'll hit it the same as we did the site in Somalia and destroy the stuff, truck and all."

"I can see a problem with your idea Colonel," observed the Prime Minister. "If it becomes known that Libya assisted us in this operation, then they will become a target for the terrorists themselves."

"They are anyway Sir to some extent. What I was going to suggest was a cover story to the effect, the Libyans had found a huge stock pile of World War II ammunition and as it was in a dangerous condition requested our help in removing it from their territory."

"Will it work?"

"No idea Sir, the only way I can see is to try it."

In the event things went a great deal better than Paul had dared to hope for. The Libyan leader agreed to meet Paul with only their respective interpreters present. The only restriction was there was to be no American involvement in any way. In truth, this suited Paul as well as it suited the Libyans. If Paul would supply twenty sets of effective protective gear, he would supply some engineers to ensure the selected landing strip was clear of significant rocks. They could use one of the Libyan army diggers, which Paul offered to fly in, along with the Libyan soldiers, to assist in the recovery, and to tow the truck to the transport aircraft, as soon as it had been made safe by Paul's crew. As a final touch it was suggested bombing the site, then should Al Qaeda try to recover it themselves all they would find would be a sterile crater. As a further gesture of goodwill, Paul offered to leave behind the advanced NBC suites provided for the Libyan soldiers helping in the recovery operation. This would enable the Libyans to deal with any future incidents themselves.

This would suit the Libyans as, if word ever got out, it could be claimed an unknown aircraft had bombed the site. The final gesture was the icing on the cake.

"Why not have one of the spy planes which had found it, watch over the entire operation to warn of any approaching terrorists?"

To everyone's amazement the entire operation went like clockwork. Two hours after landing on the airstrip cleared by the teams and a small digger from the Hercules, the C17 belonging to the All Arms Unit was on its way home, carrying the scud in its slurry tank. Most of its warhead had been left behind along with the wrecked tractor unit. Now it was obvious what had happened to the truck, it had hit an anti tank mine. As far as anyone could tell, the only one left from a mine field laid by the Italians in 1941.

As the C17 climbed away with its deadly load, followed by the Hercules, another aircraft flew over the site, given the 'all clear' by 'eagle eye four' far above; the Vulcan's bomb doors opened and its load obliterated all traces of the truck.

The entire operation proved well worth while, tests proved the VX to be identical in composition to some found in Iraq by the weapons inspectors years before. A quick check with the CIA confirmed the scud as one of the shipment intercepted by the Americans on board the unregistered ship during the invasion of Iraq, the same ship still berthed in Kings Lynn docks. The tanker which carried the missile had been manufactured in the same factory as the exploding petrol tankers which had caused such devastation. Somehow Al Qaeda had even managed to get the manufacture subsidised by the EU to help get the factory started."

"Of all the bloody cheek," exclaimed Paul when it was confirmed about the subsidy. Checks on the records revealed another worrying fact - the tank recovered was number thirty out of a batch of forty eight. "Oh shit! does this mean these bastards have all forty eight scuds which were on the ship?"

"It's beginning to look like it Paul," replied Taff. "Let's just hope they haven't got the Silkworms as well, there were sixty of them."

"Do not go there! Don't even think it mate."

"If they have, then I'd say we are in the shit up to our necks."

The other down side was they were only able to follow the other tracks for about another hundred miles, this took the trucks to an area with metalled roads used by the oil industry. Despite using every sensor and scanner they had, there was no trace of the other missile carrying trucks, they had vanished.

"We haven't missed them Paul, they are simply not in the area we have searched," reported Sebastian as the last of the data was rechecked, just to make sure.

"They must be somewhere. We couldn't have been more than a few days behind the last one. As it seems fairly certain we are the target, they have got to get within a hundred miles of London, surely they haven't loaded them onto another ship? Check the sea lanes from the Med to the Channel and run a scanner over every ship headed this way. We absolutely have to find those bloody missiles." Try as they might, not a trace could be found.

"This is bloody daft," muttered Paul at the usual morning meeting. He turned to Sebastian, "You are absolutely certain we've checked every possible ship those things could have been loaded on?"

"Absolutely certain Paul. Every cargo ship big enough to carry even a single truck which has used a North African port in the past four weeks has been checked, any of them headed in this direction have been double checked."

"Fair enough Seb, so we haven't missed them, which means we've been looking in the wrong place. The question remains, where is the right place? We have been keeping a constant check on all ports and kept up a round the clock watch for anything which could possibly be linked to these infernal things, not a bloody sniff! About all we can say is, we are fairly sure the missiles are not in their launch sites, yet."

A head popped round the door, just thought you'd like to know Boss, the PM is on his way, should be here in about an hour."

"Oh cheers," groaned Paul. "I know we answer to him, but he is getting a bit too fond of 'popping in' for my liking."

"I should think he wants a word about all the speculation in the media Paul, it's all they ever ask him about. They cannot understand how we are able to intercept so many would be attackers on their way to their intended targets. Of course the Civil Liberties Brigade are going mad over the virtually instant repatriations of captured suspects. There is trouble brewing on that front Paul," warned General Leach.

"Why for heavens sake?" he replied to the General. "Every last one we've shipped back to their native country has been caught red handed, and it is only those here illegally we have repatriated, the rest are all awaiting court appearances."

"That's another thing, what do we say when we are asked how we got onto them in the first place? You've had trouble on this exact point several times already."

"It is a bit of a pain in the arse Boss."

"One which is likely to get a good deal worse. Your reaction yesterday to, 'how did you get the pictures of their client?' did not go down very well with the judge who signed the warrant for disclosure of evidence."

"I didn't lie Sir. All I said was, 'with a camera of course'. Dozy bewigged twit, how else did he think we got it, commissioned an artist to paint it?"

It was a surprisingly subdued Prime Minister who walked into Paul's office about an hour later. "Good morning Colonel, how are things?"

"We still can't find any trace of those damned scuds. I know a lot of places they are not, but I'll admit I'm fresh out of ideas where to look next. On the plus side, we seem to have put the current crop of nutters back into their box for the time being. Manpower is our biggest single problem, we can handle our part with what we've got, as long as we are careful how we do things. It's the rest of the armed forces who come up short; there simply aren't enough trained, combat ready troops to deal with a major attack. Overall the numbers are there but so many of them are only trained to defend themselves, and even that is pretty minimal. Cooks need to be in their kitchens, getting the next meal ready for the combat troops when they return, the signallers are all working double shifts as it is, everything depends on rapid response, this means getting detailed information to the units who have to act on it in time. I know most units are supposed to have the latest data link equipment, but there is only enough of it, if they are acting in company strength. This conflict, for this is a conflict make no mistake, requires units to act in section or even half section squads. As incredible as it might sound to you Sir we have, on several occasions, actually been forced to rely on mobile phones!"

"We do seem to have been found wanting in some departments Colonel, but all things considered I think our armed forces have done rather well in containing the current terrorist threat. Of course your unit is the factor which has made all the difference."

"Good of you to say so Sir, we do however have two major problems at the moment. The first we have already covered… the scuds. We know they are out there in the hands of terrorists and, we know what they are armed with; we do not know where they are, although all indications are they are well on their way here.

The other problem is what to do with the captured terrorists? Judging from reports in the media, I'm wrong if we ship them home, at least those here illegally. I'm wrong if we hold them in an army camp just down the road, the jails are all full without this lot. I'm wrong if one of them gets shot, it doesn't seem to matter the individual had a loaded gun in his hand at the time. To crown it all, we all get pilloried if one actually succeeds with an attack, all we get is 'why didn't you stop him Colonel?' this from the same reporter, who two breaths before was complaining soldiers had shot dead two gunmen actually firing on commuters and unarmed police, at the moment they themselves were shot!"

"I do see your point, this is one of the reasons I came to see you Colonel. Many members of the judiciary are calling for your head… in their opinion you are acting unlawfully in the way you are dealing with the current terrorist crisis. The media cannot understand how you can get onto a terrorist suspect so quickly, the words 'big brother' and 'Orwellian' crop up in most articles and reports. I have been avoiding repeated requests to appear on a particular current affairs question show - the advice I am given is, now would be a good time to accept. With this in mind I will ask you, would you be prepared to appear and answer security related questions?"

"I feel I must remind you Sir what happened the last time I was on that show, the edition screened from the conference on terrorism. If you recall I had more than a slight disagreement with the now former American Secretary of State. You know I will not say how we get our information, as you said, the bloodhounds of the press know damned well it is a good deal more than enhanced CCTV footage. I don't know if you saw an article in one of the papers yesterday, I forget which one, but the reporter was speculating how many predator spy planes we had bought off the Americans and how long it would be before there was a collision with an airliner. The feature cartoon in the same paper showed 'flocks' of UAVs swooping down and picking up supposed terrorists in their talons and carrying them home, if only it were so easy!"

"So you are willing to accompany me tonight?"

"If you say be there, I really haven't got much choice have I Sir?" replied Paul. "However I will make no promises to behave. If someone is being stupid, they are likely to be told so in no uncertain terms."

"Excellent," replied the Prime Minister. "I am looking forward to a lively debate tonight, you know where and when Colonel. I must go, keep up the good work. Until this evening then."

As soon as the door closed behind the Prime Minister, Paul muttered 'pratt' under his breath and returned to the stack of folders marked for his attention.

Taff wandered into Paul's office, "What did he want, another bloody miracle by lunch time?"

"Something like it. He wants me to return to the scene of my slanging match with the Yank six months ago."

"You didn't agree? You idiot." Taff clearly wasn't happy about it. "You know he only wants you there to keep the heat off him?"

"I had sort of figured that out for myself, before he asked me."

"Oh, so that makes everything all right I suppose? You are being set up Paul, by the media as much as by the 'spin doctors' of Whitehall. Everyone wants to find out how we get our information."

"I know Taff, this is precisely the reason I'm going, to put them on the spot. We are, by any definition, at war. Enemy prisoners are repatriated as soon as possible. All captives receive the very best medical attention, if it is required. Those captured who are entitled to be in the country, along with the 'home grown' pains in the arse, are well fed, in accordance with their religious fetishes. They have freedom of worship and, for the most part, freedom of association with other prisoners.

They are shown the evidence against them, and can then make up their minds what they want to do when they go to court. Come clean, plead guilty to whatever, or not. Apart from simply shooting them out of hand, I can't see what else we can do."

"I still say you should have refused." Taff made himself a cup of coffee then sat facing Paul. "I nearly forgot why I came to see you. I thought of something we didn't check in our search for those missing tankers."

"Go on. I'll bet it is something so bloody obvious it never occurred to anyone."

"More so than usual I'm afraid. We forgot there are ferries across the Med.!"

"I don't bloody well believe it, it never crossed my mind. Hang on though, the implication of that would be driving the damned things up through France. Surely the French would spot something! The tyres would be illegal in Europe for one thing. Okay. Chase up our French contacts, find out if anyone has seen the things, I still can't believe they would take such a risk."

"I'll get it checked out. You never know, we might get lucky." Taff paused at the door. "Good luck for this evening, and be bloody careful."

"Yes, mother," replied Paul with a grin.

CHAPTER NINETEEN

Paul took his seat next to the Prime Minister, who was in turn next to the presenter. On the opposite side was a reporter who had been very outspoken against the methods, he supposed, were being used. Next to him was one of the most outspoken 'Muslim community leaders', the final chair was occupied by the very human rights lawyer Paul had stuck on a plane headed to Pakistan a week or so before.

Paul turned to the PM, "What is she doing back here?"

"I have no idea Colonel, I am as surprised as you are?"

Paul placed his slim line lap-top on the desk in front of him. "We can soon find out Sir." The Prime Minister nodded his consent. Before Paul could push the button to switch it on, a very large security man rushed up behind him and made a grab for the laptop, the man should have been more careful. Paul reacted instinctively and the guard flew through the air with the elegance of a breeze block, crashing into the mounting of a camera as he came to a halt. Two of the man's colleagues approached Paul who was now on his feet. "What was that idiot trying to do?" he asked.

"His job Colonel, give me the laptop. You should not have been allowed in here with it in the first place."

"If you are his boss, then you should have trained him to ask first, then I could have told him what I will now tell you. Dream on! There is no way on this earth I will be parted from this computer. Apart from anything else, I will need it to illustrate some points I will no doubt have to make on this show, if it ever gets started."

"I don't care Colonel, give me the computer."

"As you clearly do not understand the English language, I will make it as clear as I can, NO!"

"Then I will have to insist you leave Colonel."

"That is just fine with me old son, it will mean I can get back to my base and do something useful, like catching some more of these nut cases before they murder any more of our wives and children."

There was still nearly ten minutes before the show was due to start, both the presenter and producer had panic attacks as they saw the ratings vanish, when people switching on realised the man who had the major row with the former American Secretary of State was not on the show.

The man from the security company was unshakeable. "My orders are quite clear, no electronic items are allowed on the sets, this includes mobile phones, computers and the likes, no exceptions."

"Who gave you that order son?" asked Paul.

"My boss."

"His name?"

"I don't actually know his name," replied the jobs worth, "but he says all such items are potential security risks."

"Is he the Director General of the BBC?"

"No."

"Then give him my compliments and tell him to get down here and take my seat, seeing as he is such a security expert, otherwise he can go forth and I was going to say multiply, but on reflection we have enough idiots around as it is."

The big security guard was being helped to his feet, still uncertain as to how he had ended up on the floor. His immediate boss had given up hope of separating Paul from his computer and went to help. As he passed Paul he said, "You will be sued for damages Colonel, a formal complaint of assault will be made to the police. Our company has a strict policy concerning attacks on staff."

"Feel free, all I did was react to an idiot trying to grab my computer, which incidentally contains some highly classified files. If you are worried about your man, take him for a brain scan. They might detect one, but I doubt it."

The program controller came on the intercom, "Could we clear the set please, two minutes to transmission."

As the presenter introduced the various members of the panel, Paul completed the search on his computer interrupted by the over zealous security guard; having acknowledged his introduction he turned the screen so the Prime Minister could see it.

The questions were fairly predictable. The replies from two of the people on the other side of the presenter even more so. Sure enough, within a couple of minutes the 'Civil Liberties' activist had brought up the matter of Paul's reaction to the security guard, as well as the perfunctory manner of her deportation a couple of weeks previously. She accused Paul of being a very violent man who was quite prepared to ignore the basic human rights of anyone he happened to disagree with; confident she had made her point she sat back. The 'mullah' supported her and demanded Paul be hauled up in the Court of International Justice in the Hague for 'war crimes'.

The presenter invited Paul to respond to these accusations.

"I'd be delighted to, thank you. As for me being a very violent man, I'm a soldier and on occasions it is necessary to employ violence. The 'mad mullah' accused me of war crimes, which to me is an admission, or at least an acceptance, we are at war with these absolute morons who think they have the right to run amok in this country, killing our wives and kiddies. I have news

The Day The Ravens Died

for him, no way! As the gentleman in question is in this country illegally, I can tell him, by this time tomorrow he will be reunited with all of his wives and children. Now to little miss knotty britches. Yes I put her on a plane which took her back to her native Pakistan, and I have every intention of repeating the process in the morning. She was here illegally before, the High Court said so; the Court of Appeal upheld the judgement, yet she remained here making a lot of fuss on behalf of cold blooded murderers. Never a peep about the victims. What about the human right to live in peace and go about your daily bits and pieces without the fear of some idiot blowing you into unrecognisable fragments."

The presenter was about to say something, but Paul asked him to wait a minute, then he continued.

"Our illustrious defender of the oppressed arrived back in the UK this morning. One thing puzzles me, immigration has no record of her arrival; she is not on the passenger manifest of the flight she says she arrived on. There are, as I see it, two possibilities - one she is lying about her real name or she came in on a forged passport, she does not appear to have a visa either. There are other grounds for throwing her out as she claims to be a lawyer; this is false and she certainly didn't put this down as her profession on the passport she entered the country on last time she came."

The woman responded furiously to this, just as Paul had expected. When she paused for breath he replied. "I rather thought you might react in such a manner, so I did a bit of checking up, and guess what? This morning I obtained the exact same 'law degree' you claim to have," he produced a piece of paper from a folder, "thirty seven quid off the internet!"

There followed several vitriolic outbursts from supporters of the Mullah and the civil rights activists - many alleging, use of extreme violence by troops, nominally under Paul's command.

"Let's get things in perspective. In the course of a couple of days last week these maniacs murdered more British citizens than the Lufftwaffe killed in the blitz on Coventry during the Second World War. No-one complained the fighter pilots who tried to shoot down the bombers, or the anti-aircraft crews had over reacted. This nation's military personnel, from which ever of the armed forces, have displayed every bit as much courage in the past couple of weeks defending the ordinary man in the street. It is every bit as dangerous raiding the home of an idiot armed with an AK47, as it is trying to take out a machine gun nest. More so in many ways, as not the least of the problems facing the troops is to avoid injuring innocent women and kids, who more often than not are totally unaware the head of the household is a murdering S.O.B. Make no mistake, this country is at war, a very different war I'll grant you; one in which, because of the nature of the attackers, the soldiers work in small groups rather than the companies of a conventional conflict. Do not think for one moment a couple of days with no attacks means this is over… it is not, not by a very long way."

"I would like, on behalf of the nation as a whole, to express my gratitude to the Colonel and all the security forces for their super human efforts of the last few weeks. I would also like to take this opportunity to express my personal condolences to all the families of the police and security forces who have made the ultimate sacrifice in this conflict."

"I'm sure we all agree with the Prime Minister's sentiments on those points," observed the presenter.

"I have a question for the Colonel," the reporter spoke for the first time. "Accepting for the moment all those who have been arrested, detained what ever, are in fact active members of this insurgency, could the Colonel give us any insight into how so many have been identified so quickly. I can't help but wonder if our cartoonist had got it about right, but then there is not a single verifiable report of a U.A.V, or for that matter of a spy plane flying around. Such images as have been released could not have come from even the most advanced satellite, yet you seem to have the ability to at least track a terrorist after he has launched his attack, indeed you seem to be increasingly able to intercept them before they strike."

"The greatest advantage any commander can have is in knowing what the other guy is going to do next - that or complete surprise. I take it we agree on this point?"

The reporter nodded, and added, "Yes."

"Well, normally the terrorist has the element of surprise on his side. As far as possible we have sought to devise techniques to rectify this. We are not totally successful as yet, but we are making progress, as you noted, we are able to intercept at least some of them on their way to a target now, as opposed to chasing them after they have struck."

"But you are not going to give any indication as to how you find them?" the reporter answered his own question. "Understandable I suppose, in the light of the fiasco following the Americans declaring to the world, how they allegedly found Osama bin Laden in Bora Bora."

"I am delighted you at least understand the implications of all of this."

"I would still dearly love to know how, there is no technology I am aware of, which could give you the information you clearly have on these people. I know you have had some substantial finds of arms and explosives, could you give us an indication of the scale of these seizures Colonel?"

"Give me a moment and I can illustrate the scale of the threat posed by this lot." Paul worked on his computer for a few moments. Pointing the projector lens he uncovered at a bare piece of wall, he pushed a couple more keys. The picture showed one of the deep ammunition bunkers on the Unit's base. "All the weapons and explosives you will see in this short film are a result of home based seizures, there are upwards of thirty tons of weapons and ammunition. I am not absolutely certain of the tonnage of explosives but it is in the hundreds of tons, none of it home made."

"Bloody hell!"

The Day The Ravens Died

"Quite."

"You seem to think there is more?" asked the shocked reporter.

"Oh yes, a great deal more."

"I still do not see how you compare this with an invasion Colonel," said the presenter. "I'll grant you the numbers are beginning to stack up, but an invasion seems a bit dramatic."

Paul replied, "Just suppose for argument's sake there was a renegade bishop in the Vatican and he dispatched an armed force to attempt to overthrow our current establishment. For argument's sake, we will say this force consisted of several hundred, well equipped paratroops who were dropped in to the country all over the place in small independent groups. How would you describe such an attack? And what would you do about it?"

"It's not very likely, is it Colonel? In fact I think it is rather ridiculous to suggest such a scenario."

"Fair enough, but if you substitute a renegade Muslim leader for a renegade bishop, and the batty bishop's paratroopers for the current crop of homicidal maniacs running amok, then I think the comparison is a good one. The paratroopers would be here illegally, just as the bulk of the terrorists we have caught so far have not entered the country through normal channels."

"I do see the Colonel's point," it was the reporter who came to Paul's defence. "I can see the analogy. Alright, the religious base is different, and no-one is suggesting the paratroops would be citizens of the Vatican, I'd never thought of it in those terms, but it does make it easier to understand what is going on. Can you beat them Colonel?"

"In purely military terms… probably. But you know as well as I do, we have got to destroy the ideology and I'm not sure that can be done."

"Do you support the current wars in Iraq and Afghanistan Colonel?"

"That is a question with no straight forward answer. Saddam had to go, along with his power base. This is purely a personal opinion you must understand; in both cases I think there is too much stick and not enough carrot. As I said last time I was in this chair, there has, on occasions, been an over reliance on air strikes - a single bomb going astray can undo months of good work by the troops on the ground. The golden rule fighting any counter insurgency war is - you must get the bulk of the people on your side because they want to be on your side; this will not happen if your troops kill women and kids. It doesn't matter how accidental it may have been. You must always use minimum fire power not maximum in such conflicts. Unfortunately, in my opinion, the damage already done could take a generation to undo."

"So there is no end in sight regarding Al Qaeda attacks?"

"The short answer is I'm afraid, no."

"What would happen if the Americans succeed in hunting down Bin Laden? Surely with him gone it would spell the end of spectacular attacks?"

"I doubt it," replied Paul.

The journalist joined in again. "Won't the killing of so many leaders of supposed terrorist groups in Iran a few weeks ago, cause an upsurge in attacks?"

"Possibly, in the short term. You must remember one difference between them and dear old Sammy Bin Liner - they were feared, he is revered. Kill him and you create a martyr and there have been far too many of them already. To defeat him you must make him lose 'face', in the eyes of his followers. To do this you must ensure his plans are discredited - not easy, but it has to be done, it is the only way."

"Do you know where he is Colonel?"

"I have my ideas.... the same as every other commander of the forces ranged against him and his network have theirs. Why do you ask?"

The journalist was sure his guess was right. "So that is how you are so successful Colonel; you not only know where he is, but you have bugged his home. Brilliant.... absolutely brilliant!"

"If only," replied Paul as casually as he could manage.

The discussion changed to relations with the Americans, 'how strained were they?'

Other questions revolved around Britain's capacity to deal with the economic problems caused by the terrorist attacks and what would happen if Paul's predictions of worse to come were true?

"My sources indicate civil servants have been given the task of planning an emergency evacuation of London. Maybe the Prime Minister would like to comment on this; is it true and under what circumstances would it be implemented?"

"As our esteemed member of the press is well aware, it is any government's prime responsibility to protect the citizens of this country; it is therefore normal to have contingency plans for any foreseeable situation. Indeed, it would be totally irresponsible not to have such a plan in place."

"What would trigger the plan Prime Minister?"

"If there was to be a tidal surge which would clearly, seriously breach the flood defences, then the order to evacuate the areas most at risk would be given, as far in advance of flooding as was possible."

"Could this have had anything to do with the seizure of a ship load of explosives by members of the Colonel's unit? As I understand it, the plan was to detonate the explosives to trigger an underwater landslide to send a tsunami down the North Sea, which would have destroyed coastal communities and ultimately, inundated London?"

"How utterly ridiculous," retorted the Prime Minister.

"My research suggests it would be possible Prime Minister. Such a charge would have to be positioned very accurately, but with GPS it would not be impossible. Maybe the Colonel would like to comment?"

"It is true members of the unit which I command, boarded a ship and released someone held captive by a group claiming to be Al Qaeda. It is also true there was a considerable amount of explosives on board. As to the intended target, this would be pure speculation on my part. I will however agree, it is theoretically possible to do what you suggested."

"What form of attack are you expecting Colonel?" the journalist continued. "Is there any possibility of a major chemical attack on Britain in general and London in particular?"

"You can never rule anything out, but quite how they could mount a major, widespread attack defeats me. Maybe your 'sources' know?"

"So you will not deny it is a possibility?"

"A 'dirty' or chemical device is one scenario the emergency services train for, of course we hope it never happens, but you can never say never in this job."

In the end, the program rather lost its way after the dramatic start had sidelined two of the guests, never mind the ruck with the security guard before the program began.

Paul's parting comment more or less summed it up, "I suppose I had better prepare a statement for tomorrow after the papers are full of miss-quotes and statements taken out of context."

The Prime Minister, after the show, congratulated one of his aides for the idea of getting Paul on the show. It was just as the 'spin doctor' had predicted, such adverse comments which were made were, for the most part, directed at Paul, giving the Prime Minister an easy ride.

CHAPTER TWENTY

The following morning there was a meeting in Paul's office - most heads of the diverse sections which made up the All Arms Unit were there. A still recovering General Leach kept a fatherly eye on his 'flock'. There was one topic on the agenda. "Where the hell could the slurry tanks with the scuds inside have gone?" asked Paul.

His question was greeted with silence. "Hasn't anyone got any ideas? Damn it they can't simply vanish!"

It was Sebastian, the young officer in command of the reconnaissance squadrons who replied. "Our planes have scoured every inch of every country from the Egyptian border to the Moroccan Atlantic coast. I'll grant you we found some things we were not supposed to find, but I am certain we did not miss them. Those missiles are no longer in North Africa; equally, I am certain they are not on a ship from any possible port which is headed our way."

"Which leaves us with the improbable theory they came over to Europe on a ferry, to be driven over land to get them in range of London? But there is a serious flaw in this theory. We have checked every harbour capable of handling a truck from Portugal to Italy; none of them have seen anything which could have been the missiles. Well, apart from one in Gibraltar. A tanker brought over with cleaning fluid for the bilges of a ship under repair. This tanker has already returned to its factory in Morocco full of sludge for recycling."

"We must have overlooked something," muttered General Leach. "I refuse to believe the people behind this are smarter than you lot."

"Thanks for the vote of confidence, but if that was based on our achievements to date, I'd say it was rather misplaced Boss. Everything we have found out so far has had more than an element of luck attached to it."

"The General is right Paul, we simply have not figured out what their plan is yet."

"We know, or think we know, they are planning to attack London with scuds carrying chemical warheads. Tests on the one we recovered from Libya virtually prove it. The configuration of the missile also tells us it will have had a maximum range of about one hundred miles."

"If one gets within one hundred and thirty miles of London, the Canberras will pick it up Paul, day or night, cloudy or clear, they will spot them."

"I don't doubt you Seb, but I will still feel happier once we have located the bloody things."

For the umpteenth time they began checking the masses of photographs stacked on Paul's table. Each of them had a picture of a tanker in front of them for instant comparison, should anyone spot a possible vehicle. There was a knock on the door. Paul called out "enter" without really looking up to see who it was. When he did look up there was a stranger standing in the door way, obviously a soldier.

"And you are?" Paul asked the new arrival.

"Captain Martin Townsend Sir, reporting for duty."

Paul looked a bit puzzled, "From?"

"Hereford Sir. I'm not due here for another week really but I feel well enough, and I heard about what has been going on so I took it upon myself to come early Sir."

"Ah yes, now I remember. You got clobbered by a suicide bomber in Kurdistan a few months back, and your Boss thought it might be a good idea to do a bit of time with us to give you a longer time to recover. Come in, help yourself to a drink and pull up a pew. I presume you know General Leach, I'll introduce the rest of the motley crew once you've got a cuppa."

"Thank you Sir, I'll have a coffee if it's alright."

"'Cause it's alright, and for heavens sake drop the 'Sir', I hate it. My name is Paul and it will do fine thank you."

Clearly General Leach knew the latest addition to the unit. "I thought you were staying at your parents place in the Pyrenees to recuperate, how are they? I haven't seen them for a couple of years."

"Enjoying life Sir. Father said I was to ask when you and Lady Leach were planning on taking up the invitation?"

"I really must give Bob a ring this evening."

The young man winced as he pulled up a chair, clearly he wasn't as fit as he pretended to be. Paul watched as he sat down rather gingerly.

"Are you sure you're alright Marty?" asked Paul sounding concerned,

"It's been a bit of a long journey, but I'll be alright Boss."

"How did you get here? Surely you haven't driven in your state?"

"I drove up to Cherbourg, caught the ferry to Southampton, then drove up here."

"Mad bugger! You could have spent another two weeks in the mountains, more if you wanted it, still, welcome on board. I have to say, this is not the unit's finest hour, we have reached a bit of an impasse. We have lost forty or so scuds, well not so much lost as we can't find the bloody things! We found one buried in a sand dune in the Sahara, in the middle of a World War II mine field, just to make it interesting. We think they are being transported in demountable tanks like this one."

Paul showed him a picture of the one they dug out of the desert, still in its UN livery.

"There were a couple of them parked on the docks in Cherbourg, painted drab green but otherwise identical."

Paul shot an enquiring glance round the table, as the Captain clearly had more to say,

"Would I be correct in assuming you believe Al Qaeda are behind what ever all this is about?"

"That is the theory, why?"

"Well I didn't feel too good when I boarded the ferry, so I went up on deck for a bit. As we sailed, I saw something a bit strange. There was a huge bulk carrier at the fuelling jetty, flying a strange flag, one I didn't recognise. I could see right into her bridge as we passed, the guy I could see was wearing a Kaffiyeh."

"I'll grant you it's not often you see Arab sailors in this part of the globe, but why was this so odd?"

"The ship was named the '*Elat*'."

"Aah, I see your point." Paul turned, but Sebastian was already out of his seat headed towards the communications terminal the other side of the office.

The subconded air force officer called the control tower asking which call sign was currently nearest to Cherbourg. Wasting no time on formalities he called the crew of eagle eye five, one of the old ex RAF models. "What is your e.t.a. over Cherbourg?"

"We could begin scanning in about fifteen minutes, but if you want a proper look, we could have a problem getting home on the fuel we have on board."

"Do it," was Seb's short response. "The most detailed scans possible of the docks, use your 'sniffer' as well as penetrating radar. There are a couple of tankers sitting on the dock, we need to know what is in them. Don't worry about fuel. If a tanker can't reach you in time, I'll get you clearance to land on Jersey, even if you are dead stick, the strip there is more than long enough."

"Oh good," came back the cheerful reply, "Can we have the rest of the week off Boss?"

"Just be careful! And safe landings, out"

"I see," observed the new arrival, "one skill I am clearly going to have to master quickly is telepathy!"

In the event, the old Canberra did two orbits of Cherbourg; its cameras quickly located the tanks and locked the other sensors on to their targets. It was twenty minutes before the decoded data stream appeared on Paul's screen. The results were pretty conclusive.

"Well gentlemen, and Helga. It seems as though we have found two more scuds. Let's just hope the French will give them to us, we could learn a great deal. I'm rather glad Martin decided to join us early. This is some joining present you have given us. Hereford's loss is our gain, bloody well done."

"Thanks Boss, it's good to feel useful again."

"How long ago was it you got blown up?"

"Nearly a year. The regiment want me back as an instructor, the M.O.D. medics are trying to discharge me."

"So you thought you'd join this gang of old crocks and misfits to stay in uniform?" asked General Leach.

"I wouldn't have put it quite like that Sir but when my old Boss suggested it, at least as an interim solution, well it seemed like a good idea."

Paul had been talking to Taff, they seemed to have decided on a plan of some kind. Paul turned to Helga. "I'm afraid I'm nicking Andy again, sorry but I need his skills with these bloody chemicals. Go and find him please. He has got half an hour to get his team together, full N.B.C. gear, and one of them needs to be a fluent French speaker. A helicopter will be available by the time he's ready."

Taff came over from the communication's terminal. "The navy are not very happy Paul, they were sort of relying on *Intrepid* as a helicopter platform She also has over one hundred Marines on board. She's leaving her helicopters and landing craft as well as her two hovercraft up on the Isle of Arran. All of the Marines can be landed in one lift. As soon as they are all clear she'll head south at her best speed."

A couple of minutes later the phone on Paul's desk rang. It was the Admiralty, complaining about the unannounced withdrawal of *Intrepid* from the long planned exercise. "I must insist you order her back on station Colonel, you cannot simply remove such a vital element from a task force on a whim!"

"It's hardly a whim Sir, we absolutely must have her for a vital job which cannot wait. For the purposes of your exercise mark her down as sunk, it will add a degree of realism to proceedings. If the exercise was for real, then there is every possibility of loosing a major unit, improvise!"

An hour or so later the commander of a destroyer, in charge of a small flotilla guarding the gap between the Isle of Man and the Mull of Kintyre, was confused to say the least by a radar report of a large ship closing fast from astern. He was almost flat out in one of the navy's newest, fastest destroyers, racing to assist a frigate which had picked up what appeared to be, a submarine trying to sneak into the exercise area. "What do you mean a large ship, closing fast from astern. I'll remind you Petty Officer we are arguably the fastest ship in the fleet!"

"Then the radar is up the creek Sir, the speed the contact is closing on us, she'll be in sight in a few minutes."

A lookout on the bridge was training powerful binoculars in the direction of the radar contact. The seaman was clearly heard to utter, "bloody hell," then regaining his composure, "ship approaching rapidly from directly astern Sir."

"Where?" asked the skipper.

"Straight up our wake sir, just coming over the horizon."

"What ship?"

Timothy Pilgrim

"Don't know Sir," replied the seaman, "all I can see at the moment is a huge bow wave Sir"

By now, the reports had the skipper's full attention; the only things certain were, it was big and very, very fast. Clearly it was coming out of the Clyde, as Kintyre was still just visible as a smudge on the horizon. "Close up action stations number one."

This only took a minute as the crew were near enough at this state any way, thanks to the exercise.

The shocked look out turned to the skipper, "Sir, it's the old *Intrepid*."

"Don't be bloody daft man, she was my first ship as a junior Sub Lieutenant, her best speed was barely twenty knots with a following wind!"

"It's either *Intrepid* or *Fearless* Sir. I don't know any other ships which have lopsided funnels and a twin four point five turret on her fore-deck. *Intrepid* was part of the exercise Sir, the Navy borrowed her back from the All Arms Unit Sir."

Those on deck watched in stark disbelief as the big ship sped past on their starboard side and rapidly pulled ahead of the grey hound of the seas.

"What speed are we doing Chiefie?" asked the skipper.

"A touch over thirty three knots Sir."

"I don't know what propulsion system they have on her now Sir, but according to sonar there are no propeller noises, just a constant hiss."

"Message from *Intrepid* Sir, 'sorry to have to leave your party with such indecent haste, have a nice day.' That's all Sir."

"Send, to *Intrepid*, 'don't get a ticket for speeding, I hope your brakes work, bon voyage'."

The skipper of the Royal Navy destroyer may have expressed a wish to have gone with his old ship; had he known her mission, one cannot help feeling he might not have been so eager.

The following morning much the same group met in Paul's office.

"Right," he began, "Update on the search for these damned scuds. The harbour master at Cherbourg has been very helpful, it seems as though at least sixty of these tanks have arrived over the past few weeks. They are not unusual, as they are used in the process of cleaning the bilges of merchant ships anchored in a deep bay a few miles from the port. It seems as though this is, in effect, a parking lot for large vessels whilst awaiting charter. Before they are allowed to move they have to clean their bilges. These tanks come from a factory in North Africa, roughly one third full of a special cleaning fluid. They are, in due course, returned full of gunge for processing. The movement of these slurry tanks to and fro from the ships is by a tender, similar to the ships which supply the oil rigs in the North Sea.

In the past month, three large bulk Carriers have been chartered by a Middle Eastern company, previously unheard of. This in itself is not unusual as a company is often set up for a particular contract. However, in this case we have established all three ship charters were paid for in cash, as was the

The Day The Ravens Died

fuel they obtained from the port of Cherbourg. It would seem from the documents they supplied, two were headed to the North Eastern United States and the third one was heading for Europort, all allegedly to pick up cargoes of scrap metal. As yet we have no idea of their actual whereabouts. I can understand the difficulty of finding a particular ship in the Atlantic; it is after all a pretty large pond. Quite why we cannot locate the one supposedly heading for Rotterdam, I find harder to comprehend. We are not talking about grubby little coasters. You could cut up an American battle carrier and dump the bits in these things; they are big enough to float the QE2 in, if you removed the bulk heads. Find them Seb! This is, on the surface, the easiest to comply with order I have ever given."

"We'll keep looking Boss, as you said something so big should be easy enough to spot."

"One would have thought so," sighed Paul. "Next on the agenda, *Intrepid* will be off Cherbourg by lunch time. The French have given permission for Andy and his team of specialists to check the two suspect tanks. Quite what they will do if it is established there are chemically armed missiles in them, is anyone's guess. Predictably we have been accused of spying by some of the Frogs. I did explain we had been searching for these tanks based on intelligence gained in the Middle East. We only became aware of these two tanks when a soldier, who had been on sick leave with his parents who live in France, reported for duty and happened to see a picture of a similar tank in the course of a briefing on the search."

"The French authorities accepted the explanation Paul?" asked General Leach.

"Reaction has, I'll admit, been somewhat varied from nosey bloody English, to please check them and let us know. So it really is a case of 'suck it and see', if you see what I mean Boss."

"Just how certain are you these things have missiles in Paul?"

"I suppose there is always the chance we saw what we wanted to see, but if pressed, about ninety nine point nine percent sure Sir."

"I must admit I've never known you quite so sure about anything over the past few years."

"Frankly Sir, I am not worried about those two even if we are right, it's the others which concern me. By the looks of things, two ships have been sent to attack the Yanks, the other one to knock out London."

"Scuds are a land based missile Paul, even you know that much about them."

"I know, but try this theory for size. They have been carting them around in these modified tankers. The one we recovered from the desert had a lump of concrete in the base of the tank, or what would be the base when it was stood upright. Remember these tanks are demountable, and designed to stand on end. Now the three ships which were chartered are absolutely bloody huge things, suppose you stood these tanks on end, in say the centre hold, sixteen

Timothy Pilgrim

per ship, in a square, banded together with steel ropes. I don't know for sure, but I would have thought such an arrangement would, even in a moderate sea state, give you a platform stable enough to launch a scud, with a high probability of hitting a target the size of London."

"Sometimes you scare me Paul," commented General Leach. "You have just made something implausible sound horribly possible; the really frightening thing is, every time I can remember you coming up with one of your odd ball theories, you have been proved correct, or nearly so."

"All well and good Sir, but we haven't found the ships yet, never mind the scuds. Another thought has just occurred to me. Has anyone any idea what happened to the Silkworm missiles which were delivered to the Yemen on the same ship as the scuds?"

"No idea Boss," replied B.J..

"It might be a good idea to find out, those things have the same range and payload as a scud."

"Surely you don't think they will use them as well Paul?"

"Damned if I know Sir, but it seems to me it would be a good idea to find out."

"More work for the recons Paul?"

"It might come to it Seb, we'll try a different way first." He turned to a grey haired man in a wheelchair. "Kenny, you have good relations with some of the CIA.. Ask them if they can find out if the Yemen still have those Silkworms? They don't have to know the exact location, just see proof the Yemeni Forces actually have them, matching a serial number will do. I just need to know if they are still there?"

"Okay Paul, they owe me a couple of favours. What do I tell them if they ask why I want to know?"

"I'm tempted to say tell them about the scuds, and our theory about launching them from a ship, but it would be premature. Knowing the Yanks they would try to evacuate everywhere within a hundred miles of the Atlantic, not to mention sink anything which could possibly carry a missile. If the powers that be out there, got hold of this, there would be mass panic and total chaos, which is why I asked you to use your contacts. If I used mine for something such as this, it would be on CNN before I put the phone down."

"Anything else Paul?" asked General Leach.

"Yes Sir, and it is particularly worrying. I have here the final analysis of the chemical warhead on the scud from 'Daffies desert'."

"I thought it was confirmed, it was carrying VX Paul."

"It was Sir," replied Paul, "but it has had something added to it. It is in this report given to me by one of the 'gremlins' which inhabit our basements. There is a name here for the additive, but I can't pronounce it, never mind know what it is. It is however the worst possible scenario. This additive is an enzyme of some kind, all the technical stuff is here for any of you to read, but in this office. This document stays in here, understand?"

A ripple of acceptance surged gently around the office.

"The way it was explained to me was this - imagine a single drop of water getting into our electrics and it was guided straight to the junction box which feeds our computers. Once there it found the fuse for the trip switch which protects against power surges. Well the stuff they added to the VX does the same thing with the nerve junctions in the brain, but is specific to the neurons responsible for the breathing reflex. It literally shorts out the bodies electrical circuits which make us breathe, unlike our power grid it is more than a simple pushing of a reset button to restart the system. By the time an antidote, if there is one, was administered you would be dead. You will also be delighted to know there is no safe dose, one part per million is lethal, it can be absorbed through the skin, injested or... the quickest way to kill you... inhaled. If inhaled, the victim will suffocate because the body simply refuses to breathe. The good news is, the additive will have broken down in twenty four hours. After forty eight hours any area affected will be safe, but do not expect me to be the one to prove it!"

"Good Lord," muttered General Leach. "You are saying everyone it touches is as good as dead?"

"It seems so Sir. One other little gem has also come to light - the spreader units on these things generate a very fine mist, so each will cover a very wide area."

"What do we do about it Paul?"

"We must find the missiles, it is as simple as that, and before they are launched."

"What about the evacuation plans Paul?"

"Last I heard they were all arguing as to who had the authority to give the orders to the trains and underground to reroute everything to carry people out. Basically nothing has been done on a practical level. I suggested things like making both sides of the motorways outward bound only, with just the hard shoulder on the in bound side for empty buses and suitable trucks to pick up more people. Health and Safety vetoed that idea; we must leave it to the authorities to organise. Our job is to find those bloody missiles before they are fired."

"I've got family in London Paul, is it alright if I invite them up for a few days?" asked one of the officers present.

"I can hardly refuse can I? But don't you give them any idea as to why."

"I suppose I could say, I had heard a rumour of an attack near where they live, and I would be happier if they stayed with me and the wife for a few days."

"I'd prefer you found another reason though, because if they told even one friend it would spread like wild fire. It's a tough call, but you see my point."

"I'll think of something Boss."

General Leach grunted. "I seem to remember a certain Colonel saying things like that in the past, as I recall it was usually a cause for concern."

"Actually I have just had an idea which would solve the problem Sir," replied Paul.

"Oh Lord, here we go," muttered the General.

"I think it is a brilliant idea," Paul sounded pleased with himself. "Why not have a family day. We can easily put on an impromptu Air Show, a Free Fall Parachute display, mock attacks and the likes. The chefs can provide a buffet and barbeque; spread it over a couple of days. I'm sure of one thing Sir, our staff will function much better if they know their immediate families are safe. If we restrict it to relations from within the M 25 we'll cope easily. If need be we can always tell the families the real reason, once they are here. Right, let's see if we can work out when this is likely to happen."

It was the wheelchair bound Kenny who again came up with a clue. "You know my lot have been going over all the intercepts again, just in case we had missed something."

"Okay," replied Paul, "what have your hawk eyed lot noticed?"

"Nothing which makes a lot of sense really; we noticed a lot of references to weddings and funerals, birthdays as well, all the sort of things which normally bring families together. The odd thing was how many of them are scheduled for Friday, and all of them away from London."

"Hang on, how can Muslims be planning family funerals two weeks in advance?" asked Paul.

"It was exactly this point which caught our attention," replied Kenny.

"So based on this, you are thinking the attack is likely in two days time?"

"We haven't found any of the ships yet Paul, never mind the missiles." said General Leach.

"True, but where is the only place you could hide a bloody great ship such as the '*Elat*' or whatever they have renamed it."

"Out in the open ocean I suppose, but then it would have to come back through the western approaches, one hell of a risk as they must know by now, we are at least onto the scheme."

"I agree Taff, so if you wanted to hide a car, where would you choose?"

"A lock up garage?"

"That isn't quite what I was thinking, try a car park, bigger the better."

"You don't think they went back to their mooring among the other redundant giants?"

"Oh shit!" exclaimed Seb. "It is the one place we haven't looked! It never even crossed my mind they might have returned to the mooring." The young RAF man looked sheepish, "I'm so sorry Boss. I'll get a plane to check, as soon as possible."

"Don't feel too bad about it Seb, no-one else thought of it either. I certainly hadn't thought of it until just now."

Because several planes were scouring the Atlantic for the two ships which they thought were heading to the 'States' and these had first call on the tankers, it was late afternoon before the Canberra returning from the area south of the Azores did a quick photo run over the moored giants. Ten minutes after receiving the data stream a Warrant Officer from the photo lab presented Paul with a folder containing shots of every ship in the anchorage. "Damn it!" muttered Paul, "it's not bloody well there."

He called Martin, the new officer who had arrived the day before on secondment from Hereford to give his wounds a chance to heal. "You are absolutely certain the ship you saw was called '*Elat*'"

"No doubt at all Boss."

"Blast, I was certain it was going to be there. How the hell can something so bloody big vanish?"

"I wouldn't have thought it could."

"Neither would I. It can't have gone far, it only took on enough fuel to get to Rotterdam, its supposed destination and it's not there. We have checked, several times!"

"This lot seem pretty smart Boss."

"More likely, we're being bloody thick Marty!"

A phone on Paul's desk rang, "Yes Mate, what's up?" he asked B.J. who was Duty Officer.

"Nothing for once," came the cheerful reply. "I just thought you might like to know, *Intrepid* is on her way up the channel with both trailers on board. Andy confirms both contain scuds with chemical warheads but no fuel. Andy and the Skipper dealt with the Harbour Master and the Mayor. Keeping it local paid off, they were only too happy to get rid of the things."

"I'll bet they were," replied Paul.

"There's more Boss, the port authorities have sent everything they have on the three suspect ships. How many tanks went to each ship, when they went, who paid for the charters, the works. It's all in French but it's all there."

"Any idea why those two tanks were left on the dock?"

"As usual there is a simple explanation. They got held up by a ferry strike in the Med three weeks ago; by the time they arrived here the ship they were for had sailed for the States."

"Brilliant, I think. Thanks for letting me know."

Paul called General Leach and Taff into his office. "I think we are getting to the crisis point, the two tanks off the docks at Cherbourg are on their way here. They are on *Intrepid* heading for Portsmouth Naval yard."

"Well done Paul," said General Leach.

"Now I've had time to think about it, I'm not at all sure it is good news Sir. In fact, it could force their hand if they know we have those missiles. I think we should discreetly evacuate the Royals and, I hate to say it, the Government. Regrettably they will have to go to the 'farm'," referring to the unit's original base.

"You could be right Paul."

"I could also be wrong Taff, can you sort things out so all of those

Timothy Pilgrim

members of staff with families in London get away, so they can get their relatives up here this evening at the latest."

"Might I ask what you know and we don't?" enquired General Leach.

"I'm not sure if there is any thing else Sir, it's just the timing. The two ships we think are headed for the States must be in position by now, they have had plenty of time as has ours. Granted, we haven't found it yet though I'm damned if I can understand how we could have missed it. The French have finally cottoned on to the fact we lifted those two trailers from Cherbourg, and have sent a 'diplomatic note' expressing their displeasure at the way we did it. The cabinet office e-mailed me a copy a few minutes ago." Paul turned his computer screen so the other two could see it.

"I don't think it's anything to worry about from the diplomatic point of view," he continued. "It looks like some civil servant having a fit of pique because he wasn't allowed to foul things up."

"Clearly you are worried about it Paul."

"Damned right I am. You can guarantee it will be all over the news any time now. 'British war ship enters French harbour and steals two terrorist truck bombs,' or something similar."

"And as you are constantly reminding us, the terrorists watch the news channels too," observed General Leach.

"Quite. So what would you do if you were in their position, knowing, or at least suspecting an outfit like ours was on to you?"

"Personally I'd leave it and run home to the valleys," replied Taff.

"Or, bearing in mind these are total fanatics, say, 'stuff the plans and strike as soon as possible', do as much damage as I could, then leg it. Which would mean get in range as soon as possible, if they're not there already. This lot are dedicated to destroying our way of life, so following on from this line of thought, I don't think they are quite ready yet. They will keep out of range until they are ready."

"Why?" asked General Leach.

"Because they will know we will be aware of the maximum range of those missiles, and should we get wind of the attack, our search will concentrate on the area within range."

"Fair enough, I can follow the logic in the argument."

"Even allowing for the theory, 'assumption being the mother of all fuck ups', I think it is safe to assume they will not be able to get in position to launch in time to hit this evening's rush hour. I think they will use the hours of darkness to try to slip into position, ready to hit the morning rush hour tomorrow. I do not think they would strike over the weekend as most of the type, class, call it what you will, of people they are really after will not be in London over the weekend. Wait until Monday and the risk of discovery will have become too great, assuming once more, they are aware we have at least two of their missiles."

"So in your opinion they will strike tomorrow morning?"

"Don't you Sir?"

"You have certainly made your case to fit this scenario Paul, except for one thing. We haven't found them yet. A small but, I think you'll agree, important point."

"Of course, they could delay their attack on London until lunch time. This would allow them to hit the United States at the same time. If they hit us early, surely it would increase the risk of the Yanks spotting them to an almost certainty."

"That's a bloody good point Taff," replied Paul, "One, I'll confess had not occurred to me."

"So what do we do Paul? Suggest starting evacuation and trigger a panic of biblical proportions. The last I heard, no plan existed. The powers that be were still arguing over who could order what."

"There really isn't much we can do is there? Royalty, elected representatives, security and emergency services and I suppose medical staff....that's about it really. I suppose a lot of hospital staff will stay put, as will fire and police. If we pull out most troops based in London who will have NBC gear, they could give their kit to medics I suppose. The fire brigade have good protection, as do riot squads from the police. It's too late for any effective measures to be taken, we should have sorted this out months if not years ago."

"I don't even have to check the minutes of various committee meetings over the past few years Paul, I can remember you bringing up this very point many times over the years."

"We have got to find that bloody ship," added Taff.

"There is another problem we could do without. We are running out of Canberras, fast. It is a question of maintenance. Even with extra bodies drafted in from the RAF, the ground crews are totally exhausted, they have been working, on average, eighteen-hour days for the last two weeks. They are running out of spares, with some items the situation is reaching critical levels. Fuel is getting lower than we would like. This is down to the general disruption caused by the attacks over the past few weeks. Three of the tankers are unavailable; again it is servicing problems, staff, spares and the likes. The bottom line is, we have three unmodified Recons, one old ex RAF model, and one Tanker, either available or actually in the air, that's it."

"How did things get so bad Paul?"

"No one thing Boss. It's a cumulative thing, the amount of sorties flown to sort out all the incidents, the disruption caused to supply, by the same incidents, and of course trying to find those ships, the Atlantic is vast. Of course we know now it was wasted effort as the ships in question were out of the area we were searching before we started looking, but we didn't know that at the time and it had to be done."

"Is there any particular item we could chase up which would help matters?"

"Would you believe tyres are the main problem. As you are no doubt aware, the Recons need special tyres. It is all to do with the extreme altitude they operate at, they are filled with a special mixture of gas which you can't use in standard tyres, and you can't use them anyway as they would explode at those altitudes. There is no way round it as far as I know. The problem with the Victors is similar, no spare tyres. All three of those grounded blew tyres on landing, luckily there was no great damage or dramas. The one still available is only there because the fitters robbed the others of their best remaining tyres. Oh sure, there are supposed to be a couple of truck loads on their way but lord knows where they are."

"So we are scuppered if they move, and we have no planes up?" said General Leach.

"We are using the Tornadoes with recce pods, as well as a squadron of RAF Recons, supported by RAF Tankers .... together they add up to about two thirds of a Canberra, but it is better than nothing."

"And of course they cannot see into French waters properly, except in the narrowest bit of the channel, and we can't screen them as both AWACs are out East."

"I must confess I've been a bit naughty there Boss, I've been sending a Blackbird along the edge of French air space every three hours, at least doing this we can keep track of ship movements in the Channel."

"What do you do if, or when you do find it?" asked the General.

"Melt it. Both the TS3s are on ten minute readiness. We'll put them up at 0600hrs, use the Tanker we have available to refuel them, if nothing happens, bring 'em back after the evening rush hour, and hope we can resolve the issue of tyres over the weekend."

"That is hard on the crews Paul. Twelve hours in the air at a stretch, in one of those flying bullets."

"I know Boss, but what choice have I got? There are only three crews trained to fly the things. If we bring them back to refuel and something happens when they are on the ground they'll never get back to the Channel in time to do any good. I suppose you can blame me for not getting some of their fuel stored at more convenient air bases, but it is our old friend hindsight again. You know the tanker can only do the one sortie, its tyres are below minimum safety levels already."

"How did things get so bad Paul, I know the orders went in with plenty of time to avoid this, even allowing for the disruption caused by all the attacks, those tyres should have arrived over a week ago. I know you are busy, do you want me to chase them up?"

"If you could Sir it would be a big help."

CHAPTER TWENTY-ONE

The emergency meeting held later on the Thursday evening in the briefing room, deep beneath 'the farm' as the unit's original base was generally known, was a tense affair to say the least. Paul, flanked by General Leach and Taff told the assembled Chiefs of Staff and senior politicians all they knew about the threat to London. He had just finished explaining for the second time, why he believed the attack would come around lunch time the following day when the Prime Minister spoke up.

"Based on what you have just told us, which isn't much. You expect my government to organise a mass evacuation of London! Is it possible you are wrong?"

"Yes, it is possible. Such things are rarely clear cut, not that there is a precedent for such an attack Sir."

"If we evacuate and nothing happens we will be the laughing stock of the world. No Colonel, I will not order an evacuation unless you bring me something concrete on which to base such an order. As I understand it, as yet you have been unable to find a very large ship which you claim is carrying the missiles. Find the ship, confirm it has the weapons on board you say it has, and I will consider giving the order to evacuate."

"If we find it before they launch there will be no point in evacuating then, will there?"

"I seem to remember you saying, as well as the scuds there could be Silkworm anti-ship cruise missiles with similar warheads involved, where are they?"

"I have no idea Sir, we have however proved the existence of the scuds armed with chemical warheads. We have three of them, and there is no doubt the two from Cherbourg were headed for one of the ships we are looking for."

"Then put up all your planes Colonel, if they can do half of what you claim, they should find them easily."

"We can't put up any more Sir. We simply do not have the spares to make them serviceable. True, we could get round many of the deficiencies with little or no risk to the crews, however we cannot get round the tyre problems, and you can't pull into a lay by and fix an exploded tyre at umpteen thousand feet!"

"How could you possibly have allowed things to get to such a critical state when it was vital to have the maximum number of planes available. When I sanctioned your recall, I was led to believe you were an effective Commander who got things done, it seems as though I was misinformed."

Paul was about to explode with rage when General Leach stopped him.

"Prime Minister," began the silver haired officer, "I can tell you exactly why the unit has run out of tyres. It is the same reason several of their aircraft are still waiting for the proper engines, nearly a year after the job should have been completed. I have here," he waved a sheet of paper with a flourish, "a copy of an E-mail sent six weeks ago, to the tyre manufacturer, from the MOD ordering them to cease production of the special tyres for this unit. This order applies until an order for the MOD was complete, which would give the RAF stocks of tyres for all their aircraft for the next eighteen months. Failure to comply would result in the loss of future contracts. Now almost any tyre manufacturer can make standard aircraft tyres. Only this one has the technology to make this unit's special tyres. The blame, as is usually the case, lies within Whitehall, not here."

"Sounds as though you are trying to shift the blame General," replied one of the politicians.

"I can vouch for the authenticity of the E-mail," said the head of the Air Force. "My office was sent a copy by the tyre company querying it, a fact I was unaware of, until I asked about it prior to coming here."

"Am I to understand you are accusing civilian personnel in the MOD, of attempting to prevent this unit operating as it is supposed to?"

"I'm not accusing, Prime Minister, I am stating it is a fact. Something you are well aware of and have done nothing about, unless forced to act by the facts being made public."

"How dare you make such insinuations?"

"You say you won't act on our recommendations, fine, fair enough, but I can't help noticing you were quick enough getting your family and friends out of London today, and if you say it was a 'prudent' move I think I will be sick!"

"Regard my not issuing the order to evacuate as a vote of confidence in your unit's ability to destroy the threat before the attack is launched."

"I have never heard such blatant 'buck passing' in my life!" exclaimed Paul. "We might well have been able to justify such confidence, were it not for some hyphenated pillock with terminal piles screwing everything up. I'll tell you here and now, if a single person dies because of this, and the moron in question survives any attack, he will not survive an encounter with me, if I happen to be lucky enough to discover his identity!"

The Chief of the Defence staff decided to defuse the row before it got totally out of hand. "Tell us Colonel, if you are unable to locate these missiles and they are fired at London, what sort of casualties are we looking at, one, possibly two thousand?"

"Sir, the chemical agents we have discovered are so lethal, they have no safe level. Any contact, however slight or brief, is almost certain to be fatal. If inhaled it is a matter of a minute, two at the most before death occurs. Our calculations strongly suggest three to four tons, evenly spread, is capable of killing every living thing inside the M25. Each missile carries half a ton, plus a spreader unit. As I said earlier, we believe there are sixteen scuds on the ship, and it is possible these are backed up by as many as twenty Silkworms carrying similar pay loads. We may be able to shoot down the Silkworms using fighters, if we can get them in the right place at the right time, however there would still be many casualties in the area surrounding any crashed missile. With respect Sir, you work out the figures, I am not up to contemplating such loss of life."

"I understand your anger Colonel, and the frustration. All I can say is stay focused, and good luck; anything the Armed Forces can do to help, all you have to do is ask."

"Thank you Sir. As I understand it the only military personnel left in the capital are on essential duties, and have been suitably equipped and briefed. All available NBC kit has been distributed to the emergency services and medical personnel, is this complete?"

"I believe so Colonel," replied the senior officer.

"Thank you for that Sir. I take it as many families as possible have also been brought out?"

"All families of other ranks have been evacuated to the Guard's battle camp a few miles away from your main base, the men will be under canvas. A convoy is on its way to pick up the families of Officers and senior NCOs living inside the M25 as we speak. The men will be much more effective if they know their families are safe. If there is time, it is my intention to offer the same evacuation for the families of the emergency services. All evacuees will be housed on Military bases, which will be sealed until the outcome of all this is known. Servicemen and their dependants currently requiring hospital treatment are being moved to your medical facility here Colonel. It will be a little crowded but your staff assure me they can cope."

The politicians were furious with the Military top brass. 'How dare they embark on such an operation without consulting the Government first?'

"Regard it as an exercise Sir, it will highlight any problems for the future. If you find this unsatisfactory, then put it down to the General Staff taking care of those under our command."

When dawn broke it was clear and mild with a gentle southerly breeze, it was promising to live up to the weather forecaster's promise of a beautiful day, over most of England and Wales at least.

Paul had snatched a couple of hours of much needed sleep on the camp bed in the back office. Bleary eyed and in need of a shave, he walked slowly and painfully to his desk, stopping only to make a cup of coffee on the way, and to light the inevitable cigarette. Switching his computer on, he glanced at the latest recon. images, then began to look through the pile of files which had magically appeared overnight. It must have been nearly an hour later when he turned back to his computer. Something was niggling away in the back of his mind, but he couldn't pin it down. He checked the pictures several times and looked at a file on possible ships as the missile carrier. He suddenly experienced one of those 'eureka' moments. Stabbing at a button on the terminal on his desk he got the Duty Officer, "One of those bloody ships has gone!"

"Is that you Boss?" came B.J.'s voice.

"It was the last time I looked, one of those ships has left its moorings B.J., what coverage have we got?"

"Not a lot Boss. We are relying on Tornadoes doing hourly passes over International and our own waters, with a Blackbird doing what it can in French airspace, without upsetting them."

"Find the bloody thing B.J.," Paul sounded almost pleading.

"That could prove a little difficult Paul. There is a bank of fog and low cloud all along the French coast. Sure the planes we have out there at the moment can detect ships moving in the clag, but they cannot positively identify individual ships. A large contact could just as easily be a Ferry or Tanker, as the Bulk Carrier we are looking for."

"So we are blind?"

"Might as well be, Paul."

"Oh shit. I'm going to have to send the only Canberra up early, there's no bloody choice is there?"

"Not a lot."

Things now started to go from bad to worse. It was going to be at least two hours before the plane could take off. "Why?" he demanded.

"One of the hatches isn't sealing properly Boss, the metal has de-formed under the rubber. If we don't fix it there is a real danger of explosive decompression."

"Do whatever you have to do Seb, just get one of the modified ones operational ASAP, let me know as soon as you have a take off time."

"Will do Paul. Sorry about this, but these planes are not exactly in the first flush of youth."

"Neither am I, do your best."

The next two hours were some of the most frustrating he could remember. The world and his wife were demanding up-dates which couldn't be given, as there was nothing to up-date!

He spoke to the deputy director of the CIA, luckily it was the one he got on well with.

"Sorry I can't be more specific Carl, as soon as I get anything else I will let you know. It is looking as though they are planning to hit you during your morning rush hour. There is also the possibility of up to twenty Silkworms aimed at the same targets, which we think are Washington and New York. If you think the information on the scuds is thin, then there is even less on the

Silkworms. To compound the issue, we think they can be launched from a ramp in a standard forty foot long container, so they could be anywhere."

"You are a right bundle of laughs this morning. Give me some good news."

"I will as soon as I have any, catch you later mate."

It must have been nearly nine o'clock when General Leach wandered into Paul's office, "Anything happening Paul?"

"One of the ships we were supposed to be keeping an eye on has vanished, and we can't find it. We are fairly certain it is hiding in a cloud bank off the French coast. The only Canberra available isn't, if you see what I mean, it went U/S on pre flight inspection. The lads down on the flight line are doing their best. The gear on Blackbird can track the ships under the cloud, but can't give us the positive ID we need. The crew are bleating about having headaches and getting dizzy. They are incredible old planes but they are not made to fly in circles!"

"What about the Tornadoes?"

"They keep trying to peep under the overcast without upsetting the Froggies, but the PM is taking an unhealthy interest in the recons. All I keep getting is 'don't enter French air space'."

"The joys of command. Anything I can do to help?"

"A refill?" suggested Paul offering the General his empty cup.

"It wasn't quite what I meant, but fair enough. Any indication how long the repairs will take?"

"Shouldn't be too long now, I hope."

"I presume you are holding the strike planes until the Canberra is on station."

"It's pretty pointless sending up the TS3s without one. At the speed they fly, they couldn't hit England in cloud if it wasn't marked."

Half an hour of going through files was interrupted by what sounded like a volley of gun shots, followed by an increasing roar of a jet warming up.

"Sounds promising Boss," said Paul, the gloom lifting his demeanour a little.

The phone rang, it was Seb confirming the plane was fit for service and would be off in a few minutes.

"Thank fuck for that!"

"Quite," replied the General.

The relief was short lived, as the old plane roared down the runway gathering speed as it went, there was a muffled bang, followed by the sound of the jets running full reverse thrust. Moments later the base fire engines tore past the office window, sirens wailing.

"Oh for crying out loud!" exclaimed Paul rushing to the window, "Now what's gone wrong?"

To his dismay the nose of the Canberra was shrouded in smoke and he was sure he could see a flicker of flame under the nose.

Timothy Pilgrim

In the event it wasn't as dramatic as it looked. A tyre on the nose assembly had exploded just prior to the pilot reaching 'V2' and calling, 'rotate,' to lift the nose. Another hour was lost as the ground crews worked feverishly, replacing the wheels and the lower section of the under carriage. To save time they simply swapped the entire assembly, cannibalising from one of the other U/S aircraft.

The tyres looked even more worn than the one which had exploded, but they were the best available and would have to do.

When told of the further delay, the Prime Minister was furious and had a right go at Paul, who promptly retaliated, by pointing out it was the PM who appointed useless Ministers, who were more interested in, 'announcing new initiatives' and getting on camera, than ensuring civil servants in their departments did their jobs properly.

Undaunted by their mishap the veteran crew climbed back into their old aircraft and set off once more along the runway. This time the pilot allowed the nose to lift a little earlier than normal. Using a little extra power, the graceful old plane seemed to float up into the sky.

Lunch time was approaching by the time 'eagle eye one' was on station, with all systems operating and the data link established. The cloud was a bit thinner now than it had been, so the crew shared a moment.s banter with the crew of a Blackbird as it sped past below the old plane. The Americans asked, "Where the hell are you guys?"

"Look up, about three o'clock high."

"How high?"

"A couple of miles above you!"

"Have a nice day; see you when you get home."

Since soon after dawn, the base had been a hive of activity. A succession of American tankers had roared off, these were the 'specials' which only refuelled the Blackbirds. Other tankers scrambled from their bases in the eastern United States, to service the 'specials' which would allow the Blackbirds to scour the Atlantic for the suspect ships. Four of the super-fast Spyplanes thundered into the sky and once topped up with fuel, headed west flat out towards the next pair of tankers waiting far out over the Atlantic. The supersonic footprint they left in their wake caused a spate of complaints. Many people feared it had been an earthquake. There was a repeat performance when a pair of evil looking planes lined up at the end of the runway. The long slim aircraft with high small delta wings, with down turned tips and wide shallow 'V' shaped tails, were updated versions of the ill fated TSR2s. Painted black, they projected menace even when stationary, they were also one of the noisiest aircraft ever when taking off in a hurry, surpassed only by the unit's re-engined V Bombers and Tankers, and this pair were in a hurry!.

Paul went to the control room running the UK operations, "How's it going?" he asked.

"The data link to 'eagle eye one' is established, we'll have the images up on the display any minute now. I can patch it through to your office if you like Boss," replied the young officer running things.

"If you want me to get out of the way, all you have to do is ask me to go Captain."

"It wasn't meant like that Boss, but people get nervous when Senior Officers are around, and make mistakes which wouldn't normally occur."

"Fair point. I'll let you get on with your job, good luck you lot, keep those eyes peeled, we are depending on you."

Back in his office he watched as the feed came through, everything 'eagle eye one' could see was on his screen. The click of a button would switch the image from one sensor to another, as easily as pushing a button on a television's remote control.

"Okay, where is our ship?" he asked over the intercom link.

"We thought we had it Boss, but as you can no doubt see, the bulk carrier we have found isn't the '*Elat*'."

"Are you sure this is the ship which left its mooring last night?"

"I'm over ninety per cent certain Boss, but because of the interrupted coverage there is always a chance of a mistake. There is another one of the Super Carriers on the move, but this one seems to be moving onto the same spot the one we are following left during the night."

"Alright, keep looking." On a hunch Paul called the harbour master's office in Cherbourg and asked again about the *Elat*. The reply didn't surprise him, "Yes, she had left her mooring during the night and was headed for Europort, Rotterdam to pick up her cargo of scrap iron for the Far East."

"That is our ship General."

"You have got to be absolutely certain Paul."

"Fair enough, I'll phone the UN and check."

The ship he was looking at had UN painted in white letters on her huge black hull and UN in black letters on her funnel which was gleaming white. The name on her bows and stern was '*STELA TRADER*'

To the consternation of Paul, the UN quickly confirmed they had indeed chartered a ship called the *Stella Trader*, to pick up a cargo of wheat from Rotterdam, bound for the famine hit area in the Horn of Africa.

"Now I am confused Boss," Paul admitted. "It seems as though the UN have indeed chartered a ship with that name, and it is in the general area."

"It does complicate matters somewhat," observed General Leach. "Who are you phoning now?"

Within a minute the powerful computer had found the number for the harbour master at Rotterdam, for once Paul got lucky. "Yes Colonel, I know the *Stella Trader*, the UN charter her at least twice a year, she's due in on the tide to pick up a full load of fifty thousand metric tons of wheat. In fact I can see her, she's at anchor about four kilometres out, waiting for the tide."

"You are absolutely certain the ship you can see is the UN charter, the *Stella Trader*?"

"Yes Colonel I am sure, I'll call her to make certain for you."

"Thank you. If possible get her to give you a visual response of some kind, just in case the lot we are watching are listening in on maritime frequencies."

For what seemed the longest two minutes of his life Paul waited for confirmation, it turned out the deputy harbour master on the other end of the phone even knew the skipper of the moored merchant ship he was speaking to. "I hope I was of some help Colonel."

"You were indeed Sir, thank you very much."

"So this is our ship?"

"Looks very much like it Sir." Paul used the com link, "Where are the TS3s?"

"They are refuelling at the moment Boss, just north of the Channel Islands."

"Tell them to get their arses into gear, 'eagle eye one' will mark the target which is just about opposite to Newhaven, only four miles off the French coast."

"Are they cleared for Super-Sonic Boss?"

"And then some. Anything other than flat out and I will not be pleased, and full bomb loads on target please."

"You have spotted something we've missed," said General Leach, "I know the signs, what is it Paul?"

"Knock off the first two letters of the name Boss, what are the next four? Anyway, Stella has two 'L's and if you look closely I'm sure I can see where the paint has run down from the bottom of the 'T' in Stela.."

"Eagle eye one has just confirmed sixteen tubes, possibly demountable tanks in the centre hold Paul, we think they contain scuds. We have positive ID on rocket fuel and probably traces of VX or something very similar. The scans are not as clear as we would like due to the movement of the ship."

Paul was about to call the strike planes to see if they were on their way when the control room came on the speaker again, 'missile launch detected' and followed it with the GPS reference for the ship.

"Time to bomb release, five minutes Paul," came the voice of the lead pilot of the pair of TS3s.

There was a commotion in the outer office. To the annoyance of those in the office with Paul they were 'invaded' by most of the cabinet, led by the Prime Minister.

"I demand to know what is going on Colonel. I have had numerous complaints from the French this morning, in spite of my specific warning to you about entering French air space it seems as though you have ignored those warnings. I demand an explanation Colonel!"

Paul simply said, "Watch" and pointed at the screen. A missile climbed away from the middle of the ship into the sky and quickly vanished as its speed increased. "That was number four, just hope those planes get there before any more are launched, the first missile must be approaching London by now."

Suddenly two black planes streaked across the picture just after the fifth missile left the hold. A couple of seconds later the entire ship vanished in a brilliant fire ball.

"There is your explanation Sir. If the French authorities had been as helpful as the harbour master at Cherbourg, then there would have been a better chance of finding that bloody ship before she began to launch the missiles."

"How many casualties are we looking at Colonel?"

"I don't know do I?" was Paul's angry response.

"Paul?" Taff called across the crowded office. "Jonathon is trying to catch the last scud."

"What! Crazy sod, if his speed drops sub sonic above about twenty thousand feet he'll stall."

"Got him on screen."

"The picture from the Canberra was horribly clear, the fire ball where the ship had been had all but gone, the towering smoke cloud from the detonation was still climbing and expanding. Of the huge ship there was no sign, only a disturbed patch of water. The last scud was in the picture, still accelerating. Below it, outlined against the glowing smoke cloud, was one of the black planes - the brilliant, almost white flames of its after burners almost as long as the plane. All of those watching could see the plane beginning to wobble, a sure sign of an approaching, potentially deadly stall. At the last moment, before the pilot lost control, two small missiles flashed away from the sides of the plane. There was a cheer from the politicians as the little missiles sent the deadly scud tumbling towards the sea, still more or less intact but minus its back six feet. Paul and the others were more interested in the fate of their two friends in the falling aircraft. It was falling slightly tail down and spinning with increasing rapidity, just as it always had in the simulator, no-one had ever 'survived' a stall. Because of the angle of decent it was impossible to get sufficient air into the engines to relight them and the 'beast' insisted on falling tail first.

Everyone was willing the crew to bale out, even though they knew the 'G' force would make it next to impossible. One of the features of the TS3 was vectored thrust, at the speed these things travelled it was the only reliable way of turning them. Jonathon, the pilot, had switched off his afterburner igniters as the plane stalled, now as it descended he directed the vectored thrust nozzles fully down and hit the igniter switch. Those watching saw the burst of flame and feared the worst. In the event, this tiny amount of thrust proved just enough to push the nose slightly down. The pilot dropped one wing and the fluttering decent became a screaming dive, the engines relit and he levelled out at about five hundred feet above the sea. This time it was the military people who cheered.

Helga came into the office and headed for Paul; seeing her Paul blanked the Prime Minister as the tall blonde handed him a thin folder. Inside was a list of evacuees snatched out of London. Even as the gas clouds were sinking towards the doomed inner city, almost all the well known faces on television news programs had been rescued, as had most of the radio presenters. Most of the backroom staff at the BBC had been saved, ordered out by a handful of soldiers and sent, a car load at a time, in the direction of the M1 rather than the A40. This was too close to Heathrow which Paul was sure would be a target. For all their efforts, the soldiers were frustrated as some of the staff insisted on taking their own cars without passengers and headed off along the A40 anyway.

The Prime Minister again demanded an explanation. "Simple really, if this is even half as bad as I think it is going to be, then it will be some comfort to the rest of the population to see the usual faces on tele. and hear the usual presenters on their radios. A sense of normality will help reduce the panic."

"Paul! The Americans are on line one."

"Thanks for the warning Colonel. We got the one targeting Washington before it fired any of the scuds; one of the Blackbirds spotted it as it was removing its hatches. You were right there were sixteen on board. Just hope the stuff we hit it with was hot enough to destroy the gas. The other one launched three, Tom Cats took out two of them, the other hit around Times Square. It's bad Colonel. We have everything we've got in the air on the look out for those Silkworms, hang on. I've just had a report of the first Silkworms. You thought twenty per target. I've got to go, thanks again for the warning."

"Let's just hope our fighters are in the right place to get a shot at the bloody things before they reach major centres of population."

"I've got all three unmodified Canberras available, basically orbiting round the M25 Paul, each fighter has, as far as possible, got a Tornado bomber with it to bomb the crash site to destroy the chemicals. There is a Vulcan up as well with a full load of plasma bombs as back up."

"Well done Seb."

"Are you planning to drop bombs on targets around London Colonel!" exclaimed the horrified Prime Minister. "I forbid it! I absolutely forbid it."

"Do you think I enjoyed making the decision?" retorted Paul. "If a fighter shoots down a Silkworm, the impact will release half a ton of absolutely lethal gas. What would you rather have? A hundred or so obliterated bodies who would have died anyway from the gas, or thousands dead from the gas."

"Tell your crews not to fire Colonel until I have had chance to consult with my colleagues."

"Missile launch Paul, Isle of Grain area, got it. A container yard, on screen."

It was clear from the pictures, other containers in the yard were pointing towards London and the doors were being opened. A voice from one of the intercoms confirmed at least four contained missiles.

The Day The Ravens Died

"Where is the Vulcan?"

"Two minutes from bomb release Boss."

"Tell him to pedal quicker, my heart won't stand much more of this!"

Another Tornado shot a Silkworm into the Thames several miles down stream of the QE bridge.

"Where the hell did that one come from, not another bloody ship?"

The same Tornado followed the smoke trail; the missile had come from one of the old gun forts, built out in the estuary during the Second World War. To the consternation of the pilot he came under fairly heavy fire as he closed to investigate. He swung sharply out of range, called control and advised them of the situation. Once more he turned towards the fort, this time at ultra low level, so low he was leaving a 'wake' which was visible on the pictures from the Canberra. As this was a fighter version of the Tornado he carried no bombs. Apart from his cannon, he carried only missiles. The best he could really hope for was to keep those on the old fort occupied until the Vulcan arrived to obliterate the threat. The radar guided missiles would be of little use, but as one Silkworm had already been launched the pilot knew there must be some residual heat left on the launcher. To his relief he got a good tone as the sidewinder heat seeking missile locked onto the launcher, the missile shot off its rail and went straight into the still hot container, producing a satisfying explosion. A quick burst from his cannon had the desired effect of silencing the machine guns which had been firing at him. In fact, the exploding cannon shells did a good deal of damage, including setting fire to the fuel of one Silkworm.

His next attack was more measured, firing his last two sidewinders and spraying the fort from maximum range with his cannon until he ran out of ammunition. He had done his job well; the terrorists were prevented from firing the remaining four missiles, now it was too late. They didn't see the sinister giant delta winged plane high above, four one thousand pound bombs streaked unerringly down. When the smoke cleared all that was left were a series of glass covered supports on which the fort had been built, such was the heat generated by the plasma bombs, the rest had melted.

The Tornado had problems of its own, some of the bullets from the machine guns had found their mark and the port engine was smoking badly, so the pilot shut it down and limped home on one engine. As soon as the plane came to rest at the end of the runway the damaged engine burst into flames, the pilot got out very quickly; but the fire took hold and the RAF were another Fighter short.

The other Vulcan took off with a full bomb bay, to deal with any other sites which revealed themselves, or to 'sanitise' any sites where a Silkworm might be brought down. As things turned out, the waiting fighters brought down six of the remaining ten, the Vulcan dropped two bombs on each crash site, utterly destroying everything within a hundred yards of the impact. Whether or not anyone was killed by these bombs will never be known for certain. What is certain, had the gas been allowed to drift on the breeze many hundreds, possibly even thousands more would have died.

Of the four which got through, three were launched from a barge on the Thames, well within the area affected by the scuds. The crew of the barge were wearing sophisticated NBC suits which protected them against the immediate effects of the gas. These three Silkworms were aimed at Heathrow, so unexpected was the direction of the attack they got through. The only fighter which might have been able to have intercept them had swung away to destroy a missile, which was more or less following the M4. It ended up crashing into Windsor Great Park, its deadly cargo killing several deer before the last of the bombs from the second Vulcan destroyed the threat.

The NBC suits may have protected the terrorists from their own weapons. They were however useless against the cannon shells of an avenging Harrier which was just too late to stop the last missile. The pilot fired both of his sidewinders but the range was too great, and although they were tracking the Silkworm both ran out of fuel and exploded. Fearing there might be more missiles on the barge the pilot promptly sank it with a burst of about fifty rounds from the heavy cannon.

The final missile to get through passed east to west over the city in a gentle curve; somehow its launch went undetected and it remained a mystery where it came from, it would probably kill more people than any of the others. This Silkworm was different to any of the other missiles which got through - unlike the others it left only a minimal gas cloud in its deadly wake. The biggest menace of this warhead was contained within the hundreds of glass 'ping-pong' balls it ejected - long term these left a deadly legacy which would be next to impossible to clean up, each glass ball was packed with concentrated dioxin!

"If our estimates were correct, then the attack is over Prime Minister. Preliminary figures suggest four scuds out of sixteen got through and four Silkworms out of twenty hit their targets."

"Not good enough Colonel, not by a long way," there was an air of menace in the man's voice.

May be it was the release of tension, or maybe it was simply Paul could not stand the man. For a moment, General Leach thought Paul was going to hit the Premier.

"You have just seen what we were up against; we destroyed twenty eight out of thirty six missiles. I agree with you we should have destroyed them all, but under the circumstances I think the forces deployed did a remarkable job with what was available. My own assessment was, if we stopped half of them we would have done well."

"I witnessed chaos, panic, lack of leadership, and blatant disregard of clear unambiguous orders," retorted the Prime Minister.

"I see, you think I am going to be the scapegoat for all the dead, well old son, think again."

"Don't talk to me as though I am one of your troopers. You should have ordered up more aircraft Colonel. Less than half the Tornados were in the air, you should have scrambled them much earlier!"

"They are jets you dozy bugger, not bloody gliders which can be towed up! Every serviceable fighter and fighter-bomber in the UK was in the air around London, we even brought everything which could fly down from Lossiemouth! All the rest are overseas or grounded through lack of spare parts. Half of our own planes which were up there, shouldn't have been. You saw for yourself what happened to the Canberra this morning. If the lads hadn't been able to fix it, then we really would have been in the shit! If you need to make cuts, then cut most of the senior posts in the MOD because that's where the blame lies."

"I'll deal with you later Colonel, in the mean time I demand to know how long it will be before my Government can return to Westminster so we can oversee the clearing up operation."

"Why don't you go now? I'll even lend you some cars so you can drive yourselves, you'll have to get your own fuel though as we can't spare any."

"Paul!" scolded General Leach, "You know better than to make such comments."

"When will it be safe Colonel?"

"How the bloody hell should I know? I'm a soldier not a chemist! All I do know is, there are many thousands of dead. Until we can get men in on the ground, there is no way to know when it will be possible to even fight the many fires burning, never mind collect the dead. For all I know it might be years before it is safe, personally I don't think the stuff they used, as deadly as it is, will be very persistent, it may well have degraded within a week. There is however one problem I am aware of. According to one of my chemical experts, one of the Silkworms spread nearly half a ton of something called TCDD in a strip roughly three miles long and half a mile wide smack bang across the City. I am told TCDD is the most deadly form of dioxin, with no real treatment available and a half life of anything up to fourteen years presents us with something of a dilemma. We cannot simply wash it away, as it will end up in the river, polluting the Thames and the southern North Sea for the foreseeable future. Using flame throwers on exposed surfaces isn't an option either, as they are not hot enough; fires already burning in the area, caused mainly by crashed cars, are only making matters worse by spreading the dust and releasing PCBs, which are related to Dioxin, from burning plastics and the likes; this increases the toxicity I'm told. We have one hell of a problem for the clean up teams, they will have to wear full protective gear, because of the Dioxin, even if the other stuff does degrade quickly, can you imagine what state all of those bodies will be in, if this weather lasts as it is forecast to. Will you be leading a clearing up team? I think not!"

"I told you not to bomb any crash sites Colonel, those fire bombs of yours have started the fires we can see on the screen. If left unchecked they will destroy London."

"You might be interested to know, not one of those fires are due to our bombs, just remember our technology. We can prove where our bombs hit."

"I must have an estimate of casualties Colonel, I must have something to announce to the Nation. We must show the Government is in control of the situation following the failure of the security forces to adequately protect the Capital and its citizens."

Paul's fragile control was threatening to break, he turned to General Leach. "Please get this lot out of my office Sir so I can get on with my job. I am beginning to wish we hadn't bothered to bring them out!"

"What are you going to do to save those in the affected areas Colonel, you must get them out."

"I'll tell you what we are trying to do Sir. The plan is to evacuate everyone within a mile of the affected area, to create a buffer zone so no-one else gets killed by the gas. There are many difficulties as we have yet to determine the exact limits the gas has reached, the rate it is spreading, the rate it is degrading? There is then the problem of getting the people to leave their homes; how do we get them to safety and to look after them once they are evacuated. All these are problems you were asked weeks ago to plan for, as far as I can see nothing at all has been done in this respect. There is also the problem of preventing anyone else entering London, many of these have perfectly genuine concerns over loved ones. We do not have anywhere near the manpower to deal with these problems. Most of the emergency services were persuaded to leave inner London, this has helped a little. The best we can hope for is to limit the chaos for the time being."

"You must evacuate the city of London at least Colonel, surely you have the resources to cope with such an operation?"

"You really don't get it do you?" asked Paul. "Look at the screen, I'll zoom it in so you can see the detail. Can you see anything moving, other than a bit of smoke? What you can see are not people having a nap on the pavement, they are bodies, corpses! They will not get up and walk away.

It is like that from Croydon to Tottenham and from Stratford to Hammersmith. There is another patch around the Park Royal area as well as another strip from Staines to Rickmansworth including Heathrow. I haven't got the remotest idea of casualty totals. I will be surprised if it is less than a million! Someone is going to have to pick up every one of those bodies; it is a forgone conclusion that it will be soldiers who bear the brunt of this; to compound matters every road is jammed solid with crashed vehicles. Most contain bodies, which will have to be removed before the wrecks can be cleared. What I need from you is a clear directive stating where the mass graves are to be sited and areas to dump the cars, most of which are damaged."

"Do what you must Colonel, I will have to decide on our response to this appalling outrage."

"Get him out of here please Sir."

CHAPTER TWENTY-TWO

Bob Philips was a young engineer from Derby who had designed a revolutionary new engine He had re-mortgaged the family home to raise the money to build a prototype and test it, he had proven it worked and was reliable. It had passed all the tests with flying colours and a meeting had been arranged with the money men in the city.....on their decision his future depended. The weather men had promised another beautiful day so he had taken along his wife and beautiful little four year old daughter, he was certain he would have something to celebrate in the afternoon. His wife and little girl would meet him in Trafalgar Square sometime this afternoon. Little Emily was happily feeding the pigeons when she spotted her doting father approaching. He looked happy and had good reason to; his meeting had given him everything he hoped for, and more. With a squeal of delight the little blonde haired girl ran to his outstretched arms, "Daddy!" The pigeons flapped up in alarm then wheeled round to clear up the remainder of the food. The little girl cried out again as the pigeons fell from the sky, landing all around her, dead. A moment of confusion and her father fell forward, trying to reach the little girl who made everything worth while - he never made it, she too collapsed with a cry of fear, just out of reach of her dying father. The mother tried to reach them, she too fell, inches short of her daughter, she managed one sob, 'my baby', then she too was gone.

The busker on London Bridge spotted the two 'city gents' walking briskly towards him, and wondered what they were talking about so earnestly. Why on earth should they wear bowler hats, never mind carry umbrellas on a day like today. He decided to play the old Lovin' Spoon-full hit, 'Summer in the City'. Just as he was about to start, he became aware of people screaming away to his right. As he turned to find the reason, the lunch time crowds began to collapse, they were going down like nine pins. Glancing up all he could see was a smoke trail arcing across the sky, then, right in front of him one of the 'city gents' coughed, clutched his throat, then collapsed. His friend never made a sound as he fell across the busker's legs.

Forgetting his song the busker tried to free his legs to run, but run where; then the gas hit him too and it didn't matter any more.

The City end of the Mile End road was congested, as was usual. Somewhere, just about opposite the junction with Brick Lane was where the first gas reached the ground. A taxi driver was first to collapse; his window was wide open as it was a beautiful day which is probably why he was the first to be hit. He had just accelerated hard to beat the lights. The almost instant effect from the gas meant he was unable to stop, and the taxi slammed into the back of the car in front, splitting the fuel tank. This in itself was bad enough, unfortunately the car driver had his arm out of the open window and was holding a cigarette. He was on his way to pick up his wife and she hated him smoking in the car. The jolt of the taxi hitting him caused him to drop the half-smoked cigarette onto the road. In the space of the few seconds the petrol took to reach the still burning cigarette he had realised what was about to happen and opened the car door. His brain was racing, he must put the cigarette out before the petrol reached it. He could see it inches away from his face as he lay in the road totally unable to move.

Within the next five minutes the fire had spread, not only to other vehicles but to the buildings on both sides of the road. No-one would be responding to the automatic fire alarms, although they were the last things many people heard, no-one could hear them now.

At the Tower of London it was feeding time for the ravens. As usual a crowd had gathered to see these iconic birds. They had already had their main feed of raw meat, before any members of the public were around. This feeding was more of a daily ritual for the benefit of the public. There was a definite pecking order with the birds. The dominant male called 'Thor' always came first, closely followed by the oldest of the birds 'Gwylum', the 'king', deposed by the slightly younger and stronger 'Thor'. 'Thor' had grabbed his daily boiled egg and was contentedly pecking it to pieces as 'Gwylum' hopped up to get his mid day treat. As the 'beefeater' master of the ravens stretched out his gloved hand to feed the elderly 'Gwylum' he heard a commotion behind him. The other five ravens, waiting their turn for a treat, were unusually nervous. Then the old soldier pitched forward, almost landing on the old raven. Being on the ground, it took a few seconds longer for the gas to reach the birds. 'Thor' hopped over to join the other bird, both looked at their keeper, clearly uncertain of what was happening; both managed one defiant flap of their clipped wings before they too succumbed to the poisonous cloud.

It was difficult to determine the exact spread of the gas. Away from the main concentrations there were little isolated pockets where people lay dead in the streets. There was nothing those watching the screens could do to help, or warn some of the brave souls rushing to help the fallen, thus adding to the toll.

Paul called his signals section. "Get some of those news readers together, and fast! Transmit a warning on all BBC frequencies in the London area, as well as all the other stations specific to London, you can override. Keep it simple. 'If you see people falling over in the street, keep away from them, this is a terrorist attack'; make it clear the victims cannot be helped, attempting to do so will result in the death of anyone trying to help."

"That should start a panic Boss," was the reply.

"I know, but we have got to do something."

"Leave it to me Boss, I'll sort something out, and quickly."

"Cheers Phil."

"How soon can we get in there Paul?" asked Taff.

"No idea mate, but the shit in those rockets is a damned sight quicker acting than anything I have ever heard of, which hopefully means it is not too persistent. It can't possibly kill as quickly as it seems. Whatever it is must knock out the nervous system, those poor bastards must have realised they were dying as they lay there helpless. I'll tell you straight my friend, you and I have seen some horrible things in our time in this job, but never anything to compare with this."

Now the real chaos began. For the first time since it had been installed, the telephone system was overwhelmed. The first call Paul answered was from the British Embassy in Paris. The man on the other end was clearly agitated, demanding to speak to the Prime Minister. He had been handed a note and had been summoned to see the French Prime Minister immediately to explain the air strike by two, presumably British, aircraft which destroyed a ship in French territorial waters. There was also the question of compensation for the thousands of windows broken by the sonic booms of the planes along a fifty-kilometre stretch of coast. An explanation was also required as to why a British warship had docked briefly in Cherbourg a couple of days ago; no government permission had been given, or even requested.

"The Prime Minister is unavailable at the moment Mr Ambassador. Apologise to the French on my behalf. There simply was no time for diplomatic niceties. Our best estimates at the moment are that between a quarter and a third of all people within the M25 are dead. The missiles which killed most of the victims were launched from the ship we destroyed. You can also tell them, only four of the sixteen missiles on board struck London, and for all I know some of the remaining missiles could well have been targeted on Paris."

"It simply is not possible so many could have died, you must be mistaken."

"I only wish I was Sir. Give us an hour or two to get organised, and I will e-mail you a new number to contact your political masters. I must go, as you can appreciate we are a little bit busy at the moment."

Within a week the terrible task of clearing the bodies was getting impossible, the unrelenting heat-wave was making things even worse. Somehow, the men given the soul destroying task, had managed to open all the main routes. From the outset it had been decided, the only practical way of dealing with such a monumental task was to have a single mass grave. As unsavoury as this might be, every victim would be buried in the same huge site.

The clamour against this became so great Paul was forced to call a meeting of all the leaders of the various groups, mainly religious, opposed to the policy which was described by its detractors as 'land fill'.

It seemed as though few of those in the audience were prepared to allow Paul to explain, he simply sat back and let them rant. The media, which had a heavy presence, didn't really know what to make of it; eventually things calmed down a bit. Paul rose to speak, he barely managed to say 'thank you for coming', when one of the more extreme Clerics began shouting at him again.

"Hoy! Motor mouth, shut the fuck up!" Paul shouted back. "You've had your say, and then some. Now it is my turn. For the record, I am no happier about the arrangements for removal and disposal of the countless bodies than any of you. Conditions are absolutely terrible for the poor sods having to do the clearing up. Can you imagine having to work for two hours a day, in full protective gear breathing compressed air, as if you were a diver in this heat! The other thing they have to contend with is the state of the bodies. It was two days before we were able to even make a start because of pockets of gas. In spite of all of our precautions eleven men on the clean up squads have died. I cannot imagine anything more obscene than the sight of decomposing bodies being shovelled into the buckets of diggers, then tipped into lorries for transport to the burial site. One of you described it as a land fill site, I agree. It is a toxic land fill site which is why we selected it; there is little risk of the toxins getting into the ground water or rivers. The clay in that area is virtually impervious which is why every burial trench is lined with the stuff, it is rammed hard by the diggers before the bodies are tipped in. The longer it takes, the worse the condition of the bodies, and the greater the risk of epidemic which could kill more people than the attack did.

I have been accused of being unfeeling and insensitive to the relatives of those who died, I am going to show you all a close up of a random body, yet to be retrieved." He zoomed the view on the screen in, onto the line of workers picking their way through endless wrecked cars and buses in the city. "You can see the problems they are facing; before a vehicle can be towed away any bodies in it must be removed, and that could mean fifty on a double-decker bus. To give you a better idea, let's have a close look at a body a little further along the road, there are plenty to chose from." He zoomed in again on what had been a young woman, this identification was based on her long hair, short skirt and high heeled shoes. Again he zoomed the shot in as close as he could get on this screen, on what had been her face.

"It is quite amazing where all the flies have come from, there wasn't a living thing in the affected area for the first two days, everything was dead, now look at it, I said LOOK at it. Could you clear that up, time and time again? I don't think I could. You say I am insensitive to relatives, are you saying someone should be asked to identify a body in such a state?

Now imagine trying to get a body in that condition out of a wrecked car, or you open the driver's door of a bus or a truck, and a body, in just the same condition falls out. You can see why it is taking so long, just to clear the roads. As soon as all the bodies and wrecks have been removed from a section of road it is then pressure washed with disinfectant. Work then begins on clearing the adjacent buildings, which are also full of dead, and often still have pockets of gas trapped in the air conditioning systems.

The other problem we have to contend with is the effect this is having on the men. Not everyone can handle it day after day. Only this morning, I had to relieve one of our best sergeants, he was leading the squad clearing the bodies in Trafalgar Square. He came across what was left of a little girl, she was wearing a tee shirt identical to one the sergeant's daughter had for her fourth birthday last week. Same tee shirt, same size, same blonde hair. When he tried to move the body her arm came off! Even then he was coping, until he saw the name on her tee shirt - Emily, the same as his own little girl!"

All except the vocal militant Cleric agreed, as distasteful as the solution was to all of them, there was no practical alternative.

"If you do not order your men to provide a proper grave for every Muslim, then I will personally lead a team to recover our dead. I will not allow you to defile our dead by tipping them like pigs into the same hole in the ground as Jews and non believers. I demand you reopen all the graves you have filled, and remove all the Muslim bodies and allow us to bury them in a proper manner."

"If it were possible to give every victim a dignified funeral, according to their family's wishes, don't you think I would? You are supposed to be a leader in your community; how can any one, so devoid of a grasp on reality, rise to a position of such influence? Your impossible demands do nothing to heal the rifts appearing in the community at large, brought about by people professing to be believers in your religion. Before you start accusing me of being anti-Muslim, be aware that many of my friends, including one of my very best mates are Muslim. To me, a man's religion is his business, I genuinely do not care which faith any individual subscribes to, only the person matters. Why can't religious bigots like you accept, what is right for one person may not be right for another, it is not a question of right or wrong, merely different!"

"Then I will lead a team of my brothers to recover our dead, and you will suffer for the disrespect you have shown."

"I'll tell you here and now. You will not enter the designated area, or interfere in any way with the ongoing operation. This is the only warning you will get, heed it!"

The furious Cleric stormed out of the meeting. Paul turned to the others, "I'll concede I could have handled the situation better, and for that I apologise. Is there anything, any of you can do to prevent him and his followers attempting to enter the prohibited zone?"

An elderly Cleric rose to his feet, "He no longer listens to the council

Colonel, he seeks confrontation; his sworn intent is to see the black flags of the Hezbullah flying over the British Parliament."

"We can do without any more trouble. I suppose we can only hope the smell drives them away in the morning, if he tries to carry out his plan."

"I can only imagine how terrible it must be in London Colonel. It is almost too much to bear on Stanstead Airport, I am currently living there in a tent, along with a great many others evacuated from London."

"All I can say is, thank you for your understanding, and I promise we will get things cleaned up as fast as is humanly possible with what we have available."

"I'm sure you will Colonel, there is no dignity in death in this disaster. We must ensure there is dignity in the monuments to those who died. What, might I ask, is the plan for the burial site when all this is over?"

"Landscape the area. One suggestion is to cover the area of the burials with a layer of hard crushed limestone, so it remains brilliant white. I will make sure you are all consulted before any decision is taken."

The elderly Cleric rose again. "There is one point I would like your assurance on Colonel."

"What might that be Sir, and you do not have to rise to address me, indeed, it should be me who rises to address you."

"Respect and politeness cost nothing Colonel," replied the old man. "May I ask, where are the dead animals being buried? Not I trust with the humans."

"The orders are, they all go to Regents Park and are buried with the animals from the zoo. I cannot promise an occasional bird has not been scooped up, but clear orders on this very point have been issued. I will remind those doing the clearing up, again. I hope this is satisfactory Sir."

"Thank you Colonel for your time, I am certain I speak for all of us when I say, we now have a much better understanding of the scale of the problem. As you said, the solution is unsatisfactory, but in the circumstances it is the only practical answer."

"Thank you again, and go in peace. We all have monumental tasks ahead. I just pray we are all equal to these tasks. Good day gentlemen."

CHAPTER TWENTY-THREE

Half an hour later Paul was back in his office, most of the senior Commanders were with him, all had questions which needed answering.

"The PM is demanding to know the death toll, and wants to know when things will be back to normal. He wants to make an announcement regarding the lifting of military control at this afternoon's press conference."

"I'll be damned if I am going to sit here and add up the tally sheets, simply to give out a running total of the dead we have managed to collect. The last I heard it was approaching the four hundred thousand mark."

"Bloody hell," exclaimed General Leach, "As bad as that? And we are barely half way yet."

"I don't know if we are even a quarter of the way yet Boss, never mind half way."

"What on earth was in those missiles Paul? I know VX was the official agent, but even VX isn't as deadly as this stuff. One tiny sniff and you are history, almost instantly."

"Frankly, I haven't got a bloody clue. At least four teams are working on it, some one will come up with an answer. All I know is in the earlier report, something about an enzyme additive."

"I understand one of the Clerics kicked off in the meeting earlier Paul. What are you going to do if he and his followers try to breach the security zone tomorrow?"

"First reaction was to shoot the bastard; he isn't supposed to be in the country anyway! He's here illegally, but some dozy bloody old judge ordered his release, why? He's a convicted terrorist in a friendly state; all the usual courts agreed he should be deported. I sometimes wonder if there is any point in trying to deal with these buggers. However, our political masters have proven typically spineless, and forbidden me to authorise any action against the raving idiot which might inflame his followers."

"So what are you going to do?"

"I'll tell you what I'm not going to do, and that is, permit him to get in the bloody way! I'm hoping he won't be able to put up with the stink. I went to the control point near Epping yesterday and I could hardly breathe. I can still taste it, and I wasn't within six miles of an affected area. I honestly do not know how those men can do it day after day."

The following morning a group of about fifty militants, wearing masks, tried to enter the restricted zone. Warned of their approach they were met at the road block by a company of paratroops in riot gear. The trucks loaded with bodies and headed for the burial ground were re-routed to avoid the area, thus avoiding more aggravation. Eventually an articulated lorry with a forty foot tipper trailer approached the barrier. It was driven by a soldier, over head, no less than three media helicopters hovered hoping for a confrontation.

The trailer on this truck wasn't there by accident. Early yesterday the brakes had locked on. It was already loaded with bodies, many of which had been fished out of the Thames, and were now in a terrible condition, as were the others. A full day, standing in the baking sunshine had not improved matters. Paul called the young Captain in charge of the Paras on the road block.

"You know what to do James? Keep your boys well away from the back of the trailer, just ensure the safety of the driver."

"Will do Sir, this is not going to be pretty."

As predicted, the Militants stopped the truck and demanded any bodies of Muslims be handed over.

"I don't know if there are any in there. All I know is there are just over three hundred bodies in the back," replied the driver when challenged.

Full of religious fervour, the sealing clips where knocked off the double hinged doors and they pushed open the levers which held the doors shut. The brown and grey deluge engulfed most of those waiting to search the truck. Devious as ever, Paul had re-sited the road block over night to a spot which would be slightly up hill, just enough to produce this gruesome scene.

This was the point the plan went wrong. There was a burst of automatic fire from an AK47, several of the Paras fell. As a precaution eight of the best shots in the company had been placed around the area to cover such an eventuality. The gunman was taken out before he could fire again. It transpired, many of the militants were armed and, those not too badly hit by the deluge, began to shoot at anything which moved.

In the ensuing fire fight, four Paras ended up dead and seventeen were wounded. Every militant with a gun died, the remainder were hosed down and carted off along with the Cleric to Belmarsh, the man protesting loudly at being confined with his wet and extremely smelly followers.

All of this was, of course, captured by the cameras of the news helicopters, who, ironically had been alerted by the Cleric. The theory had been to show the inhumanity of the troops and the hoped for violence towards any protest.

The ever present Canberra far above also recorded the entire episode. This particular model was fitted with the latest version of 'big ears'. This not only recorded every word said on the ground around the road block, it also sent a data stream back to its base where computers unscrambled the individual voices as fast as the data arrived.

This would prove to be vital evidence when the case came before a judge.

Most of the country, left unaffected by the attack, was functioning more or less normally. The majority of the damage from the earlier incidents had been repaired, life went on.

Quite how most of the 'civil rights' lawyers, who regularly acted for the terrorists, had contrived to be 'out of town' at the time of the attack was the subject of considerable speculation. Was it luck? Within an hour of the broadcast of the incident, one of the Legal Eagles who had managed to get the Cleric out of jail before, was trying to see the same judge again with a petition for the release of the Cleric, who was, after all, out on bail.

The judge sitting in the temporary home for the Royal Courts of Justice, in Birmingham, to the consternation of the government lawyers, ordered his immediate release on the same bail conditions. The fact the man had clearly breached the very conditions previously set by the same judge seemed to count for nothing.

Anticipating this, a helicopter had been dispatched to Belmarsh with an armed detail on board, to collect the troublesome Cleric. A Hercules was due to leave for Basra that afternoon with all manner of bits and pieces required by the unit's detachment based there. Arrangements were underway for the plane to stop briefly in Amman, and he would be handed over to the Jordanian authorities who had applied for, and been granted, his extradition.

Predictably, this created an outcry from the Legal Eagles, and brought Paul into conflict with the courts again. Almost every day he was invited to appear on one television show or other. In the light of current happenings he agreed to appear, he had chosen the show with care. It was the same one he had been on twice before, he also knew the judge who ordered the Cleric's release was to be a guest, along with the principle Civil Right's campaigner, responsible for all the legal haverings.

"You really do have a self destruct button, don't you?" said General Leach when he found out.

"Oh, I don't know Boss, it will be a release of tension to confront those idiots. I can let fly at them, and use footage of what London was reduced to, before the clean up began. Don't forget, I can prove the mad man ordered his followers to open fire on what seemed to be unarmed soldiers. He didn't know we had sharp shooters posted just in case something like this happened. The only terrorists shot were the ones with guns, four different films of the incident all prove it.

We are now in a position to give a reasonable estimate of how much longer the area will be sealed off, most of the streets are clear now - another week will see all outside areas clear. It will be another two possibly three weeks, before the last of the buildings are cleared. Demolition of fire damaged buildings is underway and going well, this is also removing most of the dioxin, the rubble is going in a deep, sealed site. We are back filling two deep disused coal mines with the contaminated debris, the surfaces are sprayed with a waterproof sealant and the rubble fed to the deepest levels by conveyor.

I don't know how the men doing it can cope with the heat and humidity, sprayers suppress the dust, but they still have to wear protective gear.

It is just about possible to work around the edges of the affected area without a respirator, as long as you are upwind. Heathrow is functional again after a fashion, at least it is usable for bringing in relief supplies. Another week will see all of the area hit by that particular missile cleared. There are still a few streets in the Staines area and one estate out at Rickmansworth to clear. I'd say things have gone about as well as they could have, given the circumstances. We can, at least, give the people cause to hope the worst is past."

"I still say you are mad!"

The programme followed the expected format. Inevitably the topic of the Cleric's alleged abduction came up. Paul came in for a barrage of abuse from the Civil Right's campaigner, the judge was a good deal more circumspect. He did however point out, it was very likely Paul would be charged with contempt of court. A charge which, in this case, would be liable to a jail sentence.

"Oh really. Might I ask how you work that one out?" replied Paul. "Every court in the land, including the House of Lords, agreed there was nothing wrong with the extradition of a convicted terrorist back to his home country; then along you come and grant his appeal on some spurious grounds."

"They are not spurious Colonel, they are very real."

"Jordan is a friendly state, if he had been wanted for driving offences, or shop lifting he would have been sent back without hesitation, correct?"

"In all probability yes," replied the judge.

"This moron had been convicted of organising terrorists in his home country. He was here illegally, stirring up trouble we can well do without."

"That is only an allegation Colonel, he was a learned and respected scholar."

"The man was nothing but trouble. You, along with most of the rest of the nation, must have seen, by now, what happened at the road block. He told his followers to shoot the soldiers."

"There is only the soldiers' word for that, there is no proof!"

"Do you dispute the terrorists opened fire first?"

"Again it is not a proven fact, merely an allegation, and you should not brand those involved as terrorists."

"Excuse me, it is not legal to carry an AK47 around in this country, never mind use it, so there is no other word to describe these idiots. They opened fire when your lovely learned and respected scholar told them to. Listen!" Paul played the recording of the Cleric clearly saying, 'Kill the non believers', "now you can subject this tape to any test you like and I assure you it will match his voice perfectly."

"How did you record it Colonel."

"The same way we recorded everything which happened at the check point, perfectly standard monitoring equipment."

"I suspect, you set the whole thing up Colonel. We could clearly see the disrespectful way you handle the bodies of the victims, this was a justified demonstration against your treatment of the victims."

"Would you be kind enough to explain to the audience, precisely how you would have dealt with this unprecedented number of bodies. Don't forget, many of them were in cars and buses. Have you any idea of the state most of them were in, after only a couple of days, in this heat?

If you want a vision of hell, check out some of the deeper parts of the underground. With the loss of power some parts flooded, temperatures down there have reached over fifty degrees centigrade without the airflow created by the trains."

"Don't make excuses Colonel, everyone has the right to be treated with respect when they die."

"I thought everyone had the right to get on with their lives, without being slaughtered as they went about their daily business. Why don't you issue writs against Al Qaeda, Hezbullah and their likes. They are the greatest offenders when it comes to denying human rights, like the most basic one of all, to live!"

This brought a round of applause from the audience.

The judge spoke up again, "This is precisely why I ordered the Imam should not be sent back to Jordan Colonel. He will be incarcerated in inhuman conditions in a Jordanian jail."

"He is Jordanian, he is directly responsible for the deaths of those soldiers, as well as those among his followers who chose to shoot at our soldiers, he is still alive which is more than he deserves! At least he had a trial, a fair one by the laws of his country; the man is a typical coward, unwilling to face the consequences of his actions, I stand by mine in this case, he deserves what ever he gets. As for the accusations levelled at me and the men I command about the way we are dealing with the bodies, I have yet to hear any viable alternative, in spite of asking for advice."

"It is totally unacceptable, loading bodies into trucks with diggers then tipping them into a hole in the ground. Even you must agree Colonel," said the presenter.

"I do agree Sir, absolutely. The problem is, how else can we do it?"

"Individual coffins, at least body bags. Surely there must be something better?"

"I could show you a video but am loathed to do it. I will attempt to explain why. Almost all the bodies still uncollected are in such a state, it is impossible to move them, as they simply fall apart. Those which haven't already ruptured with the pressure of the gas inside, burst when disturbed. Can anyone here comprehend what this is like?"

"We hear all sorts of numbers being bandied about Colonel. You must have a fairly accurate count available to you. The ball park figure from what remains of Government sources, indicate something over one hundred thousand dead. Is this an accurate assessment?"

"In as much as, it is over the hundred thousand, yes. The question is how much over, try adding a nought and you won't be far off!"

A shocked murmur rippled round the audience. "Are you suggesting the number is nearer to one million?!" asked the shocked presenter.

"I'm not suggesting anything, I'm stating a cold hard fact, I don't suppose we will ever have a totally accurate figure, but we will be within one or two percent."

"It sounds totally impossible Colonel."

"Why does it sound impossible? We have over one thousand trucks removing wreckage, cars, and of course the bodies.

An articulated tipper truck has on average about two hundred bodies per load, most twenty four hour periods see three hundred such trucks arrive at the mass internment site. You do the sums. As the bodies deteriorate then the numbers per load increase."

"How on earth could something like this happen Colonel," asked the presenter. "Clearly you had some sort of warning, something serious was about to happen. Royalty, Members of Parliament and many of the military based in London were evacuated the day before, as were many of the emergency services. Indeed your own unit evacuated many of my media colleagues shortly before the first missiles arrived at, it has to be said, considerable risk to themselves."

"As you are well aware, intelligence is an inexact science. It is true we had many of the pieces of the plan to attack us and the American eastern sea board. Vital pieces of the puzzle were missing. I have the power to evacuate the Royals, and to advise the Military, also to advise the emergency services. The Prime Minister was kept up to date at all times. It was his call to move the Members of Parliament to an alternative location, the same is true of many of the Foreign Embassies.

I took the personal decision to evacuate as many broadcasters as possible when it became clear an attack was imminent, as, in my opinion, it was important the nation as a whole kept some sense of normality which hearing familiar voices would provide.

It was not for me to order a general evacuation of London. To be honest, with the information we did have, it would have been hard to justify. What would have happened had a general evacuation been attempted? Panic for sure, the disruption would have been incalculable. Had we evacuated, who is to say the terrorists would not have simply retargeted their missiles or, not fired at all until people began to believe it was a false alarm and returned. The truth is, we simply did not know exactly what their plans were. Although we stopped most of the Silkworms we had no intelligence on them. Granted, we had guessed they might have some of them, but it was a guess, given what we had, there was little more we could have done."

"What caused the row with the French? Our sources inform us, several diplomatic notes were sent to our ambassador complaining about incursions of

British military aircraft, presumably from your unit into their airspace. Would I be correct in assuming the ship which launched many of the missiles was in French waters?"

"Regrettably that was the case. Somehow their authorities failed to realise the urgency, but then this is always the case when pen pushers become involved. Had positions been reversed, who is to say the outcome would have differed."

"So you knew we were about to be attacked, told the Prime Minister, and nothing was done to mitigate the effects of the attack; which on your own figures suggest over one million casualties. I find this incredible."

"You say we knew; to a point this is true but we did not know when. By the time we found out, it was too late. As I said earlier, what could we, or anyone else have done?"

"Would more resources have made a difference? Going back to an earlier show, I recall a fearful row over a contract for special jet engines for some of your aircraft. Would the earlier arrival of those engines have made the difference?"

"Possibly," replied Paul, "but only from the point of view, we could have dealt with the previous bout of attacks without stretching our resources to the limit."

"Leaving nothing to deal with the threat of the missiles, which I assume, you must have had at least an inkling of, even then?"

"Again the answer is possibly, maybe we would have learned more, sooner, maybe not."

"You seem reluctant to apportion blame Colonel. It is widely known, you do not get on well with the current administration, could this effect matters?"

"I might not like this lot but it does not stop me doing my job nor, as far as I am aware, does it make any difference to the PM. Any personal animosity is put aside when it comes to matters of security, by both of us.

If there is blame, then it must be aimed at the 'bleeding hearts,' and senile old fools and their powdered wigs, allowing known terrorists to go free simply because they do not understand our technology, or appreciate, we cannot always divulge exactly how we come across a particular piece of information."

Both the judge and the civil right's activist were incensed by these remarks, which was of course the point. Each in their turn demanded to know how protecting civil rights of a suspect could affect the work of preventing attacks such as this one, both also demanded an apology.

"If either of you expect me to say sorry then you are going to be disappointed. You both overlook the most important point when we are dealing with these idiots, most of them are here illegally, this usually increases the difficulty finding them in the first place. They are here for one purpose, to cause as much trouble as possible, so when we catch one it should be a simple matter to send him, or her, home. We don't want them, they have no right to be here. If they behaved like civilised human beings they would have nothing to fear in their home country, what is the problem? Why spend our taxpayers' money to help them kill our people because this is what it comes down to?

Now in the case of our venerable legal eagle, there are several possibilities to account for his strange decisions. One, which I do not believe for a moment, is he is in league with the terrorists. There are numerous other equally unlikely explanations we will not dwell on, which leaves us with the only one which makes any sense to me."

"What is that Colonel?" asked the presenter.

"Somehow, the terrorists have gained some leverage, - blackmail comes to mind, some deep dark secret they threaten to reveal if he does not go easy on them, or more likely, they have kidnapped someone dear to the judge and say they will kill them if he does not do what they ask. Which is it Sir?"

"It is none of these Colonel, and I am shocked you could even think I could be influenced by anything you have suggested. The truth of the matter is you, and the unit you command, seem to think you are above the law. Almost every alleged terrorist you hand over has been illegally detained by you, and therefore must be released."

"How the hell do you work that out?" retorted Paul, "If we catch someone with an AK47 or an RPG, and he has been under constant surveillance since he attacked a tanker for example, what is illegal about it? We provide definitive photographs, often ballistics, in cases where guns have been used, prove someone is here totally illegally, then you let them go! Why?"

"For a start, the court needs to know how you came across the plan to attack whatever - a tanker was the example you used. We need to know exactly what source you used, to test its reliability; the court also needs to know the precise details of how you manage to get such excellent photographs of so many incidents. It is impossible to allow this evidence to be presented in a court of law as it cannot be tested. There is also the strong suspicion, much of it was gained covertly without a warrant, which is again illegal, and again renders it inadmissible."

"I don't believe I am hearing this. It may have escaped your notice, this country has been attacked. What you are saying is, if we want to give the attackers a fair trial, which is something none of their victims were offered, we have to get a warrant to watch them?"

"The law requires it Colonel, you cannot simply spy on whoever you choose."

"You are madder than the bloody terrorists, with no concept of the terrible reality of counter terrorist activities. In common parlance, you are several sandwiches short of a picnic."

"Such insinuations could land you in court Colonel, I am warning you to pick your words carefully or you will be in serious trouble, and you still haven't answered the question - how the actions of the civil right's movement interfere with catching terrorists?"

"It is the amount of time the security forces spend gathering facts to counter the normally quite spurious defences offered by these clowns, half of whom are here illegally themselves. More than a few are in league with the terrorists and most of the rest are simply ripping off the taxpayer to stuff yet more money in their over inflated bank accounts."

"The lawyers are worth a lot more than most of them receive Colonel."

"Bull shit, they are the most over paid load of useless parasites around. There is not a single member of the legal profession worth half of what the average soldier involved in clearing those bodies is paid. Anyone of those lads is worth ten times as much as the likes of you; if you don't like it tough, and the only way you will get an apology out of me for those remarks is if you join them for at least three shifts."

"This time you have gone too far Colonel."

"Have I? Or is it just a case of the truth hurts? I did not ask for this job, I had actually begun my disengagement leave when I was recalled to deal with this specific threat. How do you expect any normal person to react when they see the efforts of the security forces who are trying to keep them safe, undermined by people like you? I don't care if you don't understand how we get our information, for you to allow proven terrorists to walk free on the basis of your own ignorance is indefensible, worse still when the individual is proven to be here illegally."

"There was a risk the man would be tortured if he was returned to his home country, in this case Jordan; we are therefore bound by the European convention on human rights to give him our protection."

"Try explaining that to the relatives of all those killed over the past couple of months, I don't think you will find many who agree with you. If the individual was here legally and had been acquitted by a court, based on evidence rather than an obscure technical point, I might have a bit of sympathy, but in cases such as this one - kick 'em out."

"Absolutely not, the law is the law."

"You lot treat the law as your own personal piggy bank, you seem to think it is some sort of game, the winner being the one who can twist the meaning of the English language the furthest. I was under the impression it was about finding the actual truth, rather than some smart arse's version of it. You, and others like you, have only one course of action open to you, quit! If you don't you should be fired, with loss of all your pensions other than the basic state pension. If anyone in a normal job cocks things up as badly as you have, they get the sack, why should you be any different?"

"I take it you regard what has happened as a success on your part Colonel," asked the presenter.

"Absolutely not, however you look at it, the security forces failed to protect our citizens, we could argue forever as to who was to blame for the failure - as my principle role was to oversee the co-ordination of the efforts of the various agencies, then you have to say the failure was ultimately mine."

"I happen to know, you have had many successes since your recall Colonel. Your unit intercepted at least half of the tankers designed to explode. No one else got near to solving the riddle. I am also aware of the seizure of the ship carrying the massive explosive charge and the dramatic rescue of the captive American undercover agent from the ship. Your unit also, effectively, destroyed the pirates operating off the Horn of Africa, stealing from the UN and helping the insurgents. It is also becoming clear, your unit stopped the majority of the missiles aimed at London, and it was your information which saved millions of lives in America. New York, Washington and Baltimore would have been ghost towns had the terrorists succeeded."

"Thank you for the plaudits Sir, but you should be thanking the Marines who boarded the ship, for stopping the attempt to trigger a tsunami, just as you should thank the analysts who unravelled the pieces of the puzzle, not to mention those who collected the information in the first place, often at considerable risk to themselves. It has been my honour to command such brave and dedicated people.

From a personal point of view, I can tell you it is, in many ways, easier to be the man on the ground doing what needs to be done, than it is sitting on my backside in my office awaiting news. I never thought the day would come when I had to order troops to do a job I hadn't done, or was at least prepared to do myself. Well that day came two weeks ago when I had to send young soldiers into a dangerous environment to clear bodies; I know what it is like. I went once, and I freely admit, I could not do it, indeed I do not believe I could ever have done it under those conditions. Those young men, from the ones collecting the bodies, all the way through to the digger and bulldozer drivers at the mass burial site, deserve the highest praise and the gratitude of the nation."

"I have been doing some research of my own Colonel on the properties of VX. The results suggest we are not being told the whole truth about this attack."

"It is true; the whole truth has not been released."

Again there were murmurs from the audience, the 'civil right's campaigner' immediately jumped in with, "Typical of our military, another cover up to excuse their failures."

"Oh shut up you pretentious little prick," snapped Paul. "You have no idea what you are talking about!"

"Can you elaborate Colonel?" the presenter asked hopefully.

"Certainly Sir. Any one of those missiles, armed with a warhead consisting of VX could reasonably be expected to kill in the region of two, maybe three thousand people, five thousand if you got lucky. VX is survivable, in small doses and with the correct medical help, this stuff was totally lethal. Each missile killed one hundred and fifty to two hundred, thousand people. Yet all our tests show it was VX, clearly something was different about this stuff. Yes, we have samples of it, from two missiles we 'obtained' before they could be deployed. The top scientists are working on the problem as we speak, but as yet we have no definitive answer as to how this stuff differed. The chemicals used in the attack were totally lethal, any amount however small killed very quickly. It seems as though, within a few seconds of inhaling the stuff, the brain switched off the breathing reflex and the victims suffocated as they were simply unable to breathe. We do not know, and may never know, exactly how this happened - never mind precisely what caused it to be so deadly, other than there were traces of some, as yet unidentified, enzyme. This is the 'with held' information, we can't disclose what we do not know."

"Then surely this means the poison could not have been some of Saddam's much vaunted WMD?"

"I believe it was the source, it matches perfectly the chemical profile of some VX we know was his; if we ever identify the mystery element which must be there, then we can prove, or disprove its origin. It may well turn out to be an impurity, who knows, I am no expert on such things, which quite frankly scare the crap out of me!"

"Is there a risk of further such attacks Colonel?"

"I am unaware of any specific plan of this nature, although without a doubt there are others around, prepared to become suicide bombers. There is also the probability of more attacks with road side bombs and RPGs, possibly even gun attacks, all of which will have to be dealt with."

"So no more significant attacks are likely, in your opinion?"

"Any attack is significant if you happen to be caught up in it," replied Paul. "There are three other members of this panel, I'm sure they would like a chance to express their opinions."

CHAPTER TWENTY-FOUR

The chaos gradually subsided over the following weeks. Although occasional remains still turned up, it was generally agreed the clearing up was complete, and the mass grave site was sealed and landscaped.

At Paul's suggestion, a medal to be known as the Elizabeth Cross was commissioned - all those who served on the ground during the clearing of the bodies would receive the medal and a bounty, based on the number of hours they worked. After a lot of haggling it was agreed this bounty would be totally tax free and not counted in anyway as income.

A ceremony was held at the site of the mass grave, a single soldier received his medal and bounty from the Queen, as a representative of all those who were entitled, military and civilian alike.

It had fallen on Paul to select this representative. There was really only one choice, the sergeant who had recovered the body of little Emily in Trafalgar Square. After a couple of days to get over the trauma of discovering a little girl so similar to his own daughter, he had insisted on returning to take care of the men in his section. On asking General Leach for his opinion, Paul received a nod of approval.

"It is unfair to single out any individual, but I can see the practicalities of doing it this way, it would take all day to hand them out individually. I do have an idea though - one which will ensure everyone leaves the ceremony with their medal if not their cheque."

"This should be interesting," replied General Leach. "Let's hear it."

"As far as I can tell, there will be something in the order of twenty thousand eligible for the medal. If all senior officers of the military were present, along with all the top cops and the top brass of the fire brigade, it should be possible to organise things so everyone leaves with their gong."

"I suppose you could rope in a lot of the minor Royals as well. The only thing preventing it working is, each medal is inscribed with an individual's name."

"That isn't insuperable Boss, it's a huge area. Have the CO of each regiment present his own men with their medals, split the truckers into manageable groups with numbered ID tags - this is why we have planners Boss."

"Very true m'boy."

The Day The Ravens Died

And so it was. The ceremony went without a hitch - surprising, considering the size of the crowds and the massed ranks of the world media, security seemed low key. High above, an old Canberra orbited, beaming back streams of data to the operations room of the All Arms Unit, every terminal was manned, nothing was being left to chance. Paul sat in his office chain smoking, worrying he had overlooked something on the security screen. Someone said he should have been there to receive his medal with the rest of those involved in the horrendous task of clearing the bodies. To the alarm of the powers that be, he refused both the medal and the invitation to attend. His reasoning was simple. He had broken his golden rule of command, 'never ask your men to do something you are unable, or unwilling to do yourself'. Out of sight of the crowds the veterans of 'G' squadron from 22 SAS kept watch, in constant touch with the operations room. To assist them, almost all of the combat troops of the All Arms Unit were deployed, covering any gaps in the cordon.

All of the VIPs arrived in escorted helicopters; throughout the day tensions were high with the security forces, but as far as anyone attending the ceremony were concerned, there were no incidents. No-one associated the fatal crash, miles away on the M25, with terrorists. Quite why a range rover exploded killing all four occupants was never really explained. It was suspected it may have been a terrorist attack, but there was so little left to work with, no one could be sure. There were remnants of what appeared to be weapons, even some fragments of what could only have been bullets.

The pilot climbed out of his Harrier and walked over to Paul, who was waiting near the hangar,

"I hope I hit the right Range Rover Boss."

"You did, those things really do work. One tiny missile and something like a Range Rover vanishes. Good shot, you saved a lot of lives destroying it Mike."

"I'm glad about that. I'll tell you straight Boss, it is not a good feeling taking lives, however evil the targets might be. What on earth was in the warhead on the 'Slim Jim'?"

"The same stuff we put in the bombs we used to destroy the chemicals."

"Plasma?"

"Yep, less than a coffee cup full, looking at the results we can cut it down still more."

"Who were they Boss?" asked the pilot.

"I've only got one name, and I'm not sure how to pronounce it. What I do know is, they were a team especially sent to attack the big memorial ceremony today. Somehow they slipped through Dover undetected, I'm not going to tell you why, but there was a reason for hitting them with a plasma weapon."

"I'm glad about that Boss, I might not sleep tonight if I knew."

There was another ceremony the following weekend, this one was at the

Tower of London. The Queen and a few dignitaries attended the small service dedicated to the Yeomen of the Guard, and the famous 'Beefeaters' who lost their lives in the attack. A new squad, made up mainly of ex guards Sergeant Majors, was sworn in and a plaque with the names of the fallen Yeomen unveiled by the Queen. As the Monarch pulled back the velvet curtain to reveal the gleaming brass plaque, a young raven with a sense of occasion, managed to flap its clipped wings hard enough to perch unsteadily on the top of the small monument. It leaned forward, its bright, inquisitive eyes examining its reflection in the gleaming brass announcing its approval with a loud caaw! It flapped down and hopped off to find its friends.

Paul saw something just inside the entrance to the nearby Wakefield Tower which caught his eye. He noticed a large, solid looking glass case, in it were two perfectly mounted Ravens - one either side of a slightly less than perfect Beefeater's hat. Positioned as if guarding their master's hat, the name plates on which they were perched carried the names of 'Gwylum' and 'Thor'.

Paul turned to General Leach, pointing out the new exhibit.

"That could only happen in Britain Boss."

THE END [ALMOST]

A couple of months later, Paul once more sought the sanctuary of Loch Awe; his first morning there he decided to renew his acquaintance with the herd of deer. They were a little more wary of him than previously, hardly surprising as they hadn't seen each other for months. As he walked happily into the croft his wife reminded him, "Boots off." He chuckled as he did as he was told, breakfast smelt good. The phone rang. "I'll get it," he called, expecting it to be Marie, their 'home help' from the village.

It was Taff, "We have just been notified of outbreaks of Plague, Anthrax and Hemorrhagic Fever, Paul, a chopper is on its way."

"What! Where?" But then that's another story:---